Four Days In Easton

A Novel by

J. Michael Roper

Cover Design by J. Michael Roper & Angela Roper

Artwork by J'Von Cox

4 Augustine Entertainment Publishing

This book is dedicated to my wife, Angela,

who always has my back.

Love you.

Copyright 2017 by J. Michael Roper

This is a work of fiction. Names, characters, places and incidents either are the product of the author's imagination or are used factiously, and any resemblance to any actual persons, living or dead, events, or locales is entirely coincidental.

This book was printed in the United States of America.

CHAPTER 1

When she awoke from a restless sleep to find the shackle around her right ankle open, Lisita Gomez knew that God was with her. Divine intervention in answer to her desperate prayers could be the only reason the ratcheting lock had opened without the key. Over the last eight days she had tried everything to get the shackle off of her ankle, including smashing it on the concrete floor of the small room that was her prison and trying to squeeze it over her ankle and pull her leg free. The only results from everything she tried had been frustration, desperation, and bruised and abraded skin above her ankle. Now, mysteriously, the shackle had opened while she was asleep. An hour ago, when she dozed off into a fitful sleep, it was locked tightly around her leg just above the ankle. Now, it was open.

Lisita, a pretty, dark-haired nineteen-year-old girl from a small town in northern Mexico, jerked her leg out of the open shackle as if she expected the metal to come alive and slam back shut. The shackle was similar to a handcuff, only large enough to fit around her lower leg above the ankle. The open shackle just lay there on the bare concrete floor of the room that had been her prison for eight hellish days. Lisita scooted back on her butt to the corner of the room and sat there for a moment in the dim light, simultaneously grateful to be free and terrified at the suddenness of that freedom.

The shackle was secured to a ten-foot length of chain that in turn was bolted into the concrete floor of the small room. The walls of her cell were concrete like the floor. A single light bulb in a recessed fixture in the metal ceiling was the only light. A mattress on the floor served as her bed and a plastic bucket in the corner with a toilet seat attached served as her toilet. A plastic ice chest bolted to the wall served as the room's only seat and her kitchen. Her captor brought her ice and bottles of water to keep in the ice chest when he brought her food twice a day. He fed her once in the morning and once in the evening, usually sandwiches or something he had microwaved. She ate off paper plates, which he would take with him when she was done. He would also empty the toilet bucket in the morning. Occasionally, he would bring her a bucket of warm water, some soap, and a washcloth and allow her to clean herself up.

Lisita cowered in the corner and waited, half-expecting her captor to throw open the old wooden door of her room and come charging in like he did at least once every day. When the door opened, what happened then varied wildly, with no set rhyme or reason. Sometimes he brought her food and water. At other times, he charged in, pounced upon her, and brutalized her. Sometimes he tied her up and used whips and other things on her. Lately he had taken to bringing in a chair. He would make her sit there naked while he painted her fingernails and toe nails. He always painted them a deep, glossy red. Once he was done with that, he would rape her yet again and leave. He was always very careful to check the shackle around her right ankle and make sure it was locked and tight before he left. He would close the door, but she never heard a lock rattle on the door, so she assumed that he relied on the shackle to keep her where she was. She would hear him walk away and then the sound of him climbing steps. The steps, the sound of footsteps over her head, and the dampness of the concrete walls told her that she was in a basement or something like that. She had no idea where he went, what he did when he left, or what was outside the confines of her room.

When her captor didn't appear after what seemed like hours but was in reality only a few minutes, Lisita forced herself to move. Moving quietly, she got to her feet and crept toward the door. Her captor had taken her clothes and shoes away the day he locked her in this room and her bare skin crawled with fear as she drew close to the door. She reached the door and put her ear to the flimsy wood. She heard nothing. With shaking hands, she reached down and tried the door knob. It turned with a gentle click. As carefully as possible, she eased the door open a little and peered through the crack between the door and the jamb. The door creaked slightly, but Lisita could barely hear it over the sound of her own heart pounding in her chest.

Just outside her makeshift prison was a surprisingly ordinary basement. The walls were made of concrete blocks that were obviously old and water-stained. The floor outside the door was hard-packed dirt, proving that the concrete floor of the room where she was being held had been poured solely for the purpose of keeping someone captive. A quick glance upward revealed heavy floor joists with electrical wires, water pipes, and heating ducts attached to them. A workbench sat along one wall with tools lying scattered on its surface. Old cardboard boxes and plastic crates sat stacked in piles on the dirt floor. A neat path led from the door of the room to a single, wooden set of stairs that went up. A single narrow window let sunlight into the basement. Judging from the light, it appeared to be late morning outside.

The sight of sunlight streaming through that narrow, dirty window, triggered something in Lisita. Just outside that window was the outside world; a world with possibility of escape and blessed freedom. A desperate, animalistic instinct to flee welled up inside her. She resolved at that moment to escape or die trying. Death was far better than continuing to suffer at the hands of the man holding her against her will.

Lisita slipped out the door and made her way as silently as possible across the basement, pausing every few seconds to listen carefully for any signs of her captor returning. The second time she paused she noticed a plastic crate sitting off to the side on top of a pile of similar boxes. A piece of fabric was visible at the top of the box. Lisita turned to the box and peered inside. The piece of fabric was actually the leg of a pair of women's denim jeans. She quickly rummaged through the box and discovered that it was full of women's clothing. She didn't see the clothes she'd been wearing two weeks ago when the smugglers had led her and twenty other people across the border from Mexico into Arizona. At the end of their trek through the harsh desert, they were supposed to be given rides into Tucson to a safe house where they would be given false papers that they had been promised would help them build new lives in the United States. Instead, Lisita and four other young women had been separated from the group, loaded into a van, and taken away. The smugglers they had paid to bring them to America were actually human traffickers. In the blink of an eye, Lisita changed from a paying customer to a captive.

Once she and the other girls were in the van, they had been injected with something that had rendered her unconscious. She could remember small bits and pieces of the trip. She could vaguely remember looking through the van's darkly-tinted windows and seeing cars passing them, the desert turning to trees and fields of green, and someone making her drink from a bottle of water. The rest was a disjointed blur until she'd come to her senses in an old warehouse that smelled of chemicals. In that warehouse the man who'd been holding her captive pointed to her as she stood lined up with the other four girls. She had been bound, blindfolded, and taken away. When the blindfold was taken off, she was in the concrete room. Her new captor had forced her to strip naked at gunpoint, tied her down, and raped her savagely. He had untied her when he was done, but he had not let her keep her clothing. She had been completely nude ever since.

Lisita pulled the jeans out of the crate. There was a tee shirt and a pair of panties rolled up in a bundle with the jeans. The clothes weren't hers and were too large, but she was too desperate to care. She quickly pulled on the clothes, feeling a surge of hope as she did so. Being able to cover her nakedness made her feel a little less vulnerable. Unfortunately, there were no shoes and socks in the box with the rest of the clothes. She quickly looked through the other boxes nearby, but all she found was old papers and other junk. That was okay; she could handle being barefoot. She would run through a field of broken glass barefoot if it meant getting away.

Now dressed, she weaved her way through the stacked boxes and old junk toward the stairs. She looked up the open stairway and saw that the steps led to another wooden door. That door obviously led into the main part of the house above her. Her captor lived up there. She looked around the basement in hopes of finding another way out. The only other option was the single window, but it was too narrow for her to squeeze through. Her only options were to try to get away up the stairs or hide and wait for her captor to come down, attack him somehow, and hopefully kill him. Given her captor's size and power compared to hers, overpowering him would take a miracle. God had already given her one miracle with the unlocked shackle; she doubted He would bless her with two in one day. That left the stairs.

Lisita started up the steps, moving as quietly as possible. The stairs looked like they were fairly new, so the wood barely creaked under her ninety-pound frame. She reached the door at the top of the stairs and gently tried the doorknob. It turned easily. Slowly and quietly, she eased the door open a crack.

Cool air flowed through the crack, bringing with it the smell of bacon and eggs. It had been hours since she'd eaten; if she hadn't been terrified the smell of food would have made her ravenous. She peered through the crack and saw an open hallway that ended about twenty feet away at a front door. The interior door was open, revealing a glass storm door. Through the glass she could see part of a front porch and far beyond that trees. About halfway between where she was and the front door stood a narrow table against one wall of the hallway. Lying on the table in a flat dish was a set of what appeared to be car keys on a black key fob.

The sight of those keys and the open door at the other end of the hall caused her to lose control much like a cornered wild animal does when it spots a chance to escape. Desperate with fear, Lisita threw open the door and bolted down the hall toward the open front door at the other end of the hall. As she ran down the hall she reached out and scooped up the keys in the dish. She reached the storm door and hit the handle of it with a loud crash. The door flew open and she ran outside onto a narrow porch. Somewhere behind her inside the house she heard a startled curse and what sounded like stumbling footsteps.

With speed born of sheer terror, Lisita sprinted down the steps in front of her to an area of gravel where two vehicles were parked. She stopped long enough to frantically punch the buttons on the black key fob she had in her hands. The lights of one of the vehicles parked there blinked on and there was an electronic chirp. Lisita sprinted to the vehicle, a new-looking pickup truck, and jerked open the driver's side door. She leapt inside, slammed the door, and locked it. She fumbled the key into the ignition and turned it as she breathed a desperate prayer. The truck started immediately. Lisita jerked the truck into gear and punched the gas pedal. The truck slung gravel everywhere as it lurched forward. Lisita fought the wheel as the truck spun sideways into the grass.

She managed to get the truck turned and headed back down the home's gravel driveway just as the man who had been holding her captive ran outside.

CHAPTER 2

Easton County, South Carolina, sits in the upper northwest corner of the state of South Carolina in the foothills of the Appalachian Mountains where it shares a border with the state of North Carolina. Easton is one of the smallest counties in the state of South Carolina, covering less than 400 square miles with a population of less than nine thousand people. The biggest town and the county's namesake, Easton, had a population of less than three thousand people and was the county seat where the courthouse and other county offices were located. The rest of the county was mostly rural with a few smaller towns scattered around. Most of those smaller towns consisted of a few small businesses such as farm supply stores, diners, and gas stations clustered around a crossroads. Farming was the biggest part of Easton County's economy. Family farms raising soybeans, cotton, and tobacco had belonged to the same families for generations. Dairy and pig farms, some owned by major corporations, could also be found, but those were relatively new additions to the county's economic scene, having been drawn by cheap land and a lack of zoning restrictions.

What Easton County might have lacked in business infrastructure, it made up with scenic beauty. The county was blessed with gently rolling farmland, thousands of acres of old-growth forests, and truly beautiful views of the mountains in the distance. There was an abundance of lakes and rivers as well. The natural beauty, sparse population, and abundance of natural wildlife had made Easton a major draw for hunters and fisherman. In 2015, an article in a major hunting magazine had ranked Easton County as one of the best places in the Southeast for hunting deer, bear, and waterfowl. That article and subsequent news coverage about it had resulted in a steadily-growing hunting and fishing industry in Easton. Real estate development was also taking off, especially around Lake Charles, the biggest lake in the county and the site of a major bass fishing tournament since 2016. One new development of large, expensive new homes was already under construction on one of the lake's shores and others were planned.

Because of its location, there were no major interstate highways that ran through Easton County. Getting to Easton involved getting off the interstate and then taking smaller, two-lane highways into Easton County. The biggest highway within Easton County was Highway 41, which was four lanes for several miles near the town of Easton, the county's namesake, and then narrowed to two lanes that became increasingly curvy as you entered the foothills of the mountains. Most of the other roadways in Easton County were two lane asphalt, with some of the smaller back roads being tar and gravel and a few of the more remote roads being dirt.

It was along the two-lane part of Highway 41 that led through the open country toward the North Carolina border that a red pickup truck raced along at just slightly below ninety miles per hour. The truck, a red 2016 Ford Raptor that was practically new, weaved erratically as it raced along, sometimes going into the opposite lane. Several car lengths behind it, a tan Chevrolet Tahoe with flashing blue lights and a star with Easton County Sheriff's Office on the front doors, raced along in hot pursuit. The deputy in the Tahoe had been chasing the truck for several minutes along the back roads of Easton County. The driver of the truck had finally reached the main highway and, with the wider, newer road to drive on, had really taken off. The rolling fields and few houses they happened to pass were just blurs as the two vehicles shot down the highway.

As the two vehicles drew closer to the North Carolina/ South Carolina border, Highway 41 became a straight stretch of two lane highway for approximately five miles. At just two miles from the state border, the two lanes widened into four lanes and entered the town of Bradford. Bradford consisted of a main street with a few restaurants, gas stations, and assorted other stores. Just off the main thoroughfare there were a few residential neighborhoods, a couple of churches, and the local school complex that housed the elementary school, middle school, and high school in separate buildings right beside each other. Once you made it through Bradford's two stop lights and passed through town, the highway became two lanes again and continued that way into North Carolina. Midway between Bradford and the North Carolina border was a barbecue restaurant named Miller's BBQ Joint and a convenience store. Miller's had been in the same location for fifty-two years and was well-known for their delicious barbecue. Despite its remote location, it was always packed at lunch and dinner.

The red Ford truck blew through Bradford at eighty miles per hour with the Tahoe close behind it and gaining. Fortunately, both of the traffic lights were green at the time and the few cars that happened to be on the roadway with the two speeding vehicles were smart or lucky enough to get out of the way, allowing the pursuit to get through Bradford with nothing more than a few startled looks and pointing fingers from the people who saw them go by. Once the Ford truck was outside the town limits, the driver really floored the accelerator, allowing the powerful engine to really open up. The truck began to widen the gap between it and the pursuing police officer.

Easton County Sheriff's Office Chief Deputy Dwayne Cothran, the driver of the marked Chevrolet Tahoe, was starting to get desperate as the Ford Raptor began to widen the gap between the two vehicles. Deputy Cothran, known as "Bull" because he stood over six and a half feet tall and was three hundred pounds of rock-solid muscle, knew what the truck he was chasing was capable of. With the straight, flat road ahead and the state border coming up, the truck and its driver could very easily make it into North Carolina. By law, Deputy Cothran's jurisdiction ended at the county line. With the county line also being the border of another state, he definitely would be out of his jurisdiction and on thin ice legally in regards to continuing the pursuit of the truck. Considering the town just over the border in North Carolina had both a police department and a North Carolina Highway Patrol sub-station there, the high-speed pursuit would definitely get noticed. Other law enforcement agencies getting involved, especially ones in another county and state, might lead to questions that Deputy Cothran didn't want to answer.

With time and distance running out and his desperation building, Deputy Cothran made his move. The red pickup truck had slowed slightly because it was approaching Miller's BBQ Joint. It wasn't quite lunch time yet, but Miller's parking lot was almost full because they opened early. There were other vehicles driving into and out of the parking lot as the early lunch crowd came in. Once the truck slowed, Deputy Cothran pushed his gas pedal to the floor and closed the gap. Within a couple of seconds, the front grille guard of his vehicle was within inches of the rear bumper of the truck. Now going over eighty miles per hour, he lightly bumped the driver's side rear bumper of the Ford Raptor. This maneuver caused the rear of the Ford truck to lose traction on the roadway. The driver of the truck, startled by the impact and sudden loss of full control, jerked the steering wheel, causing the pickup truck to start fishtailing and swaying wildly. The panicked driver did what most drivers would do and drastically over-corrected.

Deputy Cothran braked as the pickup truck ahead of him swerved wildly into the parking lot of Miller's BBQ Joint. He had slowed almost to a complete stop when the truck plowed into a line of parked vehicles.

Sergeant Joel Watson, a twenty-year veteran of the North Carolina Highway Patrol, had seen a lot of unusual things during his lengthy career of patrolling the highways and byways of his home state. A tall, lean man in his mid-forties with stern features and a square jaw, he had seen the mayhem that speeding vehicles and bad drivers could inflict on the environment around them. He had seen more crushed bodies, wrecked vehicles, and broken lives than he wanted to count as he worked the roads in his home state of North Carolina. It was something he was used to. However, he wasn't used to it happening right in front of him in real time while sitting in a booth in a restaurant just over the border in Easton County, South Carolina.

Sergeant Watson was the supervisor over North Carolina Highway Patrol Troop 24 based in the town of Franklin just over the border in North Carolina. Troop 24 worked out of an office near the edge of town just a couple of blocks from the Franklin Police Department. Troop 24 patrolled Franklin County, which was just across the state line from Easton County in South Carolina. Sergeant Watson's job consisted of making sure the troopers under him were doing their jobs and doing them correctly. He also served as the field training officer for new troopers fresh out of the academy. He had one of those new troopers, a twenty-four-year-old rookie named Paul Johnson, with him today as part of the new trooper's training rotation. Johnson was finishing up his field training, so Sergeant Watson had driven over the border for a celebratory meal at Miller's. It was something he did for new troopers under his command once they successfully completed their four weeks of field training at their new duty assignment. As of tomorrow, Trooper Johnson would be in a vehicle on his own patrolling the roadways of Franklin County.

Sergeant Watson and Trooper Johnson were sitting in a booth at one of the big windows that lined the front of the restaurant. The sudden squeal of tires and brakes caused both men to turn and look through the window simultaneously. They turned just in time to see a red truck strike another parked truck in the parking lot just about sixty feet from their window. The parked truck, an older Chevrolet with tool compartments mounted on the sides and the name of a heating and air company on the cab doors, was struck so hard that the tool compartments flew open and the truck nearly flipped over before settling back down on its tires. The red truck, a Ford Raptor, then careened off the parked work truck and struck another car parked in front of the work truck. The red Ford came to rest with its nose buried in the side of the car, a Toyota Corolla. Shattered glass and chunks of plastic from torn bumpers flew everywhere.

"What the hell?" Trooper Johnson said incredulously as he watched the red Ford truck crash to a stop. Johnson had a plastic glass full of tea halfway to his mouth. The two of them had just ordered their lunch.

The look of pure shock on Johnson's face was almost comical, but Sergeant Watson didn't have time to laugh. He had noticed the other vehicle that had skidded to a halt in the parking lot just beyond the crash. The other vehicle was a marked police Chevrolet Tahoe with blue lights flashing. Watson recognized the paint scheme and decals as belonging to the Easton County Sheriff's Office, the local police force with jurisdiction. Given the speed of the crash and the position of the police vehicle, experience told Sergeant Watson that he was looking at the aftermath of a police pursuit. Years of experience in pursuing other cars had taught Watson that most police chases ended in crashes with someone, usually someone innocent, getting hurt.

"It's a chase," Sergeant Watson said as he jumped out of the booth. "Looks like the red truck was trying to outrun that deputy in the Tahoe. Come on."

Sergeant Watson hurried toward the front door with Trooper Johnson right behind him. Everyone in the restaurant was either looking out a window or trying to get to one. Several of the patrons were already hurrying toward the entrance to rush outside. "Everyone stop!" Watson barked as he rushed toward the door. Everyone hurrying toward the door froze in confusion and looked at the two uniformed troopers. "Stay in here until we can figure out what just happened," Watson said firmly. "I think the person who crashed was running from the police. There could be some bad guys with guns. Lock this door behind us." The people who were in such a hurry to get outside to check on their vehicles immediately lost their enthusiasm at the word "guns". Some of the people who were hogging the windows suddenly decided to let someone else have a look.

Sergeant Watson reached the front door, stopped, and took a quick peek through the glass. He could see the wrecked vehicles, but he didn't see anyone on foot yet. He reached down and put his hand on his holstered pistol. "Johnson, follow me," he said. He then directed his attention to a waitress standing close by. "Lock the door behind us and don't let anyone but us back in. Got it?" The waitress nodded eagerly. With that said, Sergeant Watson and Trooper Johnson eased out the door into the parking lot. They heard the harsh click of the front door lock behind them.

With his holster unsnapped and his hand on his gun, Sergeant Watson led the way around the parked cars toward where the red truck had come to rest against the Toyota. The impact had pushed the small car into the car beside it. All told, it looked like the crash had resulted in several vehicles being damaged with the most severe being the red truck itself and the Chevrolet work truck it had initially struck. Watson did not see anyone running from the red truck. Judging from the extensive damage to the front end of the truck, he doubted that anyone in the truck would be able to run too far. If the driver wasn't wearing a seat belt, he or she was probably badly injured or dead. The red Ford's front end was completely smashed with the hood being almost folded up on the windshield. The vehicle's airbags wouldn't have been enough on their own to save the driver or anyone else inside who wasn't wearing a seat belt.

Watson noticed that the deputy, a tall and heavily-muscled man with red hair, had emerged from the marked Tahoe and was moving slowly toward the red Ford. Watson was looking at the deputy's face when the deputy noticed him and Trooper Johnson approaching the scene. A look of shock flashed across the deputy's face, followed by another look that Watson couldn't decipher. "Hey," the deputy said as if it was all he could think of to say in the moment.

Sergeant Watson was about to ask the deputy if he was pursuing the truck when there was a loud thump from the cab of the wrecked Ford. Watson immediately turned his attention to the truck's cab and drew his weapon. The driver's side door of the red Ford, which the two troopers were facing, opened suddenly and the driver climbed out unsteadily. The driver of the truck was a young Hispanic female who looked about twenty years old. Aside from a bleeding laceration on her forehead and some abrasions from where the truck's airbags had deployed on impact, she did not appear to be badly injured. She wore a ragged pair of jeans and a light blue tee shirt that was too big for her small frame. She appeared to be stunned and stumbled as she took a step. Watson noticed that she was barefoot as well. Given the crash and condition of the truck, Sergeant Watson was amazed that the girl appeared to be mostly okay.

The girl stood there, less than twenty feet away from Watson and Trooper Johnson. She did not appear to even notice them. At first Watson thought that it was probably due to hitting her head in the crash, but then he realized that she hadn't noticed them because all of her attention was focused on the deputy who'd been chasing her. She was facing the deputy and the two troopers were approaching her from her right side. The deputy started toward her, prompting the girl to squat down and pick up something off the ground. When she stood up, Watson saw that it was a large screwdriver. Apparently, it had fallen out of one of the tool compartments on the truck her truck had hit. The girl held the screwdriver out in front of her menacingly with the blade aimed toward the deputy.

Time slowed down for Sergeant Watson. The girl was young and probably weighed ninety pounds at most, but she was now armed with a weapon she could use to slash or stab. The situation had definitely escalated and was in danger of spiraling out of control fast. The big deputy had stopped about twenty feet away and drawn his pistol. He had the gun aimed squarely at the girl. With his senses heightened by the adrenaline flooding his system, Watson could see the deputy's finger on his pistol's trigger. Watson stopped and aimed his pistol at the girl but kept his finger off the trigger. He had a clear shot, but the girl hadn't made a threatening move. Actually, aside from picking up the screwdriver, the poor thing hadn't moved at all. She just stood there, looking at the deputy with her eyes wide with fear and desperation.

"Stop!" Sergeant Watson yelled as he extended his pistol out in front of him in a shooting position. He kept the barrel of his pistol aimed at the ground near the girl's feet. He wasn't aiming directly at her, but he could move the gun into firing position instantly if he had to. The girl snapped her head to the right and looked at him. She seemed to notice the two troopers for the first time. Her eyes widened. "Put it down," Watson said firmly. "No one wants to hurt you, ma'am. Put the screwdriver down before something really bad happens!"

Behind him and to his left, Watson could see with his peripheral vision that Johnson had stopped and also drawn his pistol. Like his boss, Johnson had his gun held at ready, but not aimed directly at the girl. Johnson's face was flushed and he looked nervous, but his hands were steady and he looked ready for action. The girl was staring at them with wild eyes. At first her gaze was focused on the gun in Watson's hands. Then, in slow motion, Watson saw her gaze drop down to his chest. The girl's eyes widened. Watson sensed instinctively that she had noticed the difference in their uniforms and the uniform of the deputy who had chased her. Their uniforms were gray while the sheriff's deputy was black. Her face betrayed a mixture of emotions before settling on one that Sergeant Watson found very odd given the circumstances: sheer relief. Tears welled up in her eyes.

Watson assumed that the girl was either suffering from some mental illness or possibly under the influence of drugs. Either way, she seemed to be calming down a tiny bit. During the course of his career Watson had shot two other human beings in the line of duty. Both had been male and both had died. He had no desire to shoot a third person, especially a girl who looked just a couple of years older than his youngest daughter. He tried his best to look calm and reassuring. "Please, ma'am, just drop the weapon. You drop yours and I'll put mine away. We'll talk. I will help you."

The girl cut a quick look at the Easton County Sheriff's Deputy, then looked back at the two troopers. "Ay-," she started to say as she lowered the screwdriver and took a step toward them.

The deputy fired twice. From Watson's viewpoint, it played out in hideously slow motion. The girl took a step toward him and Johnson as she started to bring the screwdriver down and her hand started to open. There were two loud pops that sounded like they came from very far away. Watson saw the side of the girl's shirt jump as if someone invisible had tugged at it and then she spun back and to her right. She was already falling when the second bullet hit her and sent her sprawling onto her back on the pavement. She landed as if she were a rag doll thrown down by some angry giant.

"Damn it!" Watson screamed as time returned to normal. He turned to the deputy who'd fired. The deputy's eyes were wide and he looked like he was ready to empty all of his ammo. "She's down!" Watson barked bitterly. "Secure your weapon and I will cuff her!" The deputy slowly lowered his weapon and reluctantly holstered it. "Get an ambulance on the way now!" Watson added as he holstered his own pistol. His training said that he should keep his weapon aimed at the suspect until she was secured, but the spreading pool of blood around the wounded girl told him she wasn't a threat anymore. Besides, he'd seen the screwdriver fall from her hands a split second after the first bullet hit her.

Watson went to the girl and looked down at her. Her eyes were open, but they were already glassy and unfocused. Her mouth moved as if she was trying to talk, but only harsh, panting breaths came out. As he looked down at her with pity, the struggle to breathe stopped. Watson saw the exact moment she died. "Lord, have mercy," he said. "You poor little thing."

Johnson was immediately at his side. He looked dazed and sick. "You want me to try CPR?' he asked as he started to kneel down.

Watson waved him away. "She's gone," he said softly. "Go get some crime scene tape. We need to seal this area off."

A shadow fell over them. Both troopers turned to find that the deputy had approached. "Is she dead?' he asked in a shaky voice. Watson nodded. "She say anything?" the deputy added.

Watson thought it was a bizarre question, but the whole situation was bizarre. Five minutes earlier he'd been ordering ribs and making small talk with a waitress. Now he was standing over a girl who'd been blown away while standing fifteen feet away from him with a screwdriver. He took a deep breath as he looked at the deputy's name tag. "Deputy Cothran, you need to call your people," he said grimly. "This is an officer-involved shooting that resulted in death. Trooper Johnson and I are witnesses. This is a crime scene."

Deputy Cothran walked away from the dead girl back to his SUV. He leaned against the front fender and pulled his cell phone out of the case on his belt with shaking hands. He dialed a number from memory. It rang once and was answered.

"Sheriff," it's me," Deputy Cothran said as he looked back at the crowd gathered in the restaurant parking lot and the two North Carolina Highway Patrol officers stretching yellow barrier tape around the scene. In the distance he could the sirens of an approaching ambulance. "We have a huge problem."

CHAPTER 3

Twenty-four Hours Later

In the State of South Carolina, only two law enforcement agencies have statewide jurisdiction: the South Carolina Highway Patrol and the South Carolina Bureau of Criminal Investigation. The running joke has always been that the Highway Patrol handles the roads and the Bureau of Criminal Investigation handles everything else. The Bureau of Criminal Investigation, or BCI as it is known, is essentially the South Carolina State Police. The agency even went by that name until the state legislature changed it the Bureau of Criminal Investigation in 1965 because the governor at the time liked to call them South Carolina's FBI. Because the agency has statewide jurisdiction, the BCI investigates crimes that cross jurisdictional boundaries within the state, crimes that involve multiple local law enforcement agencies, and other crimes specifically defined by state law. The BCI also assists law enforcement agencies within the state with their own investigations, providing manpower and resources to assist local police departments who might not have the resources or expertise to investigate certain crimes that occur in their jurisdiction. The BCI's state-of-the-art crime labs and forensics investigators are an invaluable resource to law enforcement agencies of all sizes throughout a state where some police departments in small towns in rural areas literally have two officers, one of them being the chief. The agency can also provide extra manpower and other resources and equipment to local law enforcement such as Canine Units and Air Support from the agency's fleet of helicopters based near their headquarters complex in the state capitol of Columbia.

As the pre-eminent law enforcement agency in the state, the Bureau of Criminal Investigation also regulated law enforcement training and certification for law enforcement officers within the state. It was in this capacity that the agency operated the South Carolina Law Enforcement Training Academy. Anyone wishing to be a law enforcement officer in South Carolina had to go to the academy, pass their training, and be certified. This system helped to make sure that anyone wearing a police officer's badge within the state met a certain level of competency and training. Because they were responsible for training police officers and regulating law enforcement conduct within the state, the BCI also had a mandate to investigate police officers or police agencies within the state when it was needed. The BCI investigated allegations of law enforcement misconduct in any form, as well as line-of-duty shootings involving police officers. State law mandated that any officer-involved shooting of a person had to be investigated by another impartial law enforcement authority to maintain transparency and fairness.

The South Carolina Bureau of Criminal Investigation Law Enforcement Center was located a sprawling campus just outside the city limits of Columbia. The BCI's administrative buildings, crime labs, and other support services occupied one part of the three- hundred- acre spread while a small airport for BCI aircraft, a motor pool, and the police training academy occupied the rest of it. The newest building on the campus was a six-story building of red brick and glass that housed the main offices where the BCI's investigators worked and the people in charge had their offices. The current director of the BCI was John Keller. His corner office was located on the sixth floor with wide, tinted glass windows looking out over the campus surrounding him and the city's skyline.

The view through the tinted windows was actually quite striking, but at the moment BCI Special Agent Mason Holliday could care less about the view outside. He was sitting in one of the plastic chairs in the outer office/ waiting area of the director's office trying to figure out why he'd been summoned to meet with Director Keller. The BCI hierarchy had several layers of sergeants, lieutenants, captains, and others before you reached the office of the director. Getting summoned directly to the "big office" as it was called by the rank and file agents was never a good thing.

Mason, or Mace as he was called by pretty much everyone, leaned forward in his chair, a move which drew the attention of Martha Gray, BCI Director John Keller's personal secretary, who occupied the desk several feet away. Martha, an older woman in her late fifties who looked like she could be cast as "Grandma" in every Disney movie ever made, smiled at him. "Calm down, Agent Holliday," she said softly. "I don't think you're here for something bad."

Mace smiled back at her. "Martha, like I've told you a dozen times, you can call me Mace," he said. "If I'm not in trouble, then why am I here?"

"He might just want to see how you're doing and welcome you back to duty," Martha said in a low voice. "After the Laurens Incident, he probably just wants to check on you and make sure you're ready to get back to active duty."

The Laurens Incident, as it was known, had dominated the news for several days and quickly become the stuff of legend throughout law enforcement circles in the state. Three months ago, on a pleasant day in early June, a forty-five- year- old man named Lucas Turner had shot two local deputies who'd stopped him for an outstanding bench warrant for failure to pay an earlier traffic citation. Turner, a former soldier and self-proclaimed survivalist, had developed a rabid hatred for law enforcement following a two-year stint in prison for growing and selling marijuana. After shooting both deputies dead, Turner had fled into an area of swamp and thick forest in the south end of the county where he had cached weapons. A massive manhunt ensued that involved the Laurens County Sheriff's Department, the South Carolina Bureau of Criminal Investigation, and other agencies. With the thick forest, swamps, and his prior military training, Turner had avoided capture for two full days. On the third day, BCI Agent Holliday and Lucas Turner had crossed paths and the Laurens Incident was born.

On the third day, Holliday was in a BCI helicopter with the pilot, Bill Ross, and another agent named Paul Fortner. They were flying over a particularly thick area of swampy forest bordering the Enoree River searching for any sign of Turner. Unbeknownst to anyone else, Turner had managed to get his hands on a fifty-caliber sniper rifle. Turner had opened fire on the low-flying helicopter from a slight rise near the river. One of his shots passed through the copter's windshield and killed the pilot instantly. With a dead man at the controls, the helicopter had crashed within seconds. Agent Fortner had died instantly in the crash. Holliday had escaped without a single scratch. When Lucas Turner hiked to the crash site to admire his handiwork and finish off any survivors, Holliday had shot him dead in a fierce exchange of gunfire. Turner had fired over fifty shots in the running gun battle with Holliday through the thick undergrowth. Holliday had fired two shots. When it was over, Holliday wasn't hit at all. Turner had been hit once in the chest and once in the forehead.

"I'm good to go," Mason said. "Actually, I'm thrilled to be back on regular duty. Being on desk duty waiting for the state attorney general to clear me sucked."

Martha was about to reply when the door to the office behind her shoulder opened. Director John Keller popped his head out, saw Mason sitting there, and waved for him to come into the office. Mason casually stood up and walked into Keller's spacious office. There was a middle-aged white man already sitting in his office in one of the two chairs in front of Keller's large desk. The other man looked like an accountant who'd wandered into the wrong office. He was about six feet tall and stocky with brown hair going gray and somber features. He was dressed in a dark blue suit, a red tie, and polished black shoes. He stood up as Mason walked in and offered Mason his hand. "Doug Patterson," he said. "I'm from the Governor's Office.

Mason shook the man's hand. "Mason Holliday," he said. Director Keller pointed to the other chair, prompting Mason to take a seat. Keller sat down behind his desk and leaned back in his chair. Patterson sat back down as well.

"Mace, let me start out by saying welcome back to regular duty," Keller said. Keller was a handsome man with black hair parted to one side and patrician features. He had been with the BCI for thirty years and worked his way up from field agent. Pretty much everyone at the BCI respected him. "I'm sorry it took the attorney general's office so long to clear you. Ten years ago, you would have been back on regular duty two days later, especially given the circumstances involved."

"I'm glad to be back, sir," Mason said sincerely. "I just wish we hadn't lost Fortner and Ross before we got Turner."

"There was no 'we', Mace," Director Keller said. "You got Turner. There's no telling how many more officers or other innocents he would have killed with that cache of weapons and explosives he had stashed in the woods with him. You went above and beyond the call of duty and I intend to give you an award for heroism as soon as all this fades a little bit."

"I'm flattered, sir," Mace said, "but that's not necessary. Give it to Fortner and Ross."

"They will receive them posthumously," Keller said as he leaned forward and rested his elbows on his desk. "Their families will be well taken care of as well." He shook his head. "I went to the crash site. I don't know how in the world we are sitting here having this conversation. I have no idea how you survived the crash, much less that maniac coming to finish the job with an assault rifle."

For a moment Mace was tempted to look at Director Keller and blurt out the truth. *You think you wonder that?* he thought. *I've been wondering that every waking moment for the last three months. Why am I still alive with two good men with wives and kids are dead and buried? They're dead and all I got out of the deal was insomnia and way too many questions.* "I guess it wasn't my time," he answered instead.

"I know you've been seeing the staff psychologist per protocol," Keller said. "Doctor Harrison cleared you as well."

That's because I didn't tell her the whole truth, Mace thought. Following the incident, he had started suffering from insomnia, something much out of the ordinary for a man who usually slept like a rock. He would sleep for about three hours a night, then wake up and lie there staring at the ceiling. Worse than the insomnia was the recurring nightmares where he relived the crash. Worst of all was the terrible feeling that he should have died too and the questions as to why he didn't. Dr. Harrison had discussed what she called survivor's guilt and post-traumatic stress with him, but he had lied to her about what he was feeling because he was afraid she wouldn't let him return to being an investigator. Mason loved his job and he didn't want to lose it. He prayed the insomnia and nightmares would pass with time. If not, he would find his own psychiatrist to talk with.

"Yes, she has" Mace replied. "I'm ready to get back to work."

"Excellent," Keller said. "I have a special assignment for you. I need for you to follow up on a case we started work on just yesterday. It's an officer-involved shooting in Easton County. You happen to hear anything about it on the news?"

"No sir," Mace said. The sudden assignment to an officer-involved shooting investigation puzzled him. He knew that the Bureau of Criminal Investigation investigated when police officers were involved in line-of-duty shootings. However, he had never personally been involved in a line-of-duty shooting investigation as an investigator. During his ten-year career with the BCI, it was probably the only type of investigation he hadn't been involved with at one time or the other.

"Yesterday morning around eleven AM, an Easton County Sheriff's Office deputy named Dwayne Cothran pursued a vehicle driven by a Hispanic female, who is as yet unidentified," Keller said as he flipped open a folder that lay on his desk. "The female lost control and wrecked in the parking lot of a local restaurant just as a couple of miles away from the state border with North Carolina. The female then grabbed a screwdriver that had fallen from one of the wrecked vehicles as a weapon. The deputy shot her when she moved towards two North Carolina Highway Patrol officers who happened to be there for an early lunch. The highway patrol officers saw the crash and came outside to investigate. According to Deputy Cothran, he shot her because he thought she was a threat to the two other officers." Keller removed a piece of paper from the folder and slid it across the desk to Mace.

Mace leaned forward and studied the piece of paper. It was a printed picture from the scene. In the color picture, a young woman with dark hair lay on her back on some gravel. Her eyes were open and a thin line of blood flowed from the corner of her open mouth. In life the girl would have been considered cute more than pretty. In death, she just looked pitiful and frail. She couldn't have been older than twenty or so. A BCI evidence tag lay beside her head. "She's young," he said as he studied the picture.

Keller slid the folder across the desk toward Mace. It stopped at the edge in front of Mace's chair. "The Easton County Sheriff's Office notified us per state law and department protocol. We don't have a field office in Easton because it's such a small county and relatively quiet most of the time. A couple of agents from Greenville County responded and we sent a crime scene unit from here. The agents interviewed everyone involved and took statements. The crime scene unit processed the scene. All of the preliminaries are in this folder.

"It seems like it ought to be pretty open and shut, but there's a lot of unanswered questions with this one, Mace," Keller continued. "The truck the female was driving belonged to Deputy Cothran. He claims the unidentified female sneaked onto his property and stole the truck, which he accidentally left the keys in. He pursued her in his county-issued Chevrolet Tahoe until she wrecked and he was forced to shoot her. The girl had no identification on her at all. She literally had the clothes she was wearing and that's it. We've got her fingerprints and are running her through the FBI database even as we speak, but so far nothing, so she's a mystery. Also, Deputy Cothran never called the theft and pursuit in to Easton County's 911 Center. No one else in the department or county knew anything was going on until it was all over."

Mace reached out and took the folder off the edge of the desk. It was already two inches thick and would only get thicker. He opened the file and slid the photo back into it. "That's pretty odd," he said. "Usually officers in a pursuit are on the radio babbling from beginning to end."

"Agreed," Keller said. "That's not the only weird thing happening in Easton County. That's why Mr. Patterson has graced us with his presence today. Mr. Patterson is a former FBI agent appointed by Governor Richards as an adviser regarding law enforcement and homeland security issues. Governor Richards contacted me yesterday after the news about the Easton shooting came out and asked for a briefing. Shortly thereafter, Mr. Patterson called me as well." Keller looked to Patterson. "Doug, would you like to take it from here?"

Patterson smiled thinly and nodded. He turned in his chair to Mace. "Agent Holliday, what do you know about Easton County?" he asked.

"It's the smallest county in the state as far as population and area," Mace answered. "There are a few employers there, but I think the local economy mainly centers around farming. It's mostly rural, save for a few small towns. The biggest town is named Easton and it's the county seat. It's built right on the shores of the lake there. I can't recall the name of the lake off the top of my head."

"Lake Charles," Patterson said. "Easton County and the town of Easton was founded by the Easton family, who settled in the area in the early eighteen hundreds. The Easton family's descendants still live there and own several of the local businesses, including Easton Chemicals, the major employer in the county. The Easton County Sheriff's Office is responsible for enforcing the law there. The only other law enforcement agency in the county is the Easton Police Department, which covers the town of Easton. I think the Easton PD has about three officers including the chief."

"That's fairly standard for most rural counties like Easton," Director Keller interjected.

"It is," Patterson said. "Unfortunately, situations like that can result in certain law enforcement officers or agencies deciding to play by their own rules and not the law of the land. There's literally no local oversight save for a county or town council, and that's often made up of friends of the chief or sheriff. It's a recipe for disaster. Crooked cops can do a lot of harm not only to the local people, but to an entire state's reputation."

"Is that what the governor is afraid is happening in Easton County?" Mace asked.

Patterson nodded somberly. "About a month ago, the mayor of Easton contacted Governor Richards. Apparently, the mayor and the governor were college roommates and have remained friends for the last forty years. The mayor of Easton, Jacob White, owns a hotel in Easton right on the lake and is also the pastor of the local Baptist church. According to him, the county is being taken over by a biker gang and other sinister types. He believes that the Easton County Sheriff's Office is corrupt and turning a blind eye to what's happening there or actively involved in criminal activity."

"What kind of criminal activity is allegedly happening?" Director Keller asked.

"A biker gang that calls themselves The Horde has supposedly opened a new strip club on the outskirts of town," Patterson replied. "According to the mayor, the girls working in the clubs aren't local girls and some appear to be underage. Most of the girls appear to be Hispanic. The bikers and some deputies are allegedly extorting and harassing business owners in town. There's also evidence of drug activity."

"If we had known about this we could have already launched an investigation," Director Keller said with an edge in his voice. "We could have had agents all over the bar, the bikers, and the sheriff's office."

"Which is what the governor didn't want," Patterson replied calmly. "Some of these allegations are pretty serious, but they are just allegations. We have a country preacher whining to the governor because a strip club has opened where he ministers to his flock. I've looked at the crime statistics from Easton County. Arrests by the sheriff's office have stayed about the same over the last year as compared to years before. We've had no other complaints and I know your agency hasn't received any allegations of police misconduct from Easton either. This could be one bitter old man who doesn't like change."

"Or he could be the only one brave enough to speak up," Mace said.

Patterson looked at him sharply. "That's entirely possible as well, but it could very easily be the opposite. Unfortunately for the governor, there are a lot of voters in Easton and he needs to carry the upstate counties like Easton if he wants to get re-elected. Also, the Easton family are major political donors. The governor doesn't want you guys storming in like the wrath of God and rattling cages until we know there's a real problem."

"So, what exactly do you want me to do?" Mace asked.

"Officially, you are investigating the officer-involved shooting," Keller answered. "The fact that the victim was an unidentified Hispanic female like the ones who allegedly dance in the local club is very curious. That she was driving a truck belonging to a local deputy who happened to shoot her is even more troubling. I want you to go to Easton and investigate this situation thoroughly."

"And while you are there, pay close attention to what's going on around you in Easton," Patterson added. "See if there is any basis to what the governor's buddy claims. Turn over a few stones. The shooting investigation gives you guys the chance to be there without ruffling too many local feathers. After all, it's only one agent. Take advantage of the chance and find out what, if anything, is going on in Easton County."

"And if I find anything?" Mace asked.

Patterson smiled thinly and looked at Director Keller. "The governor will not stand idly by while corrupt police officers and other criminal elements threaten the rule of law. Once we know there's a legitimate problem, then you guys do what you do."

"Fair enough," Keller said. "Mace, go home, pack a bag, and head to Easton County. I'll let the local sheriff, Lynn Garrett, know you're coming to follow up on the shooting case. Check into a local hotel and investigate the shooting. During the process, see what turns up regarding the other allegations."

"Sometimes when you stir up a hornet's nest, people get stung," Mace said as he tucked the case folder under his arm and started to stand.

"Make sure the people who get stung deserve it," Director Keller said casually. "Mace, you can go. Mr. Patterson and I have a few more issues to discuss."

Mace nodded. He closed the office door behind him as he left.

CHAPTER 4

The moment Amanda Easton had been dreading for three weeks happened at a time and place where she least expected it. In the three weeks since she'd left her abusive husband, Ronny Easton, she'd been expecting him to show up and make an ugly scene. She'd fully expected him to appear and go into one of the fearsome tirades that had become a routine part of her life for the six years she'd been married to him. She'd also expected him to demand that she return and when she refused, to demand that she turn over their son, Caleb, to him. When she wouldn't let him take Caleb, she knew that he would become physically abusive and try to take him by force. The last six years had taught her that was how Ronny Easton operated. However, she'd expected that, when that inevitable confrontation happened, it would happen at a time and place where there would be no witnesses and no one to possibly help her. Ronny wouldn't risk his standing in the community by making a spectacle of himself in public and letting people see the real him. He was also a coward who was afraid that any man witnessing him attacking her might intervene. Ronny was too scared to fight a man. As the scars and bruises healing on her body could attest, Ronny might abuse a woman or a child, but he wouldn't take a chance fighting a man unless he and some of his thug friends had the poor guy outnumbered.

With her knowledge of Ronny and how he operated, Amanda had made it a point to avoid places and situations where her estranged husband could confront her on his terms. Thus far she had been lucky and, aside from several threatening phone calls and her husband following her a few times as she drove, she'd managed to keep herself and Caleb safe. That's why she was so shocked and unprepared when she saw Ronny coming as she sat at the gas pumps at Smith's Filling Station and Garage on West Main Street right in the middle of downtown Easton at just a few minutes past five PM on a weekday afternoon. In front of possible witnesses and in daylight wasn't his style, yet here he was speeding into the parking lot toward her as she was getting into her car from paying for her gas.

Amanda had just opened the driver's door of her Toyota Camry to get into the car when the squeal of tires drew her attention. She looked up in time to see her estranged husband's beige Range Rover speeding toward her and her car. Through the Rover's windshield she could see Ronny behind the wheel, his eyes on her, and a look of pure malevolence on his face. For a terrified moment she thought he was going to plow his vehicle right into her and the Camry and kill her and Caleb. Caleb, their five-year-old son, was sitting in his booster seat in the front passenger's seat. A terrible vision of the two vehicles hitting the gas pumps on Caleb's side of the car and the two vehicles exploding in a ball of fire shot through her mind. At the last possible second, though, Ronny swerved and came to a stop with the Range Rover at an angle in front of her, blocking her car in.

Amanda ducked her head down and looked into the car. Caleb was sitting in his booster seat, looking up at her with eyes full of fear. Just above his left eye was a small scar, the freshly-healed reminder of why she'd taken their son and fled to the safety of her grandfather's home. "Mommy," Caleb said softly, "he's come to get us." His lips quivered and his big blue eyes welled with tears.

The sight of their terrified son turned Amanda's fear into fierce anger. Her son was a beautiful child with his father's brown hair and blue eyes. The rest of his features, though, were hers, especially the cheeks and nose. Even more importantly, Caleb had gotten her disposition. At five, he was a generous and sweet-natured child who was also fiercely intelligent with none of his father's sadistic, mean traits. He didn't deserve to be caught in the middle of what was happening, but he was and it broke her heart. Ronny would have to kill her before she would let her baby fall into his hands.

Amanda tossed her car keys onto the front seat and hit the automatic lock button for all of the doors. "Caleb, do not unlock the doors until Mommy tells you to. Only Mommy, understand?" Caleb nodded. Amanda closed the car door and turned around to face what she knew was coming.

Ronald James Easton, known as Ronny to pretty much everyone, had jumped out of the Range Rover and was coming around the rear of the vehicle as Amanda turned to confront him. Ronny was a big guy, standing a couple of inches over six feet and weighing about one hundred and eighty pounds. He worked out regularly and it showed in his powerful arms, chest, and shoulders. He was a handsome man with blue eyes, brown hair, perfect teeth, and a sharp nose. He had a short beard and mustache as well. Most people knew him as friendly, charming, and generous. Amanda knew the real Ronny, however; the petty, spiteful man with a hair-trigger temper who abused his wife and child. That Ronny- the real Ronny- was the man coming toward her with murderous rage making his handsome face a hideous mask.

Amanda was only five feet seven inches tall and weighed a hundred and fifty pounds. She was an attractive woman with dark brown hair, green eyes, and a pleasantly curvy figure that drew a lot of looks. She worked out some, but by no stretch was she in good enough shape to fight someone like her husband, However, Ronny would have to beat her nearly to death before she would let him touch Caleb. In that moment, she could completely understand why most female animals were so dangerous when something threatened their young.

Ronny stopped about five feet away from her. "Did you think you could just run out on me?" he snarled. "And take my flesh and blood, you piece of white trash?" He was so angry spittle was dripping down his chin.

"You knocked your five-year-old son down and he cut his head open when he tried to protect me from you and I'm the piece of trash?" Amanda spat back with burning hatred. "You're the piece of trash, Ronny! If you put one hand on me, I'll have you arrested for domestic violence!"

Ronny smirked at her. "Did you forget who it is you're talking to?" he asked. "My family owns this damned county! We own the police, the county council, everything!" He made a sweeping gesture at everything around them. "Who's going to help you, Amanda? Not any of these people who are turning their heads and acting like nothing is happening. You know why? Because most of them work for me! They know I own them!"

Amanda knew that he was telling the truth, but she was too mad and scared for her son to back down. "That might be so," she answered, "but if you put your hands on me all of these people are going to see one of the all-powerful Eastons beat a woman in the middle of town in broad daylight. Then they will all get to see you for who you really are."

Ronny's face was nearly purple with rage and his hands were balled into fists. He took a step toward her. "At this point I don't care," he snarled in a low, dangerous voice. "You don't take something that belongs to me."

"He's my son too," Amanda said as she brought up her fists and got ready to fight. "You don't love him. You treat him like he's something that fell off your shoe instead of your own child. He has a scar on his face because of you! You'll have to kill me before I let you take him."

Ronny took a step toward her and drew back his fist. "Stay out of the way," he yelled as he tried to step past her. He reached out for the driver's door handle on her car.

Amanda jumped to put her body in between her enraged husband and the car. She got in his way just as he touched the door handle. Up close she could smell her husband's sweat and the strong odor of alcohol. Ronny had a problem with alcohol; when he drank he was dangerous, mean, and he had no self-control. The fact that he was already nearly drunk made this whole situation even more dangerous. Ronny pushed her back against the car and drew back his fist. Amanda raised her own hands to block the punch just as she had so many times in the privacy of their home. She hadn't been in a fight since seventh grade, but this time her son was at stake. "No!" she screamed almost directly into Ronny's face.

A look of shock suddenly appeared on Ronny's face. An expression of complete disbelief replaced it as he flew backwards. He landed about five feet away from the car on his back on the parking lot asphalt with an audible thud. While Amanda's brain was still processing that, a man appeared from somewhere off to the side. He stepped between her and Ronny and stood there.

Ronny scrambled back on the asphalt and jumped to his feet. "This isn't any of your business, Mister," he barked.

"You take one step toward this woman or her child again, you will regret it," the newcomer said calmly. "I don't know what's going on exactly, but I'm not going to stand around and watch a man your size beat a woman and take her child."

Amanda stood there, shaking with fear and adrenaline. The newcomer was a male just a few inches taller than her which put him around five nine or ten. He might have been shorter than Ronny, but the guy was built like a brick wall with the lean, powerful look of someone who could handle himself physically, not the big, show-off muscles that came from the gym and supplements like her husband had. He had a faint brown tint to his skin as if he might have Hispanic or Spanish origin. His hair was jet-black and kind of long. He wore faded jeans, a black tee shirt, and battered brown boots. His back was to Amanda and her car.

Ronny stood there facing the newcomer. "This is family business," he yelled. "You need to butt out before something bad happens." He took a menacing step forward and balled his fists up.

The newcomer grinned back at him. "I would suggest you think about your next move, Ronny," he said casually.

The mention of his name made Ronny pause. "I know you?" he asked as he stared at the newcomer.

That question never got answered. The sudden blast of a siren startled the two men and nearly made Amanda, who was watching everything unfold from just a few feet away, jump out of her skin. A gray Dodge Charger had pulled into the parking lot and stopped several feet away from the two men with the front of the car facing them, Amanda, and their two vehicles. Blue strobes flashed under the front grill and at the top of the windshield inside the vehicle. As the three of them watched, the driver's door opened and a man got out of what was now obviously an unmarked police car. The driver leaned on the top of the open car door and looked at them.

"Good afternoon," he said amiably. "Is there a problem here, guys?"

"If there is, it's none of your business," Ronny replied.

The driver smiled and stepped out around the open car door. He was about the same height as Ronny and sturdily built. He had piercing blue eyes, a strong jaw, and a mustache under a nose that looked like it had been broken a time or two. At the moment, his face was as hard as iron. He wore khaki slacks, a white dress shirt, and a gray blazer. A gold badge was clipped to the front of his belt. On his left side, just under the jacket, was the outline of a holstered pistol. "I beg to differ, sir," he said with a tight smile. "Agent Mason Holliday, South Carolina Bureau of Criminal Investigation. I arrive in town and pull up here to get some gas when I see a frightened-looking young woman with two men near her about to come to blows. Considering I am a law enforcement officer in this state, I'm obligated to investigate. Therefore, it is my business."

Ronny stepped back a few steps and glared at him. "My wife and I are estranged," he said with forced calmness. "We crossed paths and had a few words. This stranger here intervened because he thought I was losing my temper." He glared at the newcomer standing between him and Amanda. "I wasn't."

"Sir, I stepped in because it looked like this man was going to assault this woman," the stranger said. "Just being a good Samaritan and all."

"I suggest you both back off and take a few moments to calm down," Holliday said. He turned his head slightly toward Amanda. "Ma'am, who might you be and what's your side of the story?"

"My name is Amanda Easton," Amanda said shakily. "I stopped here to get gas". She pointed to Ronny. "He's my husband, Ronny Easton. I left him three weeks ago. He saw me here and confronted me." She pointed to the stranger. The stranger had turned to look at her but remained between her and Ronny. She noted that he hadn't turned his back to Ronny. Instead, he had turned to the side to face the newly-arrived BCI agent. "He came up because my husband was acting like he was about to get violent."

"You're lying," Ronny said angrily. He glared at Agent Holliday. "I'm leaving."

"Mr. Easton, you take one step and you will spend the night in the county jail," Agent Holliday said. "I decide if you can leave and when." For all of the emotion in his voice, he might as well have been discussing the weather.

Ronny puffed his chest out. "Do you know who I am?" he asked.

"No," Holliday said. "And, furthermore, I don't care who you are."

The casual nonchalance in Holliday's voice caused Ronny to visibly deflate. Coming from a family of wealth and power, he had never been spoken to like that before. He looked surprised and more than a little shaken. Amanda saw the change in his attitude and she felt like cheering inside. Because of his family's money and connections, Ronny had always been handled with kid gloves. It had been that way since elementary school where Amanda had first met him when she was six years old.

"Mrs. Easton, did your husband assault you physically?" Holliday asked. "Do you feel threatened?"

For a moment, Amanda was tempted to tell him yes. If she did, the BCI agent would probably take him to jail. The only problem was that Ronny going to jail would be pointless. He was good buddies with the sheriff, who ran the jail, meaning he would be out before the agent's paperwork was done. The criminal charge would go to local court where the judge played golf with Ronny twice a week. All it would do is further inflame the situation. She assumed the BCI agent was in town over the shooting that had happened yesterday. The local newspaper had mentioned that the BCI was involved. Once the agent left town, Ronny would make sure she paid for him going to jail.

"No, I'm okay," Amanda said softly. "If he will just leave, that will be okay."

"You sure?" Holliday asked kindly. Amanda nodded. "Very well," he said reluctantly. "Mr. Easton, you may go now," he said to Ronny.

"I'm speaking to Sheriff Garrett about this," Ronny said huffily as he started to walk away.

"Excellent," Agent Holliday said. "When you speak to him, tell him I'll be by his office soon. Thanks."

The look on Ronny's face was priceless as he stomped around to the driver's side of his Range Rover made Amanda want to laugh out loud. A few seconds later, the Range Rover drove slowly out of the gas station's parking lot. The BCI agent watched Ronny leave and then walked over to the stranger. "Hey, friend, can I see your identification?" he asked.

The stranger produced a driver's license from his front jean pocket. "My name is Sam Walker. Here's my Arizona driver's license." He handed the card to Agent Holliday.

Holliday took the card, studied it, and handed it back to him. "Mr. Walker, I saw what happened. I suspect that if you hadn't intervened, this lady would have been assaulted. Thank you."

"Yes, thank you, Mr. Walker," Amanda said sincerely. "Where did you come from? One moment I was by myself and the next, there you were."

Sam pointed toward one of the station's open garage bays. "I was over there," he said. "I was passing through and my motorcycle started giving me problems. I coasted into here in hopes they could fix it for me."

"I'm sorry that both of you got dragged into the middle of my mess," Amanda said, looking at both men. "My life is usually not quite so dramatic."

Sam smiled warmly. "I think me and this officer were both in the right place at the right time," he said. "By the way, I think your son is trying to get your attention."

Amanda spun around to see that Caleb was standing in the driver's seat and looking out the window at her and the two men. He looked more confused than scared at the two new arrivals. Amanda tapped on the window. "It's okay, Caleb. Open the door." Caleb fumbled around and hit the button unlocking the door. Amanda opened the door and he hopped out of the car. He stood there, looking at both men with open curiosity. "Caleb, say hello to the two nice men who helped Mommy."

"Hello," Caleb said softly. "Thank you for helping us. My dad is a bad man."

Sam smiled down at him. "No problem, Caleb," he replied.

Caleb looked at Agent Holliday. "Thank you too," he said. "Are you a policeman?" Agent Holliday smiled and nodded. "You should put my dad in jail. He's mean and hits us."

Amanda blushed deeply. "Caleb," she said firmly. She looked at the two men. "Sorry. He usually is pretty shy until he gets to know you. Of course, today is the day he decides to come out of his shell."

"That's kids for you," Agent Holliday said. "Ma'am, given your situation, you might want to look into getting a restraining order against your estranged husband. Next time, there might not be someone to help out."

"I will," Amanda said, even though she knew she was lying. There was no way the local judge would give her one. She reached down and took Caleb's hand. "You ready to go home, Caleb?" Caleb nodded.

"Amanda, before you leave, I assume you're a local?" Sam asked. Amanda nodded. "Good. Can you tell me if this town has a hotel? The mechanic here says he works on bikes as well, so I got lucky when I pushed it in here. However, he has to order some parts to fix mine and it might take a few days, so I'm stranded."

"That's ironic," Agent Holliday added. "I need to find one as well."

"Then you're both lucky," Amanda said. "My grandfather owns a hotel about a mile from here close to the town limits. His house actually adjoins the hotel. Caleb and I are staying there. It's the nicest hotel in town and right on the lake. Giving you two a room apiece for a few nights is the least we can do."

"Ma'am, I have a state credit card, so I don't need a free room," Agent Holliday replied. "It's your tax dollars, so you deserve to get some of them back. The hotel sounds fine. Saves me the trouble of looking for a place."

"I hate to impose," Sam said. "I'm on a solo motorcycle trip across the country, so I have camping gear. If there's local campground I'll be fine."

"The only close campground has been overrun with some biker types," Amanda replied. "There's two other hotels, but they're not exactly quality places. If you don't have money, my grandfather will either let you stay for free or let you work it off around the place."

Out of the blue, Caleb reached up and grabbed Sam's hand. "Please," he said. "Come stay."

Amanda looked down at Caleb. She had never seen her son act like that with a stranger before, especially a male. Since his father, the primary male in his life, swung between ignoring him completely or being cruel to him, Caleb usually shied away from men. She supposed it was because Caleb thought Sam was some kind of hero for helping them when Ronny showed up. "You're more than welcome," she said as she turned her attention back to Sam. "Please, I insist."

Sam pondered it for a moment. "Okay," he said, "but only for a day or two I hope."

"You can ride with me if you don't mind riding in a cop car," Agent Holliday said.

Sam shrugged. "Sure," he said.

Amanda felt a palpable sense of relief at the men's answer that surprised her. Maybe it was because their presence might mean Ronny would stay away. "Good," she said. "Let me get Caleb back in the car and belted in and you can follow me."

"I need to grab my bag off my bike," Sam said.

"I'll wait," Amanda said.

Amanda helped Caleb get in the car and back into his booster seat. She then drove her car to the edge of the station's lot and waited. She watched in the rearview mirror as Sam went to the garage bay and returned to Agent

Holliday's car with a big backpack. Sam put the pack into the Charger's trunk and then hopped into the front seat. As soon as the agent's car was behind her, Amanda eased out into traffic with the two men behind her. Once she was on the main road, she glanced over at Caleb and saw that he was looking directly at her.

"What is it, Caleb?" Amanda asked.

"It's going to be different now, Mommy," Caleb said softly. With that, he turned, stared out the window on his side, and didn't utter another word.

Amanda turned her attention back to the road. She loved her son more than life itself, but he was a little strange sometimes.

CHAPTER 5

White's Hotel was a surprisingly pretty, single story building built out of brick, timber, and native stone located at the very edge of the town of Easton. The building had obviously been built many years ago in the time before hotels were generic boxes that all looked the same. The building was a flat rectangle with only twelve rooms. The front doors of each room faced the highway and the hotel's parking lot. A stone wall with columns at the entrance and exit to the parking lot separated it from the two-lane highway. The hotel's office sat at one end of the rectangle near the entrance to the parking lot. A neat neon sign bearing the name of the establishment was mounted on the brick wall near the office's large glass windows. A metal awning, obviously old but well-maintained, extended out over a parking area right in front of the office door. The parking lot held only three cars when Amanda's Toyota with Agent Holliday's Charger following it drove into the lot.

Amanda parked in one of the empty spaces close to the front door of the office. Mace parked in the spot beside her. Almost immediately an older man with thick white hair and dark-framed glasses came rushing out of the office to Amanda's vehicle. The older man looked to be in his seventies, but appeared to be pretty spry. He wore jeans, work boots, and a denim work shirt. He reached Amanda's car just as she got out. "Are you okay?" were the first words out of his mouth. His voice was surprisingly powerful, coming from such a slender frame. The old man could have made a good living as a radio disc jockey or sports announcer.

"Grandpa, we're fine," Amanda said hurriedly.

"Jack Smith called me from his gas station," the old man said. "He told me what happened." He shook his head in disgust. "If I had been there, I would have knocked him out. A grown man shouldn't act like that."

Mace and Sam Walker were just getting out of Mace's car when Amanda directed her grandfather's attention to them. "Grandpa, luckily these two men showed up at just the right time and dealt with Ronny. This is Sam Walker. He happened to be there at the garage and came rushing over to confront Ronny before he got physical," Amanda said as she pointed to Sam. "This other gentleman is Agent Mason Holliday of the South Carolina Bureau of Criminal Investigation. He saw what was happening and pulled into the parking lot to help as well."

The older man stepped forward and extended his hand. "God bless you both," the old man said as he shook each man's hand vigorously. "I'm Jacob White, Amanda's grandfather. I own this hotel, the marina next door, and I'm also the pastor of Easton Baptist Church. Thank God you both showed up in the nick of time. Her soon-to-be-ex-husband is a piece of work. If you hadn't showed up when you did, there's no telling what would have happened."

Mace recognized the name Jacob White. The old man was the one who'd complained to the governor about possible corruption in Easton. "Nice to meet you, sir," he said. He made a mental note to speak with him privately when he got the chance. He wanted to hear Jacob's suspicions for himself.

"Glad I could help," Sam said politely.

"Grandpa, each of these men needs a room," Amanda said. "Agent Holliday will be in town for a few days regarding the shooting yesterday. Sam is stranded until his bike can be fixed."

"Gentlemen, you can stay as long as you need to," Jacob replied instantly. "It's the off season here, so we have plenty of rooms available. I won't charge you a dime."

"Mr. White, I appreciate your offer, but I have to decline the free room," Mace replied. "I have a state credit card for that, so the state pays for it. By law, I can't stay for free. Charge me the normal rate."

Jacob shook his head. "It's a shame there's a law that won't let me show some gratitude to a man who helped my family." He looked at Sam. "What about you, young man?"

"I could use a place to stay," Sam answered. "I don't have much cash on me, but I'll be glad to work for my room and board. Amanda said you might have some things that need doing."

"She was right," Jacob said. "Let me put you two fellows up in a room apiece. Also, I insist that you have dinner with me, Amanda, and Caleb tonight at my house. I live over there." He pointed to a pretty, two-story Victorian- style house that sat next door to the hotel. The house was painted a light gray with black shutters. The house and grounds were as well-kept as the hotel.

"Sir, that won't be necessary," Mace answered. "I can find a local restaurant."

"That might be harder than you think, son," Jacob answered. "Most of the local places either close after lunch or have shut down entirely. You'd have to go back into town to find anything and it would most likely be fast food. I have a local lady who cooks for me and there will be plenty."

Mace thought about it for a moment. A good, home-cooked meal did sound tempting. There was no telling how long he would have to be here in Easton, so it might be a long time before he got back home to his house in the suburbs of Columbia. "Well, if it wouldn't be too much trouble, I'll be glad to," he said.

"Count me in as well," Sam added.

Jacob smiled. "Good," he said. "Amanda, you want to grab a couple of sets of keys out of the office. We've got plenty of rooms available, so pick two."

Amanda excused herself and hurried to the office. She returned a couple of minutes later with two keys with key fobs bearing the hotel's name. "Follow me," she said. "I'll show you the rooms and then you can come back, get your bags, and get settled."

"Can I come?" Caleb asked. He had clambered out of the car and was standing beside his mother.

"Sure," Amanda said. After the events of the day, she was scared to let her son out of her sight.

"Awesome." Caleb said. He reached up and grabbed each man's hand. "Come on," he said excitedly, "I'll show you."

Amanda stood there in surprise. Caleb was normally shy, especially around adult men, but that shyness seemed to have vanished. Amanda was kind of embarrassed, but the two men looked amused. "I guess you should follow my son," she said with a smile.

Sam returned the smile. The smile softened his features and made him look younger. Amanda guessed that he was probably in his late twenties or early thirties, close to her own age of twenty-eight. "I don't think we have a choice," he said.

"Apparently not," Amanda said. "Caleb, it's Rooms 104 and 106." Caleb nodded and towed both men down the sidewalk from the office toward the right side of the building. Amanda followed along behind the two men. The first room they came to was Room 104. "Agent Holliday, this one will be yours," she said as she took the key and opened the door. She stepped back and handed Mace the key. "Mr. Walker, you can have 106. I would put you in 105 next door, but it's in the process of being painted."

"Call me Sam," Mace heard Sam say as Amanda moved on to the room that would be his. Mace stepped into the hotel room and took a quick look around. The room was surprisingly large and homey. There was a king-sized bed, a small desk along one wall, a table with two chairs, and a small counter that held a microwave and automatic coffee maker. A small refrigerator sat underneath the counter. The room appeared to be spotlessly clean as well. The room also had a sliding glass rear door. Mace walked over and looked through the glass door. Just outside the door was an individual patio area and a walkway that led to the hotel's dock and small marina. There was also an open area of grass between the patios and the water's edge with a children's play area, a basketball court, and a picnic area. Large oak trees and colorful flower beds bordered the open area. Overall, it wouldn't be a bad place to spend a few days.

Mace turned and walked back to the room's front door. He walked back outside and almost ran right into Amanda. She stopped short and the two of them stood there face to face. It was the first time since their meeting at the gas station that he'd had a chance to really notice her. Back then, he'd thought she was kind of cute, but now, up close, she was strikingly pretty. He could tell that she was checking him out as well. It was kind of awkward, but not necessarily unpleasant. "The room is nice," he said to break the silence.

"I'm glad you like it, Agent Holliday," Amanda answered.

"It's Mason Holliday," Mace said. "Most people call me Mace."

"Mace," Amanda said as if sampling the word. "It makes you sound dangerous."

"In my line of work, that's not necessarily a bad thing," Mace replied honestly. "There's some dangerous people in the world."

They were interrupted by Sam and Caleb emerging from the open door of Room 106. Caleb was chattering about some cartoon he'd watched where the good guy rode a motorcycle. Sam was paying attention as if what Caleb was saying was the most important thing he'd ever heard. Amanda broke their eye contact and turned to her son. "Caleb, give our new friends a break," she said with a laugh. "I'm sorry," she added to Sam and Mace. "I think he's still nervous from the events of the day."

"I'm fine, Mommy," Caleb said. "Sam has a motorcycle too and he's riding all over America."

Amanda realized at that moment that she knew practically nothing about Sam Walker. Agent Holliday was a police officer, so he must be a decent guy, but Sam was literally a stranger who'd showed up at the right time. He was a handsome man with kind eyes and he seemed like a nice enough fellow, but everything else about him was a question. She made a decision to find out more about him, especially since Caleb seemed fascinated by him. She supposed it was the motorcycle. Since the bikers had shown up cruising around town, her son had gotten a crash course in motorcycles simply by looking out the car window when the two of them went somewhere. She breathed a silent prayer that Sam wasn't affiliated with the thugs who'd shown up in Easton all of sudden. He didn't look the part, but appearances could be deceiving.

"Maybe at dinner in a few minutes, Sam can tell us a little bit about his travels," Amanda said with a casual look at Sam. "And maybe Agent Holliday can throw in some police stories as well."

"Sounds like fun," Sam answered.

"Speaking of," Amanda said with a quick glance at her watch. "If you two would like to follow me to my Grandpa's place next door, I suspect dinner is ready."

The four of them were walking across the parking lot toward the sidewalk that led to Jacob's house when a marked police car drove into the parking lot and headed toward them. The car was a dark blue Chevy Impala with a light bar and Easton Police Department and a large, gray badge on the front doors. The police car stopped and the driver, a burly man with a shaved head, green eyes, and a deeply-tanned face got out. He wore a black police uniform and gun belt. "Amanda," he called as he stood by his vehicle.

"Hey, Jeff," Amanda said as she walked over to him.

"A little bird told me what happened today at Smith's," Jeff said immediately. "I heard Ronny showed up and acted like a fool." Even though he was talking to Amanda, his eyes shifted to Sam and Mace, the two strangers with her. His gaze was calm but intense.

"He drove up while I was pumping gas," Amanda said. "He made a scene, but these two guys stepped in and prevented it from being more than that." She turned to Sam and Mace. "This is Sam Walker. He just happened to be passing through and was brave enough to help. This other fellow is Agent Mason Holliday from the South Carolina Bureau of Criminal Investigation. He also showed up just in the nick of time."

"Jeff Bradley," Jeff said by way of introduction. "Chief of the Easton Police Department." He shook hands with both men. As he did, he studied each man with an intensity that indicated he didn't miss much. "Welcome to Easton. Thanks for helping out Amanda. She's my cousin and one of my better friends."

"His grandmother was my grandfather's sister," Amanda explained. "We've know each other since we were toddlers. Jeff is one of the few good officers in this county. Unfortunately, he is badly outnumbered by both bad officers and criminals."

"Amanda is like an older sister to me," Chief Bradley said as he leaned against the car door. "She's a little biased. I don't think all of the cops in Easton County are bad people. I've already offered to take her husband to jail the first chance I got. To hell with the consequences."

"Chief Bradley," Mace said. "This is fortunate; I had planned to swing by your office tomorrow as a courtesy to let you know I was in town."

"Agent Holliday," Jeff said. "I assume you are here in Easton about the Deputy Cothran shooting yesterday?"

"I am," Mace replied. "Just following up, per protocol."

"You're more than welcome, sir," Chief Bradley said. "The more good officers around here the better. Are you the Mason Holliday? From the Laurens Incident a few months ago?"

"I am," Mace said with just a hint of embarrassment. "Please just call me Mace."

Jeff straightened up. "It's an honor, Mace," he said simply. "Let me know if I can help you in any possible way. I have no jurisdiction outside the town limits and my hands are full right now, but I will gladly do what I can to assist you."

"Jeff, how is Lizzie?" Caleb asked. "Is she feeling better?"

A cloud passed over Chief Bradley's face as he looked down at Caleb. It vanished almost instantly, but Mace, Sam, and Amanda all saw it and recognized it for what it was: sadness. "She's still sick, little buddy," he said as he reached out and patted Caleb on the head.

"Does her head still hurt?" Caleb asked.

"Caleb," Amanda said gently. She looked at Jeff. "I'm sorry," she said to him.

Chief Bradley tried to force a smile on his face, but it looked more like a grimace. "It's okay," he said. "Caleb, I will tell Lizzie you asked about her. I know that will make her feel better."

"Can I come over and visit her?' Caleb asked curiously. "The last time we played was at church."

"We'll see," Jeff said. He looked at the three adults. "I'll let you three get back to what you were doing," he said. His voice had grown husky and his eyes glistened. It was obvious to them that the police chief was struggling with his emotions at the moment. After a few awkward moments he simply got back into his car. He let the driver's window down. "Amanda, call me if you need me, okay?"

"Absolutely," Amanda promised. "Please give Melanie and Lizzie my love."

Chief Bradley nodded and slowly drove out of the parking lot. It was just getting dark and the lights in the lot were starting to come on. The four of them stood there and watched as the police car vanished into the gathering dusk. "He seems like a good man," Mace said to break the painful silence.

"Jeff is the Easton Police Department right now," Amanda interjected. "There used to be him and three other fulltime officers, but the other three either quit or were hired away by the Easton County Sheriff's Office. He polices the whole town by himself now. In between everything going on with the bikers and his situation at home, I don't know how the poor man manages it."

Sam looked as if he was about to ask her a question, but Amanda held up one finger to silence him and then pointed down to her son by way of explanation. Sam took the hint and dropped it. The four of them walked together in silence toward Jacob's house.

CHAPTER 6

At the exact moment Amanda and her new guests were sitting down at the table in her grandfather's dining room, Ronny Easton was sitting in Sheriff Lynn Garrett's office in the building that housed the Easton County Sheriff's Office. The Easton County Sheriff's Office was located in the center of the town of Easton on the same square block that also contained the Easton County Courthouse and the Easton County Detention Facility. The buildings were literally just yards from each other and connected by covered walkways and adjoining parking lots. The three buildings were all less than ten years old and had been built with a grant from the federal government. They all were built of concrete, stucco, and steel and looked practically the same, with the only difference being the size; the courthouse and the jail were both two stories while the sheriff's office was only one story. An attempt at pleasant landscaping around the three grim buildings had been made, but the trees, hedges, and flower beds hadn't done much to hide the stark ugliness of the architecture and the purpose the buildings served.

Sheriff Lynn Garrett leaned back in his chair behind his desk and listened as Ronny Easton, a lifelong friend and political benefactor, cursed his way through a description of his encounter with his estranged wife and the two newcomers who came to her aid. According to Ronny, the only thing that had kept him from thrashing both of the men who defended Amanda was the BCI agent's gun and badge. Ronny was within seconds of kicking some serious butt, but then he saw the BCI agent's badge and decided it wouldn't be worth it to assault an officer of the law. "If he hadn't had that badge, he'd be in the emergency room right now," Ronny said as he leaned forward in his chair and smacked the top of the sheriff's desk for emphasis.

Sheriff Garrett had to fight not to roll his eyes as he listened to Ronny's diatribe. He had known James Ronald "Ronny" Easton since first grade. Ronny had been a blowhard from day one who talked an awesome game but who couldn't or wouldn't back up his mouth with action. If his family hadn't owned half the county and their businesses hadn't provided jobs for a large number of its residents, someone probably would have beaten Ronny to death by the time he was eighteen. Throughout school Ronny had been a bully of the worst kind: one that his victims couldn't do anything about because of WHO he was. Ronny had also been smart or evil enough to surround himself with people who could back him up physically like Lynn Garrett. Lynn had always been a big guy in a lumbering ox kind of way and he wasn't above bullying others himself. Ronny, Lynn Garrett, and Dwayne Cothran, the man who was now Garrett's second-in-command at the sheriff's office, had been a trifecta of misery for many of the students going through the Easton County School District with them.

"Ronny, you did the right thing by backing down," Sheriff Garrett said as he leaned back casually in his chair. "I didn't know we would have any more BCI agents in town until their director called me late this afternoon. The agent's name is Mason Holliday and he's up here to follow up on Dwayne's incident yesterday. He'll be in town for a few days. It's just routine."

"It would have been worth going to jail to teach him a lesson," Ronny said petulantly.

Sheriff Garrett felt the first stirrings of his temper. Even though he had been friends with Ronny since they both were about seven years old, he had never really liked Ronny. He had made friends with Ronny because of who Ronny was. Even then, Lynn Garrett had been enough of a politician to recognize someone who could benefit him and predatory enough to recognize someone he could take advantage of. Lynn wasn't particularly smart, but he had always had a talent for spotting people and situations he could exploit. Still, Ronny's personality sorely vexed him sometimes. Now that Lynn had reached a point in his life financially where he didn't need Ronny so much anymore, he found he could only take Ronny's blustering in small doses.

"Ronny, that BCI agent is named Mason Holliday," Sheriff Garrett said as he turned and studied a picture on the wall of his office. It was a picture of him being sworn in at the county courthouse after being elected three years ago. It was one of his favorite pictures because it was a huge step on the path that had led him to this point in his life. He was the sheriff of Easton County, and thus the most powerful police official in the county. That position, along with connections to some very bad people and a complete lack of any moral scruples, had made him wealthy beyond his dreams. "If half of what I read is true, he probably would have stomped you into the concrete, then arrested what was left for making him sweat doing it."

"I don't think…," Ronny started to say.

Sheriff Garrett's temper surged. A man could only take so much of Ronny within a short time. "That's right, you don't think!" he said fiercely as he bolted to his feet and leaned across the desk. Standing up, Sheriff Garrett was a big man with wide shoulders and a heavy paunch. He had been an all- state linebacker in high school and the power still showed in his chest and shoulders. His thick body, blonde flat-top haircut, and emotionless eyes lost behind thick cheeks and a large nose made him a very intimidating person when he was angry. Ronny shrank back visibly in his seat, even though Ronny was a couple of inches taller than the sheriff and in better shape. "Jesus, Ronny! Your wife, a woman you've been screwing around on and treating like a dog for years, up and leaves you. How many times have you sat there and told me that you wish you could be rid of her? Well, you get it and now you're acting like a fool!"

"She took my son!" Ronny whined.

"The son you don't like and you ignore constantly?" Sheriff Garrett retorted. "You can't stand being a father. What's the big deal?"

"He's mine!" Ronny answered. "You don't take what's mine! I'm Ronny Easton!"

Sheriff Garrett forced himself to sit back down in his chair. He took a couple of seconds to compose himself. When he spoke again, his voice was lower, but it still shook with anger. "So that's it, huh? You don't care about the kid; you just don't want someone getting the better of you." He shook his head. "Ronny, my friend, we have talked about her and this situation. You will get Caleb back from her. By the time your lawyer and Judge Cooper are done with her, Amanda will be lucky if she gets two days of supervised visitation a month. How many times have I got to tell you? The deck is way beyond stacked in your favor. Let this play out. All you have to do is be cool. Being cool means not attacking your estranged wife in public in front of witnesses! And especially not in front of a damned BCI agent!"

"I didn't mean for it to happen," Ronny protested. "I happened to see her there at the gas station. That smug look on her face pushed me over the edge."

Sheriff Garrett had known Amanda since the two of them were kids. Amanda had always been pretty, but she wasn't conceited or smug in the least about it. He had thought about asking her out many times during their teen years. Secretly, he'd always hated the fact that Ronny ended up marrying her. She would have made a fine Mrs. Garrett. "You should have just kept driving."

"Maybe," Ronny said. "It's not just about the kid, Lynn. She could get half my stuff. Her lawyer has the right to dig into my finances, including the company books. You know what could happen with that if her lawyer gets a good accountant who's smart enough to dig a little."

Sheriff Garrett leaned back in his chair, ran a hand over his face, and sighed. "We'll cross that bridge when we come to it," he said. God, he hoped that didn't happen. If their business partners got wind of that, Amanda, her lawyer, and several others would meet sudden, violent ends. The thought of what the animals he was in business with might do to a pretty girl like her was enough to make even him squeamish. "Maybe the best bet would be to let her win this one, Ronny. Pay her off and let her keep the kid. It would save us all a lot of trouble."

"No!" Ronny snarled. "I want that bitch to live in misery. You don't leave me and you don't take what belongs to me!"

Sheriff Garrett took a deep breath. At this time, Ronny and the company he owned were vital to the criminal enterprise that was making them all a tremendous amount of untraceable cash. Their business partners wouldn't let Ronny's domestic problems mess up a good thing. Ronny needed to chill out, but he'd known Ronny long enough to know that wasn't happening. Not for the first time, Sheriff Garrett wondered if Ronny suffered from some type of mental disorder that made him lose his mind if he thought someone else was getting the better of him somehow.

"Okay," Sheriff Garrett said. "Ronny, I'm asking nicely. Please chill out with this until the BCI finishes their investigation and gets out of town. Judge Cooper gets his money tonight. He's already said he would grant you temporary custody. As of tomorrow, you've got your son back. You know that will make her miserable."

Ronny smiled at the thought of making Amanda miserable. "I want to see the look on her face in court tomorrow," he said. "The thought of that has been the only thing that keeps me going."

"Yeah," Sheriff Garrett said. Once again, he had to fight the urge to get up from behind his desk, walk around, and knock Ronny completely out.

"On a side note, how's the situation looking for Dwayne?" Ronny asked. He shook his head and smirked. "Man, we both told him he was playing with fire. I guess he got burned, huh?"

Sheriff Garrett sighed loudly. The situation with Dwayne Cothran, his chief deputy and best friend, was vexing him even more than Ronny was. Dwayne and he had been inseparable friends since grade school where they had bonded because they were the biggest kids in class. The two of them had been football stars in high school and even gotten jobs in the sheriff's office together as deputies ten years earlier. Dwayne was a mountain of a man, standing over six and a half feet tall with three hundred pounds of rock -solid muscle that would have made a professional bodybuilder jealous. Unfortunately, he was also pretty ugly, with a flat face, big ears, eyes that seemed to bulge from their sockets, and wiry red hair that stuck out in a short afro. As if his appearance wasn't a big enough problem with the ladies, Dwayne was also a little weird when it came to women. He didn't seem to like them very much at all for anything other than sex.

Several months ago, as part of his payment from their business partners from south of the border, Dwayne had started requesting women. Their Mexican business partners, who were known as the 'Baja Cartel', were trafficking in women as well as drugs and other illegal items, so it really wasn't a problem for them to pay off one of the crazy gringos with a girl or two. Sheriff Garrett had tried to talk Dwayne out of it, but Dwayne had insisted. The sheriff had a pretty good idea of what was happening to the girls, but he didn't press the issue. Dwayne could be truly frightening, even to him. However, he had warned Dwayne not to let his sexual appetite interfere with other business. The Baja Cartel would not look on something like that kindly.

Unfortunately, that was exactly what had happened yesterday. One of Dwayne's toys had managed to get away, steal his truck, and make a run for it. Thankfully, Dwayne had caught her before she was able to find someone who would listen to her and believe her story. Unfortunately, he had been forced to kill her in broad daylight in front of numerous witnesses, including two North Carolina Highway Patrol officers. However, by pure happenstance, it had played out like a justifiable shooting by a sworn law enforcement officer doing his duty. The girl had stolen a vehicle, wrecked it, and then lunged toward two other cops with a weapon, forcing Deputy Cothran to shoot her. That's the story Dwayne, and by association Sheriff Garrett and the entire sheriff's office, was sticking with. Now the South Carolina Bureau of Criminal Investigation was involved and snooping around.

To say that Sheriff Garrett was stressed at the moment was an understatement. Not only was he having to deal with the legal aftermath of what was officially an officer-involved shooting, he also had to make sure the official narrative stood up to the resulting investigation. He had to make sure that Dwayne kept his story straight, got rid of any evidence that might make anyone question that story, and played the part of a good cop forced to do the unthinkable. Even more than that, he had to make sure that there was not the faintest hint of the illegal activities that were making him, Dwayne, and a fair share of the other folks a lot of money. Last, but definitely not least, he had to make sure the cartel was happy. It was a juggling act, and dealing with it left him very little time or desire to deal with Ronny Easton.

"I think he'll be okay," Sheriff Garrett replied. "It looks like a good legal shooting."

"He about screwed us all up," Ronny opined.

"I agree," Sheriff Garrett said. "Make sure you don't add to the problem, Ronny."

"After tomorrow, I'll be fine," Ronny answered.

CHAPTER 6

Leona, a slim woman in her forties who worked for Jacob White as a combination housekeeper, cook, and hotel front-desk employee during the busy season, had cooked an excellent meal of fried chicken, mashed potatoes, and an assortment of fresh vegetables. She served the meal in the dining room of Jacob's rambling Victorian-style house and then went home for the day, leaving Jacob, Amanda, Caleb, and the two new arrivals to enjoy the food. The five of them settled down at the long wooden table there and helped themselves. Not much was said as they dug hungrily into the food. Even Caleb, who had been a regular chatterbox with his new friend, Sam, was silent as they ate.

The dining room window overlooked the hotel office and part of the parking lot. Through the lighted office window, they could see the young woman who worked there part-time in the evenings manning the check-in counter. Dusk had turned to full darkness outside when Amanda broke the silence. "So, Sam, you said earlier that you're just passing through?" she asked.

"Yes," Sam replied. "I had always dreamed of seeing America. Circumstances worked out so I had some money and free time, so I bought an old motorcycle, fixed it up, packed a few things for the trip, and set off. I've been traveling all over the country, just seeing the sights. So far, I've seen twenty-three states. I've been in South Carolina for the last two days. "

"That sounds amazing," Amanda replied. "I think everyone dreams of hitting the road like that at one time or the other."

"It's been really interesting," Sam replied. "Although I must say, today was the first time I've ended up in a domestic situation."

"Young man, I would like to thank you for getting involved," Jacob said as he pushed away his plate. "Her hopefully-soon-to-be-ex-husband is an abusive thug. I'm a man of God, but part of me wishes you had kicked his rear end."

"You have to excuse my grandfather," Amanda said. "He and my grandmother raised me after my parents died in a car accident when I was seven. He's a little overprotective."

"I wish you had too," Caleb chimed in with his mouth full of food.

"Caleb Elijah Easton!" Amanda said sharply. "That's your dad you're talking about."

"Sorry," Caleb said, even though he didn't sound in the least bit sorry. He went back to using his fork to move around the green beans on his plate.

"You're right, Amanda," Jacob said. He looked at Mason and Sam. "My son was her father. When he and her mother were killed, we got custody. She is my granddaughter, but my late wife and I raised her. Since my wife, Debbie, passed away, Amanda and Caleb are all I've got left. So, yes, I am very protective of them both. I begged her not to marry Ronny Easton. The Lord commands that we should love everyone, but I must confess that I don't even remotely like Ronny Easton, or any of the Eastons for that matter."

"And why is that, sir?" Mace asked. He had really enjoyed the food. As a bachelor who worked long hours, he didn't often get a chance to cook such meals and the home-cooked meal was a welcome respite from microwave food and takeout. Now, with his stomach full, he was interested in finding out what had prompted Jacob White to call the governor and seek help.

"The Easton family has lived in this area since the early eighteen hundreds," Jacob said after a quick sip of iced tea. "From what I know of county history, the Easton ancestors were good people who were apparently good at business. They prospered, starting a number of local businesses and were generous to the community. The family started a textile plant, a trucking company, and a chemical supply wholesale company that provided jobs for a lot of people in the county. It was all well and good until all of the old, decent Eastons died off and Big Ron, Ronny's father, took over. Big Ron wasn't exactly the business type. Instead, he spent most of his time gambling, drinking, and living like a king. Because of his mismanagement, the trucking company and textile plant closed down. All that was left was the chemical company and it was struggling.

"Big Ron died two years ago on the gaming floor of a casino in Las Vegas from a cocaine-induced heart attack," Jacob continued. "Shortly thereafter, Ronny took over the business. He seems to have a good head for business because the company, Easton Chemicals, is doing better, but that seems to be all he's good for. He's been a lousy husband and father."

"Mr. White, what is this biker gang I keep hearing about?" Sam asked. "The reason I ask is because of the response I got when I first arrived at the garage where I met Amanda and her estranged husband. Mr. Smith was pretty short with me until he realized that I wasn't involved with them. Once he realized that, he was very nice."

"They call themselves The Horde, at least that's what the patch on the vests they always wear says," Jacob replied. "They just showed up one day and bought an old farm property a few miles outside of town. Later they bought a bar right outside town limits, remodeled it, and opened up a strip club. The county council approved a zoning change literally overnight. I've always heard that was Ronny Easton's doing. Anyway, their name is accurate. They're a horde alright; a horde of thugs and criminals with no respect for themselves or anyone else. Ever since they arrived, they've been a blight on this whole county.

"Jack Smith, the owner of the garage you spoke with, was one of the first people to have a run-in with some of them," Jacob continued "Shortly after they arrived in town, some of them came to his station. They were showing out and being rude, so he asked them to leave. They beat him up pretty bad. That's why he hates them so bad. He keeps a shotgun behind the counter of his station now. He's a tough old bird and he swears that he'll shoot them if they ever try anything at his place again."

"Wow," Sam said. "What did the police do?"

"It happened in town, so Chief Bradley investigated it," Jacob said. "He requested help from the sheriff's office, but they wouldn't help him. One man couldn't go out to that farm where they are all camped by himself because he would probably not survive the trip. Also, poor Jack couldn't give a good description of the ones involved because he couldn't remember some of it. Poor man was in the hospital for over a week. Besides, all of the bikers look pretty much alike: long hair, beards, tattoos, etcetera."

"We met Chief Bradley a little while ago," Mace said. "He seems like a good man. Why wouldn't the sheriff's office assist him with his investigation?"

"Because they are all a bunch of crooks," Jacob said bitterly. "They turn a blind eye to everything the bikers do. If you drive by that club the bikers run you'll find girls there working who are obviously under-aged. You can also watch people sell drugs outside in the parking lot in broad daylight. I've seen those bikers riding around with pistols hanging out of their pockets walking right by sheriff's deputies and the deputies ignore it. I've personally seen the sheriff's marked cruiser in the parking lot and he wasn't there making arrests, if you know what I mean."

"Mommy, what's a strip club?" Caleb asked as he turned to Amanda.

The four adults had been so wrapped up in the conversation that they had forgotten a five- year- old was at the table with them. Amanda turned a faint shade of red. Sam made a sound that might have been the start of a laugh but a glare from Amanda silenced him immediately. Mace couldn't help but grin. Jacob grimaced and shrugged apologetically.

"I'll explain later, "Amanda said to her son. She glanced down at her watch. "Meanwhile, it's time for you to take a bath and get ready for bed, young man." She directed her attention back to the adults. "Gentlemen, excuse us while I help him get ready for his bath. I'll be back in a few minutes. Come on, son."

Caleb looked like he wanted to protest, but changed his mind and jumped out of his chair. He already looked a little sleepy and his tiredness after what had to be an exciting day for him had made him docile. "Will I see you tomorrow, Mace?" he asked as he started down the hall connected to the living room. Mace nodded. "And what about you, Sam?" he added over his shoulder.

Sam nodded and held up his closed fist. Caleb fist-bumped him as he went down the hall with his mother following him.

"So, Jacob, you think the sheriff's office isn't necessarily doing their jobs when it comes to dealing with the bikers?" Mace asked. "Do you think it is individual officers or the whole department? They have what, twenty or thirty people in the whole department?"

"I served on county council for a couple of terms before I became mayor of the town," Jacob said. "I helped oversee their budget, so I know a lot about them. The whole sheriff's office has thirty-two people, including Sheriff Garrett. They've got about twenty-one deputies on patrol, four detectives, Sheriff Garrett, his second-in-command, Dwayne Cothran, and the remaining people are clerks and secretaries. Most of them have been with the sheriff's office for years and are good people. I personally suspect that the sheriff, Cothran, and maybe seven or eight others might be involved. When I say involved, I mean to some extent ranging from taking bribes to ignore certain things all the way up to active involvement in criminal activity."

"And what makes you suspect those particular ones?" Mace asked

"Mace, I'm seventy-four years old," Jacob said. "Save for four years of college and three years in the U. S. Army, I've lived my whole life in this county. I've been the preacher at the local church for fifty years and my family has run the hotel here for all my life. I know this county and everyone in it. As a pastor, I'm the one people confide in, and I keep my eyes and ears open. I know all the rumors and town gossip. Since Lynn Garrett became sheriff three years ago, a core group consisting of him, Cothran, and a few others have all of a sudden started spending a lot of money. I'm talking new cars, boats, motorcycles, even building new houses. All of this from a department whose highest paid employee is the sheriff and he makes fifty-one thousand dollars a year."

"I can see where that might make a person wonder," Sam interjected.

Jacob nodded. "Garrett and Cothran only got jobs at the sheriff's office because they were local football heroes," he added. "Seven years after walking through the door as a rookie deputy, Lynn ran for sheriff and defeated the incumbent, a good man who'd been our sheriff for twenty years and done a great job. He did it by spending tens of thousands of dollars he somehow came into on newspaper ads and such. He even had commercials on local television. The fact that his best friend was Ronny Easton didn't hurt either. Ronny had a meeting with all of the employees at the chemical company and suggested they vote for Garrett."

"And you think Sheriff Garrett is in pretty deep with the bikers?" Mace asked.

"Mason, is your interest personal or professional?" Jacob retorted. "I know you're here to investigate that young lady getting killed yesterday. Based on what I've heard, the whole thing seems kind of shady."

"I am here to investigate the shooting involving Deputy Cothran," Mace answered. "I really haven't formed an opinion on the matter yet."

Jacob started to say something else, but he was interrupted by Amanda's return. She had pulled her hair up into a ponytail and rolled up her sleeves. "Sorry it took so long, she said. "Caleb either likes taking a bath or hates it. It depends on what day it is."

"I'm single with no children, so I'll take your word for it," Mace said with a smile. "He seems like a good kid, though."

"He's my life," Amanda said as she leaned against the doorway. "The fact that his father was so mean to him is one of the many reasons why I'm here."

"I must confess that, given some of the things I've heard tonight and the way he acted today, I'm developing a pretty low opinion of your husband," Mace said. "He doesn't seem like the type of man a lady like you should end up with. If you don't mind my asking, how did you two end up a couple?"

"He flirted with me constantly in high school and we dated a few times," Amanda said. "I went to the University of South Carolina in Columbia and got a degree in nursing and my nurse's license. I planned to be a pediatric nurse and then maybe go on for my master's degree. I came home after I graduated for a little vacation. Ronny heard and tracked me down. I was young and stupid. He was rich, good-looking, and treated me like a queen. I fell for it, we got married after seven months of dating, and I went off to live in his big house few miles from here."

"All of this despite her grandfather and grandmother begging her not to," Jacob added with a sideways glance at Amanda.

"After the wedding, he changed completely," Amanda said, somewhat defensively. "He went from Mr. Wonderful to being physically, mentally, and emotionally abusive literally overnight. He was very possessive, jealous, and spiteful. It's almost like he had to have me to prove something, and then once he got me, he didn't have to put on a show anymore."

"Sounds like a classy guy," Sam said from his chair. "The police chief obviously isn't a fan of his either."

"No," Amanda replied. "Jeff hates him because Ronny's a bully and Jeff hates bullies."

"What's the issue with the chief's daughter?" Sam added. "I noticed the awkwardness earlier when the subject came up."

"He has a six-year-old daughter named Lizzie," Amanda said. "She has a brain tumor. Based on the location of the tumor and type it is, it's inoperable. She's not going to make it."

"I hate to hear things like that," Mace said grimly.

"Jeff's a fine man," Jacob added. "As mayor of the town, I'm his boss. He does what he can regarding the bikers and all of the problems their arrival has caused here. People used to come to Easton for the peace, quiet, and scenic beauty, but now the only people we get are looking for drugs, prostitutes, and everything else bad you can name." He shook his head sadly. "I've been praying a lot for Jeff and his family, this whole county, and my own family." He looked at Amanda. "I've about wore my knees out praying about tomorrow."

"What happens tomorrow?" Sam asked.

"I have a hearing tomorrow morning at nine A.M. in family court," Amanda said. "My husband's attorney has requested that Ronny be given temporary custody of Caleb because I am an unfit mother. It goes without saying that I'm terrified that Caleb will have to go back with his father."

"I doubt that will fly," Mace said. "Knowing what I know about family court procedure here in South Carolina, your husband would have to have some pretty damning evidence against you proving that before they would take Caleb away from you this early in a separation."

"The family court judge is Judge Roy Cooper," Amanda said. "He's good friends with the Eastons. There's also been rumors over the years that he can be easily swayed to your side if the money is right. I'm sure Ronny has already spoken with him and some money has changed hands. I'm not optimistic."

"I saw that fancy Cadillac the judge drives outside the strip club as I was driving past about two hours ago," Jacob said bitterly. "I'm sure he's there clearing his mind so he can be fair and impartial tomorrow." He rolled his eyes. "That was sarcasm, if you haven't figured that out."

"Do you have an attorney?" Sam asked.

"A lawyer here in town named Hiram Bean," Jacob replied for Amanda. "He's an old friend and a fine lawyer, but he knows it's an uphill battle, to say the least. He tried to get a venue change to a judge in a neighboring county, but Judge Cooper overruled him. In this state, a family court judge has a great deal of power."

"They do," Mace agreed. "If he rules against you, have your attorney immediately appeal."

"He's already said he would," Amanda said. "But Caleb would have to be with Ronny while that was happening. Ronny would treat him like crap just to spite me the whole time. He doesn't care about Caleb. This whole farce of a hearing is just a way to torment me."

No one knew how to reply to that and an awkward silence descended in the dining room. Somewhere back down the hall they could hear running water and Caleb splashing in the bathtub. "I need to go check on him," Amanda finally said. She turned and walked down the hall, leaving the three men sitting at the table.

"I hope it goes better than she expects," Sam said quietly.

"I've been praying steadily," Jacob answered. "I know the Lord knows what He's doing. We just have to have faith."

"Well, it's getting late," Mace said. "I think we all have a long day ahead of us tomorrow." He stood up from his chair. "Sir, the food was delicious. Let me at least help you clean up."

Jacob rose from his chair. "That's alright," he said with a wave of his hand. "I'll take care of it. Mace, good luck with the start of your investigation tomorrow. Maybe this whole thing is the answer to my prayers regarding something being done about the problems we have in this county. Sam, I suspect I can find you some chores to do to earn your keep until your bike is fixed."

Sam had also risen from his chair. "I'll be glad to help out," he said heartily. "You've been very kind to me and I appreciate it. I'm good with my hands and don't mind working hard."

Jacob ushered the two men through the kitchen toward the back door where they'd entered earlier. "Sam, what type of work did you do before you set off to see the country?" he asked

"I was in the military," Sam answered.

Jacob intended to follow up with a question regarding which branch of the military Sam had served in, but at that moment the cell phone in Jacob's shirt pocket began to ring. He took it out and glanced at the phone's display screen. "This is one of my church deacons,' he said apologetically. "I need to take this. His brother has been very ill and I suspect it's not good news."

Mace and Sam thanked Jacob for his hospitality and left through the back door. Both men were lost in thought and didn't speak as they made their way to the hotel next door and their individual rooms. They shared one last polite nod to each other as each man reached the door of his room, unlocked it, and went inside.

Barely an hour after the two men had retired to their rooms, a single figure appeared in the darkness outside the hotel. The figure moved as silently as a wraith along the back of the hotel until he reached the deep shadows of the trees along the edge of the lake. He paused for a moment to get his bearings. Satisfied that he knew where he was going, he stood there for a few moments longer, breathing deeply and enjoying the night air and the sounds of the lake lapping against the shore close by. It was very peaceful and the feel of the night air on his skin was most pleasant. He had been places where a cool breeze and the presence of water would have been a gift from God Above and he savored it.

He would have willingly spent hours there enjoying the different sensations and indulging his senses, but he unfortunately he could not. There was business he needed to take care of. He had a list of names to make his way through and a plan to set in motion. That was why he was in Easton County, not for pleasant scenes and friendly people. Everything else would have to wait.

He took one last, long breath and smiled. "Let the games begin," he said as he walked away into the night.

CHAPTER 8

Easton Police Chief Jeff Bradley lived in a secluded house on a slight hill several miles from the town where he worked. The two- story house with white clapboard siding and a wraparound front porch sat in the middle of a cow pasture nearly a half a mile from the main road down a gravel driveway. The house had been a rundown old farmhouse when he and his wife, Melanie, bought it eight years ago shortly after getting married. Jeff had started renovating it as soon as they moved in and over the years had almost completely rebuilt the structure. The original floor plan and exterior had stayed the same, with the only addition he had ever made being a covered rear porch that looked out over the field behind the house and the distant trees. There were a couple of oak and pecan trees right at the edge of his yard, but after that it was just open fields and nice views. The new back porch, outfitted with a hand-built porch swing he'd made in his shop, was Jeff's favorite place. He often retreated there when he needed to be by himself. Lately, it seemed like he'd been spending more time outside on the back porch than he had in the house. The porch at night had become his place to try to sort out the emotional turmoil that was tearing him apart.

Jeff sat on the porch swing and looked out into the darkness that surrounded his house. The half-moon lay a soft glow over the pasture behind the house. He could see the faint shapes of a few cows huddled together on the other side of the barbed fence at the edge of his back yard. Jeff had always found the cattle's soft, nighttime lowing combined with the chirruping of the cicadas in the trees to be very soothing and peaceful. Many times, he and Melanie had sat in the porch swing listening to the sounds and holding each other. Even during the day, the view across the green fields with wildflowers scattered here and there was pretty. The view of the flowers, birds in the trees, and the cows had also made the porch swing a favorite spot of their only daughter, Lizzie. She would often sit out there with them, swinging happily while telling him and Melanie about what she'd learned in kindergarten or some Disney movie she'd watched.

The thought of Lizzie caused a lump to swell in Jeff's throat and his eyes start to sting. He fought the tears valiantly, but it was to no avail. A single tear slid from each eye and dripped down to his chin. He wiped them away with one hand. At this point, he didn't know who or what he was crying for anymore. Sometimes he thought it was over the loss of those happy, simple days when everything was good and everyone was happy and healthy. Those days were gone now, never to return. They had been stolen away by the brain tumor that was now growing inside his daughter's head. Along with those happy days, that same vicious, merciless tumor had stolen the peace and contentment that had once ruled Jeff's home. Even now, in his daughter's bedroom, that same tumor was busy stealing Lizzie's life. According to the doctors, the tumor would succeed on its unholy mission sometime within the next few days.

The thought of Lizzie's illness and coming death caused a fierce, restless anger to surge through his body. Suddenly unable to sit down any longer, Jeff stood up and walked to the edge of the porch. He leaned against one of the wooden posts that supported the porch's roof. He looked up at the night sky beyond the edge of the roof overhang. Because they were so far out in the country, there was no light pollution and in the clear night sky it looked like every star in the universe was on display. Normally the sight would instill him with a sense of awe, but tonight it just made him even angrier. It was hard to believe that a God who could create something so beautiful would also create brain tumors in little kids.

There was a soft creak behind him and he turned. Melanie had slipped out and was standing there at the back door. She knew he liked the darkness, so she hadn't turned on the porch light. Her face was hidden in the shadows. He was actually glad that it was; Melanie was a pretty woman, but the stress of Lizzie's illness had left dark circles under her eyes and a pained look on her face. That hurt look was all too familiar because he saw it in the mirror every time he looked at his own face. He didn't like being reminded of it. "Yes, baby?" he asked over his shoulder.

Melanie walked over and stood beside him. She slipped one arm around his waist and rested her head on his shoulder. "You okay?" she asked softly.

"Is that a rhetorical question?" Jeff asked in a weak attempt at humor. "I think we both know neither one of us is okay."

Melanie squeezed him tightly. "I know, honey," she said. "I just came out to let you know she's asleep now. She really enjoyed the story you read her."

"I know," Jeff said. He'd started reading aloud to Lizzie every night when she was a baby. Even though she was too small to understand the words at first, his daughter had seemed to love the sound of his voice and would go to sleep almost immediately. He had continued to read to her even though she was beginning to read herself now that she was older. It was their nightly ritual. It was one of the things he was going to miss the most when she was gone.

"Did the hospice nurse say anything about her eyes when she came by today?" he added. Two days ago, Lizzie's eyes had started turning in, making it look as if she was intentionally crossing her eyes trying to be funny. Lizzie's doctor had told them what symptoms she would exhibit as the tumor progressed. Eye issues had been one of the symptoms he'd mentioned.

"Mary said it was from the tumor pressing on the brain stem," Melanie said. Mary was the hospice nurse who came by at least once a day to make sure Lizzie was comfortable. "She said it happens close to the end. She expects that Lizzie will go to sleep soon and not wake up. Once that happens, it's a matter of hours. The good news is that Lizzie won't be in any pain. She'll slip away in her sleep."

Jeff wanted to scream, rant, rave, and curse at the thought of his precious daughter dying in her sleep, but he knew it was pointless. His pitching a fit wasn't stopping the inevitable. Plus, he was afraid that, if he lost control that bad, he might not be able to regain his composure or senses. That's all Melanie needed: her only child dead and her husband locked up in a psychiatric ward. "So, I might have just read my baby her last story?" he asked hoarsely.

"No idea," Melanie said in a voice that was scarcely above a whisper. She looked up at his face. "Does it make me a bad mother because I want this to be over? I'm tired of her suffering and I'm tired of having to watch my baby die by inches." Her voice cracked and became a sob. She put her hand over her mouth as if to stifle it, but failed.

Jeff looked down at his wife's face. In the pale moonlight he could see the wet tracks that the tears she'd been silently shedding had left on her cheeks. He turned, pulled her to him, and hugged her fiercely. She buried her face in his chest. Quiet sobs racked her body as she sagged into him. "Is it bad that I've stopped asking God to cure Lizzie and instead asked that He let her die quickly and without pain?" he asked softly.

Melanie pulled her face from his chest and looked up at him. "You still pray?" she asked. "I quit talking to God the day Doctor Adams told us that Lizzie was terminal. I can't find it within myself to be on speaking terms with a God that would let this happen."

Jeff stood there and held his wife. "Me and Preacher White talked about this yesterday," he finally said. As Mayor of Easton, Jacob White was Jeff's boss, but he had also been Jeff's pastor since Jeff was a child. Jeff's family had attended the Easton First Baptist Church since he was born. Jeff, Melanie, and Lizzie had continued to go there as a family. "Jacob said that everything happens for a reason and that God always has a plan."

A suppressed sob shook Melanie's slender frame. "Do you really believe that God, if He even really exists, made a plan that involves our six-year-old daughter dying?" she finally asked. "What kind of God does that?"

Jeff really wanted to answer Melanie's question. It was the same question he'd asked himself a few thousand times since Lizzie's diagnosis, and he'd never gotten an answer to it either. Maybe one day, far in the future, the two of them would understand why they were facing this horrible ordeal, but for now there were no answers to be found. All he and Melanie could do was hold each other, cry, and wait for the inevitable moment when their only child lost her battle.

The two of them stood there in the darkness, holding each other tight, lost in a sea of immeasurable pain.

CHAPTER 9

Judge Roy Cooper was drunk and he knew it. He'd just spent four hours drinking steadily and ogling the new girls at The Boy's Club, the strip club on Highway Forty-seven outside the town of Easton. Normally he could handle his liquor, but the pretty girls and free-flowing alcohol had caused him to lose track of how much he was drinking. He hadn't realized how drunk he actually was until he'd gotten up from his VIP table to leave. The spinning room and clumsiness were the first clue as he staggered out of the club to his car. Once at his car, it had taken him ten minutes to open the car door, get in the vehicle, and start the engine. Now, as he drove his Cadillac down the dark highway toward his house, he could tell that he was swerving all over the road. He'd run off the road onto the grassy shoulder twice already and he'd barely made it a mile from the club. The only thing that had kept him from crashing into the trees along the side of the highway was the jolt of his car running off the roadway. The noise and motion had snapped him out of his haze in just enough time to get his car back onto the road.

Most people in Roy's condition would have been petrified of getting stopped by the police and arrested for drunken driving, but the very idea of that happening just made Roy smile. Even if the police did spot him and stop his vehicle, the officers wouldn't do anything to him. They would probably just give him a ride home. After all, he was Judge Roy Cooper, Chief Magistrate of the Easton County Magistrate Court. As such, he was the most powerful legal official in the entire county. He ran the criminal and family court systems in Easton County. There were four other magistrates in the county, but they all answered to him. He not only presided over his own caseload, he also assigned the other four magistrates their caseloads. He could decide who heard what cases on what schedule. He could overrule the other magistrates under him. In short, he had complete control over most legal matters brought before the courts in Easton County.

As Chief Magistrate, Roy was well-known to local law enforcement, particularly the Easton County Sheriff's Office. He counted Sheriff Lynn Garrett and several of his deputies as personal friends. The sheriff and he would go deer hunting together at least twice a season. Sheriff Garrett and his men wanted to stay on his good side, so they overlooked it when he enjoyed his liquor too much and drove. The way the deputies saw it, if the judge wasn't wrecking his car, he was okay to drive. They had also protected Roy when his love for pretty women and total lack of self-restraint had come back to haunt him. Sheriff Garrett and Chief Deputy Cothran had visited more than one angry father or furious husband and convinced them not to make an issue out of something Roy had said or done to their daughter or wife. Not many men were willing to withstand the sheriff's threats and Deputy Cothran's size and furious temper to make an issue out of Roy's dirty mouth or grasping hands. The husbands and fathers, thoroughly cowed, had accepted a half-hearted apology from Judge Cooper delivered by the sheriff and dropped it.

As if his lust for alcohol and pretty women wasn't enough, Roy also had quite a reputation for being corrupt. It was well-known within certain circles that his decisions could be influenced in your favor with the right incentives. Cash discreetly slipped his way was his personal favorite, but sexual favors from a pretty women was a close second. A short, fat man in his late-forties with a receding hairline and a bulldog face, women weren't exactly beating a path to his door, but as a judge with the power to help or hurt them, many were more than willing to endure his attentions for however long it took to get their desired result. More than one divorce case or criminal case had been decided in a woman's favor following a private meeting in the judge's chambers at the courthouse or at the house on Lake Charles where the judge, who was divorced, lived alone. Most of the local lawyers who tried criminal cases in front of Judge Cooper also played the game, even going so far as to factor in the cost of a bribe to the judge as part of their legal fees for certain kinds of cases.

Ronny Easton had made it a point to cover all of his bases when it came to his divorce hearing in front of the judge tomorrow morning. As soon as Amanda had left him, Ronny had contacted a local family lawyer who was a particular friend of Judge Cooper and well-versed in how the judge liked to operate. The lawyer had filed papers requesting an emergency hearing regarding the custody of Amanda's and Ronny's son, Caleb. The lawyer had then placed a call to his good buddy, Judge Cooper, and requested that he hear the case personally. Ronny's lawyer had also let the judge know that Ronny really wanted the case to go his way and that he was willing to do whatever he needed to do to make that happen. A few coded messages were exchanged, and that was what had brought the judge to the bar tonight. While the girls and liquor kept Judge Cooper entertained and happy, Ronny's lawyer had slipped into the club, walked up to the judge's VIP booth, and shaken his hand as if to greet him. In actuality, he had slipped Judge Cooper a carefully-folded envelope filled with cash. If the free lap dances and liquor weren't already enough, the envelope sealed the deal.

Roy took one hand off the wheel long to enough to pat his pants pocket. The fat envelope was still there and the feel of it made him smile. He had gotten five thousand dollars from Ronny in order to rule in his favor at the hearing tomorrow, much more than he normally demanded for a petty divorce case, but Ronny had the money to pay it. Judge Cooper had been friends with Big Ron Easton before his untimely death. Big Ron's power and influence had helped Roy go from a country lawyer barely getting by on petty criminal cases and divorces to being a magistrate and then to chief magistrate. Now Big Ron was dead and any particular favors he'd owed the senior Easton had died with him. Besides, Judge Cooper wasn't particularly fond of Ronny Easton; he'd always considered him a punk who'd been fortunate enough to be born to the right people. Cooper had been born to ordinary, working folks and had worked his way through college and law school with odd jobs, so he was not really fond of people like Ronny who thought the world owed them something.

There were a couple of other reasons he'd demanded so much from Ronny as well. Ronny's wife's lawyer was Hiram Bean, a man the judge personally detested and possibly the best lawyer in the county. When he ruled against Amanda Easton, Bean would appeal the decision to the state circuit court, which was the next level above magistrate's court. That appeal would be heard by a completely impartial judge in a neighboring county that was within the state circuit for their area of the state. Roy was going to have to make his decision in Ronny's favor look impartial and based on case law if his decision was going to stand on appeal. Even if his decision to award temporary full custody to Ronny was overturned, he had to make it at least look like it was a simple legal error and not what it actually was. In short, he was going to have to actually hit the law books early tomorrow morning before the hearing and do some work. Lastly, Bean's appeal might draw unwanted attention to how the judge conducted his court, meaning he might have to play it all straight and legal for an undetermined amount of time. The money from Ronny would offset potential losses from bribes he would be unable to accept if such scrutiny came.

Roy's attention to his driving had only wandered for a couple of seconds while he touched the envelope in his pocket, but it was enough. As Roy directed his attention back to his driving and the roadway in front of his car, he caught a fleeting glimpse of something in the road ahead. He caught the briefest of glimpses, but it was enough for his alcohol-addled brain to realize that there was a man standing directly in front of his speeding car right in the middle of the road caught in the glare of the headlights. With that realization also came the certainty that he was about to run over the man standing in front of his car. Even while Roy's brain was still processing the thought, his body was reacting instinctively. His hands jerked the steering wheel to the right while his right foot came off the gas pedal and tried to hit the brake pedal. Unfortunately, due to the alcohol in his system, his right foot didn't hit the brake pedal. Instead his foot came back down on the edge of the accelerator. While he was still fighting the wheel his car, a Cadillac CTS sedan, surged forward onto the shoulder of the road and then into the trees beside the road.

To Roy, the next few moments were a blur. He felt the powerful sedan surge forward almost like a horse trying to throw its rider. The headlights showed the shoulder of the road and then a wall of greenery coming toward him way too fast. There was a horrible crash, an explosion of white, a burst of brain-numbing pain that made him scream aloud, and then a series of loud cracks that sounded way too much like wood splintering. There was another burst of pain that made the first one pale in comparison. Mercifully, that burst of pain brought darkness with it.

When Judge Roy Cooper opened his eyes, it was to a world of agony. At first the excruciating pain filled the world around him, but after a few seconds it seemed to center in his legs. He tried to move his legs, to get them away from the pain, but attempting to move them only made the pain worse. He screamed in anguish and started to crumple forward, but only succeeded in smacking his face against the steering wheel and the now-deflated airbag hanging from it. He tried to push the steering wheel away, but only ended up pushing himself back in the seat and getting a look at the front windshield. The glass was a spider web of cracks. Through what little area of glass he could still see through, he saw the crumpled metal of the hood and what looked like the trunk of a huge tree beyond it.

I wrecked, Roy was his first thought, followed immediately with *I've got to get out of this car before it blows up.* That thought brought sheer panic with it. He fumbled for the door handle, found it, and tried it. The handle worked and the door opened a little, then stopped. He tried to push against the door, but moving unleashed a wave of agony that left him gasping and with tears flowing down his face. He did manage to open the door far enough for the car's interior light to come on, giving him a chance to get a look at his legs. He instantly wished he hadn't. His pants legs were soaked with blood and a large section of bone protruded from the center of his left thigh through his pants. The jagged bone was at least four inches long. His right leg wasn't much better. His lower right leg had a forty-five degree angle in it between the ankle and his knee. Another bone protruded through his pants right below the knee.

"Oh God!" Roy gasped as he surveyed the damage to his legs. It didn't take an orthopedic surgeon to see that his legs were badly broken, and that was just the part that was visible. He needed an ambulance and he needed one fast. The pain seemed to have numbed a little, making him wonder if he might be slipping into shock. If he was, he had to get help before he passed out. He reached down to his belt and fumbled around for the cell phone he wore clipped to his belt. Thankfully, he found it immediately. His hands were shaking as he jerked the phone out and typed in the number sequence that unlocked the screen.

Roy was about to dial nine one one when the driver's side door of his car was wrenched open. "Thank God," he cried as a figure appeared there in the open door, "I need help." Roy had no idea where the person trying to get to him had come from; he hadn't seen any other approaching lights from where the road was behind him. Maybe it was the moron who'd been standing in the road, the one who'd caused him to wreck. He could tell that the figure was a man, based on the width of the chest and the hands that had forced the door open. He could also see the outline of his head hovering outside in the darkness, but his face was hidden in the shadows.

The man reached inside and took the cell phone from Roy's shaking hands. "Judge Roy Cooper?" he asked almost conversationally once he'd taken the phone away out of Roy's reach.

"Yes," Roy nearly sobbed. It was someone who recognized him, so it must be a local. He tried to see who it was exactly, but the tears in his eyes from the pain were distorting his vision. "Please help me! I've broke both my damned legs!"

"You have," the man at his open car door said agreeably. "It's obvious that they are definitely broken. Does it hurt?"

The terrible pain caused Roy's temper to flare. It was bad enough that he'd wrecked, but it was even worse that his rescuer seemed to be a blithering idiot. "Hell yes, it hurts!" he nearly screamed. "Mister, are you going to help me or not? Jesus H. Christ!"

"Yes, Judge, I am going to help you," the man said casually. "I'm going to help you by telling you your future. You've got one chance to listen, so I suggest you listen carefully. Do you understand?"

In intense pain and now more than a little afraid, Roy unleashed a string of curses at the man he'd thought was rescuing him, calling him every vile name in the book and a few new ones he invented on the spot. "Do you know who I am?" he shrieked. "I'll have you arrested and I'll put you under the jail! I swear to God!"

"You're in no position to threaten anyone, Judge Cooper," the man outside the car door said as he hovered there in the shadows. "And furthermore, if you want me to help you before you go into shock and die from blood loss and trauma, I would suggest you shut up and listen." The man held up Roy's cell phone so Roy could see it in his hand. "All I have to do is take this and walk away. I figure you'll last about twenty more minutes. That's twenty more minutes of pain and fear, followed by a reckoning for the terrible things you've done. Make your choice now, Your Honor."

The way the man said "Your Honor" made it sound like a slur. Roy had no idea who the man hidden in the darkness just an arm's length away was, but he was at his mercy. Given the number of people Roy had wronged during his legal career, the list of possible suspects was considerable. Unfortunately, at the moment he had Roy's life in his hands. If the fellow did walk away with Roy's phone, there was no way Roy could summon help. The judge didn't know which one was more terrifying at the moment: the man tormenting him as he sat there injured and helpless or the thought of being left there to suffer and die. "Okay, man," he whined. "I'm listening."

"Good," the man said. "Judge Cooper, I am going to call you some help. The ambulance and the fire department will come. They will get you out of your car and rush you to the hospital. At the hospital, you'll be rushed into surgery. You'll spend a couple of weeks in the hospital and then you'll face a long, painful recovery. You will most likely limp and suffer some pain in your legs for the rest of your life. Let that serve as a reminder so that you never forget this night and this meeting. You with me?"

"Yes," Roy groaned. He didn't care if the guy just a few feet away in the darkness outside the car recited The Gettysburg Address if it meant he was going to get some help. As soon as he was able to, Roy was going to tell Sheriff Garrett what had happened here tonight. When the sheriff found whoever his tormentor was, he planned to make sure the sheriff hurt the man really badly.

"Very good," the man replied. "As soon as you are physically able to make the call, you are going to call your secretary and have her type your resignation letter and submit it. You are resigning from your position as Chief Magistrate. After tonight, you will never serve as a judge again in any capacity for any court. Not only will you never serve as a judge again, you will surrender your law license and not even practice law again. You understand?"

"What's this got to do with me being a judge?" Roy nearly screamed. "Why are you doing this? WHO ARE YOU?"

"I'm doing this because you are corrupt," the man said. "You have sold the law and justice to the highest bidder. You have let the guilty go free and imprisoned the innocent, all in the name of greed, lust, and power. This is your only warning, Roy Cooper. If you don't do what I say, I will return. If I return to you, what happened here tonight will seem like a pleasure compared to what will be next. You understand?"

Something about the man's voice cut through the cloud of weakness and pain to the center of Roy's brain. There, something instinctual and primal told him that the man meant what he was saying. Not only did he mean it, he was fully willing and able to carry out his threats. Roy felt his bowels let go and he couldn't tell if it was from the pain from his injuries or pure, primal fear. "Yes, sir," he sobbed in pain and humiliation.

"Good answer," the man said. "Go to sleep now, Roy."

Roy's brain was still trying to figure out what the man meant by "Go to sleep" when the man reached over and thumped the jagged end of the femur bone sticking up out of Roy's left thigh. It was a light contact from the man's middle finger, much like someone flicking another person's ear as a joke, but the effect was magnified thousands of times due to the contact with the shattered end of the bone. The horrible jolt of utter agony from the contact to the bone caused Roy to pass out instantly. He sagged to the side and lay across the console between the front seats, out like a light.

The man in the darkness turned and walked away from the smashed Cadillac back to the shoulder of the road. Once he was back at the road, he dialed nine one one and waited. "There's been a car crash on Highway Forty-seven about three miles east of the town limits," the man said as soon as an emergency dispatcher answered. "You can see the vehicle from the road. There's a man trapped inside and he looks like he's hurt really bad. You better get an ambulance and the fire department on the way. Tell them to hurry."

The emergency dispatcher began asking him questions, but the man disconnected the call without answering. The judge's car was easily visible from the roadway to any passing vehicle, so finding him wouldn't be a problem. With help on the way, the man dropped the judge's cell phone on the shoulder of the road and strolled away into the night.

CHAPTER 10

Mason Holliday sat in a booth at a small diner just inside the Easton town limits named, aptly enough, The Diner. It was a small place located in an old brick building that faced the highway leading into town. It had probably once been a storefront of some kind. The seating inside was a mixture of booths along the large, front windows, a few tables, and a counter with stools. The walls were brick and hand-hewn planking and they were decorated with an eclectic mix of old pictures of the town, old farm implements, and memorabilia from the local high school's athletic teams. Behind the counter a couple of cooks dressed in jeans, white shirts, and aprons were busy at the griddles and stoves while a couple of waitresses wearing jeans with tee shirts bearing a picture of The Diner's sign on the back hurried around taking orders and filling coffee cups. It was the type of small, local place that Mace liked because it was usually locally owned, meaning the food was good because the owners didn't want their neighbors talking bad about them. A lot of time spent traveling to different places in the state had taught him that every community had one such place. In Easton, The Diner seemed to be it.

It was about eight thirty in the morning and the dining room was about half full as Mace finished up his breakfast. The food was very good, just as experience had told him it would be. He pushed his plate away and was about to motion for the waitress to bring his check when he saw a familiar car pull into the parking lot outside the window at his booth. He sat waiting as Amanda Easton got out of her car and hurried into the restaurant. The two waitresses and the older woman running the register at the counter all spoke to her as she walked through the door. Amanda returned the friendly greetings and then paused to look around. She spotted him and hurried over to his booth. Mace noted that she was nicely dressed in a nice blouse, gray slacks, and low heels, as opposed to the jeans from yesterday. She looked as if she were on the way to something important.

Amanda walked to his booth and looked down at him. She looked happy and very relieved. The smile, along with the nice clothes, looked really good on her, Mace thought. "Hi, Agent Holliday, I saw your car in the parking lot as I was driving by. I thought I would stop and give you the news. May I sit?"

Mace returned the smile. "Only if you promise to call me Mace from now on," he replied. "Agent Holliday makes me sound like I'm sixty years old."

Amanda gave him a slight smile in return. "Okay, Mace," she said. She sat down across the table from him. One of the waitresses, a redheaded, heavyset girl, hurried over to ask if Amanda wanted anything. She declined, so the waitress took Mace's breakfast dishes and left. "Well, you certainly look official today," Amanda said once the waitress was gone.

Mace had left his suit back at the hotel. Today he wore olive drab tactical pants with a matching shirt. The shirt had the BCI badge embroidered in silver thread over the left breast and Agent M. Holliday embroidered on the right breast over the shirt pocket with the same thread. A pair of highly polished black tactical boots on his feet, his holstered pistol on his left side, and his official state badge clipped to his belt completed the outfit. "This is what we call our duty fatigues," Mace said. "It's a lot more practical and comfortable than a business suit most of the time. Besides, I'm not the only one who's dressed up today."

"I wanted to look nice for the hearing this morning," Amanda explained.

"That's right, you have the emergency family court hearing this morning," Mace said. "Your husband was trying to get custody of Caleb." He couldn't believe that he had almost completely forgotten that, but he had spent a sizable amount of time last night sitting in his room and reading the file on the Deputy Cothran shooting. The details of the case and the lack of sleep must have made it slip his mind.

Amanda smiled. The smile lit up her face and easily made her the prettiest woman in the room. "It was supposed to be this morning at nine," she said. "I was actually on the way to my lawyer's office near the courthouse when he called my cell. The hearing has been postponed until further notice, possibly for several weeks at least!" Her happiness was a palpable thing. "I'm not going to lose Caleb! Thank God!"

Mace couldn't help but return the smile. "That's great," he said sincerely. "What happened?"

"Judge Cooper was in a bad car accident last night around ten o'clock," Amanda answered. "He ran off the road and hit a couple of big trees. He was injured pretty badly and will be out for quite a while, if he ever returns at all. That's why the hearing was cancelled."

"Well, that's good for you and Caleb," Mace replied. "I'd be willing to bet that the judge probably has a different take on it, though."

"That's true," Amanda said. "I probably shouldn't be so happy at someone else's misfortune, but I can't help it! Does that make me a bad person?"

"No, it makes you human," Mace answered. "I'd be happy if I was in your shoes as well."

"Wait, it gets even better," Amanda said gleefully. "I called a girlfriend of mine who works as a nurse in the emergency room at Easton Regional Medical Center, where Judge Cooper was taken, to try to get some details. She said that when the judge was brought in, he had an envelope with five thousand dollars in cash stuffed in his pants pocket. My friend had to count it and list it on their intake sheet where they track incoming patient's personal property."

That piqued Mace's interest. "Really?" he asked casually. "That's a lot of money to be carrying around in an envelope on your person."

"I know," Amanda replied. "The kicker is that the money still had a wrapper on it from the Easton Regional Bank, the local bank here in town. That's where my husband and I had our joint accounts. That made me start wondering, so I logged onto their online banking. Ronny has a personal account that he doesn't know I know about. I found the log-in information and password for it one day when I was cleaning his home office. Guess how much he withdrew from that account the day before yesterday?"

"My police powers of deduction tell me that it was probably five thousand dollars," Mace said as he leaned back in the booth.

"Dead on the money," Amanda said triumphantly. "I called Hiram, my lawyer, and told him what I had discovered. He was thrilled at the news. He said that, even if it was a coincidence, it still looks like Ronny could have gotten it to bribe Judge Cooper. Think about it: Cooper is an old family friend, Ronny takes five thousand dollars in cash out of the bank, and the next day the judge has five thousand dollars in cash on him from the same bank Ronny uses." She slapped the table. "What are the odds?"

Mace couldn't help but smile at her happiness. "My job taught me a long time ago not to believe in coincidence," he said. "It just boggles my mind that, if what you think happened is actually true, Ronny didn't bother to take the bank wrapper off the cash. However, I've seen a lot of cases get solved over something stupid and trivial like that, so…," he added with a shrug.

"With Ronny, it's a combination of stupidity and arrogance," Amanda surmised. "He thinks he's smarter than he actually is. He also firmly believes that he is untouchable because his last name is Easton." She rolled her eyes. "God, I must have lost my mind when I started dating him, much less married him. I'm an idiot!"

"Don't be so hard on yourself," Mace chided. "We've all done things we regret; it's part of life. What else did your lawyer say when you told him what you'd found?"

"He plans to use that to demand that Judge Cooper and all other judges in this county recuse themselves," Amanda said. "That means that all hearings regarding my divorce and custody of Caleb will have to be heard by a judge from outside the county. Best of all, he's going to request an ethics investigation of Judge Cooper. Is that something you guys do?"

"No," Mace said. "That's handled by the South Carolina Commission on Judicial Conduct. They have their own investigators. We do assist them sometimes if they ask for help, but that's not very often. They've got some good people there and they're very thorough."

"Good," Amanda said. "I hope they do investigate him. He's a crook and has been one for years. They won't have to work hard to find anything on him."

"I'm glad it worked out for you," Mace said sincerely. "I could tell you were scared to death about your hearing last night. You look like a different person today, much more relaxed."

The redheaded waitress came over and brought Mace his check. She offered him a refill on his coffee, but he declined. The waitress moved on to the rest of her customers, leaving him and Amanda alone. "It is a huge relief," Amanda replied. "Since I don't have the hearing, I'm going back to work on my resume'. Luckily, I'm still a licensed nurse. There are some openings at the hospital here, so maybe I can get a job there. I need to stay here until my divorce goes through."

"I'm actually on my way to the hospital when I leave here," Mace said. "I'm meeting with the pathologist that did the autopsy on the girl the police shot."

"That's a pretty strange situation," Amanda commented. "Even the local newspaper, which usually avoids being critical of the sheriff's office, seems to be baffled by how it went down."

"It's odd," Mace admitted, "but that's one of the many reasons I'm here. I'm supposed to find answers to all of the questions."

"Well, I think you're the man for the job," Amanda said. "Just to be completely honest, last night after you left I Googled your name. I thought it sounded familiar and I was trying to find out why."

"What did you find?" Mace asked, even though he knew the answer.

"I read about what happened in Laurens earlier this year," Amanda said. "I remember seeing that on the news." She looked at him intently. "You must be very brave and tough to survive something like that."

"Or lucky," Mace replied laconically. "I survived a helicopter crash where everyone else died and a madman shooting at me with an automatic weapon without a scratch. Sometimes I can't even believe I'm still alive."

"Well, I'm glad you are," Amanda said. "You saved me yesterday. Apparently, either you or Sam is good luck because my luck seems to be changing."

"I'll take that as a compliment," Mace said. He glanced at his watch. "I would love to sit here and talk with you all day, but I need to get started on my investigation."

"I just wanted to share the good news with someone," Amanda said as she slid out of the booth and stood. "I hope everything goes well for you today. Hopefully, you'll find the truth."

"That's the goal," Mace said. He watched her leave the restaurant. He continued to watch as she climbed into her car and drove out of the parking lot. Only after she was gone did he slide out of the booth and head for the cashier to pay his check.

CHAPTER 11

The Easton County Morgue was located in the basement of the Easton Regional Medical Center, the sprawling hospital complex that occupied nearly two blocks close to the center of town. The morgue had its own separate entrance off Hammond Street with a small parking area. A single set of concrete steps with a steel handrail led to a small platform in front of a single glass door with Easton County Morgue on the glass. Several feet away to the left of the office entrance was a single garage door that allowed entrance for ambulances and mortuary vehicles. A small sign with Authorized Vehicles Only Please Do Not Block on the wall beside the garage door attested to that fact, as if someone would decide to drive the family sedan into the vehicle bay behind the door if the sign wasn't there to sternly warn them away. The exterior walls were all gray concrete and painted cement blocks. Even though it was a pretty, sunny day, the place still seemed dreary. All in all, it looked like every other morgue Mace had ever had to visit: a grim, official place where the business of dealing with the dead was handled.

Mace parked the Charger in one of the spaces marked for visitors and went inside. He carried the case file folder with him, tucked under one arm. The glass door opened to a small area with a counter and a glass barrier with a speaker in it. Another gray-painted metal door faced the interior of the lobby from the same wall as the counter. A pleasant-looking woman sat behind the counter and the glass window. She looked up from her computer when Mace walked through the door and approached the counter. "May I help you, sir?" she asked. The name plate on the edge of the counter behind the glass identified her as Wanda.

"Hello, Agent Mason Holliday, South Carolina Bureau of Criminal Investigation," Mace said as he stood at the window. "I have a meeting with Doctor Joe Patterson in reference to a homicide that happened yesterday. I called yesterday."

"Yes, I spoke with you," Wanda said. "Dr. Joe is waiting for you. Open the door when it buzzes." She pressed a button somewhere on her desk. The metal door buzzed impatiently. Mace grabbed the knob and opened the door to reveal a tiled corridor with drab, gray walls and several doors along it. Wanda emerged from the first door to his right as he walked into the hallway. "Third door on your left," she said as she pointed down the hall.

"Thanks," Mace said as he walked past her. He followed her directions and went to the third door. He opened it to reveal a single, large autopsy room with green tile on the walls, a concrete floor, and an autopsy table with surgical lights over it. A sheet covered a form on the table. The surgical light fixture also supported a small digital video camera system that allowed the autopsy to be filmed. Brilliant fluorescent lights illuminated the rest of the room beyond the autopsy table. The rest of the room held a couple of tables close to the autopsy table with various instruments the pathologist used for autopsies, scales, and various containers for evidence. There was also a single desk with a computer. The large metal door of the refrigerated room used for body storage took up most of one wall. The room had the unique smell that all such places seemed to have; a mixture of disinfectant, meat, and bodily fluids.

A small, wiry man with thinning silver hair and high cheekbones sat in the chair at the desk. He wore green scrubs and a neat white lab coat. He stood up when Mace opened the door. "Agent Holliday?" he asked as he extended his hand. "I'm Joe Patterson, the medical examiner for Easton County." His voice was a pleasant baritone that echoed in the large room.

Mace shook his hand. The man's hands were cold and smooth. "Nice to meet you, Doctor Patterson," he said. "As I said in my call yesterday, I'm here regarding the female killed yesterday by the sheriff's deputy."

"Yes," Dr. Patterson said brusquely, "I just finished up her autopsy about an hour ago. I was typing up the report of the findings when you arrived." He stepped past Mace and motioned toward the autopsy table. "Hispanic female, no identification, shot following a police chase when she tried to stab another officer?"

"That's the gist of it," Mace said. He laid the file folder down on the closest bare tabletop he could find. The file folder contained copies of the original incident report filed by the BCI agents on the scene yesterday, copies of witness statements, and some of the photographs taken by the BCI forensics team. He opened the folder and removed one of the photos. In it the dead girl lay on her back in the parking lot with her face turned toward the camera lens almost as if she were intentionally looking at the camera. In the photo, a dried stream of blood ran from the corner of her mouth down the side of her face and her eyes were open.

Dr. Patterson walked over to the table and removed the sheet draping the small form on it, giving Mace his first look at the girl in real life. He was shocked by how small she actually was. The limp form lying on the table looked like she ought to be no older than fifteen. She was also very slender, as if she hadn't been fed properly in a long time. "She's a little thing," he said almost reflexively.

"I know," Dr. Patterson remarked. "She weighed ninety-one pounds and her height was five feet three inches. Without an identification and solid birthdate, I would estimate her age between eighteen and twenty, max. That is an estimate; she may actually be younger."

Mace moved around the table and carefully studied the body. The familiar y-shaped incision on the front of the torso from the autopsy had been stapled shut, making it look like the girl had a zipper running down the front of her body. The zipper-like appearance of the staples and the waxy pallor of death made the girl look like some type of macabre Halloween decoration. "So, what are your findings, Doctor?" he asked as he slowly circled the autopsy table with his eyes riveted on the body. "You can spare me all of the medical terminology if you'd like. There will be enough of that in your report, I imagine."

Dr. Patterson nodded. "I'll save that for the coroner's inquest," he said. "To put it simply, this woman was shot twice, with both shots hitting the left side of her torso between the left armpit and her hip. One of the bullets passed through between two ribs, entered her left lung, tore a hole in the bottom of her heart, and then hit a rib on the other side and stopped. The other bullet struck a rib on her left side, breaking it, then angled down and struck her pelvis after tearing through her intestines. The shot that hit the heart was the one that killed her. She bled out internally within seconds.'

Mace nodded silently as he continued to study the body. "I assume you documented all of this with photos and video?" he asked softly. Dr. Patterson immediately looked offended and started to say something, prompting Mace to hold one hand in a placating gesture. "No offense intended, sir. I've been involved in other investigations where the local coroner used the town mortician to do autopsies. And yes, it went about as well as it sounds like it would, so I'm in the habit of asking." In South Carolina, county coroner was an elected position for which anyone could run as long as they met certain minimal requirements. In the not-too-distant past, that had resulted in complete incompetence and outright negligence. It was only in the last few years that the state had started mandating that coroners have some law enforcement training and medical training and that all autopsies be performed by a certified medical examiner.

Dr. Patterson relaxed a little. "Agent Holliday, I am a fully trained medical examiner with an M.D. from the Medical University of South Carolina. I am also a board-certified forensic pathologist. I don't work for the county coroner; I work for the hospital. And I have twenty years of experience."

"I assumed as much," Mace replied evenly. "However, hard experience has taught me that I need to ask sometimes. As I said, no offense intended."

"None taken," Dr. Patterson said. "I've met some of the county coroners during continuing education classes in Columbia, so I get it. Yes, I have pictures and video attached to my report. I can print out the report or email it to you."

"Email is fine," Mace said pleasantly. "What other observations did you make, Doctor?" During his circuit of the autopsy table, he had stopped at the girl's feet and was studying them intently.

"There is evidence of rough sexual activity in the vagina and anus," Dr. Patterson said. "A lot of bruising and small tears, as well as some scarring that indicates that some of it had happened in the past. This young lady was either very sexually active with a number of rough partners or there was one person who regularly abused her and who was extremely forceful with her."

"Did you take swabs?" Mace asked as he turned from concentrating on the girl's feet to grab a pair of latex gloves from a box on a nearby table.

"No," Dr. Patterson answered honestly. "Given the circumstances of her death, I did not. We're not dealing with a female found dead under mysterious circumstances. This woman was shot by a police officer in full view of multiple witnesses. The signs of rough sexual activity I found could be the result of a sexual assault, but they could also be the result of consensual sexual activity with a partner or partners who liked to get rough. As I imagine you know, some people enjoy such things."

Mace nodded. Real life wasn't like television, where the medical examiner could take one look and instantly know just what they needed to know so the police could make an arrest within the show's one hour run time. In real life, medical examiners and police investigators had to examine all of the evidence and see where it led them. Medical examiners and forensics technicians didn't run countless, very expensive tests on dead bodies and evidence unless other evidence indicated that performing that test was needed. Given the seemingly clear-cut chain of events leading up to the young woman's death, he could understand why Dr. Patterson hadn't performed the tests.

"I did note the abrasions on her left leg slightly above the ankle," Dr. Patterson said as he pointed to her leg. "There's a band of bruising and abraded skin there. It looks like she might have been bound with something there."

"I saw that too," Mace said as he pulled on the latex gloves. "Almost looks like she might have been shackled or something similar." He paused and carefully examined the girl's feet and hands. "But nothing of note on the wrists or other leg, oddly enough" he added. "Was she clothed when they brought her in?" he asked.

"She was dead at the scene," Dr. Patterson said. "After the crime scene people were done, the ambulance crew placed her in a body bag and brought her straight here. I removed her clothes and bagged and tagged them as evidence. It's secured in our evidence room with a chain of custody form attached. All she had on was a pair of jeans, a pair of panties, and a tee shirt. No bra, no socks, and no shoes."

"I noticed in the scene photos that she was barefoot," Mace said. "I also noted that no shoes were found anywhere at the scene." He walked to the foot of the exam table. "I noticed the soles of her feet. They are very smooth and relatively clean with no cuts or abrasions. Supposedly she stole the deputy's personal truck from his front yard and drove away with him in pursuit. Based on Google maps, his home is in the middle of nowhere with the closest house being nearly a mile away. Where did she come from? If she walked and was barefoot, her feet should show it."

"Maybe she was riding with someone," Dr. Patterson opined. "Maybe she was in a vehicle with her boyfriend, they argued, and he made her get out of the car. She might have left her shoes in the car. Also, she might have been right at the deputy's house when that happened. She may have had only a short walk."

"It's possible," Mace said distractedly. "Was there anything odd about her clothing at all? Anything you noticed at all that jumped out at you?"

"Her clothes were too big for her, even the panties," Dr. Patterson said as he leaned against the closest table. "Way more so than if she had simply lost some weight. They might have been hand-me-downs someone gave her, but most females are very particular about their underwear. Even if they are forced to wear hand-me-downs, their underwear is usually their own and it fits. I have a wife and teenage daughter who wear the same size in clothes, including underwear. They will exchange outfits, but never their underwear." He shrugged. "It was just kind of struck me as odd. That and the nail polish."

Mace had also noticed the polish on her fingernails and toenails. The girl's nails appeared to have been manicured and were all painted a bright, glossy red. It was incongruous, given the girl's ragged, over-sized clothes and appearance and it had immediately grabbed his attention. "I noticed that," he said. "Her finger- and toenails look like they were professionally manicured. That's a pretty distinct color as well."

"It's called Fire Engine Red," Dr. Patterson said. "You can get it at the local Wal-Mart and drugstores. Like I said, I have a teenage daughter, so I know these things."

Mace removed a small notepad from his shirt pocket and scribbled the name of the color down. "That's strange," he said. He directed his attention back to Dr. Patterson. "I guess I've seen enough, Doctor. I'll take her clothing with me. Once you're done with your report, you can email it and the pictures to me." He produced a business card and gave it to Dr. Patterson.

The doctor took it and slipped it into the pocket of his lab coat. "Have you guys identified her yet?" he asked as he moved to cover the girl's body back up with the sheet. "If this young lady is the age I think she is, then she's only a couple of years older than my daughter. I would imagine there's someone worried about her. We should know her name so we can notify her family."

"The other agents fingerprinted her yesterday," Mace said. "Nothing came up in the FBI's database. They are also going to run her prints through the Department of Homeland Security and Immigrations and Customs Enforcement in case she's an illegal. Interpol and the federal police in Mexico are also an option. Hopefully, we'll find out who she is, followed closely by what she was doing in Easton County."

"I also have to confess that I don't know how to feel about her being shot by Deputy Cothran," Dr. Patterson said as he finished arranging the sheet over the body on the table. "I don't know the man personally, but I have seen him before out in public. He stands out because he's so tall and muscular. Seriously, the guy looks like he could be a professional wrestler in the WWE. It is hard to believe that someone his size had to resort to shooting someone her size. I mean I heard she had a screwdriver in her hand and was threatening him, but still...."

Mace didn't reply to that. Most people who had never been in law enforcement had a hard time understanding why police officers sometimes used deadly force. Most people had no idea just how deadly a person armed with a weapon other than a gun, such as a bladed weapon or blunt object, could be in a confrontation. A lot of police officers were in graves because of bad people with weapons other than firearms. "I haven't met Deputy Cothran yet," he finally said. "I plan to interview him later. Once I've got all of the evidence, the state attorney general decides if it was justified or not."

"Well, I wish you luck. I hope you find out who she is and what her story is," Dr. Patterson said.

"That's the plan," Mace said.

CHAPTER 12

Jacob White wore a huge smile as he drove his Toyota Tundra pickup truck along West Main Street in Easton. Sam couldn't help but notice the old pastor's smile from where he sat in the passenger's seat. Sam had been with Jacob since shortly after eight that morning, assisting him with a variety of tasks around the hotel and the adjoining marina. The old man hadn't had much to say during the first part of the morning while the two of them were repairing the wooden handrail that ran along one of the docks. However, that had changed a few minutes after eight when Jacob's cell phone rang. The caller was Amanda with news of the judge's car crash and the cancelled hearing. The news that Caleb wouldn't have to go back to his father for the foreseeable future had seemed to remove a terrible, invisible burden from Jacob. Jacob had visibly relaxed and his usual spry manner had returned. As the morning had progressed, the two men had whittled down the list of chores. Maybe it was the rapid progress of the work, the earlier good news about the hearing sinking in, or just that it was a nice day out. Whatever the reason, Jacob had become positively cheerful as the morning flew by.

It was now a few minutes after eleven in the morning and he and Sam were heading into town. Jacob wanted to pick up some needed items at the local building supply store and then run by his office at the Easton Town Hall to sign some paperwork. Sam was simply along for the ride. A comfortable silence had settled in the truck's cab between the two men as Jacob drove and Sam studied everything outside the window on his side. Jacob had discovered that Sam wasn't much of a talker as the two of them had worked together all morning. That didn't bother Jacob; some people just weren't conversationalists. Even if he wasn't a talker, Sam seemed like a decent guy, he was a hard worker, and Caleb seemed to like him. That was good enough for Jacob.

Jacob and Sam were driving in traffic when three men on motorcycles passed them on Sam's side of the truck. All three men wore jeans, tee shirts, and sleeveless black leather vests with The Horde in red letters over a figure embroidered in the center of the vest. The figure was a hooded skeleton with a bloody sword in one bony hand and a battle axe in the other. The words

Motorcycle Club were in red letters beneath the patch. The similarities between the men ended with the way they were dressed. Two of the men were lean and tough-looking with long hair and they rode older Harley Davidsons with most of the chrome removed and replaced with black components. The other biker was bigger, with heavily-muscled arms covered with tattoos, a bushy beard, and a ponytail almost down to his belt. He rode a chopper with an extended front wheel and a garish paint job on the gas tank and fenders. The fat man on the chopper rode in the lead with the other two men flanking him as if he was the leader and the other two men were his flunkies.

Jacob and Sam both watched as the bikers passed them and headed farther down West Main. "They are up to no good," Jacob said grimly as he drove. "If you see one of them by himself, he usually keeps a low profile. If you see two or more together, that usually means they are looking for trouble. Every incident we've had where someone in town has had a bad run-in with them has involved two or more of them. They're all just overgrown bullies who think they're tough when they have their victims outnumbered."

"How often does that happen?" Sam asked as he continued to look out the window. "The confrontations with people in town, I mean."

"We've never had a problem with anything like this before," Jacob said. "One day, about fifteen of them riding in a pack just showed up and took over a campground outside of town. At the beginning, there was a few incidents, mainly reckless driving and the bikers mouthing off to locals. Everyone just hoped they'd move on. Next thing anybody knew, the bikers had bought a rundown farm and set up house there. They followed that by buying up the building that houses their strip club. Now it looks like they are here to stay. The incidents are getting worse. They've roughed up a few local people and stolen a few things. It's almost like they are an occupying army."

"And the sheriff won't do anything?" Sam asked.

"Not in the least," Jacob said bitterly. "His men won't touch the bikers. I don't why for sure, but I assume they must be paying the sheriff and some of his people off. You know, bribing the cops to leave them alone while they run their criminal enterprises."

"Do you think that's true?" Sam asked as he settled back in the truck seat.

"One of the ladies in my church has a daughter who's gotten involved with one of the bikers," Jacob said. "Her daughter told her that her new boyfriend confided to her that the bars, the prostitution, and the drugs they sell is only a small part of a bigger picture. Supposedly, the bikers and the sheriff's office are on the same team, both working for a third person or organization. The bikers and the sheriff's people are protecting something."

"Do you believe that's true?" Sam asked. "It seems like crooked cops could protect something like that without the bikers."

"I've pondered on that," Jacob said as he changed lanes. Even though it was in the middle of the morning on a weekday, traffic in town was sparse. "The threat of crooked cops would keep most of the people in line, but what about the really bad people? You know, those hardcore criminal types that aren't afraid of the cops, even crooked cops. Maybe the answer to armed, dangerous thugs is other armed, even more dangerous thugs."

"Makes sense," Sam said. He had suddenly learned forward and was peering through the windshield. About a block ahead, he could see the sign for Smith's Garage. "Say, Jacob, if it isn't too much trouble, could we stop at garage and let me check on my bike? I want to see if Mr. Smith has found the parts he needs."

"I was planning to stop by there anyway," Jacob replied. "I need to get some gas. Later on today I'm going to run out to Jeff Bradley's place to check on him and his family."

"He's the police officer we met last night?" Sam asked. "The town police chief?"

"That's him," Jacob said as he slowed and started to turn into the parking lot of Smith's. "I think he's the only real, honest lawman we've got left here in this county. He's by himself since all of the other town officers have either been lured away by the sheriff's office or got scared and quit. As if that's not a big enough load, he's dealing with his daughter being sick. I don't know how much more the man can take."

Sam saw the three motorcycles sitting at one of the gas pumps as Jacob was turning his truck into the parking lot. The bikes were parked at the pump closest to one of the open garage bays. The three bikers were not with their bikes. Instead they had walked over and were standing at the open garage bay closest to the main entrance to the convenience store part of the gas station. An older man who looked to be close to his sixties stood in the open garage bay confronting the three bikers. Sam recognized him as Jack Smith, the owner, who he'd spoken to yesterday when dropping off his bike. All four men looked tense and angry. "Oh Lord," Jacob said softly.

"Oh Lord what?" Sam asked as Jacob pulled up to the gas pump right behind the motorcycles.

"This can't be good," Jacob said ominously. "Some of the bikers jumped Jack before and beat him up pretty bad after he asked them to leave his store. He swore it wouldn't happen again. Jack's a good man, but he's got a temper. This isn't going to end well."

"Then we need to intervene before it gets out of hand," Sam said. "Drive over there and park close to them. Maybe the arrival of some witnesses will convince them to leave."

Jacob drove his pickup truck over and stopped right in front of the bay close to the confrontation. The three bikers and Jack all glanced over when Jacob parked and shut the truck off. Sam opened his door and got out and Jacob followed. "Hey, what's going on?" Jacob asked as he approached the small group of tense, angry men.

"You need to get back in that truck and drive away," the biker closest to Jacob and Sam warned as he eyeballed them with contempt. The biker was a young man with long hair, a scraggly mustache, and a tattoo visible on the side of his neck. He had the lean, vicious look of a feral dog. "This ain't none of your business."

"I'm the pastor of the church here and the mayor of this town as well," Jacob said calmly. "I could tell as I drove up that you fellows are arguing. I just want to calm the situation down if I can before someone does something they regret."

"They want me to turn on the pumps so they can fill up their bikes," Jack Smith said angrily. "They have to pay first before I turn on the pumps. It's that way for everyone else and it's that way for them."

The bigger biker, the one with the beard and ponytail who rode the chopper, took a menacing step toward Jack. "Old man, I done told you we ain't everybody else," he snarled in a voice with a Deep South accent. "You turn on the pump so we can fill up and then we'll pay."

"So you can ride off without paying?" Smith shot back. "That's not happening, young man. Every time some of you bikers come in here you steal or destroy something. I don't want any of you in my business anymore. I'm not turning on the pumps! Now get before I call the police!"

"If you put your hand on a telephone, I will stomp you through this pavement," the biker said. "Get in there and turn on the pumps before you get taught a lesson about respect."

Jacob took a step forward. As a preacher, he couldn't stand by and simply watch while a member of his church and a good friend was in harm's way. "Okay, fellows, maybe all four of you should calm down a little," he said calmly. "I don't want to see anyone get hurt or in trouble over a few bucks worth of gasoline."

Jacob had barely got the words out of his mouth when the tattooed biker closest to him, the one who'd told him to go away, spun and punched him squarely in the gut. The punch was completely unexpected and delivered with a lot of speed and power from the biker, a veteran of numerous brawls in bars and back alleys all over the country who knew how to punch and make it count. Jacob, who was the same size as the biker but much older and in worse shape physically, was caught completely by surprise. The blow knocked all of the breath out of him. He gave a strangled cry and crumpled to the pavement.

As Jacob collapsed to the pavement, there was a few seconds of stunned inaction. Jack, the owner of the gas station, gaped in shock. "You hit Preacher White," he said incredulously as he stared at the biker.

The tattooed biker opened his mouth to say something, but before he could get out a single word, Sam's fist caught him squarely in the jaw, breaking the jawbone, sending several of the biker's remaining teeth flying, and snapping the biker's head to the right. Before the biker, who was known by the name "Snake", could even register the impact and pain from the blow, Sam followed it with a snapping kick right to the biker's groin. Snake made a sound that was something between a scream and a groan before he collapsed to the pavement. He struck his head on the concrete and was knocked out completely, a small mercy given the agony of his cracked jaw and injured testicles.

The other two bikers reacted instantly to the attack on their fellow gang member. The biker with the beard bellowed like an angry bull and charged at Sam while flailing wildly. Sam ducked beneath the biker's wild roundhouse punches and came up behind the biker. He grabbed the big biker's ponytail and hauled back on it, sending the biker falling to the ground on his back. The moment the biker landed on his back Sam stepped forward and kicked him in the side of the head much like a football player trying to kick a field goal. There was a resounding thud and the biker stayed down. The final biker, the smallest of the three men, had backed away almost to Jacob's parked truck. When Sam turned to confront him, the biker, a wiry man with black hair and a scar on his left cheek, whipped out a knife and flipped the blade open. He stood there, waving the knife menacingly from side to side.

Sam moved away from the biker he'd just knocked out and looked at the biker with the knife stoically. "You've got two options here," he said casually. "Option one is to put the knife away, pick up your two friends, and get out of here. Option two is go ahead and attack me with that knife. If you go with number two, I'm obligated to warn you that I will take that knife from you and I will kill you with it, right here, right now." For all of the emotion in Sam's voice, he might have been discussing a new recipe he'd just learned.

The final biker lunged forward with the knife extended. With lightning quickness Sam caught his extended wrist, twisted it, and pulled the biker forward off balance. As the biker pitched forward, Sam turned to the side and sent the biker flipping onto his back. With the downed biker's wrist in an iron grip, Sam straddled the biker's chest and sat down, pinning the biker to the pavement with him on top. Sam then bent the biker's wrist so that the point of the biker's knife blade was aimed at the biker's own chest. He began to push the blade down toward the biker's chest. The biker fought back mightily, thrashing his feet and bucking his hips to throw Sam off, but Sam didn't budge. Seeing that wasn't working, the biker struggled to keep the knife's point form reaching his body. The muscles in his arms bulged as he pushed back against Sam, but the blade still continued inexorably downward.

The blade was maybe four inches away from the biker's chest when Jacob staggered to his feet. "Sam," Jacob said sharply, "stop this madness right now!" He was holding his abdomen and breathing heavily. His face was still white with pain.

Sam stopped pushing the knife blade down and looked at Jacob. Unlike the straining and wild-eyed biker he was on top of, Sam looked almost serene. "He made his choice," Sam said calmly. "Let him face the consequences of his decision. That's what creates people like him and his buddies; the consequences of their actions take too long to catch up to them."

Jacob took a step forward toward Sam. The other two bikers were slowly regaining consciousness and starting to move. "Sam, as a man of God, I can't stand here and let you kill him," he said imploringly. "He's not a danger to you anymore. Look around you, son. There's a bunch of people seeing this."

Sam looked around. Jack Smith was standing off to the side with a cell phone in his hand, probably in the midst of calling the police. There was a shopping plaza next door to the garage and a number of people in that parking lot had stopped and were watching the brawl. Traffic on West Main Street had also stopped. Some people had even gotten out of their cars to get a better view. He saw cell phones in some of the bystanders' hands, meaning he was probably being recorded. "Please, son, none of these guys are worth going to prison for the rest of your life," Jacob said.

With a sigh, Sam looked down at the biker. "Open your hand and let the knife go," he said to him. "I'm going to take it away from you and then I will get off you. You can take your friends and leave. If you try anything else, I promise you that the last thing you ever see will be your guts hitting the pavement in front of you. You understand?" The biker muttered something unintelligible under his breath, but then nodded. He reluctantly relaxed. Sam snatched the knife away. "Now, turn your head and look over at the man your friend hit." he commanded harshly. The biker cut his eyes over toward Jacob. "The only reason you're alive is because he asked me to show you mercy. I suggest you thank him."

"Thank you," the biker grunted. He didn't sound very sincere.

Sam stood up and stepped away from the biker. He closed the biker's knife and slipped it into the pocket of his jeans. The biker slowly got to his feet while watching Sam warily. Sam backed away a few steps. "Now get your friends and leave," he said. The biker turned to his two injured friends. The bigger one had regained consciousness and was sitting up. He looked both dazed and angry. The other biker, the one who'd hit Jacob, was just beginning to stir. He emitted a series of loud groans as he tried to move. The third biker nodded to Sam, backed away, and went to check on his friends. Sam watched warily. The third biker spoke with the other two briefly, then dug a cell phone from his pocket and called someone.

"Jacob, you okay?" Jack Smith asked as he walked over to the preacher. Jacob still had his hand on his stomach, but at least his color was returning. Jacob nodded. "I suspect that other biker is calling his buddies," Smith added as he pointed at the biker on the cell phone. "I called Chief Bradley and he's on the way."

Chief Bradley arrived in his Easton Police Department marked cruiser within a couple of minutes. Bradley jumped out of his car with one hand on his gun as he surveyed the carnage. After a few seconds, he cautiously approached the bikers. By then the big one with the ponytail was on his feet. The other one was sitting up and holding the front tail of his shirt to his busted mouth. The third one was still holding his cell phone. Unlike his injured buddies, he was all bad attitude with the chief. Chief Bradley spoke with them briefly. Sam and walked over to stand beside Jacob and Jack Smith. Judging from the chief's body language, the conversation with the bikers wasn't going very well at all. He finally turned and walked over to where Sam and the others stood by Jacob's truck. "Gentlemen," Chief Bradley, "would someone like to tell me what just happened?" He jerked his thumb over his shoulder. "Those nice gentlemen over there don't seem to have much to say about the matter."

"Those punks rode up here and parked at the gas pumps," Jack said. "They demanded that I turn on the pumps for them without them paying up front. I told them I wouldn't and we got into a confrontation. Jacob and this young man rode up and tried to calm things down." He motioned with his chin towards the bikers. "That one over there with the busted mouth turned around and hit Jacob in the stomach. Sam here jumped in to help Jacob and kicked their asses. All three of them."

Chief Bradley looked at Sam warily. "Is that true?" he asked Sam.

Sam shrugged. "That's one way to put it," Sam replied. "I would say that I saw one of the bikers assault an unarmed, older man for no reason and, as a concerned citizen, I was forced to intervene."

"Damn right!" Jack said enthusiastically. "He intervened so much that he stomped all three of them!" He clapped Sam on the back. "It's about damned time too."

"Mayor, is that true?" Chief Bradley asked, turning his attention to Jacob.

"Yes," Jacob replied weakly. It was obvious the powerful blow to his stomach was still causing him distress. "We came by so Sam could check on his bike repairs. We drove up right in the middle of Jack and those three arguing. I tried to talk some sense into them, but that one sucker-punched me right in the stomach." He pointed to the biker with his shirt pressed to his mouth. The shirt was soaked with blood and the biker was having to lean on his bigger friend. "Sam jumped in to defend me."

"Sam, it seems like you stay pretty busy defending people," Chief Bradley said as he cocked his eyebrow at Sam. He glanced over his shoulder at the three bikers. "The evidence would seem to indicate you're pretty good at it."

"Seems like there's a lot of people around here that need defending," Sam said evenly. "Sorry for the mess, but I couldn't stand around and let them beat up an old man. No offense, Jacob."

"None taken," Jacob replied.

"You want to press charges for assault?" Chief Bradley asked Jacob. "What about you, Jack?"

Both men looked at each other and then shook their heads. "I don't think it would help the situation. They learned their lesson, thanks to Sam," Jacob said. Jack apparently shared the same sentiment, especially about the bikers learning their lesson. He kept looking over at the bloodied bikers and grinning.

"Sam, I'm going to have to write a report just in case," Chief Bradley said. "The way my luck runs, one of them will fall over dead an hour from now from their injuries. Can I see some identification?"

Sam reached into his back pocket, removed a battered leather wallet, and produced his driver's license. The chief took it and looked it over. "Arizona?" he asked. "You're a far piece from home."

"I like to travel," Sam said. "Chief, am I going to be arrested?"

Chief Bradley shook his head. "Not by me," he said. "This is what we call a mutual combat situation. They could try to press charges if they want, but then you guys could also press charges, so nobody wins. I'll explain that to them, but I doubt they'll try to press charges. They are the type who'll try to handle it themselves, so you need to be careful while you're here in this county, Sam."

"I don't expect to be in Easton too much longer," Sam said. "I'm just waiting on Jack here to finish fixing my motorcycle."

"It should be ready tomorrow," Jack said. "I'm waiting on UPS to bring the parts today." He once again clapped Sam on the shoulder. "By the way, the repairs are on me as thanks for what you did here today, young man."

"Keep a low profile until then, Sam," Chief Bradley said. "Hang out while I write down your information. I'll write a report just to cover my butt. They could get a copy of my report and go to a county judge to try and get a warrant. They won't get one though, especially since Judge Cooper is out of commission. I'll be back in a few."

Sam and Jacob leaned against Jacob's truck while Chief Bradley went to his car and retrieved a clipboard. The chief wrote down Sam's information and brought his license back over to him. Sam was putting his license back in his wallet when several motorcycles drove into the parking lot with the roar of engines. The approaching bikers immediately went to their fallen comrades. Several of them glared balefully at Chief Bradley, Sam, and the others while the remaining ones saw to their injured comrades. It didn't take a genius to know that if not for the presence of the armed police officer, the newly-arrived bikers would probably have tried to avenge their friends. Chief Bradley and Sam returned the stares. One of the bikers, a dangerous-looking character with a shaved head, aimed his phone at Sam and the chief. He obviously snapped a few pictures of them before hopping on his bike and riding off.

The injured men were able to get on their bikes, with the exception of the one with the broken jaw. He hopped on a bike with another biker. Another biker who'd ridden double over to the station jumped on the injured biker's motorcycle and drove it away. As they drove away several of them extended their middle fingers to the police chief and the others. Within a couple of minutes, it was as if the incident had never happened.

"That went better than I figured it would," Chief Bradley said as the last motorcycle vanished down the street. "Of course, I doubt this is the end of it. They won't let this go. You might better head back to Arizona as soon as humanly possible"

"But Chief, I'm just now making friends here," Sam retorted.

Chief Bradley glanced over and saw that Sam was smiling. He made a silent vow to check on Sam's background as soon as he could. No ordinary man went through three bikers like a hot knife through butter and then acted like it was no big deal. "I'm not kidding," he said. "You put yourself in harm's way the minute you touched one of them."

"I'll bear that in mind, sir," Sam said.

Chief Bradley shook his head and walked back to his car with a sigh.

CHAPTER 13

Mace met Sergeant Joel Watson of the North Carolina Highway Patrol in the parking lot of Miller's Barbecue Joint at a few minutes past eleven in the morning, almost forty-eight hours to the minute after Sergeant Watson had witnessed the shooting that occurred there. Sergeant Watson was sitting in his vehicle, a marked Dodge Charger similar to Mace's unmarked one, at the edge of the parking lot when Mace drove into the lot. Sergeant Watson got out of his car and waited as Mace parked close by and got out. Mace walked up, introduced himself, and the two lawmen exchanged a brief handshake. Mace immediately liked Watson; the veteran highway patrolman looked like the kind of guy who'd be a good man to have around when something bad happened. He had that air of relaxed confidence and steadiness that inspired the same in others.

"Thanks for meeting me, Sergeant Watson," Mace said after the mutual introductions. "I'm assigned to follow up on the shooting that happened here two days ago. I asked you to meet me so you could walk me through everything that happened from your viewpoint. I also called Trooper Johnson, but to my understanding he's tied up in court today."

"That's correct," Sergeant Watson said. "He's in a hearing from a case he made as a city police officer before he came to work for us. He'll be available later if you need to speak with him as well."

"I've already read his statement and yours as well," Mace said. "They are pretty much the same, as far what you witnessed. You're the one I really wanted to meet with because you were closer to the action, so to speak. There were a couple of key differences in your statements that I wanted to ask you about."

"That's fine," Sergeant Watson said. "I'm familiar with the process, so I'm glad to be of assistance."

"I don't want to waste too much of your time, Sergeant, so I'll get started," Mace said. He opened the file folder he held to reveal a diagram of the crime scene as drawn by the BCI forensics team that responded to the scene shortly after the shooting. The positions of the vehicles involved, including the deputy's vehicle and the truck the victim drove, were noted, as well as the locations of the people involved. Measurements related to objects in the diagram and their proximity to each other were also noted. He laid the diagram on the hood of Watson's car. "This is a diagram of the scene as our forensics unit found it," Mace said. "Does it look accurate?"

Sergeant Watson examined the diagram in silence for several minutes. Several time she glanced up and looked across the parking lot as if replaying everything in his mind. "Yes," he finally said. "That's pretty much it, I'd say." His voice had taken on a more somber tone, as if reliving the events pained him.

"Okay," Mace said. "Would you mind walking me through what happened once you and Trooper Johnson came outside?"

"I don't mind," Watson said. "Now?"

Mace nodded. The parking lot was about half full already. Even though the area where the crash and shooting had happened was no longer blocked off, no one had parked in the area, even though the affected parking spots were good ones close to the restaurant's front doors. Maybe it was because there were still painted marks on the ground, put there by the forensics unit to mark certain points and evidence. Perhaps it was some animal instinct deep inside people's brains that sensed that violence and death had occurred there and they subconsciously avoided it. Whatever the reason, Sergeant Watson had a clear area and he was able to quickly guide Mace through the events that had transpired during the shooting. Mace made careful notes on the legal pad he held as Watson talked.

Watson's demeanor was efficient and professional as he moved through the parking lot showing Mace where all of the relevant individuals were when the shooting took place. However, his demeanor changed when he reached the spot where the girl had breathed her last. Some dark stains remained on the asphalt where her body had fallen. It could have been oil or some other liquid from one of the vehicles that had parked there before or after the girl's body was removed or it could have been blood. Regardless of what it was, standing there looking down at the stains made Sergeant Watson struggle to keep his voice even and professional. "You have to excuse me," he finally said. "The girl who was shot looked like she wasn't much older than my youngest daughter. Seeing her die wasn't exactly easy to stomach."

"I understand completely," Mace said, "and I'm sorry for making you have to relive this so soon. I'm just trying to find out what exactly happened."

"I understand," Watson said. "Have you guys identified her yet?"

"No," Mace said. "As you know, she had no identification on her. We haven't had much luck on her fingerprints yet either. I will find out who she is, though."

"I hope you do," Watson said. "Agent Holliday, you mind if I ask you a question?"

"Not at all," Mace said.

"How did she end up driving the deputy's personal vehicle?" Watson asked. "I know what I've heard on the news and what the deputy was saying. He claims she stole the truck out of his yard after he accidentally left the keys in it and he chased her."

"That's what he said in his official statement," Mace replied. "I haven't interviewed him in person yet."

"Oh," Sergeant Watson said as the two men turned and walked back to their parked cars, "I guess that makes sense."

The skepticism in the veteran officer's voice was unmistakable. Mace already knew what was going through the other man's mind; it was the same thought he'd had as soon as he read Deputy Cothran's statement. "But what cop leaves their keys in their car and the door unlocked?" he said out loud.

Sergeant Watson stopped and turned to face him. "I thought the exact same thing," he said. "I've been a cop for twenty years and I've see some cops do some pretty dumb things, but most cops are pretty conscientious when it comes to things like that. Most cops I know consider it the ultimate shame is they become victims of a crime."

Mace had noted the same thing among his fellow law enforcement officers. Being a cop and being victimized in a crime was almost as bad as a firefighter accidentally burning their own house down. It was embarrassing, to say the least. "To be completely forthcoming, Sergeant Watson, there are plenty of unanswered questions regarding the entire situation. Now, I have another question for you. This one is off the record and it stays between me and you," Mace said.

The two men had reached Sergeant Watson's cruiser. Watson leaned back against the fender. "Fire away," he said.

"Would you have shot her?" Mace asked. "You are the officer who was closest to her. Deputy Cothran said that he shot her because he felt that you, a fellow officer, were in danger. What's your opinion of that? Did you feel like you were in imminent danger?"

Sergeant Watson looked down at the ground for a few seconds as he considered the question. "I hate Monday -morning- quarterbacking another officer," he said. "That's a slippery slope. He had a different line of sight than me, so he was seeing things from a different angle." He glanced past Mace to the spot in the parking lot where Deputy Cothran was standing when he fired.

"I completely understand that," Mace said. "It's a tough question. I'm essentially asking you, as a veteran law enforcement officer, if you think he was justified in shooting the suspect."

Sergeant Watson exhaled. "Personally, I would not have shot her," he finally said. "From where I was, she looked like she was about to drop the weapon. There was nothing in her body language that indicated to me that she wanted to attack me."

Mace had interrogated a lot of criminal suspects during his career with the BCI. Experience had taught him to recognize the point when someone wanted to talk, to get something that was bothering them off their chest. He was seeing that now in Sergeant Watson. He didn't think for a moment that the veteran lawman had lied to him about anything so far, but he could tell that something wasn't sitting well with him. "Sarge, there's something bothering you about this whole situation. Please tell me what it is. I don't care if it's your impression, some gut feeling, or just your honest opinion. I made a few calls and spoke to some mutual friends at the North Carolina Department of Public Safety. They all spoke highly of you. They all said you're a good cop and a good man. That makes your take on this very valuable."

Sergeant Watson digested this somberly. "Alright then," he said reluctantly. "This is something that has been eating at me since this happened, Agent Holliday. I want to ask you a question: What suspect running from the police in a pursuit wants to see another police officer?"

"None I ever dealt with," Mace answered.

"That girl crashed the truck she was using to try to escape getting arrested," Sergeant Watson said. "She climbs out of the wrecked truck and she sees two other cops coming toward her, as well as the officer who was chasing her to begin with. Every other suspect I've ever dealt with had an 'oh crap' look in that situation, followed by either anger or fear. This girl looked like that for a moment, but then you could tell she was glad to see me and Johnson. I saw the look on her face when she saw that my uniform was different from Deputy Cothran's. At first it was surprise, but then it was sheer relief."

Mace had not heard this before. Sergeant Johnson's official statement had been all about the facts; who was where, what happened, and what he personally saw and heard. There was nothing about his personal interpretation of the girl's facial expression because it wasn't a measurable, verifiable thing. There wasn't a judge or lawyer alive who would let him give his own view on what he thought another person was thinking. A person's motive to do what they did was often one of the hardest things to determine in a court of law. Sergeant Watson had been a cop long enough to know that and that's why such things weren't in his statement.

"That young lady was glad to see us," Sergeant Watson continued. "Can I prove that in court? No, I can't. But I'm telling you I have never seen someone do that before when confronted by more cops."

Mace could tell that what Sergeant Watson was saying had been bothering him immensely. The man was practically quivering as he spoke. "There was one other thing in your statement I was curious about," Mace said. "You put in there that the girl spoke with you or tried to speak with you."

"It looked like she was about to drop the screwdriver she was holding," Watson said. "She started to say something that sounded like 'Aye' or maybe 'Hey' but then the deputy fired. When she was shot she was literally about ten feet away from me. I was looking her right in the face." Watson turned and looked back at the spot where the girl's body had lain. It was obvious from the look on his face that he was replaying it all in his mind and he didn't like the memory.

"You have any idea of what she was trying to tell you?" Mace asked.

"No clue," Watson said. He turned to Mace. "You think the girl was Mexican, maybe an illegal alien?"

Mace nodded. "Given her appearance, the lack of identification, and other things, I suspect she was," he said. "Why do you ask?"

"There's a biker gang in these parts calling themselves The Horde," Watson said. "Some of my troopers have had run-ins with them just over the state line. I've heard that they're involved in human trafficking, mainly young girls from Mexico and Central America. I just wonder if she was one because of something my daughter mentioned."

"What was that?" Mace asked.

"My youngest daughter is a junior in high school," Sergeant Watson said. "She takes a Spanish class. Last night she overheard me venting to her mom about this whole situation. I've always made it a policy to not bring my job home, but this whole shooting has really affected me. It's messed with my head in a big way. Even more strange, it bothers me more than the two line-of-duty shootings I've been involved in personally. Weird, huh?"

"You were closer to the girl than anyone else," Mace said. "You were looking her in the face when she was shot. It changes everything. Believe me, I know. A few months ago, I was talking to the pilot in one of our choppers when the bad guy we were hunting shot through the cockpit window with a fifty-caliber sniper rifle he'd bought illegally. The pilot, a friend of mine, was literally looking over his shoulder into my face when the bullet came through and hit him in the chest. That stays on my mind. It keeps me awake at night even now."

"I thought I recognized your name when you called yesterday," Sergeant Watson said. "The thing in Laurens. That was you?"

"Afraid so," Mace said.

"Then you understand," Watson said. "Anyway, my daughter heard me telling her mom about the girl trying to say something to me before the deputy shot her. I mentioned how it sounded like 'Aye' or something similar. My daughter overheard us and she brought up an interesting point. In her Spanish class, they learned the word 'Ayuda'. Ayuda is Spanish for help."

"So, you think she was asking you to help her?" Mace said.

"Based on her body language and facial expression, I do," Sergeant Watson replied. "Legally, given how close she was to me with a weapon in her hand, Deputy Cothran probably had the right to shoot her, but just because something is legal doesn't make it right."

"What kind of help do you think she wanted?" Mace asked.

"I really think she wasn't running from the police as much as she was running away from that deputy," Sergeant Watson said. "Something about this stinks to high heaven. You're a cop, you shoot someone, and the first thing you ask another officer is if the person you just shot said anything? What the hell?"

Mace had read about Cothran's question in Sergeant Watson's statement. It was one of several things he intended to question Deputy Cothran about when he interviewed him. "I caught that," Mace said. "I intend to find out the truth, Sergeant. By no means is this an open and shut case of justifiable force."

"I hope you do," Watson said. "As I said, this one really bothers me."

"I think that's enough questions for the day," Mace said. He glanced down at his watch. "Since we are here, would you like to grab some lunch? I've heard this place is great."

Sergeant Watson shook his head. "Thanks for the offer, Agent Holliday, but I need to get back to my office. I've also kind of lost my appetite for the food here for a while. Too many bad memories."

"I understand," Mace replied. "Thanks for meeting me here."

Watson nodded. "If there's anything else you need, you have my number."

With that, Sergeant Watson climbed back into his car and drove away. Mace stood there and watched as he drove out of sight. Once he was gone, Mace took out his cell phone and dialed a familiar cell phone number. The number belonged to Billy Winslow, an older BCI agent who was the agency's expert on biker and assorted other gangs. A gruff but cheerful voice answered on the other end. "Hey, Billy, it's Holliday," Mace said. "Just the man I needed to talk to. You ever heard of a biker gang calling themselves The Horde?"

"Unfortunately, yes," Billy said. "I've got a file on them."

Mace leaned against the fender of his car. "Excellent," he said. "I'm in Easton County investigating an officer-involved shooting. Got time for a few questions on the phone?"

"I can do you one better," Agent Winslow said. "I'm on my way back from Charlotte where I was putting on a seminar for some agencies in North Carolina. If you're in Easton County, you're only about an hour from me now. I don't mind a detour, so I can meet you somewhere. How's that?"

"Excellent," Mace said. "There's a public library in the town of Easton. Meet me there in maybe an hour or so?"

"See you there," Winslow said.

CHAPTER 14

Sheriff Lynn Garrett sat in the front passenger's seat of his county-issued unmarked Chevrolet Tahoe and stared morosely out the window on his side. He was tired, angry, and more than a little worried. He had always been a man who prided himself on being able to handle things, no matter what fate threw his way. He had a natural talent for taking situations and making them work to his advantage and it had served him well. Sheriff Garrett wasn't particularly smart, but he did possess an animal cunning and penchant for getting lucky when he needed it. Those attributes, coupled with a complete lack of morals, ethics, or conscience, had helped him go farther in life than many people had ever thought he would and made him richer than he'd ever dared to dream. Now, due to other people's stupidity and just plain bad luck, it seemed like everything he had worked so hard to build was crashing down around him at the worst possible time. The Easton County Sheriff's Office- and he, by default- were under a lot of scrutiny from outsiders. Now, more than ever, he needed everything to run like a well-oiled machine. Unfortunately it wasn't, by any stretch.

The last several hours had been a prime example of just how screwed up everything was getting. Shortly before midnight he'd received a call from one of his deputies with the news about Judge Cooper's crash and injuries. Normally, he could have cared less- the judge's tendency to drive drunk was well-known, so an accident was bound to happen eventually- but the judge was claiming that someone had run him off the road and threatened him. With that news, the sheriff headed to the hospital. He wasn't able to find out anything more because the judge was already in surgery by the time he arrived. The only thing he had learned was that the hospital was already buzzing with the news of the large sum of money found on the judge's person. Thanks to the small-town rumor mill, everyone would know about it by noon the next day. In the right hands, that news could be dangerous. Rumors were the least of the sheriff's concerns regarding Judge Cooper's accident, however. If someone really had caused the judge to wreck his car, then Sheriff Garrett would have to find out who and why. It could be something as simple as someone the judge had ruled against in a past court case or it could be something more sinister.

Unable to learn anything else from the judge, Sheriff Garrett had headed back home and dropped into bed about five A.M. for what he hoped would be a few hours of sleep. Unfortunately, sleep had eluded him. He'd spent the three hours lying in bed and simply staring at the ceiling while his mind churned through different scenarios involving the main thing that was stressing him out: Cothran's shooting incident. That situation could go several different ways and most of them weren't good. If the Bureau of Criminal Investigation and the state attorney general believed Cothran's story about the shooting and the events preceding it, it would be declared a justifiable homicide in accordance with state law. If the attorney general reviewed the case and decided to charge Cothran, then he could go to court and a jury may or may not decide the shooting was justified. The real concern was that Agent Holliday and the BCI might dig deeper into the events leading up to the chase and shooting. If that happened, it could be a disaster for Cothran and himself. Given the people they did business with, both of them probably wouldn't make it to jail, much less trial.

After three hours of staring at the ceiling and trying to figure out how to make everything work out, Sheriff Garrett had finally given up and gotten out of bed. A quick shower, some breakfast that had given him indigestion, and the drive back to the office had followed. He'd barely made it to the office when Ronny Easton had called him. Ronny was livid about Judge Cooper wrecking his car and the custody hearing being cancelled. Garrett had listened to him whine for a few minutes before giving him a few mumbled assurances that everything would work out and hanging up on him. As usual, dealing with Ronny had put him in a bad mood, if it was even possible to get in a worse mood than he was before the call. He was really starting to hate Ronny. The day would come when they no longer needed Ronny. When it did he planned to personally deal with Ronny. The thought of putting a bullet through Ronny's sniveling face was enough to actually cheer him up some.

He'd spent a good part of the morning meeting with Deputy Dwayne Cothran in his office. Technically, Dwayne was on administrative duty while the shooting was being investigated, meaning he couldn't be out on patrol or doing anything else in uniform, so the sheriff had let him come in to work in street clothes to act as his driver and assistant. In reality, it gave the sheriff a chance to sit down with Dwayne and make sure that he had his story straight and that he was doing everything possible to make sure the BCI didn't uncover the truth. It was a difficult undertaking, to say the least. Lynn Garrett and Dwayne Cothran had been best friends since grade school, where they'd bonded over their mutual love of bullying others. Dwayne had always been big and strong, but he wasn't that smart. However, he was ruthless, completely fearless, and extremely loyal. Dwayne was the first person the sheriff had brought in when he realized that taking bribes and working with his current business partners paid a great deal more than being a cop. Dwayne was the muscle behind the sheriff and he was like a rabid pit bull that the sheriff could turn loose on whoever he needed to. With the sheriff as the brains and Dwayne as the brawn, the two of them were making more money than they had ever dreamed.

Things seemed to go well with his talk with Dwayne. The big deputy understood that he never should have let the girl get away, killing her in front of witnesses was a potential disaster, and that they were in full damage control mode. The two of them went over his story regarding the events leading up to the shooting and the shooting itself until the sheriff was sure Dwayne had his story straight. Dwayne had also assured him that he was in the process of getting rid of all possible evidence linking him to the dead girl and the other girls before her. Despite all that, about halfway through their talk, Sheriff Garrett had come to a grim realization: Dwayne, his best friend and ally, was a too much of a liability.

Now, as Dwayne drove him to meet with the leader of the bikers, Sheriff Garrett stared out the window and wondered why he hadn't seen something like this coming. Dwayne had never really been normal, especially when it came to girls and sex. Lynn had figured that out in middle school when Dwayne had shown him the treasure trove of pornography that he'd collected. Lynn wasn't squeamish, but some of the more violent bondage magazines his best friend obsessed over were enough to turn his stomach. Dwayne hadn't dated much in school, mainly due to the fact that he did and said things that freaked most girls out. He'd dated even less since high school. Actually, Sheriff Garrett couldn't remember the last time he'd seen Dwayne with a woman who wasn't a prostitute. The real red flag should have been when Dwayne started getting one of the girls the bikers smuggled through the county for his personal use. The sheriff had known deep in his guts what was really happening, but he'd let it keep happening. Now it had come back to haunt him.

Dwayne turned off the paved highway onto a dirt and gravel road that cut its way through a thick forest of pine trees. The road ended at a small clearing in the middle of the woods where the gravel met red dirt where the land had been cleared. The road and the hundred acres of forest around it belonged to Sheriff Garrett. The clearing would soon be the site of a new log home the sheriff planned to build there. It was an excellent place to meet if you didn't want to be seen. The closest neighbor was over a mile away and there was almost no traffic on the highway that led to the property. The privacy and solitude were the reasons why Sheriff Garrett had bought the land.

A single motorcycle sat parked on the gravel in the clearing with the rider leaning against the seat smoking a cigarette. The rider, a muscular man of medium height with a shaved head, piercing green eyes, and a flat nose that looked like it had been broken a time or two, looked up as the SUV pulled in and parked several feet from him. Full sleeve tattoos covered both exposed arms and extended up each side of his neck almost to his ears. Even from a distance, the man looked dangerous. He took one more insolent puff of his cigarette before dropping it and smashing it out with his boot. The biker, who Sheriff Garrett knew only as Stoner, was the leader of The Horde, the motorcycle gang the sheriff did business with. Stoner didn't look like he was in a pleasant mood. His intense gaze never left the SUV and the two figures as it parked and Dwayne shut off the engine.

Sheriff Garrett looked at Dwayne. "Stay in the truck," he ordered as he opened his door. "This is between me and him."

Dwayne glared out the window at Stoner. Stoner and Deputy Cothran had met several times before in clandestine meetings such as this one and from the first meeting it had been hate at first sight. For some reason the two men had instantly disliked each other and neither man could really articulate why they felt that way. It was something instinctive and primeval, almost like two alpha wolves meeting up in the wilderness and trying to kill each other simply because that's the way they were wired. The sheriff had realized almost from the first meeting that, if a meeting was going to go smoothly, Dwayne and

Stoner had to be kept away from each other. When they were in close proximity to each other, the tension in the air was palpable.

"If you need me, give me a sign," Dwayne grumbled in his low voice. "I don't trust that tattooed freak."

Sheriff Garrett nodded and closed the car door. He walked over to Stoner. The biker leader had called him earlier and demanded this meeting. Stoner's call and the request for the sudden meeting was yet another thing that had so far made this day terrible. When Stoner requested a meeting, it was never good. Stoner ran The Horde in Easton County and the entire upstate of South Carolina. The Horde actually worked with the Baja Cartel. The Baja Cartel, based in northern Mexico, smuggled drugs, weapons, and human beings into the United States. Once those things were across the border into the United States, the biker gang was responsible for getting the smuggled drugs, weapons, and human beings where they were supposed to go. The gang also collected the cartel's money for said illegal activities, laundered it when possible, and got it back into the cartel's hands. Getting summoned to a meeting with Stoner was like being called to the principal's office when you were in grade school: nothing good usually came out of it.

"Howdy, Sheriff," Stoner said in an accent that was all Texas. "I appreciate you coming."

"Did I have a choice?" Sheriff Garrett asked. "Your phone call made it pretty clear that my attendance was mandatory."

Stoner smiled, revealing surprisingly nice teeth. "You're right, Sheriff, your attendance wasn't a request. We needed to talk immediately because I'm not very happy right now."

"And why is that, Stoner?" Sheriff Garrett asked with a calmness he didn't really feel. Ever since Dwayne had let the girl get loose and ended up killing her, Lynn had been expecting a meeting like this. The shooting had brought an outside law enforcement agency into Easton County to investigate the incident. Outside law enforcement agencies couldn't be controlled the way the sheriff's office was controlled. The outside law enforcement agency might find something no one wanted found. The Cartel was paying Lynn Garrett a lot of money to make sure that law enforcement stayed out of the way of the criminal enterprises that The Horde was operating for them in Easton County. Now, thanks to the shooting, the status quo was in jeopardy.

"We've had some things happen in the last couple of days that I'm not very happy about," Stoner said. He motioned toward the parked Tahoe where Dwayne sat with his chin. "Your pet there has done messed up. Now, there's a big investigation going on, thanks to him. We don't need some outside cops snooping around."

"Hey, he didn't have a choice," Sheriff Garrett said. "The girl got away and he was after her. It's just sheer bad luck that she happened to wreck right where there were other cops from another agency. At least he was able to get her before she talked to those North Carolina troopers."

"But he let her get away in the first place," Stoner said tersely. "When that freak started asking for a girl, we warned him that he was responsible if it blew up in his face. Well, guess what? It did. Now he's under investigation."

"But he's probably going to be cleared," Sheriff Garrett replied. "Given the situation, the shooting played out perfectly. It looks like the girl stole his truck, he chased her, and then had to shoot her to protect other officers. It looks like a clear case of a justifiable homicide by an officer performing his duty."

"He'd better hope so," Stoner said. "My worry- and the cartel's- is that the BCI won't buy the part of the story where the girl mysteriously comes out of nowhere and happens to find his truck with the keys in it. That freak has gone through what? Five girls? You know he killed them all. That's a big problem, given the situation."

"Are you really standing here and bitching to me about killing people?" Sheriff Garrett said incredulously. "Your gang and the people you all work for have probably killed more people than cancer."

Stoner's face hardened. "That was business, Sheriff," he spat back. "Your pet deputy there is nothing but a serial killer hiding behind a uniform. I could care less how many women he rapes or kills, as long as it doesn't interfere with business. The problem is that he got sloppy, one of his toys got away, and now the situation might get out of hand."

"If it does, we'll handle it," Sheriff Garrett said. He could barely believe that he was standing there defending Dwayne, especially considering his earlier realization that Dwayne was a problem, but he couldn't back down to Stoner. Stoner and people like him were like mad dogs; if you showed the slightest fear or hesitation they would be all over you.

Stoner smirked, which made the sheriff want to punch him in the face. "What's this 'we' you're talking about?" Stoner asked. "If this goes south, it's your problem. Remember when you decided to get in this game? You were warned."

Sheriff Garrett did indeed remember that moment in his life. He remembered it like it was yesterday. Almost from the moment he'd graduated from the police academy and started working the roads of Easton County, Lynn Garrett had been looking for ways to line his pockets. At first it had been as simple as taking a folded twenty-dollar bill to not write a traffic citation. That had graduated to shaking down drug dealers and illegal gambling houses. Pure luck had led him to stop a van for a burned-out tail light on a narrow two-lane back road in the middle of nowhere. The van was being driven by a white man but was loaded with Hispanic-looking men and women. It had taken Lynn about three minutes to realize that the van was full of illegal immigrants and the man driving the van was a human trafficker. Lynn, along with his back-up, Deputy Cothran, had relieved the van driver of over a thousand dollars in cash and a bag of meth. "If you want to run this through my section of this county, there's a toll," Lynn told the driver before releasing the van and everyone in it.

From then on, it was easy for Lynn and Dwayne to identify and stop the human traffickers, even when the smugglers used different vehicles and tactics. During one stop, they had found the panel van empty of human cargo, but with nearly a hundred thousand dollars under one of the seats. The driver of that van was Stoner. Unlike the other drivers, Stoner was almost cheerful when Lynn and Dwayne pulled him over and found the money. Stoner had warned him that he could take the money, but if he did he wouldn't live long enough to spend it.

The other option was to give Stoner his cell phone number and to wait for a call. The call would be to discuss a business proposition that would make the money in the van seem like chump change. Stoner's cool confidence and the matter-of-fact way he delivered what was essentially a threat made Lynn decide to let him go on his way with the money.

Three days, Lynn's phone rang and he was told to meet someone at an old church on the same back road where he'd stopped Stoner. Lynn and Dwayne had waited there in the dark until a BMW drove up. Stoner and a slender male dressed in khakis, a dress shirt, and expensive-looking cowboy boots were the sole occupants of the BMW. The other man introduced himself as Garcia and with his slim frame, nice clothes, and manicured nails, he looked the part of a rich playboy. The look was misleading; Garcia was a high-ranking member of the cartel and his job was to solve problems. At that point, Deputies Lynn Garrett and Dwayne Cothran were a problem and Garcia was there to find a solution. Garcia gave Lynn two choices: Be on the payroll or be eliminated. If he chose to turn down the money, he would be killed in a manner that would send a message to others who might get in the cartel's way. In return for taking the money, Lynn and Dwayne would turn a blind eye to certain criminal activities in Easton County and also make sure other cops didn't get too nosy. Garcia had given the two of them five minutes to think about it.

Lynn and Dwayne were huddled up thinking about it when Stoner walked over to them. "Take the money," he told them. "They prefer not to kill cops because it draws a lot of heat, but they will if that's what it takes. Play the game and get rich. We will do our part to keep a low profile. You two will be just an added layer of security."

"Why are you guys coming through Easton County?" Lynn had asked. He was genuinely curious at the time as to why they would be smuggling drugs, people, and cash through a backwoods county like Easton instead of one of the major cities.

Stoner had simply smiled. "You just answered your own question," he said. "Cops expect stuff like that in certain places. You two just got lucky once, figured out what was happening, and got greedy. You two are hyenas slipping up to drink at the same watering hole as the lions."

"What's to stop us from killing you both and acting like this never happened?" Dwayne asked. Even then there had been unspoken animosity between Stoner and Dwayne. It had only gotten worse as the years passed.

"I don't think you guys are that stupid," Stoner replied. "If something happens to us, both of you, along with your families and friends, will die in ways that will be talked about around this hick county for years to come."

Lynn and Dwayne had chosen to take the money. They did their part to keep things running smoothly for Stoner and the cartel. A few years later, Garcia met with Garrett and ordered him to run for sheriff so he could keep a tighter grip on things. The cartel was planning on a major expansion and traffic through Easton County was going to be increasing. Lynn had earned some extra points with them by bringing Ronny Easton into the fold. Ronny's chemical business was an excellent means for the cartel to smuggle their illegal cash back into Mexico. Still, the tension remained between Sheriff Garrett, the bikers, and the cartel, most of it based on the mutual distrust that criminals had for cops, even crooked ones. That tension made for some dicey negotiations at the best of times. When something was going wrong, it was like walking through a minefield.

"I believe we will be okay," Sheriff Garrett said. "If not, I will handle it, like I said."

"Needless to say, since that big freak can't keep his pet projects locked up, he's not getting any more women from us," Stoner added. "Letting him pick a girl had conditions and he blew it."

"Understood," Sheriff Garrett said testily. There was no point in arguing with Stoner, especially considering that he agreed with him. "Anything else?"

"Three of my guys got beat down earlier today," Stoner said.

"Excuse me?" Sheriff Garrett said incredulously.

"Three of my men got beat down today in downtown Easton," Stoner said impatiently. "They had words with the owner of Smith's Filling Station about turning on the gas pumps. That old guy that's the preacher, the one who owns the hotel and dock. What's his name?"

"Jacob White?" Sheriff Garrett asked.

"Yes," Stoner said. "He came up with some young dude with him. One of my guys took offense at the old man not minding his business, so he punched him. The young dude lit in on my guys and took it to them. One of them has got a busted jaw and probably won't ever father any children. The other two will recover."

"I don't know of any young man that hangs out with Jacob White," Sheriff Garrett said. "I'm familiar with most of the locals. Can you describe him?"

"I can go one better," Stoner said. He produced a smart phone from his jean pocket, punched a few buttons, and pulled up a photo. He held up the phone so the sheriff could see it. "I took this when we went out to pick up my boys," he said. "One of them called us after the fight and we rolled out there intending to even the score. The only thing that stopped us was that there were too many witnesses."

"Guy doesn't look that big," Sheriff Garrett said as he studied the picture. The guy in the picture looked like he might be six feet and weigh a couple of hundred pounds. He looked thick across the shoulders and arms as if he worked out, but other than that he looked pretty average. His face was clearly visible in the picture as if he had intentionally posed for the photograph.

"My guys said he used some kind of kung fu stuff on them," Stoner said. "He must be pretty badass because the three guys he beat down are all pretty tough."

"What do you want me to do?" Sheriff Garrett asked.

"Find out who he is for me," Stoner said in a tone that made it clear it wasn't a request as much as an order. "Do it all nice and legal-like so our fingerprints ain't on it. The Horde is going to deal with him personally, but I need to know if he's a local or some stranger."

"Why does it matter?" Sheriff Garrett asked.

"That's the other reason for this meeting," Stoner said. "I got word from further up the chain that one of the cartel's rivals might be making a move to try to eliminate them and take over. They've had a few of their guys down Mexico way go missing and get found later dead with obvious signs of torture. Someone's gathering information, possibly for a large-scale move. That could spill over here. We need to keep an eye on any new strangers in town. This guy beating down my guys might just be a coincidence, or it could be the start of something worse. I want to know who this guy is. Who better to do that than the local sheriff?"

"Send the picture to my phone," Sheriff Garrett said. "I'll handle this personally."

Stoner nodded and got back on his bike. "Anything else you need, Sheriff?" he asked.

Sheriff Garrett was silent for a few moments. "If I need to handle a certain problem, it's going to have to look like an accident or suicide," he said as he cut his eyes back toward the unmarked Tahoe where Dwayne sat. "Anything else would just invite more scrutiny."

Stoner grinned as if he'd just gotten good news. "That's why they have Garcia," he said. "He solves problems. Big Boy there is definitely in his wheelhouse." With that, he started his bike, gunned the engine, and took off, peppering the sheriff with dirt and small pieces of gravel.

Sheriff Garrett watched him ride away, then turned and trudged back to the truck.

CHAPTER 15

South Carolina Bureau of Criminal Investigation Agent William "Billy" Winslow was a character, to say the least. A tall, lean man who bore a close enough resemblance to the actor Sam Elliot to make people do a double-take, Billy had been with the BCI for thirty-two years. He had served in a variety of positions during his career and excelled in all of them, but he'd really found his calling working undercover and infiltrating biker gangs throughout the southeastern United States. During the course of his career he'd infiltrated several different gangs and investigations he'd either initiated or been involved with had shut down several criminal gangs, some with national reach. Now in his late fifties and getting close to retirement, the BCI had put him in an office and made him responsible for gathering and compiling information on biker and street gangs. He also taught at the state criminal justice academy teaching police officers about gangs. In short, he was a treasure trove of valuable insight into that particular criminal underworld and Mace knew that he'd gotten lucky by catching him close enough to Easton County to come meet with him in person.

The two of them were meeting at the Easton County Public Library, an old brick building that was once the main passenger depot for the train line that passed through Easton. The building had been beautifully restored, modernized, and turned into the local library. Mace had chosen the library because it was easy to find and, just as he expected, they had meeting rooms he could use to meet Agent Winslow. Fortunately, one of those meeting rooms was available and the head librarian was more than glad to let the two BCI agents use it. The meeting room they ended up in had a small table with four chairs and big, arched windows that looked out over an expanse of manicured lawn. The other wall, which faced into the library, was glass with adjustable blinds to ensure privacy. With the door closed and the blinds closed, Mace and Agent Winslow sat down at the table across from each other.

"Billy, I really appreciate you coming this way to meet me," Mace said sincerely. "I probably could have gotten what I needed over the telephone, though, and saved you the drive."

Billy leaned forward and rested his elbows on the table. "I didn't mind the drive at all, Mace," he said. "I'm retiring in about six months. I plan to spend a lot of time hunting and fishing and I've heard this place is great for both, so I didn't mind a chance to get a look for myself. Besides, all I was doing was heading back to my office. I'm not really an office kind of guy. You just gave me a chance to actually be helpful."

"I figure you will be," Mace said. "You know I'm here following up on an officer-involved shooting that happened a couple of days ago."

"Saw it on the news, so I know the general details" Billy said.

"There's a biker gang that's taken up residence here in this county," Mace said. "They've bought property and opened up a strip club just outside the town limits here. They call themselves The Horde. I haven't personally seen any of them, but I have been running around interviewing people so I haven't exactly looked. I suspect the girl who was shot might be an illegal immigrant. One of the witnesses to the shooting was a North Carolina Highway Patrol officer. He told me that The Horde is allegedly involved in immigrant smuggling. That's why I made the call to you."

Billy nodded. "I've got some information on The Horde," he said. "There's not a lot of information on them out there because they are one of the smaller gangs in the United States. The best estimates give them maybe three hundred members nationally, mainly in the southwestern United States, with most in New Mexico and Arizona. Another reason there's not much information on them is because they keep their mouths shut. Members of The Horde don't talk to the cops when they get busted. I stay in touch with a lot of cops who work gang intelligence like I do and we swap info constantly. If a member of The Horde has ever flipped, I've never heard of it. Their guys are pretty hardcore, with a lot of them being ex-military."

"What kind of illegal activities are they usually involved with?" Mace asked as he scribbled notes on the legal pad he'd brought in with him.

"That's where it gets interesting," Billy said. "Pretty much all of the national biker gangs are involved in some type of illegal activities. Usually it's running drugs and weapons. Their favorites are crystal meth and cocaine. Many of the biker gangs are involved with international criminal organizations that are smuggling the drugs and weapons into the United States, like the Mexican cartels and the Russian mafia up north. It's mainly a business thing, with the bikers buying from the other criminal organizations and using their people to distribute the drugs or whatever else. The different organizations also usually stay out of each other's way and off each other's turf. It keeps disputes down to a minimum."

"Makes sense, "Mace said. "Crime makes for some strange bedfellows."

"You ain't kidding, brother," Billy said sardonically. "From what we know about The Horde, they are one of the few biker gangs that actually is involved in a close working relationship with one of the drug cartels in Mexico. The cartel in Mexico calls themselves the Baja Cartel because that's where they are located in northern Mexico. When I say The Horde has a close relationship with them, I mean The Horde acts as the cartel's arm in the United States. It's not simply a case of a biker gang buying drugs from a cartel, selling the drugs on the street, and then pocketing the money. The Horde actually works for the Baja Cartel. The gang is essentially a sub-contractor for the cartel. That's pretty unusual because most bikers won't actively work for the cartels."

"Why is that?" Mace asked.

"Racism," Billy said cheerfully. "I think that's a big part of it, to be completely honest. Most bikers are red-blooded, flag-waving, ex-military, good-ole-boys. They look down on the Mexicans and consider them trash. But I also think that another reason they try to keep the cartels at arm's length is fear. Most of the Mexican cartels are freaking crazy. Just watch the news and see what happens in Mexico every day. They had what, thirty thousand homicides in Mexico last year? People in Mexico have to drive to work under highway overpasses that have bodies hanging from them every day. The local cartels drop off trash bags full of heads at the local police stations. Hell, the Mexican military had to get involved because the police were either outgunned or corrupt, and the cartels attacked the military! The cartel will go after you, your family, your friends, and pretty much anything else you love if you mess with them. These people put videos online of them cutting people up with chainsaws. That's not exactly the kind of people I would want to work with if I had a choice."

"So why is The Horde involved with them?" Mace asked.

"Because The Horde had to find a niche if they were going to survive in the dog-eat-dog world or criminal motorcycle gangs," Billy said. "Some of the national gangs have five thousand members or more. I don't mean guys who put on a vest with a patch on it and try to hang out and act tough; I'm talking hardcore, gun-toting felons who will do what they are told with no questions asked. Those big gangs control ninety percent of the drug trade and huge swaths of the country. If you get caught in the wrong place wearing the wrong colors, you'll be considered lucky if you just get put in the hospital in intensive care for a few weeks. Usually, you'll disappear. Your vest with the club patch on it will be sent to your leader as a message to stay out of their territory. Also, if you try to move too big a quantity of drugs, you'll get noticed. The Horde had to find someone to back them and some way to make money that wouldn't get them obliterated by another gang or put them too high on law enforcement's radar."

"If they can't run drugs, that narrows what they can do to make serious money," Mace said. "If they came from the Southwest and they're in bed with a cartel, what does that leave?

Billy grinned. "The Horde traffics in human being," he said. "The Baja Cartel runs dope and money like all of the other cartels do, but they also are heavily involved in human trafficking. The cartel's coyotes smuggle paying customers across the border and The Horde takes it from there. The Horde delivers the new arrivals to wherever they are going in America. They also have their hands in prostitution, strip clubs, and pornographic films. Many of the young females that are smuggled into this country end up as sex slaves working as prostitutes."

Mace digested this information. That would explain the lack of identification and the signs of sexual abuse on the dead girl. Given the allegations of corruption involving the sheriff's office, it was very possible that Deputy Cothran had been involved with the dead girl in some manner before the chase and the shooting. He could have been involved with her sexually as a paying customer or, if he was truly corrupt and being paid off by the bikers, he could have been the one actually transporting her from one place to another. That seemed more plausible than Cothran's story.

"The Horde also runs some drugs, but mainly pills and some crystal meth," Billy continued. "Human trafficking is their real value to the Baja Cartel, followed by laundering the cartel's cash. They were smart enough to make themselves valuable to the cartel by finding ways to launder the money legally. They do that by owning legitimate businesses where they can do some creative accounting and make the cartel's illegal money look legit. They get a percentage off the top for doing that, of course."

"Like a strip club or a bar?" Mace asked, even though he already knew the answer.

"Aw man, bars are great ways to launder money," Billy said enthusiastically. "A bar is primarily a cash business with a lot of ways to doctor the books. There's no way any auditor can prove or disprove that you sold a certain number of drinks or had a certain number of customers, unless they put cameras on every aspect of your operation. The strip club you say the gang runs here actually would benefit them on two levels. They can launder money while simultaneously putting the girls they brought in to work to make money. It's a win-win situation for the gang and the cartel behind them."

"The government keeps an eye on international financial transactions, especially ones going to certain countries," Mace said. "Realistically, how much money could they ship back to the cartel without it raising red flags?"

"That's one of the biggest problems criminal organizations have," Billy replied evenly. "Suppose you're making millions of dollars in cold hard US currency every day. That's cash you can't put in the bank in most countries because it's dirty. Also, there's only so much you can launder and send back home from America without some nice gentleman from the IRS or FBI showing up wanting to know how a restaurant or bar in the middle of nowhere is making tens of thousands of dollars a week. The cartels' answer is to try to smuggle the cash back into Mexico. That's actually much more difficult than you would imagine for them. Remember, we're not talking about a few thousand dollars in hundred-dollar bills; we're talking millions of dollars in bundled cash, literally shipping pallets stacked with crates packed with money."

"I've seen the news footage of some of the raids in Mexico," Mace said. News footage of Mexican soldiers standing in rooms stacked floor-to-ceiling and wall-to-wall with bundles of money was commonplace on the cable news channels. "It's amazing. I remember reading somewhere one of the major drug cartels would lose millions of dollars a month to bugs and rodents eating the bills because of where they had to stash the money."

"Smuggling cash is hard because it has a certain size," Billy added. "A single dollar bill is going to take up a certain amount of space, no matter how you try to fold it or shrink-wrap it. Now imagine the problem that millions of bills represent to someone trying to sneak it somewhere. The Border Patrol intercepts millions of dollars every month that people are trying to get into Mexico. You think the cartels get creative smuggling drugs? You should see some of the ways they try to smuggle cash. The Border Patrol has found tunnels with electrified trains like they use in mining. They've busted guys flying bundles of cash over the border using drones. It's crazy."

Mace sat quietly and let all of that sink in for a few moments. "Why do you think The Horde has decided to set up shop here in Easton County?" he finally asked. "If you had to venture a guess, that is."

"They stay away from major cities," Billy opined. "All of the things about a big metropolis that make it easy for criminals to blend in also make it so there's a bigger law enforcement presence with more oversight. More people requires more cops. A small, rural county like this would be an excellent place for a criminal organization to set up shop. The old, backwoods busybody is a stereotype. Most people who live out in the sticks mind their own business until something is a problem for them personally. I grew up in a small town about this size in Georgia until we moved when I was fifteen, so I know whereof I speak."

"I've been hearing allegations that the local sheriff's office is on the take and working hand in hand with the bikers," Mace said. "Several local citizens, as well as the town police chief, have told me that. It would explain where this mystery girl the deputy shot came from. I haven't interviewed him in person yet, but I've read his preliminary statement. Between me and you, I'm just not buying his story about how he ended up in the car chase that resulted in him shooting this kid."

"Is it just you up here, Mace?" Billy asked with a hint of concern in his voice. Mace nodded silently. "Why in the hell did they send you into a situation like this by yourself?" Anger had replaced the hint of concern.

"I know you will keep your mouth shut, Billy," Mace said, "so I'm going to level with you. Investigating the shooting was just a good excuse for me to come here and snoop around. The town mayor is an old buddy of the governor and he called him begging for help. Officially, I'm following up on the use of force. Unofficially, I'm here to see if some of these allegations might be true enough to warrant a full scale BCI investigation."

Billy scowled. "Mace, I know you can take care of yourself, but based on what I know, The Horde isn't someone to take lightly. You better be careful. If they really are involved and you start getting close, they probably want take that lying down."

"Yes," Mace answered. "I plan to be careful. If I find something concrete that proves that the local police and the bikers are working together, I'll call in the troops."

"You do that," Billy said. He glanced down at his watch. "You need anything else from me?"

"No," Mace replied. "I just keep hearing about The Horde, so I wanted to know what I was dealing with. I knew you would know something."

Billy smiled and shrugged. "It's what I do," he said. "I guess I better head back to Columbia. God forbid my office chair gets cold."

The two BCI agents left the conference room together. Mace thanked the librarian for letting them use it as he passed the main desk. "Where you heading to now?" Billy asked as they reached his car.

"I'm probably heading back to the hotel I'm calling home for now," Mace replied. "I've got a lot of paperwork I need to fill out over what I've found out today."

Billy climbed into his car, an unmarked Dodge Durango. "You be careful here, Mace. Seriously. The Horde makes people disappear."

Mace nodded. "I will, but careful only goes so far."

CHAPTER 16

When Mace drove into the hotel parking lot twenty minutes after leaving Billy and the library, the first thing he noticed was a familiar beige Range Rover cruising slowly through the parking lot close to the front of the building. He recognized it immediately as the same one from the ugly confrontation when he'd first arrived in town yesterday. It belonged to Ronny Easton, Amanda's estranged husband. As he drove closer to the SUV, he could see Ronny inside behind the wheel. Ronny's face was turned toward the front of the hotel, away from the highway and where Mace had just entered the parking lot. Judging from the way Ronny was craning his neck, he was obviously looking for something or someone. It didn't take a rocket scientist to figure out that he was probably looking for either Amanda or Caleb. Ronny was probably furious over the emergency custody hearing being cancelled and he'd come here looking for a chance to confront his wife again.

Mace felt the first faint stirrings of anger as he drove through the lot toward the office and Ronny's vehicle. He had only known Amanda for maybe twenty-four hours, but so far he'd seen nothing in her that warranted being treated the way her estranged husband treated her. Granted, in private she might be totally different, but no one deserved to be stalked and bullied. Also, Mace had always been really good at reading people and, based on what he'd seen so far, he didn't think Amanda had a mean or bitter bone in her body. Based on everything he'd seen or heard so far, it looked like Ronny was the problem. He shook his head in quiet amazement. It had never ceased to amaze him how some of the worst people in the world always seemed to find someone to be in a relationship with them. He'd heard the old adage about love being blind, but he sometimes wondered if love was deaf and insane to boot. That a woman as lovely as Amanda could end up with someone like a Ronny Easton amazed him.

Mace drove the Charger up behind Ronny's Range Rover and beeped the horn. Through the back windshield he saw Ronny jump and then look in the rearview mirror. Ronny did an almost comical double take and then accelerated rapidly away. The Range Rover fled the parking lot with a squeal of tires and then took off down the highway back toward town. For a moment, Mace was tempted to give chase and pull him over, but then he thought better of it. He had enough on his plate without having to deal with Ronny Easton.

Mace parked in a spot close to the office, grabbed his briefcase, and got out of the car. He walked down the sidewalk to the door of his hotel room. He was opening the door to his room when he heard a child's laughter coming from further down the sidewalk where it opened to the lawn, the dock, and the lakeshore. The sound of laughter was followed by what he recognized as Amanda's voice. Mace put his briefcase on the desk in his room and went back outside. He paused long enough to make sure the door was locked before he walked down toward the lake. As soon as he emerged into the late evening sunshine, he saw Amanda sitting on a wooden bench on the grass near the dock. Caleb and Sam were several feet away on the dock. Both of them had fishing poles they had gotten from somewhere and Sam was baiting the hook for Caleb, who seemed to find the sight of Sam trying to put a worm on the hook hilarious. Jacob stood at the closest picnic table. The older man had fired up the grill there and was busy grilling. A variety of containers and an ice chest sat on the picnic table.

Amanda was the first to see him. "Mace," she called as he walked up. "How are you?"

Mace walked to the bench. "Hey," he said. "It looks like everyone is having a good time." He felt awkward standing there with his badge and BCI fatigues on while everyone else was dressed in jeans and having fun.

Amanda motioned for him to sit down on the bench beside her. "Have a seat," she said as she slid over a bit. "I was just sitting out here watching my son traumatize all of the fish in the lake."

Mace sat down on the other end of the bench. The bench was small, leaving only a few inches between the two of them. Even over the smell of cooking food from the grill, Mace could smell the flowery scent of her perfume. She smelled wonderful. "Thanks, Amanda," he said. "It looks like they are having a ball."

"My grandpa and Sam finished all of the chores they had," Amanda said. "It's a pretty day out, so Caleb begged for Sam to go fishing with him. Caleb has his own pole and we had a few others in the storage room, so Jacob grabbed them and here we all are. Once we got here, he decided we should cook out." She looked over toward Jacob at the grill, but her eyes and Mace's eyes locked. The gaze lingered for several seconds before she broke it. "I think we might be having an impromptu celebration over the hearing being cancelled. I think we all thought today was going to go a lot differently than it has."

"I don't want to rain on anyone's parade," Mace said as he lowered his voice, "but when I pulled in your husband was cruising through the parking lot. It looked like he was looking for someone."

Amanda's sunny demeanor immediately vanished. "I'm not surprised," she said with a sigh. "He's left me a couple of voicemails on my phone already. He sounds about half drunk and wired. He actually accused me of somehow causing the judge's car accident." She shook her head. "I seriously think he'd losing what little mind he had."

"Since the judge is out of commission, have you reconsidered trying to get a restraining order on Ronny?" Mace asked. "It might be easier than you think this time, especially if you have audio evidence of his behavior in the form of voicemails. I'll gladly go with you to magistrate's court. I did see him stalking you. Also, my presence might sway the judge."

Amanda lapsed into silence while she thought about it. "To be completely honest, Mace, I'm trying to do everything I can to not provoke him." She tilted her face up to the sun and closed her eyes. "I know I'm married to him and he is the father of my child, but living here, away from him, has made me realize just how toxic our relationship was. He's a bad person and he makes me so angry! The sad part is that I think the biggest part of the anger inside me is actually me being mad at myself. I don't think I ever really loved him. Now I just want our marriage to be over as quickly and easily as possible."

Mace leaned back against the back of the bench. The evening sun was warm and pleasant and looking out over the lake was very peaceful. Sitting there made bikers, dirty cops, and dead girls seem like something from another universe. "Unfortunately, it's not going to be that easy," he finally said. "He will always have certain rights as Caleb's biological father. Fighting for sole custody will be a long, expensive process and chances are he will end up with at least some custodial rights."

"I know," Amanda said softly. "The thought of him alone with Caleb terrifies me." She turned to look at him. "You ever been married, Mace?"

"Nope," Mace replied. "I've dated a few women and even got kind of serious with a certain one. We dated for several months and even lived together for a little while. We ended up breaking up just when I was thinking about proposing. That was about year ago."

"Really?" Amanda asked. "It sounds like you were pretty serious. Do you mind if I ask what happened?"

"She was a teacher in a private school in Columbia," Mace said. "She claimed that being in a relationship with a cop stressed her out. Apparently the best way to relieve stress is to screw the doctor dad of one of your students and have him write you illegal prescriptions for painkillers. I knew nothing about this until a buddy of mine investigating the doctor over the prescriptions he was writing tipped me off about an hour before they arrested the doctor and her. They arrested them both in a hotel room while they were both naked. Needless to say, when she posted her bail and got out of jail, her car with all of her stuff packed into it was parked in the jail lot waiting for her. I haven't seen or spoken to her since, and that was well over a year ago."

"Wow," Amanda said softly, "all of a sudden, I don't feel so bad about marrying Ronny."

That struck Mace as funny and he couldn't help but laugh. The laughter was contagious and Amanda joined in. "So you've got a sense of humor," Mace said when he finally quit chuckling. "I like it."

Amanda blushed lightly. "I'm more than just a damsel in distress," she teased. "I have a personality and everything."

"And a charming one at that," Mace said. "Honestly, I needed a good laugh. I haven't had one in a while."

"Glad I could help," Amanda answered. "I haven't laughed in a long time either. It felt good. Anyway, I'm glad you came back early. Jacob wanted to invite you to join us for the cookout. We're having hamburgers, but they are homemade and he makes great potato salad."

"I would love to," Mace said. "Is this part of the celebration about the hearing being cancelled or was it already planned?"

"My grandfather is ecstatic about the hearing, but there's another reason he's in a great mood," Amanda said. "He'll never admit it, but he's happy about what Sam did in town today."

"What did Sam do in town today?" Mace asked as he cast a look back toward the dock. Sam and Caleb sat side by side on the edge of the dock with fishing poles in their hands. "I've been running around all over the place all day interviewing different people, so I have no idea what you're talking about."

Amanda quickly told Mace the details of Sam's and Jacob's encounter that morning with the three bikers at the garage. Mace listened intently, casting occasional glances toward Sam's back. "My grandfather said it was like nothing he's ever seen, but bear in mind he's a pastor, so he probably has limited experience when it comes to brawls. Still, the gist of it seems to be that Sam knows how to fight and isn't afraid to."

"The problem now is that most biker gangs don't take members getting beaten up in public very well," Mace said worriedly. "I suspect Sam might have put himself in danger."

"I thought the same thing," Amanda replied. "I've already told him that, but he told me that he's not worried about it. The funny thing is that people have been calling my grandfather ever since it happened and asking him to tell Sam 'good job'."

"Really?" Mace asked.

Amanda nodded. "That's not all. He told me he's had numerous calls from people in town asking if he knows how your investigation is going," she said. "I guess that speaks volumes about how tired the people in this town are of letting criminals run things," she said. "They're actually happy when someone stands up to the bad guys."

"Speaking of bad guys, I need to ask you about something," Mace said reluctantly. "The question might be offensive, but it's an angle I need to pursue. I'm asking this as Mace to Amanda, not Agent Holliday to Mrs. Easton."

Amanda scooted around on the bench so she was facing Mace. "Oh, Lord," she said, "I can hardly wait. Go ahead."

"You've mentioned before that your husband has a close relationship with Sheriff Garrett," Mace said. "Have you ever seen anything that might lead you to believe your husband was involved in any type of criminal activity?"

"You mean besides possibly bribing the judge in our custody hearing?" Amanda asked.

Mace grinned. "Well, besides that," he said.

"What have you found, Mace?" Amanda asked with concern in her voice. "Is he involved in something that might put Caleb and me in danger?"

Mace held up his hands in a calming gesture. "Whoa, take it easy, Amanda," he said instantly. "I have not found anything bad. The reason I'm asking about Ronny is because of the company he keeps. He's good friends with a sheriff who's rumored to be crooked and it looks like he might have bribed that judge. All of that makes me wonder if he might be involved in other shady things. I was just wondering if you, as his wife, had ever seen anything that made you wonder if Ronny was up to something."

Amanda sat in silence for several moments thinking. "Do you remember last night when I told you how Ronny changed almost as soon as we were married?" she asked reluctantly. Mace nodded. "I realized pretty quickly that a lot of things about Ronny Easton were an act. One of the first things about him that I realized was all a lie was the family's wealth. Ronny's father indeed inherited a fortune, but Big Ron, as they called him, was a terrible businessman, a degenerate gambler, and a cocaine addict. By the time I married into the family, they were struggling. They weren't in any danger of starving, but the big house and fancy cars were all a façade. The big house had bare spaces on the walls where they had been forced to sell off artwork, the fancy cars were parked because they couldn't afford to insure them, and the big house was as dark as a cave because they had to keep the power bill low."

"So they were broke," Mace said. "You didn't catch on to that while you were dating?"

Amanda blushed. "Not a clue," she said. "Ronny played me for a fool in so many ways. In hindsight, there were several things I noticed that should have tipped me off, but I was young, thought I was in love, and I trusted him."

"You're talking to a guy who was going to propose marriage to a woman who was trading her body to feed her prescription drug addiction," Mace said gently. "Everyone gets fooled sometimes."

"You didn't fall so completely you married her and had a child with her," Amanda said.

"That was pure luck," Mace replied with complete honesty. "I hate to admit that, but it's the truth."

"We're a pair, aren't we?" Amanda said sadly. "Anyway, out of all the businesses in this county that had once had the Easton name on them, the only one that was still running was Easton Chemicals. The only reason it was still open was because the man Big Ron had put in charge of it years earlier was actually pretty good at what he did and Big Ron died before he could bankrupt it draining off the profits to fund his lifestyle. That business was all the family had left."

"That's the business Ronny runs now?" Mace asked.

"When Big Ron died, Ronny was content to let John Clary, the guy who'd been running it for years, keep running it," Amanda said. "Big Ron's life insurance policy saved the family from ruin. Then, out of the blue, Ronny walks in one day, fires Mr. Clary, and takes over the business. This was about two years ago. Easton Chemicals signs some big contracts to provide chemicals to other companies, and suddenly business is booming."

"So what about that situation made you suspicious?" Mace asked.

"Ronny is no businessman," Amanda said firmly. "This is a guy who had to have his mother manage his checkbook for him until he married me so he wouldn't write bad checks. Also, this is a guy who possibly bribed a judge and left a trail of evidence proving it that the Keystone Kops could follow. All of sudden he's a business genius? I just don't buy it."

Mace was about to follow up with another question, but they were both distracted by the sound of Jacob calling everyone over to the picnic table. "I think we might need to finish this conversation later," Amanda said. "I'd hate for the food to get cold."

"I look forward to it," Mace said sincerely as the two of them stood up. "I enjoy talking with you. Getting answers to my questions is just an added bonus."

Amanda's reply was a sweet smile.

Later that night, Mace went to Sam's room and knocked softly. Sam opened the door almost instantly. "Hey, Mace, what's up?" he asked.

"Hey, Sam, can I come in?" Mace asked.

Sam nodded and stepped aside to allow Mace to enter. The layout of his hotel room was the same as Mace's. The television was on and the bed was rumpled as if Sam had been stretched out on it watching television. Other than that, the room was as neat as a pin, with Mace's backpack resting in one of the room's two chairs. Some neatly folded clothes sat on top of the backpack. "What's up?" Sam asked.

"I wanted to talk to you about the confrontation with the bikers this morning," Mace said once Sam closed the door behind him. At dinner earlier,

Jacob had repeated his story about what happened at Smith's Garage, even going so far as to stand up and re-enact some of it. He had gotten so wound up that Amanda had finally had to ask her grandfather to calm down.

"I really didn't have a choice," Sam replied casually. He was dressed in jeans and a plain white tee shirt. He looked relaxed and rested. "After one of them sucker-punched Jacob, I had to step in and defend him. That biker really laid into him. I'm surprised he didn't have to go to the hospital."

"From the way Jacob was telling it, you evened up the score and then some," Mace said. "I'm impressed. Not many guys could fight three people at once and win."

"It was surprisingly easy," Sam said modestly. "People like them think they have safety in numbers. They are so used to everyone being afraid of them that they get relaxed. They were so surprised that someone actually fought back for a change that they were easy pickings."

"Jacob said you used some kind of martial arts moves on them," Mace said. "You trained in that sort of thing?"

"I grew up in a bad area where you learned to fight pretty fast or you were everybody's victim," Sam answered as he pulled out the remaining chair from the table and sat down. "The rest of it I learned as a soldier."

"I remember you mentioned you were in the military," Mace said. "What branch did you say?"

"I didn't," Sam said with a smile. "It was army, though."

"Ah," Mace said. He noticed that Sam didn't use the formal title of United States' Army or even 'the army'. Most of the other veterans Mace knew used one or the other when talking about their military careers. It struck him as a little odd, but he didn't press the issue. "Anyway, I just wanted to advise you to be really careful until you can put this place in your rearview mirror. From what I know about The Horde, they can be dangerous. You might should keep a low profile from now on."

"I figured," Sam replied. "I know the type, but I appreciate the friendly advice nevertheless. However, my concern now is what will happen I leave. If they can't get me, I'm worried they might come after Jacob, Amanda, or Caleb."

"That's crossed my mind as well," Mace replied honestly. "I hope they aren't that stupid, but I suspect I may go by and suggest politely that they keep their distance."

"It would have to be you," Sam said. "The local sheriff and his men can't be trusted. That seems to be the general consensus of the people who live here. It seems like the town chief, Bradley, is the only honest cop left around here. Perhaps the agency you work for can investigate the allegations of corruption around here and do something about it."

"I'll go wherever my investigation leads me," Mace said.

"I don't doubt that at all," Sam said. "I feel bad for the people who live here. What are you supposed to do when the people who are supposed to be the good guys really aren't? Who do they turn to then?"

"Apparently, you," Mace said, only half-jokingly. "Jacob said earlier at dinner that a number of townspeople have called and asked if you could stay. From the way Caleb acts around you, I think you already have a number one fan."

"Caleb is a great kid," Sam said. "I really think he's just thrilled to have a male figure in his life who's not abusive. Regarding the townspeople, I think they just want someone around here who's not afraid and not bought off by the bikers."

"That's what I think about Caleb," Mace said. "I suspect you're right about the townspeople as well."

"I promise to watch my back and be careful, Mace," Sam said. "Anything else?"

"Nope," Mace said as he turned and opened the door. "See you tomorrow, Sam."

Sam walked to the door behind Mace. "Mace, you be careful as well. Some people get vicious when their secrets are being brought to light," he said right before he closed the door behind Mace.

Mace simply nodded and walked back to his room.

CHAPTER 17

The Boy's Club, the strip club owned by The Horde, sat by itself barely a half-mile outside the Easton town limits. The building had always been a bar, having opened as what locals called a "beer joint" in the early-seventies when a local man named Scooter Thompson had built the concrete block building, installed a few neon signs, named it Scooter's Bar, and opened for business. In the years since it had opened, Scooter's Bar had always been a local watering hole where folks stopped to grab a beer, shoot some pool, and dance to country music from the jukebox. There was an occasional fight, a few arrests every now and then for drunkenness or drugs, and sometimes the crowd got rowdy, but overall Scooter's Bar wasn't much trouble to the good people of Easton. The Thompsons had lived in Easton County for ages and were generally good people, so Scooter's foray into entrepreneurship was tolerated, if not actually embraced. In return, Scooter kept the trouble at his place to a minimum, paid his taxes, and helped the locals blow off steam every now and then.

That, like so many other things, had changed with the arrival of the biker gang calling themselves The Horde. The bikers had taken over Scooter's Bar, running off the regulars and giving the local bar such a reputation for danger that everyone but the bikers stopped going there. Within just a few weeks of the bikers taking over Scooter's, Scooter Thompson, the man who had owned and ran it since it opened, sold it to a man named Joe Stoneman. Joe Stoneman was known as Stoner, and he was the leader of The Horde. Scooter Thompson refused to discuss the terms of the sale of the business he'd owned for over forty years, a business he'd told friends and family that he planned to run until the day he died. However, just shortly before Scooter sold the bar to Stoner he'd been admitted to the local hospital after a severe beating that had left him with numerous stitches and a broken arm. Shortly after the sale was complete, Scooter Thompson and his wife Marybelle had moved out of Easton. Allegedly, it was to be closer to their son and his family who lived in Georgia, but everyone knew the truth: Scooter Thompson had been forced to sell his beloved bar and he was ashamed.

Once Scooter's was under new ownership, the bar's name was changed to The Boy's Club. Local contractors were hired to come in and renovate the building. The gray concrete block exterior walls were given a coat of stucco and painted. The interior was enlarged, a stage complete with stripper poles and a lighting system was added, the bar area was made bigger, and more seating was added. The iconic Scooter's Bar neon sign was replaced with neon signs advertising live nude girls and happy hour. The gravel parking lot, which had once held a dozen cars on a busy night, was suddenly packed, with overflow parking taking over the empty field next door. Many of the cars in the parking lot bore out-of-state plates. Even on slow nights they were pretty busy. On busy nights there would be a line of men of all shapes, races, and sizes trying to get into the bustling bar.

There was no line to get into the door tonight, mainly because it was just a few minutes past one in the morning on a Wednesday night, or more accurately, a Thursday morning. The bar had closed at midnight and the bouncers, two burly members of The Horde, had tossed all of the remaining customers out and locked the front doors. The girls had left as soon as the place closed, some back to their respective homes and others back to the farm where The Horde made them live in a rundown single-wide mobile home and treated them like pieces of property. The parking lot out front was empty now, save for three motorcycles that belonged to the two bouncers and Stoner, the man who ran both the biker gang and the bar. Traffic on the highway was practically nonexistent at this hour, meaning the chance of some passerby seeing something suspicious was miniscule. In short, it was the perfect environment for what was about to happen.

At the back of the building, one of the bouncers was standing outside the rear door that led into the kitchen, smoking a joint and urinating loudly on the side of the fenced enclosure that housed the building's trash containers. The biker, a big man with numerous tattoos on his exposed arms and chest, was so busy relieving himself that he never noticed the figure slip from the shadows behind him. He sensed the figure behind him just a split second before the short length of metal pipe the figure held crashed into the back of his skull. The only sounds were a solid thud as the pipe impacted his skull and a grunt as the biker went down like a house of cards in a breeze. The biker landed on his side, completely unconscious. His attacker removed a roll of duct tape from a pocket and used it to bind the biker's hands and feet. Satisfied the biker was unconscious and immobilized, he put a strip of the tape over the man's mouth. With him out of the way, the man from the shadows moved to the open door.

The back door led into the bar's small kitchen. The man moved through it silently, pausing every couple of seconds to listen. He held the two-foot-long piece of metal pipe he carried down by his side so that if someone did confront him the weapon wouldn't be the first thing they saw. That might give him a precious few seconds of surprise that he might need. The kitchen held only a greasy flat-topped griddle, a deep fryer, a refrigerator, and a couple of hanging racks for pots and utensils, but it was all jammed into a relatively small space. Given the condition and cleanliness of the equipment, he doubted that the place had earned the A rating from the health inspector that was displayed so prominently on the on the board by the bar's front window. Just walking through the kitchen was almost enough to give him food poisoning. Of course, he doubted that people came to the club for the food, so it was probably irrelevant.

He continued through the tight kitchen area to the door that separated the kitchen from the bar area and the rest of the club. The door was made of plastic with a clear plastic window at head height. It swung freely in its frame so that servers going back and forth didn't have to turn a knob or latch. It was also obviously new. He stopped at the door and peeked through the plastic window. Going through the door would bring him out at the end of the bar and into the floor area beside the raised stage area where the strippers performed. Fortunately, the place was dimly-lit with the only illumination coming from lights behind the bar and a few lights around the stage area. He could see a single hallway leading off the main seating area. He assumed that was the location of the restrooms and probably a doorway leading to the backstage area and the dressing rooms for the girls. That assumption was verified when a second biker emerged from the hallway zipping his pants and adjusting his belt. The second biker was a short, stocky man with a heavy gut and a full beard. He had an unlit cigarette between his lips. He walked to the bar and sat down with a bored expression on his face. After a few seconds he turned on his bar stool and looked at a single door on the opposite side of the seating area from the bar.

When the biker turned his attention to that door, it gave the man in the kitchen the chance he needed. He eased the door open as quietly as possible and slipped out into the darkness there at the end of the bar. Three quick and silent steps brought him up behind the biker on the bar stool. He didn't use the iron pipe to knock this one unconscious; he was afraid it would be too loud in the closed confines of the building. Instead, he placed the pipe down on the bar as he moved with one smooth motion and slipped his now empty arms around the biker's throat from behind. "Dude, I ain't in the mood to play," the biker grumbled as the arms reached around his throat. He quickly realized that it wasn't his fellow biker playing a joke when the arms clamped down with full strength. The move, called a rear naked choke by most mixed martial arts fighters, clamps down on the carotid artery and windpipe, cutting off both blood flow and oxygen to the brain. The sudden dip in blood pressure that results from the pressure to the artery causes unconsciousness within a few seconds, long before the lack of oxygen becomes an issue. It is quiet and brutally effective, but not lethal. The victim usually wakes up within minutes with a splitting headache

The biker bucked backwards and came off the bar stool in an attempt to shake his attacker free, but the man's grip was like iron. The biker tried to cry out while simultaneously trying to elbow the person behind him in the ribs to break the hold on his throat, but all he managed was a weak cry barely above a whisper and a minor impact to his attacker's abdomen that had no effect. Within ten seconds, the biker slumped to the floor, jerked a couple of times, and then blacked out. His attacker lowered him the rest of the way to floor and left him lying there on his back. Incredibly, the biker still had the unlit cigarette held between his lips. His attacker plucked the cigarette out of the biker's mouth and tossed it away. "You should quit. Those things will kill you," he whispered to the unconscious biker as he quickly bound the biker's hands with the duct tape. He bound this one's hands in front of him with just a couple of laps with the roll of tape. He wanted this one immobilized, but not to the point where he couldn't save himself once the man initiated the second part of his plan.

The man finished binding the biker's wrists and stood up. He turned his attention to the door the biker had originally been looking toward when he came up behind him. It was the bar's office. He started toward the door just as the door was opened from the inside and a figure emerged.

Joseph Mark Stoneman, who had been called Stoner since he was a fourteen- year- old juvenile delinquent on his first trip through a juvenile detention facility in his home state of Texas, was a survivor. He'd learned how to fight and how to survive thanks to his upbringing by an alcoholic father and a drug addict mother in a trailer park in West Texas. Dirt poor and with practically no adult supervision, Stoner had learned at a very early age that if he was going to survive he was going to have to do whatever was necessary. Unfortunately, whatever was necessary had become a life of crime. Naturally intelligent, a quick learner, and with no moral restraints at all, he was good at being a criminal, just as some people were talented musicians, star athletes, or brilliant scholars. He was such a good criminal that now, at the age of thirty-two, after having been involved in some type of criminal activity since the age of ten, he had only been arrested and convicted twice in his whole life. The first time was a six- month stint in a juvenile detention facility at the age of fourteen for breaking into a pharmacy and stealing pills. That's where he'd gotten the name Stoner. The second was a two- year stint in prison in New Mexico after severely injuring another man in a bar brawl.

That two- year stint in New Mexico had been a life-altering experience. For one, he'd realized that he hated being locked up. Not enough to stop being a criminal, but enough to vow never to go to prison again. Secondly, because it was there, in prison, where he'd first met one of the founding members of The Horde named, ironically enough, John Jones. John had taken him under his wing and taught him many things while Stoner served his time, including how to be a better criminal and how to fight. After Stoner's release, John's word had gotten him into The Horde where he rose quickly through the ranks. Now Stoner was the number two man in The Horde, second only to the man who'd originally founded the gang. Stoner ran the gang's operations on the eastern side of the Mississippi River. He was also instrumental in the gang starting to work with the

Baja Cartel. That partnership with the feared cartel had garnered the gang newfound respect in the criminal underworld and more money than ever before.

Unlike most of his biker compatriots who drank regularly and used pretty much every drug available, Stoner had always made it a point to stay fit physically and mentally. He rarely drank and when he did it was rarely more than a shot of liquor or a couple of beers. He also refused to partake of the drugs the gang ran for the cartel. Stoner also worked out regularly, doing calisthenics and lifting weights in the old barn at the farm where the gang lived. John, his mentor in prison, had taught him very early on that if he was going to stay alive and free in the world he'd chosen to live in he had to be ready to outfight and outsmart other people at a moment's notice. That lesson had been pounded into him literally when he got jumped by some fellow inmates on his second day in prison in New Mexico. That was the first time he met John. The grizzled old biker had intervened and saved Stoner simply because he didn't like the inmates who had jumped the new kid, not out of any particular affinity for Stoner at the time. Their friendship was born that day, however, and John became the father Stoner never had.

Stoner's survival instinct kicked in the instant he saw the strange man dressed in black coming toward the office door as he opened it. Stoner, who was owner of the bar on paper, was in the office counting up the night's receipts. He had just finished and was coming out of the office when he saw the stranger. At the same moment he saw the stranger he also saw Blue, the fellow Horde member who served as one of the bar's bouncers, lying there unconscious in the floor behind the approaching biker. Stoner's mind was still processing that image as his animal instinct to fight and survive kicked in.

Stoner jerked back into the office and slammed the door. The office was small, barely big enough for the desk that faced one wall and a single filing cabinet in the corner opposite the door. The office door Stoner had just slammed back shut was the only way in or out of the room, so Stoner was effectively trapped. However, the door was new, made of steel, and set in a heavy steel frame that had been added when the bar was renovated. The door was thick enough to stop most small arms fire. The door also locked automatically every time it closed, thanks to the lock in the doorknob. Even better, it had a deadbolt lock with a finger latch, so he could lock himself in the office when he counted money or simply when he wanted to be alone and uninterrupted. Barricading himself in the office would give him time to figure out the best way to handle the situation. He didn't know who the stranger outside in the bar area was or what he wanted, but Stoner figured it wasn't something good. The stranger could be some fool who thought he could rob the bar or he could be an assassin. As he'd warned the sheriff earlier that day, one of the cartel's enemies was possibly making a move on them. Anything was possible.

Stoner was reaching for the deadbolt latch when a tremendous force struck the steel door from the other side. To Stoner's astonishment, the door flew open with the shriek of metal and slammed into him. The force of the door knocked him backwards and his back struck the wall behind him. Reflexively, Stoner kicked out as hard as he could at the man coming through the door. His boot caught the man squarely in the abdomen. The man crumpled forward and grunted. Stoner bounced off the wall and used his momentum to throw a punch at the newcomer's face. The man expertly blocked the punch and countered with a straight punch to Stoner's ribs. The punch felt like being kicked by a mule, but Stoner fought off the pain and fought back savagely. All he needed was to drive his attacker back through the doorway back into the bar area. That would give him the precious seconds he needed to grab his gun off the desk. Stoner's gun, a Colt 1911 forty-five caliber semi-automatic pistol, lay under the zippered bag containing the night's receipts. If he could get it, his attacker was done for.

Bellowing like a madman, Stoner unleashed a flurry of punches and kicks toward the man. The man in black blocked most of them, but the act of blocking them had the desired effect of giving Stoner a little more space. With one final straight kick, he managed to force the man back out through the open doorway. With that, Stoner spun to his right and lunged for the pistol. He grabbed it off the desk just as the man came back through the doorway. Stoner started to bring the gun up to fire at his attacker but the man caught Stoner's wrist with one hand and prevented him from bringing the gun to bear. The two of them grappled for the gun with both hands, with Stoner trying to aim it at the man and the man trying to keep the gun from being used against him.

It boiled down to a test of pure strength. Stoner was strong, but the man in black was stronger. No matter how hard Stoner fought, his arm wasn't budging an inch. The man in black had a grip like a vise and was incredibly strong. Not only could Stoner not bring the gun to bear on his assailant, his own arm was being relentlessly forced down. Stoner tried to lunge forward and head-butt the man in the face, but the man twisted his face and head away out of range. Stoner then tried to kick out in hope of striking his attacker in the legs or groin, but their bodies were so close that he couldn't bring his leg up without risking giving his attacker better leverage. The two men were locked in a stalemate with control of the gun on the line.

As they struggled Stoner got his first good look at the man attacking him. It took a moment for his mind to recognize the man and make the connection. "You?" Stoner snarled.

"Turn the gun loose," the man replied. "I came to talk, not to kill you."

"No way, man!" Stoner snarled. "I should have killed you when I had the chance."

With that, Stoner tried to jerk his arm with his hand on the gun away from the man's grip. Unfortunately for Stoner, his finger was close enough to the trigger to snag it as he made the sudden move. There was an ear-shattering boom within the close confines of the office and Stoner felt a white-hot jolt of pain tear through his left thigh. His left leg crumpled beneath him as a forty-five caliber slug ripped through the flesh of his thigh, shattered his femur, and exited out of his leg behind his kneecap. Stoner gave an agonized scream. The shock of the pain caused him to immediately release his grip on the gun. In a split second the gun was snatched from his hands by the man in black. Stoner fell to the floor and looked down in horror at his thigh. Even worse than the agony was the sight of thick blood jetting from the hole on the inside of his left leg. It was gushing out of him like water through a garden hose.

Stoner lay in the office floor and put one hand over the spurting blood. He could feel the warm wetness against his palm pulsing there with its own terrible pressure. He looked up and saw that his attacker now held the pistol in his hand and the gun was aimed right at his face. For some reason, the gun looked really far away, almost as if he was looking through a telescope. His head was starting to spin and he could feel his heart pounding in his chest. "You've killed me, you son of a bitch," he said. "Finish it."

The man in black instead lowered the gun. "I didn't kill you, Stoner," the man said calmly. "You did. You're the one who pulled the trigger, not me."

Stoner tried to think of something else to say, but before he could the world turned black. Unconsciousness was followed within seconds by a couple of gasping breaths as the loss of blood volume caused his body to shut down. Within three minutes of accidentally shooting himself while fighting over the gun, Stoner was dead.

The man in black watched as Stoner died. His face betrayed no emotion whatsoever as he watched the gang leader's final seconds. Once it was over, he turned and laid the gun on the closest table. He walked back to where the biker he'd choked out lay in the floor. The man was just starting to stir. The man in black kicked him in the ribs. The biker groaned loudly and his eyes fluttered. "Your leader is dead," the man in black said as he looked down at the stirring biker. "Get up and get out. You and the rest of your gang are out of business. Twenty-four hours from now, any member of The Horde found in this county will regret it. You understand? "

The biker, who went by the street name Blue, groaned and nodded. His eyes fluttered open and he tried to look at the man in black but the man was already walking away back through the bar into the kitchen. A few seconds later he heard a loud crash as if something had been knocked over back in the kitchen. Blue must have faded out again because the next thing he knew he opened his eyes and the bar was filling with thick smoke. He managed to sit up and turn his head toward the kitchen. The move caused his head to pound and his neck muscle to scream in protest. He could see orange tongues of flame licking at the walls near the door leading to the kitchen. The man who'd attacked him had set the place on fire.

Blue's hands were still bound with tape, but he was able to stagger to his feet. He noticed that the office door was open and the light inside was on. He saw Stoner lying on his back in the office and the pool of blood around him. Some of the blood had drained out through the doorway and out onto the tiled floor of the main section of the bar. Blue staggered over to the door to check on Stoner. One quick glance at Stoner's open eyes and deathly pale face told him the man was dead. With the smoke thickening and his eyes starting to burn, Blue turned away and lurched toward the front entrance to the bar. The smoke and heat were getting unbearable just as his hands found the panic bar on the front door that unlocked it. He pushed on the bar and threw his weight against the door. The door opened and he stumbled outside into the cool night air. He staggered a few more feet and fell onto the packed gravel.

Blue stayed on his knees for a couple of minutes, coughing and spitting out the taste of the smoke. Once he was sure he could breathe, he looked around, fearful that the man who'd attacked him and killed Stoner might still be in the vicinity. The parking lot was empty, save for the three bikes that belonged to him, Stoner, and Jimmy, the other bouncer. Blue had no idea where Jimmy was or if he was even still alive. The last time he saw him Jimmy was going outside to throw some trash into the cans out back. Blue looked back at the front door. When he'd plowed his way through it, the door had locked open. The increased air flowing through the open doorway had added fuel to the fire inside. Thick black smoke and flames were starting to roll from the front door.

Blue got up and moved further away to escape the increasing heat and flames. Once he was safe, he brought his wrists to his mouth and tore at the duct tape around them with his teeth. He was able to free his hands quicker than he thought he would. Once his hands were free, he fumbled in his jeans pocket for his cell phone. He found it and used it to dial nine one one. As soon as he was done with that call, he dialed a second number. That number was to one of his fellow Horde members. He was calling to break the news about the attack and Stoner's death but, more importantly, he wanted some back-up in case the man who attacked him decided to come back.

The Boy's Club was completely engulfed in flames by the time the first fire truck pulled into parking lot.

CHAPTER 18

His world is a spinning blur of colors as the helicopter plummets from the sky. Blue sky, white clouds, then green as the tops of the trees below come rushing at them through the cracked windshield of the cockpit in front of him. The helicopter pitches and bucks and spins as the pilot's dead hand drops away from the controls. Through his headset he can hear screams, but he doesn't know if they are coming from him, the pilot, or Paul, the other agent in the helicopter with them. His stomach drops almost as if he is on a rollercoaster that is plummeting down a steep track. Thankfully he is strapped into his seat and the straps prevent him from being tossed around in the cabin or out the open door on the side. Paul, his good friend and fellow agent, isn't so lucky. He hears one last scream and then Paul is flung out the door into the open air. The fall jerks the headset off Paul's head and leaves it dangling by its cord. The empty headset bounces around in the cabin by his face. He hears the thrashing as the rotors beat the air and scream in protest to the angle of the dive. The green wall of the trees is getting closer, so he does the only thing he can do and closes his eyes.

Mace jerked awake and sat bolt upright in bed, flailing. For a moment he didn't know where he was or what was happening, but then he realized that he had been having a vivid dream. He was in bed and not back in the helicopter. He reached down and touched the bed beneath him and then ran his hand over the covers to make sure it was all real. It was, so he breathed a grateful sigh of immense relief. The worst thing that could happen now was falling out of bed a few feet to the carpeted floor. Considering he'd survived a major helicopter crash, rolling out of bed didn't scare him in the least.

He reached over and fumbled with the lamp on the bedside table. The light flooded his hotel room and brought with it the knowledge of where he was. He was in his room at White's Hotel in Easton County. He reached up with a shaking hand and brushed it over his face. He was soaked in sweat and breathing as if he'd just ran a marathon. He glanced at the digital alarm clock beside the lamp. It was almost one thirty in the morning. He had been asleep since maybe ten thirty. It was only three hours of sleep, but as of late three hours was nothing to sneeze at. It was actually the longest he'd slept without dreaming since the helicopter crash and shootout in Laurens. Since the incident he'd been sleeping for only an hour or two at a time before the dreams started.

Mace took a several deep breaths and willed himself to calm down. He slowly climbed out of bed and walked to the bathroom. In the bathroom he splashed cold water on his face and then dried his face and whole body with a towel. The sweat had soaked the boxer briefs he slept in, so he went to his suitcase and changed his underwear. Now wide awake, he thought about watching some late night television or maybe rereading his notes from the day's interviews to see if he'd missed something. Neither option really appealed to him. He was too wound up from the dream to lay there and watch television and there was nothing in the files he hadn't already read countless times. Maybe some fresh air would help calm him down. He pulled on a pair of jeans he'd brought with him and a tee shirt. He walked over to the sliding glass door, unlocked it, and stepped outside into the cool night air.

It was a beautiful night outside. The lights at the dock and the lake shore were on timers and had shut off at midnight, leaving the patio outside his room and the grassy area beyond it dark. The clear sky overhead was lit with stars and a light breeze with just a hint of chill wafted across his skin. He breathed deeply and soaked in the silence. The fresh air and wide open space helped drive away the last, claustrophobic vestiges of the horrible nightmare. He sat down in one of the plastic chairs there on the patio and let the momentary peace sink in. He was surprised to feel himself getting drowsy again. He had been having different versions of the same nightmare for months and usually he couldn't even imagine going back to sleep for a long time after each occurrence. *Maybe I'm turning a corner and getting better,* he thought hopefully.

Something out of the corner of his eye caught his attention off to his left. He turned and saw a single shaft of light that illuminated a small section of the patio. The light was coming from the crack between the curtains over the sliding glass door of Sam's room. Apparently the lights in Sam's room were still on. That was kind of unusual given the late hour and it piqued Mace's curiosity. He didn't know much about Sam, given the circumstances of their meeting, but he seemed like an okay guy. Still, there was something about him that made Mace uneasy. It was nothing he could put his finger on, just a gut feeling.

That feeling in his gut prompted his next move. Mace silently stood up from the chair and walked over to the sliding glass door of Sam's room. He paused there and listened for several seconds. He did not hear any movement or any other sounds from inside the room. Slowly he eased forward and peeked through the crack between the curtains into the room. From his position he had a clear view of the interior of the room. Sam lay on the bed on his back with his eyes closed and his head turned to the side facing the window. His eyes were closed and his chest rose and fell evenly. A book lay on the bed beside him as if it had fallen and landed there right beside his body. It didn't take a genius to realize that Sam had apparently been reading and dozed off into a peaceful sleep.

Mace drew back and walked back to his patio and the chair. He sat back down in the chair and stared off into the darkness. He felt like some kind of weird stalker for spying on Sam. The man had done nothing to arouse his suspicions. In fact, Sam had been nothing but nice to him, Amanda, Caleb, and everyone else. The man had even put himself in danger when he defended Jacob. Even now, just seconds later, Mace really couldn't explain why he had peeked into Sam's room. It was just a weird urge that came out of nowhere.

Mace sat there in the darkness and pondered on his recent behavior. He had been acting and feeling a little different ever since arriving here in Easton. Deciding to peek in Sam's window wasn't the only thing lately that was completely out of character for him. He had always made it a personal policy to never get too involved with the people he encountered in his job. Categorizing the people he encountered as he investigated the cases he was assigned as either victims, witnesses, or suspects kept everything simple. He'd seen good cops get too invested in cases out of sympathy for the victims or anger at the bad guys. It invariably cost the cop that happened to something, either professionally or personally. Because of the potential costs involved, he'd always lived by a single saying that he quietly repeated to himself at least once a day. "It's my job," he repeated each day, usually in the mornings as he looked into the mirror. He did this each day to remind himself that what he did wasn't personal. Being a cop, investigating crimes, and putting bad guys in jail was his profession and he was very good at it.

So far in his career that attitude had served him well. However, since arriving in Easton, he'd found himself drawn into a situation that threatened to break his wall of objectivity. That situation was Amanda Easton and her family drama. Ever since encountering the situation yesterday between Amanda and her estranged husband, he'd found his usual stoic demeanor tested. He'd only known Amanda Easton for a little over twenty-four hours, but he found himself really drawn to her. Something about her made him want to spend time with her. Even though she was an attractive woman, it wasn't really a physical thing. He just really liked talking to her and enjoying her company. He also really liked young Caleb. Just seeing how the kid interacted with him and Sam made it clear that the kid was hungry for a positive male role model in his life. It was sad that Ronny, his biological father, was such a terrible person. Mace had disliked Ronny Easton from the moment he met him during the filling station encounter. Now, after hearing from Amanda and others about the type of person Ronny really was, Mace had to admit he liked the man even less, if that were possible. He found himself really hoping that Amanda had a good attorney to help her with the divorce and Caleb's custody situation. He wanted them both to be safe and happy.

Mace also had to admit the shooting he was investigating was bothering him. Something about the whole situation seemed off to him. Seeing the body there at the morgue had left him with a lot of unanswered questions about who the girl was and what had happened to her before her fatal encounter with Deputy Cothran after the pursuit. His interview with Sergeant Watson had only added more questions. Mace had learned a long time ago to listen to older, more experienced cops and also to trust his instincts about people and situations. Sergeant Watson's story on his encounter with the girl before the shooting was particularly troubling to Mace. Watson was convinced that the girl wasn't trying to hurt him right before the deputy shot her. That said a great deal, especially coming from the police officer who was literally within arm's reach of an armed assailant. Mace was going to have his first interview with Deputy Cothran in just a matter of hours. He was looking forward to it because he had a lot of questions he wanted answered.

Mace sat there in the darkness, listening to the night sounds and trying to sort out his thoughts. After a while, his eyelids grew heavy and he found himself starting to doze. Normally a nightmare about the crash kept him awake and wired for hours, but now, for some reason, he could barely hold his head up. Surprised but grateful, he got up and went back into his room. He locked the sliding glass door behind him, closed the curtains, and stripped off the jeans and tee shirt he had put on. He checked his alarm once more to make sure he had it set and then turned off the lamp beside the bed. He climbed under the covers and settled in, fully expecting to spend the rest of the night staring at the ceiling like he had so many nights before.

He was asleep within seconds. This time he didn't dream at all.

CHAPTER 19

Dwayne Lee Cothran, lifelong friend of Sheriff Lynn Garrett and Chief Deputy of the Easton County Sheriff's Office, lived alone in a remote farmhouse several miles from the town limits of Easton. Surrounded by over a hundred acres of land that had been passed down through his family for generations, the small, renovated farmhouse he called home sat by itself at the end of a gravel driveway that was over a quarter mile long. Thick trees screened the house from the highway at the front and thick forest surrounded it on the other three sides. His nearest neighbor's house was to the east and over a mile away. Around the house where Dwayne lived were fields and pastures that had once nurtured the Cothran family farm's crops and livestock. Now the fields and pastures were overgrown and served no other purpose than serving as a buffer between Dwayne and the rest of the world. That didn't bother Dwayne in the least; he had always hated farming and he needed the privacy for what he called his "hobby".

Dwayne's hobby was holding young women captive, sexually abusing and torturing them, and then killing then when he was tired of them. However, he did not limit himself to just women. He was a serial killer and he'd claimed six victims over the years. His first victim was an old man named John, who occasionally worked on the Cothran farm when extra hands were needed at harvest time. When Dwayne was fourteen, John had walked into one of the barns that used to stand behind the house and caught Dwayne torturing a stray cat he'd caught. Disgusted, John had made him release the cat and then started toward the house to tell his father. Desperate to keep his strange urges secret, Dwayne had smashed John over the head from behind with an axe handle. Already tall and strong at fourteen, Dwayne's blow had killed John instantly. He'd covered up the crime by carrying the old man up into the barn's loft and then throwing the body down head first. He'd tossed the old axe handle under some hay bales close by. A well-acted, frantic rush to the field to get his father and a made-up story about seeing John fall from the loft had brought his father rushing to the barn to find the dead man. Given John's reputation as a local drunk, John's death was ruled an accident after just a cursory investigation by the local sheriff. Later that night, alone in his room, Dwayne had masturbated to the best orgasm he'd ever had in his life up to that time.

His next victim was a prostitute who propositioned him in a bar while on a recruiting trip to the University of Florida. Dwayne' size, power, and fearlessness had made him a star linebacker in high school and resulted in a number of major colleges looking at him for their teams. Dwayne had strangled her in an alley behind the bar after she'd performed oral sex on him and then tossed her body into a dumpster. He'd sweated that one for a few days, fully expecting the cops from Florida to nab him, but nothing had happened. The case was still unsolved to this day. He'd never gone back to Florida, or to college for that matter. He'd stayed in Easton and worked a number of jobs until his best buddy, Lynn, talked him into applying at the sheriff's office. To his surprise, he'd gotten hired. The rest, as they say, was history.

Dwayne had managed to keep his urges in check since becoming a deputy, thanks mainly to being able to view violent pornography on the Internet. Sometimes, if the urge got too powerful, he'd resort to visiting prostitutes in neighboring states or arranging rendezvous with willing, submissive women he met in underground Internet chat rooms. Trapping and torturing various stray animals also helped when the urges got too bad. Just as he'd reached a point where the satisfaction from those activities wasn't sufficient, he'd entered into his new business relationship with the cartel and the bikers. The women they gave him as part of his payment had literally saved the day by keeping him from acting out plans he's made to abduct women in counties close to him. If he'd been forced to engage in such a high-risk plan, it would only have been a matter of time before he was caught and his secret revealed.

Sometimes the sheer irony of it all was enough to make Dwayne smile. He was sworn law enforcement officer, duly trained and certified by the State of South Carolina to uphold the law, but he was a serial killer. He had no qualms at all about labeling himself a serial killer. His father had always said "If it walks like a duck, looks like a duck, and quacks, it's most likely a duck." Dwayne raped and killed people for sexual gratification or just the sheer fun of it, he had killed six people, and he didn't plan on stopping. Therefore, he was, by the FBI's definition, a serial killer. It was who he was, and he was okay with that. Let psychiatrists and behavioral experts figure out why he was the way he was if he was ever caught.

The thought of getting caught secretly terrified Dwayne. Getting arrested for multiple murders in South Carolina would get him the death penalty. Dying didn't bother him as much as the thought of living on death row in prison. Being on death row would mean being locked up in a ten by ten foot cell for twenty-three hours a day with only one hour per day outside for exercise. Even that one hour was spent locked inside another high-security enclosure. Being locked up like that could last for years while his sentence was automatically reviewed and appealed. Even if he insisted on no appeals, it would still take years to execute him. As much as Dwayne loved being free to do whatever he wanted, being locked up would be a living hell. Dwayne had made a silent vow to himself many years ago when he'd first started indulging his secret urges that he would die before he let himself be put in prison. If the day ever came where he was going to be caught, he planned to either kill himself or make someone else kill him.

So far in his life he hadn't had to worry about getting caught. It seemed that luck was with him when it came to satisfying his dark urges. The first two times he'd killed someone he'd gotten away with mostly due to either good luck or incompetence on behalf of the authorities. The easy supply of untraceable victims courtesy of his relationship with the cartel was another stroke of pure luck. The escape of his last victim, Lisita, had almost been a disaster, but then good luck had reared its head again when she wrecked his truck before she got away. Granted, having to shoot her in front of two other cops could be seen as a stroke of misfortune, but overall the girl's escape had ended about as well as he could hope for. The girl was dead in a way that looked justifiable and his secret was safe for now. If the girl had gotten away and told her story, he would be either be dead or sitting in a cell right now.

Dwayne's actions during the last twenty-four hours had been devoted to making sure the truth stayed hidden. As soon as he'd gotten back home following the interviews with the BCI agents immediately after the shooting, Dwayne had started getting rid of evidence in case the investigators didn't buy his story about the events leading up to the chase and the shooting. He'd spent several hours dismantling the cell where he kept his victims. The shackles, chain, and other contents of the cell were in a burlap sack weighted with rocks that now rested at the bottom of a river several miles away. The cell itself had been cleaned with bleach and a pressure washer, then filled with boxes of junk and old furniture. The concrete cell now just looked like another part of a cluttered basement full of unused junk. He'd also gone through the rest of his house and thoroughly cleaned it just in case, paying special attention to any areas the girl might have touched when she fled. In short, he'd done everything humanly possible to make sure there was no trace physical evidence that the girl had ever been inside his house.

Now all that was left was the single black plastic trash bag Dwayne carried with him as he walked through the darkness. A single flashlight he held lit the way as he walked through the knee-high weeds toward the hole he'd dug earlier in the day. The hole was nearly three feet deep and about fifty yards from the rear of his house through the overgrown field that had once been a field of corn. The bag contained articles of clothing from his previous victims and computer drives containing pictures he'd taken of the girls for his pleasure. Most of the pictures were of the girls tied up with terrified looks on their faces. There were also pictures of the girls modeling their newly-painted fingernails and toenails. Dwayne had several fetishes, but brightly-colored nails was his favorite. Something about a woman with painted finger- and toenails drove him crazy with lust. He had no idea where that particular fetish came from, just as he had no idea why he was the way he was, but it had always been a thing with him. The bag also contained several bottles of nail polish and the manicure kit he used when he painted his victims' nails. It would have been hard to explain bottles of nail polish in the home of a single male with no female relatives or girlfriends.

The evidence contained in the bag was enough to earn him a trip to the death chamber four times over. Numerous serial killers had been caught because they kept mementoes of their victims that became evidence of their crimes when found by the police. As a cop he knew that, but he couldn't make himself get rid of the stuff. The items contained in the bag were keys to treasured memories. He could no more imagine throwing away his keepsakes than a parent could imagine throwing away their child's baby pictures. That's why he'd decided to put the items in a couple of thick plastic trash bags and bury them here. The items were out of his house, but he still knew where they were. Once the heat passed, he could dig it all up and have it all back for his enjoyment. He felt sure that the thick plastic bag would protect the stuff from the elements until he could recover it.

Dwayne gently placed the bag in the hole and smoothed it flat. Once that was done, he carefully shoveled the loose earth he'd piled to the side back into the hole. He covered the bag in a couple of feet of dirt. Once the hole was filled, he carefully smoothed out the earth and then scattered some grass and underbrush over the fresh dirt to camouflage the hole. Once that was done, he examined the area carefully with his flashlight. The hole was barely discernible from the surrounding area. Last of all, Dwayne used his hands to scatter the dirt he hadn't used to refill the hole around in the surrounding area.

Satisfied, Dwayne grabbed his shovel and headed back to his house. The shovel went back into the tool shed. Once he was back inside, he retrieved his cell phone from the kitchen table. He had three missed calls from the sheriff. He swore loudly when he saw the missed calls. It was well after two in the morning and calls from the sheriff at this hour usually meant trouble. So much for his plan to get some sleep so he would be on his toes for his interview with that new BCI agent tomorrow.

He stood and gazed out the kitchen window toward the field he'd just come in from as he called the sheriff back.

In his haste to bury the bag containing his precious mementoes, Dwayne had failed to notice something. The black trash bag had a small tear in it along the bottom. The way Dewayne placed the bag in the hole and the darkness prevented him from seeing the rip, which was less than two inches long. If he had noticed it he would have immediately retraced his steps to make sure that none of the items he was so intent to hide had fallen out. Blissfully unaware of it, however, he covered up the bag and left.

The tear was the result of the bottom of the bag he carried catching a single thorn on the rose bush his late mother had planted by the back steps many years ago. Dwayne hadn't even noticed it when the bag snagged on the thorn and it made a small rip in the bottom of the bag, nor did he notice the single small item that fell out of the bag through the rip. The item now lay on the grass a few feet away from by the back steps looking lost and forlorn.

CHAPTER 20

"So run that by me one more time," Sheriff Lynn Garrett said to the biker known as Blue. Blue sat on the rear bumper of an Easton County Department of Fire and Rescue ambulance with a chemical ice pack pressed to the back of his neck. His fellow biker, Jimmy, was in the back of the ambulance on the stretcher. Jimmy had a bandages swathing his head, thanks to a wicked gash on the back of his skull courtesy of the iron pipe that was used to knock him unconscious behind the bar. A paramedic sat in the back of the ambulance with him. The paramedic was busy shining a small penlight into Jimmy's eyes and taking his vital signs. Although Jimmy was conscious at the moment, he was still groggy and confused about what happened. Aside from a sore neck and pounding headache, Blue was relatively unharmed and lucid, therefore he was the only one capable of telling Sheriff Garrett what had transpired inside The Boy's Club. Blue had already told the sheriff what happened once, but Sheriff Garrett wanted to hear it again. Considering the bar was now a half-burned wreck and Stoner, his business associate and the leader of The Horde, was lying dead in the floor inside, Sheriff Garrett was more than a little anxious to hear how it went down again.

"Jimmy went out back to take the trash from the kitchen out," Blue repeated patiently. "The front door was locked and the bar was empty. Stoner was in the office doing the books. I was chilling out at the bar and having a beer. Next thing I know some guy comes up behind me, grabs me in some weird kung fu chokehold, and starts choking me out. I fought like crazy but he had the drop on me. Next thing I know, I wake up and this dude is leaning down over me. He tells me he killed Stoner. He also tells me that if he catches any of us in this county twenty-four hours from now, we're dead. Then he vanishes back through the kitchen. Next thing I know the place is on fire. I make it outside and call for help. The fire department people found Jimmy tied up out back when they got here."

The story was the same version Blue had already told him once, but the sheriff still found it hard to swallow. He turned and looked across the gravel parking lot at The Boy's Club. The parking lot was lit as bright as day, thanks to the spotlights on the fire trucks that filled most of the parking area. Fire fighters in protective gear and breathing apparatus scurried around the building. Ladders leaned against the front and side walls and numerous fire hoses lay snaked across the lot. Most of the hoses disappeared into the bar's open front door. The building itself was heavily damaged with one half, the half that housed the kitchen, storage area, and dancers' dressing rooms, completely gutted. The fire fighters had managed to cut the fire off and save the section where the office and Stoner's body were. Stoner's body still remained inside. The first fire fighters on scene had found the body, but been smart enough not to move it once they verified that the biker was already dead. Several Easton County Sheriff's Office vehicles, both marked and unmarked, were parked off to the other side of the parking lot. The vehicles belonged to both patrol deputies and the sheriff's two investigators. They were waiting for the fire department to release the scene to them so they could begin investigating the homicide that had occurred within it. Sheriff Garrett had already spoken to the fire chief. The chief expected to release the building within the next fifteen or twenty minutes.

Sheriff Garrett's mind reeled as he watched the activity unfold across the parking lot. He could barely believe that someone had overpowered the two bikers, killed Stoner, and then burned the bar. No, not really someone, because someone could be considered plural and possibly mean more than one person. According to Blue, it was one guy who had pulled this off. Garrett could understand one person maybe surprising Blue and his buddy, Jimmy- Hell, both of them were probably half-drunk and tired from getting free favors from the girls- but Stoner was another thing entirely. Sheriff Garrett considered himself a good judge of men and he'd relegated Stoner to the mental file he'd labelled People Not To Piss Off Unless Necessary after the first time he'd met him. Not only had one guy managed to kill Stoner, the same guy had managed to do it at the bar, The Horde's own turf.

Sheriff Garrett spun back to Blue. "You sure this was one guy?" he asked the biker.

Blue somehow managed to look both miserable and furious simultaneously. "It was only one that jumped me," he said. "I only saw one when I came to. Jimmy don't have a clue how many. He remembers throwing the trash in the can and the fire fighters dragging him out of the way behind the building."

"I already talked to your buddy," Sheriff Garrett said angrily. "He's still got bells ringing in that lump of crap he calls a brain. Damn it, are you sure it was just one guy? Somebody came to YOUR bar, on YOUR turf, killed YOUR leader, and tried to burn the place to the ground." Sheriff Garrett made it a point to emphasize the word "your" because he wanted to insult the biker in front of him. The gang and his own crooked deputies were supposed to make sure things like this didn't happen. What had happened here tonight made them all look like incompetent idiots. That definitely wasn't the image you wanted to represent to the people they worked for.

Blue stood up from the tailboard of the ambulance so he was almost face to face with the sheriff. "You trying to be funny, Sheriff?" he asked coldly. "I get your point. Don't you think it would look better for me if I lied and told you it was three or four guys?" He motioned with his chin over the sheriff's shoulder toward the grass field across the highway from the parking lot. That field was occupied with about thirty of Blue's biker gang members. The sheriff had already seen the bikers. They all looked angry and ready for war. Someone had taken down their leader and they wanted someone to pay. "How you think this makes me look to my people?"

"You look like a bitch," Sheriff Garrett replied just as coldly.

"You think?" Blue shot back. "I'll be lucky if I make it through the next twenty-four hours without getting beat down or killed because I was supposed to be protecting Stoner and I blew it. I'd be better off if the dude had messed me up bad so I could at least claim I went down fighting." Fear had started to creep into Blue's voice, almost as if his situation was dawning on him as he spoke. "All I saw was one guy. He came up from behind me. All I can tell you is he was strong as an ox. I never stood a chance once he locked down on my throat."

"So what did this Superman look like?" Sheriff Garrett asked. "You said he leaned down over you and talked to you. What did he look like?"

"That's the weird part," Blue said nervously. "I was just coming to. I remember looking up at the dude and seeing his face. I can't remember what he looked like, though." He ran his hands over his face. "I can tell you the guy was big and strong as hell and that he was a white guy, but no matter how hard I try I can't picture his face in my head. It's crazy! Maybe my brain was all messed up from him choking me out."

Sheriff Garrett felt his own frustration building, but he tamped it down. He knew that Blue was indeed in a lot of trouble with his fellow bikers over what had happened here, so it would have been in his best interest to claim more than one attacker. It would have looked even better if Blue was able to give his fellow bikers and the sheriff a description or something else to go on. This was a situation where lying would have been beneficial to Blue. The biker even looked like he was telling the truth. "Stoner warned me earlier today that he'd heard that one of the other cartels might be making a move," the sheriff said. "You heard that?"

"Stoner told us that after he came back from a big meeting with the wetbacks in charge," Blue said. "He told us to keep our guard up and our eyes open. Matter of fact, what happened in town yesterday morning where that dude jumped a couple of our guys kind of had him on edge."

Sheriff Garrett glanced over at the burned-out bar. "It looks like he should have paid attention to his own warning," he said.

"We've had five of our people beat up, the bar's burned down, and Stoner's dead," Blue said. "Things were quiet and running smooth here until that stranger that hangs out with that old preacher showed up. Some of the boys want to go find this guy and have a few words with him."

"Me and Stoner already talked about that yesterday," Sheriff Garrett said. "I'm going to have some of my guys pick him up and bring him in for a few questions. He had a run-in with you guys yesterday and all of a sudden this happens?" He made a sweeping gesture with his hand toward the bar. "Weird coincidence, if you ask me."

"Just find out who he is," Blue said. "Don't keep him in jail, if you know what I mean."

"If I think he's working for a rival group, I'll deliver him to you on a silver platter," Sheriff Garrett said. "In the meantime, keep your people close to the farm and make sure all of them are armed. We've got a shipment going out tomorrow. I'm going to tell Ronny to increase security at the plant. We all need to be on high alert. Right now it seems to be focused on you guys. Has The Horde ticked off any rival gangs?"

Blue looked around to make sure no one was in earshot. "No way, man," he said in a low voice. "Ever since we got this sweet deal going with our friends south of the border, we've played nice with everyone else and they've played nice with us. We'd have heard by now if it was a rival club making a move."

"Keep your eyes and ears open," Sheriff Garrett said. "One thing I don't want to see is your people riding around with guns visible. You understand? I've got the BCI in town following up on the shooting yesterday, so the last thing I need is a bunch of bikers riding around carrying weapons. Your people need to stay home until we figure out who's doing what."

"I'll keep the tribe on the reservation as much as I can," Blue promised, "but they want blood over what happened tonight."

"They'll get it," Sheriff Garrett promised. "If I think the preacher's new friend is involved, I'll let you know. If I can't get the answers I want from him all nice and legal, I'm sure you guys can get it out of him."

The arrival of another vehicle interrupted the two men's conversation as Deputy Cothran's marked Tahoe pulled into the parking lot and parked close to the ambulance. Cothran, dressed in jeans and a tee shirt with ECSO Deputy on the back of it, got out of the vehicle. "We'll finish this later," Sheriff Garrett said to Blue as Cothran walked up to them.

The sheriff caught Dwayne by the arm and pulled him away to the side of the ambulance. "I called you three times," the sheriff said angrily. "Where the hell you been?"

"I was finishing up some cleaning," Dwayne said calmly. "The kind of cleaning you recommended yesterday morning in your office."

It took a moment for the sheriff to remember that he'd told Dwayne to make sure there was no evidence of the girl at his house just in case the BCI started digging deeper than expected. "You sure you got everything?" he asked.

Dwayne nodded. "I don't foresee any problems," he mumbled. "I was hoping to get a good night's sleep before my interview tomorrow." He glanced at his watch. "I mean this morning. What happened here?"

"Someone attacked the bar, disabled two bikers, and then killed Stoner in his office," Sheriff Garrett said. "It might be a rival gang making a move on them and us."

"Oh no! Not my buddy, Stoner," Dwayne said sarcastically. "We were just getting close."

"I know it breaks your heart," Sheriff Garrett said. He swore under his breath. "This couldn't have happened at a worse time either. We've got your deal going on, the shipment about to go out, and now this."

"I've got my end handled," Dwayne said arrogantly.

"I've been thinking about that," Sheriff Garrett said nervously. "Just to be safe, maybe you should take an attorney with you. From what I understand, this Agent Holliday is pretty sharp."

"I ain't worried," Dwayne said with a smirk.

And that's why I am, Sheriff Garrett thought as he looked up into Dwayne's flat, lifeless eyes. A cold chill shot down his back and he had to fight the urge to shudder. Something in his gut told him that their luck had turned bad and was going to get worse. If he was going to survive, he was going to have to be proactive.

"Good," the sheriff said with a fake smile. "I wasn't worried."

About twenty minutes later, Sheriff Garrett retrieved a cell phone from the glove compartment of his unmarked SUV. It was a cheaply-made flip phone that came loaded with a set number of minutes for calls and texts; the same kind that was for sale in every convenience and department store in America. The phone was completely untraceable because it was easily available and could not be linked to any specific person or account unlike a regular cell phone with paid service from a cell phone company. Commonly called "burner phones", they could be used once and then disposed of, enabling untraceable communications between parties who didn't want someone else to know they were communicating. For those simple reasons, the phones were a boon to criminals and a scourge to law enforcement.

The sheriff switched the telephone on and dialed a number he'd memorized. The phone began to ring on the other end. The sheriff sat there looking through the front windshield while the telephone rang. Over at the front door of the bar, Dwayne and one of the detectives were talking to the fire chief. The ambulance was pulling away with the emergency lights switched off. The fire fighters were disconnecting and rolling up their fire hoses. The activity outside was almost calm, unlike the sheriff, whose heart was pounding in his chest and whose hands shook slightly as he held the phone to his ear.

The phone was answered on the third ring by a man with a faint accent. It was just before two in the morning in Easton County. Sheriff Garrett had no idea what time it was in Mexico or wherever the man who answered the telephone was, but the guy sounded alert. "I need to speak with Garcia," Sheriff Garrett said through lips that were suddenly dry.

CHAPTER 21

Mace's pleasant mood from his first decent night's sleep since the Laurens Incident and a delicious breakfast at The Diner started to slip away as soon as Chief Jeff Bradley walked into the restaurant and headed right for his booth. Chief Bradley looked tired and grim, but he radiated the same focused intensity he had the first time they'd met in the hotel parking lot. "Good morning, Agent Holliday," Chief Bradley said when he reached the booth, "may I sit?"

"Absolutely," Mace replied as he slid his empty plate and cup out of the way. "What can I do for you, Chief?"

Chief Bradley took a seat across the table from him. The waitress approached and asked if he wanted anything. The chief declined politely and the waitress walked away. The chief looked at Mace. "Have you heard the news about last night?"

"I've overheard little bits and pieces from the locals in here this morning who were talking about a fire at the strip club just outside town," Mace said. "Is that what you're referring to?" The restaurant had indeed been buzzing with the news and gossip when Mace came in for breakfast earlier. Most of the conversations on the subject seemed to be speculation regarding if the fire was intentional or an accident. Some of the gossip centered on the death of the man reputed to be the leader of The Horde. Some said he'd been shot, others said he'd died from the fire. Most of the locals seemed almost happy about it. That indicated clearly to Mace just how tired everyone was of the bikers' presence in their community.

"Yes," Chief Bradley said. "Around one this morning, someone knocked out one of the bikers who works security at the bar while he was outside emptying the trash. The attacker gave the guy a pretty bad concussion and a nasty gash on back of his head. A second biker inside was supposedly choked unconscious with some sort of martial arts hold. The attacker then went into the bar office and killed a man who goes by Stoner. He's the manager of the bar on paper. My source tells me he was shot once in the femoral artery, apparently following a struggle, and with what appears to be a gun that belonged to him. The attacker left the gun lying on a table close to the office door. The attacker then warned the biker he choked out. He told him that any of his fellow bikers caught in Easton County after twenty-four hours would be killed."

"Wow," Mace said. "Chief, how do you know all of this? Isn't the bar outside of town and under the sheriff's jurisdiction? I didn't think you and the sheriff exactly had a great working relationship."

"My brother-in-law is the battalion chief over the Easton County Department of Fire and Rescue," Chief Bradley said softly. "He responded to the fire. He overheard pretty much everything the bikers told the sheriff and what the sheriff's men were saying. Like pretty much everyone else, he thinks the sheriff and most of his people are crooked and in bed with the bikers, so before he allowed the sheriff's people access he went inside and looked around. He saw everything."

"Really?" Mace asked curiously. As an investigator, he was intrigued. For Easton County to allegedly be such a quiet, sleepy, rural county, there sure seemed to be a lot going on lately.

"Yes. The sheriff's men came in and ran all the fire personnel out," Chief Bradley continued. "They got an attitude, claiming it would mess up the crime scene. I imagine you know that a crime scene where there's been an actual working fire is already contaminated, mostly by the fire itself."

Mace nodded. "I'm aware," he said. "As far as I know, my agency hasn't been contacted by the sheriff's office requesting assistance, so either they feel they can handle it and don't want help or they don't want us snooping around anymore than I already am over the shooting incident."

"Knowing the sheriff, it's most likely B," Chief Bradley said morosely. "Anyway, I went by the hotel hoping to catch you there. Amanda saw me and told me you'd just left. She also told me that you might be here eating. I saw your car and figured I would stop in to speak with you."

"Something tells me that you didn't just stop here to give me the local news," Mace said amicably. "What's really on your mind, Chief?"

Chief Bradley nodded. "You don't miss a trick, do you?" he said in admiration. "Am I that obvious?"

"Not really," Mace answered. "Everyone I've met speaks really highly of you. They say you're a good cop, possibly the only good cop left in these parts. I think you trust me because I'm not from around here and I have a reputation for being a good cop, same as you. I figured you wanted to talk about recent events here. Like I said, a lot seems to be happening for such a supposedly quiet place. First, we have our run-in with Ronny Easton, local bully extraordinaire, then the judge, now the bar. Seems like it's a bad week to be a bad guy around here."

Chief Bradley nodded. "Yep," he said, "I've had the same thought. Your encounter with the great Ronny Easton was just good luck for Amanda. If you and Sam hadn't been in the right place at the right time, Amanda would probably be in bad shape right now. As far as Judge Cooper, it's a small community and I've heard about the alleged man who ran him off the road and then tortured him after he was injured. I think there's some validity to that because the judge's phone was found a good piece away from the crash and someone did call 911 from the cell phone to report the wreck. My sources at the hospital tell me that Judge Cooper gets panicky if he's left alone in his room. Supposedly, he's told his secretary that he's retiring and plans to move out of the county."

Now it was Mace's turn for admiration. "I'm not the only one who doesn't miss much," he said appreciatively. "For a one-man police force, you seem to have a lot of sources around."

Chief Bradley shrugged. "It's a small community," he said once again. "Everybody knows everybody and everybody talks. The small-town grapevine can be an awe-inspiring thing. I promise you that."

"So, what else are your sources telling you?" Mace asked.

"I'm not hearing much other than that about the judge," Chief Bradley continued. "I just find it odd that we have two strangers show up in Easton County. Those two strangers are you and Sam Walker. Suddenly, bad things start happening to people who richly deserve it, almost from the moment you two set foot in town. Ronny gets put in his place and Amanda gets saved from getting assaulted. A mysterious man causes the judge to wreck his car and then assaults him, resulting in the judge getting caught with what's pretty obviously a bribe in his pants' pocket and making him suddenly decide to retire and get out. Your new friend Sam goes through three bikers in the middle of town in broad daylight like they were made out of paper. Now the leader of the biker gang is dead and the business they owned- a business that was most likely a front for criminal activity- burns to the ground."

"Maybe it's just karma," Mace said in an attempt to be funny.

Chief Bradley rolled his eyes. "All of this stuff starts happening almost immediately after Deputy Cothran kills that girl and you and Sam arrive in town. Now it could be that someone is looking to avenge the girl. I like to think that if she had any family or friends in Easton they would have claimed her body by now and you would know her name, so that kind of rules out the vengeance theory."

"The shooting was national news," Mace countered. "It might not be someone local. Someone could have realized what happened to their sister, daughter, or whatever relation the girl might have been and come here seeking revenge. The question there is why go after the bikers and the judge? I could understand going after the deputy before anyone else."

Chief Bradley leaned forward and placed his elbows on the table. "What if the bikers brought the girl here and put her in a situation where Deputy Cothran had to kill her? People have noticed that a lot of the girls in that club were Hispanic. How do we know Cothran isn't next?"

"I don't think you really believe that theory, do you?" Mace asked. "Cut to the chase, Chief. You suspect it's either me or Sam."

Chief Bradley looked Mace directly in the eye. "Agent Holliday, I don't suspect you at all. There are two new people in town. One of them is a respected South Carolina Bureau of Criminal Investigation agent who was sent here from Columbia to conduct an investigation. That much is verifiable fact.

The other person is a drifter, a man who says he's just riding across America on his motorcycle and happened to end up in Easton. This drifter, Sam Walker, is built like a Greek god and knows how to fight well enough to beat the crap out of three pretty-good-sized bikers in broad daylight in the middle of town. The, about fifteen hours later, someone takes out two bikers, and kills a third one. Not to mention the incident with Judge Cooper happened the night after he showed up in town with you. So, let me ask you, Agent Holliday, who would be on your radar if you were in my shoes?"

Mace digested all of this. "I can see your point," he said. "I must confess that there are some things Sam has said in general conversation that made me wonder what his deal is. Those things, along with the fact that he seems to be blissfully unconcerned that he has ticked off a very dangerous group of criminals in The Horde, have made me a little suspicious."

Chief Bradley looked relieved. "Good," he said. "I didn't know how you would take what I planned to tell you. I about halfway suspected you would be think I was stupid."

"Not at all," Mace said honestly.

"There's another thing that made me suspect that Sam Walker isn't who he claims he is," Chief Bradley said. "I responded to the fight at the garage yesterday. I got Sam's identification and used it to fill out my report. It's an Arizona driver's license. Later yesterday, I ran the name and driver's license number through the Arizona Department of Motor Vehicles out of curiosity. It came back as not on file. Supposedly that name and number do not exist in their state database."

This information deeply intrigued Mace. "Is it possible you copied down the number wrong?" he asked.

"Anything is possible," Chief Bradley said, "but I'm pretty sure I got it right." He leaned back against the back of the booth. "I think Sam's identification is fake. I don't know who he is or what he's up to, or if he's even up to something. He's on my radar and waving a great big red flag. I'm also really nervous about him being around Amanda, Caleb, and Jacob. I mean, if he's beat up five guys and killed one, he's not someone I want around. "

Mace completely understood the chief's point of view. Sam Walker seemed like a really nice guy, but many killers seemed like nice guys until you got in their way. Many notorious serial killers and Mafia hitmen had lived seemingly normal lives where they were good neighbors, community volunteers, and all-around good guys to the people around them. Still, something bothered him. "Chief, what time was the attack at the bar last night?"

"Around one this morning, based on what I'm hearing," Chief Bradley answered.

Mace felt a vague sense of relief when he heard the time. "Well, I guess we can rule out Sam as the one responsible," he said. "At about one this morning I couldn't sleep, so I walked out onto the back patio of my hotel room at White's to get some fresh air. I noticed the light still on in Sam's room. It's one room down from mine with a similar back patio and sliding glass doors. I went to the sliding glass door of Sam's room to see if he was up and wanted to shoot the breeze to help me unwind a little. Through the crack between the curtains, I saw Sam lying asleep on his bed. It looked like he'd dozed off while reading a book. I can verify that at one this morning Sam Walker was in his hotel room asleep."

Chief Bradley accepted this news stoically. He mulled it over for a several moments. "You sure about the time?" he asked.

"Without a doubt," Mace said without reservation. "Also, Sam has no means of transportation because his bike is in Smith's Garage. The location of the strip club is what, three or four miles from the hotel? The judge's car crash was several miles away as well."

Chief Bradley looked a little embarrassed. "I hadn't thought about that," he said sheepishly. "I feel like an idiot now."

Mace felt bad for the chief. The man had some weird things going on in the community he served, not to mention the presence of the biker gang and the possible crooked cops helping them. That he not only was concerned but trying to figure out what, if anything, was happening was commendable in its own right. "You shouldn't," Mace said firmly. "Sam even had me a little suspicious, as I said. This job has made me quit believing in coincidences, so I commend you for your curiosity. In your shoes, I would be doing the same thing you are."

"The driver's license possibly being fake was the kicker for me," Chief Bradley said.

"It could be that you wrote down something wrong when you were looking at his license or it could be a computer glitch on their part," Mace said. "Computers can do weird things and people make mistakes. I got a letter a couple of years ago from the state department of motor vehicles saying my license was about to be suspended for an unpaid traffic citation. The problem was that I'd never had a traffic citation. I made a few calls and came to find out that someone had reversed a couple of numbers when punching in the license number of the guy who actually got the ticket. Stuff like that happens."

"I know," Chief Bradley said.

"Sam might not be responsible for what happened at the club last night, but someone is," Mace continued. "Someone was also involved in the incident with the judge. Something is still going on around here."

"Yay," Chief Bradley said sarcastically. "That's just what I needed right now. Hopefully whoever it is will keep it out of my jurisdiction."

"I understand that," Mace said. "On a personal note, Amanda told me about your daughter's illness," he added. "I'm very sorry."

"Thank you," Chief Bradley said softly. "It's been very tough on my wife and me. No parent should ever have to watch their child suffer."

"There's no hope?" Mace asked.

Chief Bradley shook his head and his eyes glistened. He took a moment to compose himself before he answered. "There's always hope, but at this point in the game it would take a miracle to make a difference. You and I have both been around long enough to know that miracles are in short supply in this world. We don't expect her to make it too much longer."

"No one would blame you for being at home," Mace said. "Jacob White and the people of this town would completely understand. Your duty to the public can wait."

"I only leave when Lizzie, my daughter, is asleep and the nurse is there with my wife," Chief Bradley said hoarsely. "Lizzie sleeps most of the time now. It's the result of the meds they give her for pain and the tumor pressing on the part of her brain that regulates sleep. Everything I ever wanted or needed to say to my baby girl I've already said to her because we've been expecting her to not wake up for a while now. Sometimes I think the pain she sees in our faces hurts her more than the tumor. Putting on this uniform and getting out of the house for short spells is the only thing that keeps me from breaking into a million pieces in front of Lizzie and my wife."

"I can understand that," Mace said. "I wasn't judging you, Jeff."

Chief Bradley looked grateful. "I've read about what happened to you in Laurens with the helicopter crash and the gunfight," he said after a short silence. "Do you ever wonder why you made it and the other guys did not? You ever wonder if everything that happens is part of God's plan or if it's just random luck, good or bad?"

Mace leaned forward. "I ask myself those questions constantly," he replied. "I once heard a man say that if he could ask God Himself one question, it would be 'Why?'. Not why this or why that. Simply why. I think I understand that comment now more than ever. Why am I here? Why did this happen or not happen? That's the reason I was awake last night and can vouch for Sam. I have trouble sleeping because I wonder the same things."

Silence settled over the booth as the chief considered what Mace had said. "Maybe one day we'll find the answers," he finally said. He glanced at his watch. "Until then, I have other things to deal with. I'll quit bothering you now, Agent Holliday." He slid out of the booth and stood up.

"Please call me Mace," Mace said. "All my friends do and as of right now I consider the two of us friends. If there's anything I can possibly do for you personally or professionally, please call me." He produced a card from his shirt pocket. "This has my personal cell number on it. Call me if you need me. Even if you just need to talk. I mean it."

Chief Bradley took the card out of Mace's hand and pocketed it. The two men shook hands. "The same applies to you, Mace," he said. "I'm always willing to help."

"I'll bear that in mind," Mace said sincerely. "I have to go interview Deputy Cothran this morning. By the time this is over, you might be the only friendly face in uniform left in this county."

"Between you and our mystery man, we might actually make a difference around here," Chief Bradley said as he turned and walked out of the restaurant.

Mace watched through the front window as Chief Bradley made his way back to his car in the parking lot and left. He sat there for a few moments longer, thinking. Something about the chief's parting words was bugging him, but he couldn't quite put his finger on it. He thought for a few moments longer and then it came to him. The chief had used the pronoun "we" when talking about Mace and the possible vigilante. *Why would you phrase it like that, Chief?* he thought.

CHAPTER 21

It was a peaceful, beautiful morning outside White's Hotel. Sam was helping Jacob put his suitcases in the back seat of his truck when the two police vehicles drove slowly into the parking lot. One of the vehicles was a marked Chevrolet Tahoe with light bars and the sheriff's office's insignia on the front doors and the other was an unmarked blue Chevrolet Impala. Amanda, who stood nearby with Caleb, noticed the two vehicles first and pointed them out to Sam and Jacob. "I wonder what they want," Jacob said as Sam slid the last suitcase onto the back seat and closed the rear door. Jacob was heading out of town for a few days for a Southern Baptist religious conference in Charleston. Sam was helping him with his luggage before starting the list of chores Jacob had asked him to work on. Amanda and Caleb had come out to tell him goodbye for his trip.

"No idea," Amanda replied nervously. "It wouldn't surprise me if Ronny has tried something else since bribing Judge Cooper failed."

The deputy driving the Tahoe was visible through the front windshield. They saw his eyes lock onto them and then he drove toward them slowly. The blue Impala followed. The Tahoe stopped several feet away and a uniformed deputy emerged. The blue unmarked sedan also pulled up and stopped beside the Tahoe. "All of you keep your hands where I can see them," the uniformed deputy said loudly. He stayed behind his open truck door with his hand on his gun.

"You can see our hands, Jimmy Cleveland," Jacob said reasonably. "I don't think there's any need for you to yell or to have your hand anywhere near your gun. There's a woman and her child here."

Jacob's calm demeanor seemed to make the deputy, a tall man in his late twenties with a pronounced spare tire and pinched features, angry. "Just do what I tell you," he snapped. "This is official business."

By then the driver of the unmarked Impala had emerged. The driver was a stocky older man with blonde hair and a thin mustache. He had the flushed features of someone who either had high blood pressure or drank too much. Unlike the deputy, the driver wore khaki slacks and a short-sleeved dress shirt. He wore a holstered pistol on his hip with a badge clipped to his belt beside the weapon. "Calm down, Cleveland," he said. "Preacher White didn't mean no harm."

The driver walked over to stand in front of Jacob and the others. "Preacher," he said amiably, "we're sorry to bother you on this fine morning." He turned his gaze to Sam, Amanda, and Caleb. His eyes lingered on Amanda in a way that made her very uncomfortable. "Mrs. Easton," he added.

"Detective Roberts," Jacob said tersely, "what brings you and Jimmy to my doorstep this morning?"

"That's Deputy Cleveland," the uniformed deputy said loudly.

Detective Roberts cut the deputy a sideways look that silenced him. The deputy still stood behind the open door as if he needed to use it for cover. "There was an incident last night at The Boy's Club, the bar on Highway Forty-one a few miles from here," he said. "You folks hear anything about it?"

"I saw it on the morning news on television," Jacob replied. "I saw that the place caught fire and someone was killed. As a matter of fact, we were talking about it over breakfast just a few minutes ago."

"The news didn't have the whole story because we've kept a tight lid on it," Detective Roberts said. "Someone attacked the place, took out two of the bouncers, and then killed the manager of the place in his office. They shot him and he bled out."

"I'm sorry to hear that people were hurt or killed," Jacob said. "I'd be lying if I said that losing that den of iniquity bothered me, though. That place never should have been allowed to open to begin with."

"That's your opinion and you're entitled to it," Detective Roberts said. "Being a preacher, I didn't exactly expect you would be all for it. We are in the middle of trying to figure out who committed assault, murder, and arson, though. That's why we are here."

"Excuse me?" Amanda said incredulously. "What's that got to do with us?"

"It has nothing to do with you, Mrs. Easton or you, Preacher White," the detective replied. He directed his attention to Sam. "We would, however, like to speak with you, sir."

Sam looked surprised. "What does this have to do with me?" he asked.

"Well, it's common knowledge that you had a confrontation with some members of the biker gang yesterday at the garage in town," Detective Roberts said firmly. "You've already had one violent encounter with them. That could be a motive for a little follow-up revenge. We'd just like a chance to talk with you and ask you a few questions about that encounter and your whereabouts last night."

"The encounter at the garage was him defending me when the bikers attacked me," Jacob said fiercely. "Chief Bradley investigated and no charges were filed. Regardless, it's not against the law to defend yourself or someone else in this state."

"You need to calm down, sir," Deputy Cleveland said loudly to Jacob. "We're trying to keep this polite and professional."

Jacob glared at the deputy. "You don't come onto my property, accuse my guest of a crime, and then tell me to calm down, son."

Detective Roberts held up a hand in a placating gesture. "Everyone calm down," he said. "Preacher, we didn't come here to accuse this young man of a crime or arrest him for one." He looked at Sam. "I don't even know your name, sir. I heard about what happened yesterday at the garage and that the young man responsible was staying here at the hotel."

"My name is Sam. Sam Walker," Sam replied evenly. "I'm the guy involved in the fight yesterday." Unlike pretty much everyone else there, he was incredibly calm.

"Mr. Walker, I'm Detective Jack Roberts with the Easton County Sheriff's Office," Detective Roberts said cordially. "I'm one of the people investigating what happened at the bar last night. I would like to speak with you. Because of what happened yesterday, you are considered a suspect in what happened last night."

"Then speak," Sam said.

Detective Roberts cocked an eyebrow. Most people, when they found out they were considered a suspect in a serious crime, were anxious to start talking. Some of them practically babbled. The tall, young man facing him looked like he'd just heard a rather boring weather report. "Mr. Walker, I need for you to come to the sheriff's office with me to be interviewed. We want to ask you some questions. We also need to photograph and fingerprint you."

"Why do you need to do that?" Sam asked.

"We need the photo in case we find someone who saw someone suspicious there," Detective Roberts said. "We can put the photo in a photo lineup for potential witnesses to view. It saves us the trouble of possibly dragging you in physically to stand in a lineup. The fingerprints give us something to compare prints recovered from the scene to. It's all a formality. Most people don't have a problem with it unless they have something to hide."

"Well, I have nothing to hide," Sam said.

"Good," Detective Roberts said. "If you would like to come to the sheriff's office with us for a quick chat, we would appreciate it."

"Don't go, Sam," Jacob said firmly. He looked at the two cops. "I don't trust the sheriff's office and anyone who works for it."

Deputy Cleveland scowled fiercely and Detective Roberts looked wounded. "Preacher, that's uncalled for," the detective said. "We're just trying to do our jobs here."

"You all haven't done your jobs when it comes to what's happening in this county for a long time, so why start now?" Jacob shot back. The old pastor was shaking with anger and righteous indignation.

"It's okay," Sam said as he turned to Jacob and Amanda. Caleb stood by his mother's side, taking in everything with wide, frantic eyes. He was too young to understand exactly what was happening, but even he could feel the sudden tension in the air between the adults. "Jacob, I haven't done anything wrong. I definitely didn't shoot anyone. I'll go with the detective and answer his questions. It's not that big a deal. I doubt I'll make much headway on that to-do list you left me, though" he added with a bemused smile.

"Then I'll go with you," Jacob said. "I'll give you a ride to the sheriff's office."

Sam shook his head. "You have to get to your conference in Charleston," he said. "You're one of the keynote speakers. I understand that's quite an honor. Don't miss it for something this trivial."

"He's right, Grandpa," Amanda spoke up. "You're involved in things for all three days of the conference. Go on to it. I'll give Sam a lift to the sheriff's office. I'll also keep you updated on what happens via cell phone. I promise."

"Sam can ride with me," Detective Roberts said. "When we're done, I'll drop him back off here."

"It's not a problem, Amanda said hurriedly.

"I'm not asking," Detective Roberts said as all pretense of politeness vanished from his voice. "Sam, you need to come with me now."

Sam looked at Detective Roberts appraisingly, then shifted his gaze to Deputy Cleveland. He seemed to be examining the two men. "So, I thought I wasn't being arrested," he finally said.

"You're being lawfully detained as part of an investigation," Detective Roberts said. "Technically, it's not an arrest. The Supreme Court said so. Now, play nice and I won't handcuff you. You can even sit in the front seat with me."

"Oh, goody!" Sam replied sarcastically. "Amanda, I'll be fine. If I need anything I will call you. Can I have your cell phone number?"

"Absolutely," Amanda said. "Let me write it down for you." Jacob grabbed a piece of paper from his truck and a pen. Amanda quickly scribbled down her cell phone number and gave it to Sam. Sam stuck it in the pocket of his jeans. "Call me if you need anything. Do you want me to have my lawyer meet you at the sheriff's office?"

Sam smiled. "No," he said, "I'm not worried." He shook hands with Jacob. "Have a safe trip, sir. I'll be fine, so don't worry." Last of all he looked down at Caleb. "I'll be back in a few, little buddy," he said. "We'll catch some more fish." Caleb nodded, but then buried his face in his mother's leg. Sam patted him on the head.

"You ready to ride?" Detective Roberts asked.

"Sure," Sam said. He walked around to the passenger's side of the detective's car. Roberts followed him to the side of the car. He quickly and expertly patted Sam down for weapons before he opened the passenger's side door for him. Sam got into the car and the detective closed the door. Roberts walked around and got into the car in the driver's seat. Sam waved as the detective started the car and drove away out of the parking lot.

Amanda, Jacob, and Caleb watched as the two police vehicles drove out of the parking lot. "I think I'm going to call Mace," Amanda said quietly to Jacob once the vehicles were gone. "He'll probably want to know this happened."

"Mom, will Sam be okay?" Caleb asked so softly that Amanda barely heard him.

Amanda stood there, unsure of the answer.

CHAPTER 23

Mace slowed his car almost to a crawl and glanced at the screen of the GPS unit attached to the windshield of his car just above the dash. Given that BCI agents frequently had to travel all over the state, the agency had equipped each vehicle with a small GPS unit to help agents find locations when they were in unfamiliar territory. The GPS unit was attached to the windshield with a suction cup mounting bracket that put the unit right in the driver's view. According to the small arrow on the screen, Mace should be right on top of the address he'd programmed into the unit as he sat in the restaurant parking lot after breakfast nearly a half hour ago. The address was Deputy Dwayne Cothran's home address. According to the arrow, it should be right in front of him to his right.

Mace looked back through the windshield. He noticed the mailbox first, then the gravel driveway right beside it. It was the only mailbox and driveway that he'd seen on the narrow, two-lane country road he'd been driving on since turning off the main road four miles back. All he'd seen since making that turn onto the road he was on now was trees, a couple of pastures surrounded with rusty, barbed wire, and one old farmhouse way out in the middle of an overgrown field. That house had obviously been vacant for many years with a collapsed roof and most of the walls overgrown with kudzu. He had yet to see another vehicle or another human being on the road. He guessed that was a good thing because it didn't look like the road was wide enough to allow two vehicles to pass each other if he should encounter one. With the thick forest on both sides and the narrowness of the roadway, he might as well have been in a tunnel.

Mace stopped, put his car in park, and got out of the vehicle right at the entrance to the driveway. He stood there in the open door of his car and looked up and down the road. According to the Deputy Cothran's statement, his pursuit of the girl he'd ended up shooting had started at his home when the girl stole his truck out of his front yard where he'd parked it. Supposedly he'd accidentally left the keys in the vehicle. His whole encounter with the girl he'd killed was allegedly just happenstance. Somehow the girl had ended up in his yard at the exact same time that he accidentally left his keys in his new truck. The girl had then stolen the truck, forcing him to pursue her in his police vehicle which he also kept in his yard because the sheriff's office provided their people with take-home vehicles. The chase had ended with a wrecked truck and a dead girl. As Mace stood there, looking and listening, all he could hear was the sounds of birds in the nearby trees and the hum of his car's engine. All he could see was a road so empty and barren that he might as well have been the last person on earth. To Mace, the fact that this road was an excellent place to dump someone you wanted to be rid of supported the deputy's strange story. At the same time, the road was way out in the middle of nowhere and he had yet to encounter anyone or any vehicles on the road. That could be seen as something that cast doubt on the story.

Mace glanced at the number on the mailbox and verified that the number was the deputy's home address. It matched. He noted that the house was not visible from the roadway. All that was visible was a curve about twenty yards down the driveway from the entrance off the road. He noticed a No Trespassing sign nailed to a tree right beside the mailbox. The sign was metal and looked like it had been there a while but was clearly legible. He got back into his car, turned into Cothran's driveway, and drove slowly forward. The driveway was gravel and he could hear the loud crunch of the stones under the tires of his car as he drove. The thick forest continued on each side of the driveway as he crept forward. He reached where the gravel roadway curved and continued around the curve. Once around the curve the forest stopped and became an open field with only occasional clusters of trees and wild undergrowth of briars and other weeds. It looked like the fields had once been cleared and cultivated, but then allowed to grow wild. He continued forward.

According to the car's odometer, he was nearly two-tenths of a mile off the road when he finally saw Cothran's house about twenty yards ahead. The gravel driveway reached the front of the house and widened into an area of packed earth and gravel that was wide enough for a couple of vehicles to park side by side. Off to the side was an area of dirt that looked like it was used as a turnaround for cars that parked in the gravel area in front of the house. The house was probably around twelve hundred square feet, with beige vinyl siding and a black-shingled roof. A small, covered front porch extended about half the length of the house. A set of wooden steps with a handrail went from the porch to the gravel parking area in front of the house. There was a small lawn in front of the house and at the sides. The lawn was neatly trimmed in the area around the house, but then turned into the same wild undergrowth as the fields that stretched around the house. Mace assumed the lawn extended to the back yard as well.

There were no cars visible in front of the house. Mace hadn't expected to find anyone home; Cothran supposedly lived alone and he was probably already at the sheriff's office where he was supposed to be interviewed by Mace about half an hour from now. Mace had driven out to the deputy's house before interviewing him because he wanted to see the actual location where the entire event started in person. He had read Cothran's statement to the BCI agent who originally interviewed him. Mace had found it helpful in the past to go and actually see a location in person. It helped to be able to picture things as he was interviewing a person. Seeing it in person was much better than pictures or video. The BCI forensics team had come to the deputy's house and taken some still pictures a few hours after the shooting incident. Cothran had given them permission to do so and had never retracted that permission, so technically Mace had the right to be there.

Mace stopped the car at the edge of the wide gravel parking area, turned off the engine, and got out. He walked to the front of his car and stopped to study the gravel area and front of the house. Ruts in the packed gravel indicated where two vehicles had been parked side by side. Judging from the ruts, the vehicles would have been parked about ten feet from the bottom of the steps leading up to the porch. That was more than close enough for Cothran to hear his truck start from inside the house, even with the windows and door closed. Upon hearing it, he could have rushed outside, seen his truck driving away, and pursued it like he claimed. That wasn't difficult to believe. For Mace, however, it was the only thing about the deputy's statement that wasn't hard to believe.

Ever since reading Deputy Cothran's original statement and studying the case file, Mace had been consumed with questions about certain things in the statement. Now, studying the scene in person, those questions only multiplied.

The deputy's home was in the middle of nowhere on a very lightly travelled road with just the entrance to the driveway, a mailbox, and a no trespassing sign visible. What was difficult to determine was how the girl ended up here and what her motive was for stealing the truck. Had someone literally thrown her out of a vehicle on the remote road and she walked here to the house seeking help? Where were her shoes and why did her clothes not fit? If she had walked a great distance, her feet would have been in rougher shape than they were when he examined her body at the morgue. Also, if she came to the house seeking help, she would have seen the deputy's marked SUV sitting right beside the truck she stole. Why not knock on the front door and ask the police officer for help?

Mace pondered these questions as he walked slowly through the graveled area to the foot of the front steps. He stood there studying the front porch and the rest of the front of the house. "The girl is in trouble," he said softly, thinking out loud. "She walks down the driveway and sees a cop car and a truck parked here. Maybe she's an illegal and doesn't want the police involved. She sees the truck and looks in the cab. The keys are in the ignition so she tries to steal the truck. Unfortunately, she's heard and the chase starts." He looked around at the overgrown fields and nearby woods. Given the remoteness of the place, Deputy Cothran might have been confident that his truck wouldn't be stolen, so he often left the keys in it as it sat in the yard. It was possible, he supposed, but not very smart.

Mace walked away from the foot of the steps along the front of the porch. Deputy Cothran apparently didn't have a dog because the forensics team had not encountered one while taking pictures here at the house a couple of days earlier. Still, Mace kept his eyes peeled as he continued along the front of the house. The last thing he wanted was to encounter a big dog with a lot of teeth and attitude. He had no desire to harm an animal that was just trying to do what it thought was right. He didn't hear or see anything as he continued along the front of the house to the corner. He turned the corner and walked along the side of the house. He kept his eyes on the ground as he walked. He had no idea what he was looking for. The forensics team had scoured the area and hadn't noted anything that might shed some light on the case. The BCI forensics team was good at their jobs; if there had been anything, they would have found it.

Mace reached the back corner of the house and walked around it into the back yard. The back yard was the same as the front, a neat expanse of cut grass that extended about twenty feet from the rear of the house where it became a wild tangle of overgrown weeds and briars. The tangle of overgrown foliage continued to the wood line about a hundred feet or so away. A single oak tree sat in the middle of the back yard with its outstretched limbs almost touching the roof at the back of the house. A swing made from a rope and an old tire dangled from one of the thick limbs. Judging from the appearance of the rope, it had been there for many years. Mace knew that Deputy Cothran lived alone and was a bachelor, therefore the swing must have belonged to the home's original owners.

Mace walked along the back of the house to where a set of wooden steps led up to a back door. Someone had planted rose bushes there on each side of the steps. The rose bushes had spread out as they grew and now extended up the side of the house beside the door. The door appeared to be new and had a heavy deadbolt lock on it. Mace's eyes swept the ground as he walked, searching for anything out of the ordinary. A faint hint of color in the green grass a couple of feet away from the base of the steps caught his eye. He stopped dead in his tracks and focused on it. Whatever it was, it was red. It stood out brightly in the green of the grass. He reached over and nudged at it with the toe of his shoe. The object moved out from beneath the grass and lay there in the sunlight.

It was a small bottle of nail polish. Mace felt his heart rate speed up the second he realized what it was. He retrieved a pair of latex gloves from the pocket of his fatigues and pulled them on as he squatted down for a better look. "Why hello there," he said softly as he examined the bottle without touching it. "Why are you here at a confirmed bachelor's place?" He could not see the label on the bottle, but it obviously was the same shade of red as the dead girl's fingernails and toenails.

Mace stood up and hurried back around to his car parked in front of the house. He opened the trunk of the car to reveal a couple of plastic storage boxes. He removed a digital camera from inside one of the cases and an evidence bag from the other one. He went back around to the back yard, turned on the camera, and shot several photos of the nail polish bottle lying there on the grass. He made sure to take a couple of photos showing the bottle's location in regards to the rear steps and back of the house. Once he was done with the photos, he used his gloved hands to pick up the bottle and examine it. According to the tiny label on the bottom front of the bottle, the color was called Fire Engine Red. There was no price or store sticker on it, but it wouldn't be hard to figure out where it was sold locally using the barcode on the bottle. He put the bottle in the plastic evidence bag he'd gotten from his car and sealed it.

He continued to hold the evidence bag as he carefully examined the area around where the bottle lay on the grass. On one of the rose bushes beside the step, a single thorn held a tiny piece of black plastic barely half an inch in size. Mace took several photos of the rose bush and the piece of plastic snagged on it. He removed the piece of plastic and put it into another evidence bag. Once that was done, he looked around the back yard for several more minutes but found nothing else.

Carrying the two bags, Mace returned to his car and secured them in a plastic storage bin he used for that purpose. He glanced at his watch as he got back into his car and started the engine. He had about twenty minutes before his scheduled interview with Deputy Cothran at the Easton County Sheriff's Office building. He had plenty of time to make it back there in time for the interview, but part of him wanted to turn on the lights and siren and get there as fast as possible. He could hardly wait to talk to Deputy Cothran.

Mace was pulling into the Easton County Sheriff's Office parking lot when his cell phone rang. He took it from the case on his belt and looked at the screen. It was a local number with the name Amanda Easton above it. He tapped on the screen and answered the call. "Agent Holliday," he said.

"Mace, it's Amanda," Amanda said. "There's a situation going on that I think you should know about. Something has happened with Sam."

"What's up?" Mace asked as he pulled into a parking space. Mace listened as Amanda told him about Sam being taken in for questioning by sheriff's deputies. "I'm at the sheriff's office," he said when she was finished. "I'll handle it."

CHAPTER 24

Sam Walker sat in a chair at a small table in one of the interview rooms on the first floor of the Easton County Sheriff's Office. The chair was green and made of hard plastic that made sitting there for long periods of time uncomfortable. He supposed that was intentional in order to make the person sitting there eager to talk and get the interview over with so they could leave. The interview room itself was small with painted block walls done in a light beige color, an acoustic tile ceiling, and faded green industrial-style tile on the floor. A mirrored window occupied one wall beginning about waist high on a tall man and extending to just a few inches below the ceiling. Sam figured that it was one- way glass that allowed people in the adjoining room to watch what was happening inside the interview room. A video camera and microphone occupied one corner of the room at the ceiling so everything could be recorded. The table where Sam rested his elbows was old and made of gray-painted metal.

Detective Roberts sat across the table from Sam. His chair was upholstered and had wheels on it, giving him a much more comfortable seat and perhaps putting him at an advantage over the person he was questioning. That didn't seem to be working too well at the moment for Detective Roberts however. He'd been questioning Sam for the last hour and he had made no headway at all. Most people, if they had been brought to the police station, photographed, and fingerprinted like Sam had been, would be talking a mile a minute to try to prove their innocence and get to go home. Aside from politely answering the detective's questions with short, concise answers, Sam hadn't said a word. Roberts was used to scared people talking their heads off and he was getting frustrated.

"You know I could put you in jail right now, don't you?" Roberts said as Sam leaned casually back in his chair. "I could charge you with disorderly conduct over the fight at the garage in town yesterday and keep you in jail for several days if I wanted."

"I understand that," Sam replied evenly, "but you haven't. That makes wonder why. Maybe it's because you know it wouldn't stick. Maybe you know your agency is under a lot of scrutiny right now over the tragic event a couple of day ago. Maybe you secretly agree with what I did by fighting those bikers. Which is it, Detective?"

Roberts sighed wearily. Not for the first time he wondered just how deep a hole he'd dug for himself when he joined the group of people taking bribes from The Horde. He'd always known that the day would come when he'd regret it, and now it seemed that day was coming faster and faster. The BCI was in town over the Cothran thing and someone had injured Judge Cooper, killed the leader of the biker gang, and burned their place down. If the BCI didn't buy Cothran's story and started digging into the sheriff's office, they were all screwed. Some of his fellow cops hadn't exactly been discrete with their newfound wealth. It wouldn't take the BCI long to question how a deputy supposedly making thirty-five grand a year could afford new cars and a condo in Myrtle Beach. Once the BCI started asking questions, the cops involved would rat out each other. Roberts knew his coworkers well enough to know that was a certainty. There would just about be a foot race to be an informant and hopefully get leniency from the state prosecutors.

Even more troubling to Roberts was the thought of possible scenarios that didn't involve the BCI. He had been a cop long enough to know that he and the others were in bed with some truly bad people, the kind of people who wouldn't go to jail quietly when a bunch of dirty cops started singing like birds to save their own dirty hides. If the whole house of cards came down, Roberts and several other people could end up dead in order to keep them from being witnesses. As if the bikers and who they worked for weren't scary enough, there was another player in the game, the person or persons who had taken out the judge, killed that biker and burned their place of business. It looked like the bad guys were going to war and Detective Roberts could end up in the middle. That scared him far more than getting arrested for taking bribes. Prison or a shallow grave from an unknown assassin's bullet weren't exactly two good choices.

Sheriff Garrett had asked him to bring in the man sitting in front of him. Detective Roberts was supposed to find out who he was, what he was doing in Easton County, and what his issue was with the bikers. Officially, Sam Walker was a person of interest in the killing and arson at the bar. Unofficially, Sheriff

Garrett and others feared that the man sitting across the table from him in the interview room was an assassin sent by one of the cartel's numerous enemies. That's why Sam had been photographed and fingerprinted. Even as he sat there, his fingerprints were being run through the FBI's database. His pictures had been delivered to Sheriff Garrett in his office. Roberts had no idea why the sheriff wanted them personally, but he did and Ron couldn't say no.

"I'm the one asking the questions here!" Detective Roberts said irritably.

"And you're doing a fine job," Sam said amiably. "However, no matter how many ways you ask me the same questions in an attempt to trip me up, my answers are the same. I got in a fight with the three bikers yesterday because they attacked Jacob White, a man who has been nothing but nice to me since I got stranded here. I managed to beat them up because, luckily, I know how to fight. I had nothing to do with what happened at the bar last night. During the time frame you say it happened, I was asleep in my room at White's Hotel. I won the fight yesterday, so I have no reason to seek revenge."

"Doesn't it seem a little coincidental that several hours after you get in a fight with the bikers, someone burns down a business they own and kills their leader?" Roberts asked.

"Maybe me beating them up made someone realize that they weren't invincible," Sam replied calmly. "I've noticed there seems to be a lot of ill will in the community here about the bikers and their strip club. Perhaps someone saw their chance."

"We are working our way through a list of suspects," Roberts said. "You were on it. That's why you're here. We're trying to eliminate people off the list."

"How many other people on that list of suspects get their pictures and fingerprints taken?" Sam asked. "That's pretty invasive for someone who's on a list of multiple suspects."

"We try to be thorough," Roberts answered sarcastically. "If you don't have anything to hide, you shouldn't have a problem with it."

"I don't have a problem with it, Detective Roberts," Sam said sweetly. "You know what else I don't have? A means of transportation. That club is located about five miles from the hotel. If I went there, I would have to walk there and back."

"That's not hard," Roberts said as he glared at Sam. "You look like you are in good shape. You could probably run it with no trouble in forty, forty-five minutes."

There was a knock at the door. Roberts stood up and opened the door. He stuck his head out into the hallway and talked briefly with someone. "Stay put," he said to Sam. "I need to speak with someone out in the hallway."

Sam nodded and leaned back casually in his chair.

Out in the hallway, Detective Roberts found himself face to face with BCI Agent Mason Holliday and Deputy Cleveland. Deputy Cleveland's face was red and he looked like he was mad enough to spit nails. Agent Holliday's face was calm and pleasant, but he had an air of implacability about him. Roberts's keen detective skills told him that Deputy Cleveland had tried to keep Agent Holliday from making his way to the interview room and it hadn't gone well for him. Agent Holliday held a briefcase in his hand. Deputy Cleveland also held what appeared to be a computer printout.

"Yes?" Detective Roberts said. He suddenly felt very nervous as he stood there with Agent Holliday. He looked like a friendly, laid-back kind of guy, but his reputation as both an investigator and someone not to anger preceded him.

"I told him he couldn't come back here," Deputy Cleveland spat. "He wouldn't take no for an answer."

"It's no problem," Roberts said with a fake smile. "A fellow law enforcement officer is always welcome, especially one as well-known as Agent Holliday. I hope Deputy Cleveland didn't offend you, Agent Holliday. He's a rookie and gets a little overzealous sometimes."

Mace smiled. "There's not a problem," he said. "I told the desk officer that I needed to speak with the detective who brought Sam Walker in from White's Hotel for questioning about the incident last night. He referred me to Deputy Cleveland, who insisted that you were not to be disturbed. Once I explained to Deputy Cleveland the fine line that separates doing your duty and obstruction, he allowed me to come and speak with you. I have information that might be helpful to your investigation."

"Really?" Detective Roberts said. "What information might that be, Agent Holliday?"

"If I may ask, Detective Roberts, what time did the incident at the bar occur last night?" Mace asked.

"According to the two witnesses who survived, between one AM and about one thirty," Detective Roberts said.

"I'm also staying at White's Hotel," Mace said. "I'm in the room next door to Mr. Walker's room. I was up late last night working on my case file for the Deputy Cothran shooting and I stepped outside to get some air. I went out the sliding glass door of my room to the patio area. Sam Walker's room is next to mine. I saw a light on in his room so I glanced through the crack between the curtains that cover the sliding glass doors of his room. I clearly saw Mr. Walker lying asleep on his bed. This was at around one fifteen in the morning."

Detective Roberts digested this information for a few silent moments. Sheriff Garrett was convinced that this Sam Walker character was involved somehow and that's why he'd sent Roberts and Cleveland to bring him in. The sheriff wasn't going to be happy with this development. "You sure on the time, Agent Holliday?" he finally asked.

"I am," Mace answered. "I specifically recall looking at my watch and noting the time because I couldn't believe I had lost track of time that bad while I was working on my notes. I wish I could tell you who was there at that bar, but unfortunately all I can tell you is who wasn't. Sam Walker wasn't."

"You can understand why we brought him in for questioning, given the fight with the bikers yesterday morning," Detective Roberts said. "He was definitely a person of interest. Had we known what you just told me, we could have eliminated him right off the top."

"I'm not questioning your actions, Detective," Mace said disarmingly. "I completely understand why you did what you did. I probably would have done the same thing. Aside from arriving in town around the same time and sharing one of the few local hotels, I don't know the man that well, so you may have good reasons for your suspicions."

"If you don't mind my asking, how did you know he had been brought here?" Detective Roberts asked. "I'm just curious."

"Amanda Easton called me on my cell phone," Mace answered honestly. "She has my cell number from where I checked into the hotel. I think Sam being taken in scared her. She knows I am an officer of the law and she just wanted me to be aware that the man who is essentially my next-door neighbor for a few days might be a dangerous man." The last part of what Mace said was a little white lie; Amanda had actually been afraid that Ronny Easton was behind Sam getting taken away and wanted Mace to try to help him.

"Well, thank you for the information, Agent Holliday," Detective Robert said with enthusiasm he didn't really feel. "I will release Mr. Walker and arrange for him a ride back to the hotel. I'm glad we were able to rule him out as being involved. He seems like a nice guy."

"Glad I could help," Mace said. "Now, if you will excuse me, I need to find the main conference room where I'm meeting Deputy Cothran."

"First floor, main hallway, second door on the right just before you reach Sheriff Garrett's office," Roberts said helpfully.

Mace thanked him and turned and walked away down the hall toward the stairs. Detective Roberts watched him go. "He's a smartass," Deputy Cleveland said sullenly once Mace was out of sight. He handed Roberts the computer printout he held in his hand. "Walker's fingerprints came back. He's clean."

"Agent Holliday might be a smartass, but he's a dangerous smartass," Detective Roberts said. "As long as he's in town snooping around, we're all in danger." He shook his head in disgust. "Cothran might have screwed all of us when he shot that girl and put us on the radar."

"Why you say that?" Deputy Cleveland asked. Cleveland was also on The Horde's payroll. The deputy wasn't making as much illicit money as Roberts was, but his palm was definitely getting greased, just like most of the other people at the sheriff's office. Most of the ones taking bribes took them for the same reason Roberts did: It was seemingly easy money for not doing anything other than turning his head at the right time and acting like he hadn't seen a thing. Unfortunately for Roberts, he'd discovered after a while that the easy money didn't bring ease with it. He'd started taking an extra thousand dollars a month under the table from Sheriff Garrett about three years ago because saying no meant losing a job he'd had for fifteen years at the time. The extra money had come in handy many times, but knowing he was committing a major felony under state law had brought with it sleepless nights, ulcers, and a monthly prescription for anti-anxiety medications.

"Having him in town means he might find something he doesn't need to find," Roberts explained. Sometimes talking to Cleveland was like explaining things to a five- year-old kid. "If he does, we all might end up in jail."

Deputy Cleveland started to ask him another question, but Roberts wasn't in the mood to talk with him anymore. Before Cleveland could get it out Detective Roberts turned and went back into the interview room. Sam Walker was sitting there patiently when Roberts entered the room and closed the door behind him. "You got lucky," Roberts said without preamble. "BCI Agent Holliday is staying at the same hotel you are. He claims he saw you through your window last night sleeping in your room at the time the incident happened at the bar."

"Oh?" Sam said casually. "That just proves what I've been telling you all along, Detective Roberts."

Detective Roberts sank back down into his chair across the table from Sam. He was suddenly tired and he could feel sweat dripping from his armpits under his shirt. He ran his palm over his face and realized that he was starting to sweat from his forehead as well. He also felt nauseous and his chest was tight. He realized that talking to the BCI agent had unnerved him. If a casual, seemingly friendly conversation with a BCI agent could affect him so badly, he couldn't even begin to imagine how bad he would do in an actual interrogation if his illegal deeds came to light.

"Sir, are you okay?" Sam asked curiously.

"I'm fine," Roberts said irritably. "You're free to go, Mr. Walker. Hang on a few and I'll give you a ride back to the hotel."

"If it's okay, I think I'll decline your generous offer," Sam said. "I think I'll just walk to Smith's Garage from here. He is supposed to have my motorcycle repaired today. If it is, I suspect I might be leaving town."

With Sam's words, Detective Roberts felt a grim sense of foreboding strike him out of the blue. It was a sudden, visceral feeling that bad things were about to happen. It was similar to the vague feelings of anxiety that had started tormenting him since he'd started taking money from the bikers, only much worse and much more focused. He had no idea what caused the sudden feeling, but he had to force himself to not stand up and run out of the room screaming. "You sure?" he croaked as he fought to pull himself together.

"Yes, it's a nice day outside and the garage is only a couple of blocks away," Sam replied as he stood up. "If it's not ready, I have someone I can call."

Roberts had planned to just tell Sam to hit the road, but he stopped at the last moment. "You be careful out there," he said to his own surprise. "The friends of the bikers you beat up yesterday are probably out looking for you to get revenge. If your bike is fixed, get on it and get the hell out of here as fast as you can and don't look back."

"I'm not afraid of them," Sam said firmly. He extended his hand. Roberts took his hand and shook it. "I appreciate your concern, Detective. I can tell you are a good man inside. I wish you the best."

Roberts wanted to say something, but he was afraid that if he opened his mouth he would burst out crying. *What in the world is wrong with me?* he thought. He was starting to wonder if he might finally be losing his mind. Instead he simply nodded and released Sam's hand. Sam walked by him, opened the interview room door, and walked out. He closed the door behind him.

Ten minutes later Detective Roberts was standing in Sheriff Garrett's office in front of his desk. The sheriff sat behind his desk, looking grim and exhausted. Roberts had just finished briefing the sheriff on his interview with Walker and Agent Holliday's alibi for the man. The photo of Sam Walker that was taken when he was brought in lay on the sheriff's desk. "His fingerprints came back as not on file," Roberts said to the sheriff. "He's never been arrested or fingerprinted anywhere in the United States. His alibi for last night is a freaking BCI agent. I don't think he had anything to do with what happened at the bar last night."

"He arrives in town and everything goes crazy," Sheriff Garrett said bitterly. "It's either him or the BCI agent. That's the only two new people around."

"Maybe it's someone local," Roberts countered. "Maybe it's just bad luck. Maybe we should shut everything down until the BCI gets finished with what they are doing. I'm not going to lie, Sheriff. I'm getting nervous."

Sheriff Garrett glared across the desk at him. "You knew the deal when you wanted in on what we have going," he said. "Do you really think I can call these people up and go 'oh by the way, the millions of dollars you pay us to ship to you illegally every month won't be coming for a while because we're nervous'? How do you think that's going to go?"

"I think they would prefer that as opposed to the whole operation getting shut down and all of us ending up in jail," Roberts answered.

Sheriff Garrett looked at the detective like he'd just grown three heads and started speaking in tongues. "You really think they care about us as people?" he said. He rolled his eyes. "You can't be that stupid."

"Then what do you want me to do?" Roberts asked plaintively. "I don't believe this Sam Walker fellow is involved. I know he beat the crap out of the bikers yesterday, but I don't think he had anything to do with the bar last night. I let him go. I couldn't hold him with a BCI agent affirming his alibi, especially not with that agent here in the building right now."

Sheriff Garrett looked down at the photo on his desk. "Maybe he didn't do the bar," he said. "The Horde still owes him for what he did to their brothers yesterday. The cartel is also sending one of their guys here to help find out who's behind what's happened recently. If this Walker character gets lucky and gets out of Easton County without the bikers spotting him sometime in the next couple of hours, he might make it. If he stays in Easton, he's screwed."

"Can I go now, Sheriff?" Detective Roberts asked. "I did what you wanted."

The sheriff sat back in his chair and studied Roberts. "I don't recall you ever being so high-strung when I give you your envelope every month," he said. "You look like a nervous wreck. Considering Dwayne is in the conference room being interrogated by the BCI, I should be the one who's a wreck."

"I got two hours of sleep last night before I got called in about the bar," Roberts said. "I feel like crap right now. I think I might be coming down with something."

"Go home for a few hours," the sheriff said. "Get some sleep and pull yourself together."

Roberts was relieved when the sheriff said that. He really did feel terrible. His head was pounding and his chest was tight. "What are you going to do, Sheriff?"

"I'm going to sit here and hope to God Dwayne doesn't bring us all down," Sheriff Garrett said grimly.

CHAPTER 25

Mace sat in the conference room on the first floor of the Easton County Sheriff's Office and gazed serenely across the long oak table that occupied the center of the room. Master Deputy Dwayne Cothran, the second-in-command of the sheriff's office, sat directly across the wide table from him. It was the first time Mace had ever seen Cothran in person. He'd heard that Cothran was a big guy, but after seeing him in person Mace realized that 'big guy' was an understatement. The guy was huge, standing over six and a half feet tall and weighing close to three hundred pounds, most of it solid muscle. Mace assumed that Cothran's uniforms had to be specially made to fit over his massive arms, legs, and torso. Looking at him, Mace was immediately reminded of the medical examiner's comments a couple of day earlier at the morgue about Cothran looking like he belonged in a wrestling ring. The way the man was built reminded Mace of a more muscular version of the legendary wrestler Hulk Hogan. The man must have lived in the gym when he was off duty.

Cothran sat across the table from Mace and stared insolently back at him. His face was flat and emotionless. For all of the emotion he showed, he might as well have been dozing on his couch instead of waiting to be interviewed about a violent encounter that left a young girl dead. Mace noted this and found it odd, but it wasn't the only odd thing he noted. He distinctly felt like he was being sized up as an opponent by the big deputy and that Cothran immediately didn't like him. Mace didn't care, but at the same time he didn't want Cothran to develop an adversarial attitude right out of the gate. It would make interviewing him and finding the truth that much harder. Mace had expected some tension in the room, but what Cothran was putting out was off the charts.

Mace reached down and pressed a button on a small, black rectangle about the size of a business card clipped to the front of his shirt. The rectangle, which was less than half an inch thick, was a digital video body camera. The small camera could record up to two hours of high quality video and audio from Mace's point of view across the table at the deputy. He smiled disarmingly. "Deputy Cothran, I'm Agent Mason Holliday with the South Carolina Bureau of

Criminal Investigation," he said. "As you know, I'm here to follow up on the statement you made shortly after the incident where you shot the unidentified female you pursued. Do you understand that's why I'm here?" Cothran nodded morosely. "Do you also understand that I've switched on my body camera, so you're being recorded right now as we speak and will continue to be recorded for the entirety of the interview?"

"Yes," Deputy Cothran answered flatly. His voice was surprisingly high for such a large man.

"Okay, let me go over a few legal things with you," Mace said. He launched into the familiar speech he gave everyone he questioned in which he advised them of their legal rights regarding being questioned, their right to an attorney, and their right to end the interview process at any time. Deputy Cothran acknowledged that he understood his legal rights. Mace then had him sign the necessary legal forms waiving those rights and affirming that he agreed to be questioned. Last of all, Mace reminded the deputy that he was being recorded by the body camera he wore and also by a small digital recorder that Mace placed in the center of the table between them. Cothran signed the forms Mace slid across the table to him, then slid them back to him. Mace put them in the folder he'd brought.

"Okay, Deputy Cothran, tell me exactly what happened from the beginning," Mace said.

"Read my original statement," Cothran said flatly. "It's all in there."

Nasty attitude right out the gate, Mace thought. *Well, here we go. This is going to be fun.* "I did," Mace said calmly. "I know you've had a couple of days to settle down a little and I wanted to see if you recalled anything else you might not have put in your original statement. I know your first statement was taken just a few hours after the shooting, so I figured you were still affected by that. It's not uncommon to remember more after you've settled down."

"It's all there," the deputy replied almost instantly. "I'm not going to sit here and let you try to trick me into getting myself in trouble."

There was an edge in Cothran's voice that rankled Mace, but he didn't let it show. He remained calm and pleasant. "I promise you my goal is not to get anyone in trouble, Deputy. I'm just trying to make sure we have all of the facts straight before I turn over this file to the state attorney general's office in Columbia," Mace said. "They are the ones who decide if the shooting was a justifiable use of deadly force. I just gather the relevant info and give it to them. Just to lighten the mood, can I call you Dwayne?"

"No, Deputy Cothran is fine," Cothran snapped. "We're not friends."

"Fair enough," Mace said. "So, you're sticking with your original statement regarding the shooting and the events leading up to it?"

"I am," Deputy Cothran said smugly. "That's all I have to say."

"Okay," Mace said. "Do you mind answering some questions to clarify as few points for me, though?

"That depends," Cothran replied with a smirk. "Ask and see how it goes."

"You stated that you were in your house getting ready to come to work when you heard your truck start outside," Mace said. "You ran outside just in time to see your truck being driven away, so you pursued it in the marked Chevy Tahoe you drive on duty. You take this vehicle home, correct?"

"Yes, to all of that," Deputy Cothran said in a bored voice. "All of that's in my statement already."

"I drove out by your house on the way here," Mace said. "I parked in your driveway and walked around your property to try to place things in my mind."

Deputy Cothran stiffened instantly and his face turned red. "You went on my property? Who gave you the right to go on my property?"

"You did," Mace said without missing a beat. "You gave us, the BCI, permission to go on your property to take pictures and gather evidence the day of the shooting. You never retracted it."

"You should have let me know," Deputy Cothran snapped. "I'm not happy about you going on my property without me knowing it."

"You know it now," Mace snapped back. "I'm still trying to figure out where this young lady who stole your truck came from. Your place is really out in the middle of nowhere on a road with practically no traffic. Your house is hidden from the road and you have a no trespassing sign beside your driveway. I'm trying to understand where she came from and why she decided to approach your place out of all the places she might have gone. Did you hear any other vehicles outside?"

"I don't know where she came from or what she wanted," Deputy Cothran said. "I didn't hear any other vehicles. Somebody might have let her out on the road or she might have walked from somewhere. I don't know."

"That's a rough walk for a girl with no shoes," Mace shot back. The so-called friendly interview had now become anything but that. What Mace had found at the deputy's house had only elevated the doubts he already had about the deputy's story. Given Cothran's nasty attitude, Mace decided to take off the gloves. "Down that long gravel driveway, I mean. Her feet were in really good shape considering how far she must have had to walk and where she had to walk."

Cothran sat there silently for several moments. Mace could almost hear his brain working as he fumbled for an explanation. "Somebody might have given her a ride," he finally said. "She might have left her shoes off so she could sneak up on the house and steal my truck. Maybe she had a partner in a car out on the road who took off when he saw what was happening."

"That's possible," Mace countered. "But you parked your marked police vehicle right beside your truck, didn't you?" Mace didn't give him time for an answer. "Obviously a cop lived there. What car thief in their right mind would walk right up in a cop's yard in broad daylight to steal a car? Especially when their police vehicle is parked right beside the truck they want to steal? Even if they had the balls to do that, why wouldn't they do something to disable the police SUV? Common sense would indicate there's a chance they would be seen or heard when they took off in the truck. Why not do something to make sure you couldn't chase them if that happened? Something as easy as flatten one tire, maybe?"

Cothran was getting mad. It was obvious in the redness of his face and the way his massive arms tensed as he leaned forward on the table. Mace was glad he had his pistol on his hip. Given the deputy's size, if he tried anything physical Mace planned to shoot him outright. Mace wasn't a coward, but fighting someone Cothran's size in an area the size of the conference room was a recipe for disaster. Cothran was wearing his uniform but no gun because his gun had been seized as evidence following the shooting and he was supposed to be on administrative duty until his case was resolved. The lack of a weapon didn't make him any less dangerous, given the circumstances. Mace figured it was even odds the deputy probably had a gun in an ankle holster.

"You're asking me to explain someone's motivation," Cothran said through clenched teeth. "I don't know why that female did what she did. Maybe she was stoned out of her mind on drugs."

"Nope. I've read the toxicology report from the medical examiner," Mace said. "No drugs or alcohol at all present. She was stone cold sober."

"Maybe she was a lousy crook," Cothran retorted.

"Maybe," Mace fired back, "but then she didn't have to be a master car thief considering you left your keys in the truck and the doors unlocked." He grabbed a copy of Cothran's original written statement and made a big show of flipping to the relevant page. "That is what you claim, that you accidentally left your keys in your truck. Right?"

"Yes," Cothran answered gruffly.

"So, your keys were in your truck all night? You stated you drove your personal truck the night before on an errand. Once you arrived home, you forgot and left the keys in the truck," Mace said with a quick glance at the written statement in his hand. "Is that correct?"

"Yep," Cothran answered.

"That's so weird," Mace answered. "The keys were in the truck's ignition and were taken and bagged as evidence by the forensics team at the scene of the shooting. There's a notation on the evidence form by Agent Wilson from the forensics team that says that he had to remove one key from the key ring recovered from the ignition. It was the key to the front door of your house and you requested it because it was the only key you had to get in and out of your house." Mace looked directly across the table into Cothran's eyes. It was unsettling, like looking into the eyes of a rattlesnake that desperately wanted to strike. "Is that notation correct? Did Agent Wilson do that for you?"

"It's in your notes," Cothran said warily. "You know the answer."

"I do," Mace answered. "If your only house key was on that key ring and you left it in your truck all night, then how did you get into your house when you arrived home that night?"

"Huh?" Cothran asked stupidly.

"If your key stayed in the truck's ignition, how did you get into your house when you got home the night before the shooting?" Mace repeated slowly. "Did you unlock your front door and then go back to put your keys in the ignition?"

The look of self-righteous anger had vanished from Deputy Cothran's face, only to be replaced with a combination of confusion and the dawning realization that he had messed up bad. "I must have been confused about the sequence of events," he finally stammered. "I just got mixed up. I think I may have gone back to my truck for something after I went in my house."

"Think? THINK? Mace said, raising his voice. "I think your story doesn't make any sense, Deputy Cothran. I think it doesn't make any sense because you're not telling me the truth about what really happened. You hear me? I think you've been lying the whole time."

"You're wrong!" Deputy Cothran said so vehemently he nearly rose out of his chair. "Why would I lie? I'm telling you it was a simple mistake about the timing of certain things. Like you just said, my mind wasn't right after I had to shoot that poor girl."

"I think you're lying because you knew that girl," Mace answered fiercely. "What's the real story? Was she your girlfriend? You two have an argument that got out of hand and she took off in your truck? You chased after her and she wrecked it. Did that make you so mad you shot her? Is that what happened?"

"Hell no!" Cothran replied.

"Maybe she's a local prostitute you hired and brought back to your place," Mace said. "The medical examiner says there's evidence of sexual activity. I think you took her to your place, you two had a disagreement about money or maybe you were a little rough on her, and she sneaks out and takes off in your new truck. That pisses you off and you chase her. She wrecks your truck. You see the other officers and know that she's going to rat you out, so you shoot her."

"She was going to stab that other officer with a screwdriver!" Cothran said angrily.

"That officer says he never felt threatened," Mace said, raising his voice just like Cothran had. "He said the girl was trying to surrender right before you fired!"

"He's a damned liar!" Cothran yelled as he slammed his fist down on the conference room table. The whole table shook from the impact.

The conference room door was behind Mace. Just outside it in the hallway, he heard footsteps. The steps stopped, meaning someone was probably outside the door in the hallway. He wasn't surprised; he was sure their raised voices could be heard elsewhere in the building. "I don't think he is," Mace said, lowering his voice.

Deputy Cothran sat back down in his chair. He was so angry his body was quivering. "He is," he said petulantly.

There was light knock at the door behind Mace and then it opened. Mace looked over his shoulder just as Sheriff Lynn Garrett stuck his head inside the room. "Guys, is everything okay in here?"

"Not really," Mace replied evenly. "This is actually good timing. Could you step in here and close the door please, Sheriff?" Mace didn't bother to turn his head. He had met the sheriff for the first time just prior to speaking with Detective Roberts earlier. He hadn't been impressed. Sheriff Garrett seemed nice enough, but he had that fake charm more suited to a politician or a used car salesman than a lawman.

Sheriff Garrett stepped into the conference room and closed the door behind him. He looked troubled. "Yes, Agent Holliday?"

Mace directed his attention to Deputy Cothran. "Deputy Cothran, you've stated for the record that you don't know the as-yet-unidentified female you shot two day ago. In your statement, you say that your only encounter with her has been the incident where you shot her following the pursuit and crash. Do you continue to stick with that statement?"

"Yes," Deputy Cothran said flatly.

"This girl has never been in your house or anywhere else on your property that you know of?" Mace asked.

"That's correct," Cothran answered.

"Okay," Mace said. "When I viewed the girl's body at the morgue, one thing that jumped out at me was her painted toenails and fingernails. They were freshly painted bright red. It got my attention because it was so unusual given the condition of her clothing." Mace reached down into his briefcase and retrieved the plastic evidence bag he'd brought in with him. He placed it down on the table in front of him. "Deputy, I found this in the back yard of your house right at the foot of your back steps. It's a bottle of nail polish. It appears to be the same color as the color on the girl's nails. I'd be willing to bet our crime lab can see if it's the exact nail polish that's on her nails."

Every bit of the color drained from Deputy Cothran's face. He opened his mouth as if to say something, but nothing came out for several long seconds. "I have no idea where that came from," he finally said.

"I told you where it came from," Mace said. "Weren't you listening? "

"I have no idea why it was there," Cothran stammered. "Maybe she snuck around behind the house before she stole my truck and dropped it by accident. Like I said, I've never seen it before in my life." He stood up and glared across the table at Mace. "This interview is over. If you talk with me anymore, it will be with my attorney present."

Mace also stood up. "Fair enough. I was getting tired of your lies anyway," he said. He turned to the sheriff, who stood with his back against the wall by the conference room door. "Sheriff Garrett, I want to officially put you on notice. I believe that Deputy Cothran here isn't being completely truthful regarding the events leading up to the shooting incident he was involved in two days ago. If that is so, then it calls into question the actual use of force itself."

Sheriff Garrett's face paled and he glared daggers across the table at Cothran. "That's a pretty serious allegation, Agent Holliday," he said slowly, "especially considering it's based on finding a bottle of nail polish near someone's home."

"That, along with some other factors, is enough to convince me that a much more in-depth investigation into this matter is needed," Mace said fiercely.

"I see," Sheriff Garrett replied. "Agent Holliday, if you would excuse us, I need to speak in private with Deputy Cothran."

Mace nodded. He retrieved his digital recorder from the table, switched it off, and put it back into is briefcase. He switched off the body camera he wore and put it in the briefcase with the recorder. The file folder from the table followed. Mace closed the case and turned to the sheriff. "I'll be in touch, Sheriff," he said as he walked by the sheriff and out the door of the conference room.

Sheriff Garrett watched from the doorway as Holliday walked down the hallway toward the entrance to the lobby. Once he was sure the man was gone, he closed the conference room door and turned his attention to Cothran. "What the hell just happened?" he snarled furiously.

Cothran looked dumbfounded. "Lynn, I have no idea where or how he got that," he answered. "I made sure there was nothing in my house. That's what I was doing for hours yesterday before you called me about the bar."

"He's onto you," Sheriff Garrett said as he fought to keep his voice under control. His whole body was shaking, but he couldn't tell if it was rage or fear. "Jesus Christ! All you had to do was stick with the story we came up with and make sure there was no evidence. How could you mess that up? Are you retarded?"

Cothran stiffened as if the sheriff had touched him with a live wire. "What did you just say?" he growled menacingly.

Sheriff Garrett knew that he had pushed the wrong button. Dwayne had always been a little slow and he'd been picked on about it mercilessly until he'd started growing in the third grade. The word 'retarded' had been used as a weapon against him until Dwayne had grown so big and mean that anyone using it risked serious injury if not worse at his hands. Using that word against Dwayne now was like waving a red flag in front of a bull. Still, the sheriff was so furious he didn't care.

"Take the rest of the day off, Dwayne," Sheriff Garrett said. "Just go home and chill until I call you."

"What are you going to do?" Cothran asked.

"The shipment goes out later today," Sheriff Garrett said. "That's our primary concern. Once that's done, I'm going to try to find a way to fix this mess so we all don't go down."

"Should I get a lawyer?" Cothran asked. Some of the rage had slipped from his voice. Now he just sounded angry and anxious.

"I need to make some calls," Sheriff Garrett replied. "I'll let you know."

Deputy Cothran nodded and stormed past the sheriff out of the conference room. Sheriff Garrett closed the door behind him and locked it.

Once the door was locked, Sheriff Garrett sat down at the table and rested his aching head in his hands.

CHAPTER 26

Amanda came out of the hotel office as Mace was parking his car in the hotel lot. She hurried to his car and met him just as he got out. "Hey, I was about to call you, Mace. You didn't happen to see Sam anywhere on the way here?" she asked.

"No," Mace replied as he closed the car door. "What's going on?"

"He called me to tell me that he was being released by the sheriff's office," Amanda said worriedly. "I told him I would come pick him up. He told me not to bother because he wanted to walk. He planned to go by and check to see if his bike was ready at Smith's. If it wasn't, he would walk home."

"I spoke to the detective at the sheriff's office like I promised," Mace said. "He told me they would be releasing Sam shortly. That was around nine forty-five or so." He glanced at his watch. "It's eleven now. What time did he call you?"

Amanda looked at the cell phone in her hand. "About ten minutes after ten," she said. "It's a couple of miles to the sheriff's office, so he should have made it here by now. I'm getting kind of worried."

"Take it easy," Mace said. "He probably stopped at Smith's and started talking with him or he could have stopped to get something to eat. I'm sure he's fine. How did he sound when he called you?"

"He sounded normal, maybe a little relieved," Amanda said. "Thanks for intervening in that."

"I'm just glad I happened to notice he was in his room sleeping through the crack in the curtains," Mace answered. "Talk about fortuitous timing. I just happen to notice the man's in his room just when it mattered."

"I'm so glad it worked out," Amanda said sincerely. "I just wonder where he's at. Caleb was wondering too."

"I suspect he's fine, Amanda," Mace offered. "Give it a little while longer and try his cell phone."

"I don't have a number for him," Amanda replied. "The number he called me from a little while ago didn't register on my cell phone's caller ID for some reason. He didn't list a cell number when he signed into the hotel either."

"That's kind of odd," Mace said. "I tell you what. I've got some paperwork to do regarding my interview with Deputy Cothran this morning. If Sam hasn't shown up in another hour or so, we'll go look for him."

"Thanks, Mace," Amanda answered. "I think the situation with the bikers has me a little worried."

"Sam can take care of himself," Mace said as he grabbed his briefcase from the backseat of his car. "He's proven that. I'll be in my room working on this mess. Let me know if you hear from him before an hour has passed okay?"

There was a knock on his door just fifteen minutes later. Mace opened the door to find Amanda standing there. "I called Jack at the garage and asked if he'd seen Sam. He said Sam came by and picked up his bike about an hour ago. He told Jack he was going to put a few miles on it to test it, so he's probably out riding."

"Good," Mace said. Actually, the news was more of a relief than he'd expected. A grim sense of foreboding had settled upon him since leaving the sheriff's office and he didn't know why.

"Just figured you wanted to know," Amanda said. "I'll let you get back to what you were doing."

Amanda turned and started to head back to the hotel office. "Hey, Amanda, would you and Caleb like to go out and grab some pizza this evening? I could use a break from this paperwork."

"I'm working in the office because Lorena is out sick," Amanda said. "Plus, it might look bad for me with me being separated and all from my husband."

"I didn't even consider that," Mace said as his face flushed with embarrassment. "I apologize. I feel like I might have overstepped my bounds."

Amanda smiled. "That doesn't mean we can't order a couple of pizzas and have them delivered to the office," she said. "We all need to eat. Easton might not have much, but we do have pizza delivery. How about we meet up in the office around six."

"I'd like that," Mace said with a smile.

"We would to," Amanda said. "See you then."

CHAPTER 27

The man with dark hair kept his baseball cap pulled down low as he walked through the Easton Chemicals warehouse. The massive warehouse and attached loading dock area sat at the southern edge of the town of Easton. A smaller, separate two-story brick building beside the warehouse served as the administrative offices for the company. The warehouse, office building, and parking area for both buildings were all surrounded by a ten-foot-high fence topped with razor wire. A separate fence separated the business office and their parking lot from the warehouse and its adjoining parking. There were two separate gates into the facility, one in front of the office building for employees and visitors and one at the rear of the warehouse used by tractor trailers transporting chemicals to and from the warehouse and warehouse employees. Access at each gate was controlled by a guard shack located in the middle of the roadway that led through the gate. The guard house at the front gate, the one for office employees and visitors, was manned by a friendly, older local man named Dave who'd worked for Easton Chemicals for years. The rear gate, the one for tractor trailers, was staffed by off-duty Easton County Sheriff's Office deputies. Supposedly the deputies were just moonlighting for extra money. In reality, they were there to protect the warehouse against anyone from the outside trying to get too nosy.

Given the high fence with razor wire and the armed guards at the gate, it should have been harder for him to get into the warehouse. However, it was almost absurdly easy. The Easton Chemicals warehouse was surrounded on three sides by streets. The back of the warehouse faced an overgrown field and a set of long -abandoned train tracks that locals in the surrounding neighborhoods used as a pedestrian shortcut to walk to a nearby street that had several stores, bars, and restaurants on it. A single walk through gate about three feet wide faced the old train tracks. The gate was securely locked with a new chain and padlock. However, the chain-link fence that made up the gate was old and the wires that held it to the frame were even older. To make it even easier, because the gate sat at the rear of the building in an area far away from the loading docks, parking lot, and break area, no one ever came back there.

Very few of the current employees even knew the gate was there. None of the crooked deputies who were paid to keep the place secure knew about it at all.

He already knew about the gate at the rear of the warehouse. A casual stroll from one of the side streets across the empty train tracks brought him to it. One hard push against the gate's chain-link fence broke it loose from the frame of the gate itself and made a nice gap for him to slide through sideways. He paused long enough to push the fencing back in position before walking away slowly and casually. Someone would have to literally walk up to the fencing and pull on it to tell it was ever loose and had been moved.

The man in the baseball cap walked around the corner of the warehouse and came to a metal door set into the side of the building. The ground in front of the door was packed earth and patchy grass. An old metal can was full of cigarette butts and several more were scattered on the ground. The side door and the area around it was used as the smoking area by some of the warehouse workers. The man tried the doorknob and it turned easily in his hand. He eased the door open and stepped into the warehouse. The inside was darker than the outside with the only light coming from a few widely-scattered lights high in the ceiling and a few scattered skylights. Plastic and metal drums sat around on wooden pallets lined up in neat rows. There were also rows of pallets with paper bags neatly stacked and shrink-wrapped on them. A strong smell of chemicals permeated the air. Further into the interior of the warehouse were huge racks of metal shelves with boxes of various sizes stacked on them.

According to Easton Chemicals' website, they were a wholesaler of chemicals for industrial and other uses. Their customer list included everything from Fortune 500 companies, small businesses, and a number of government and educational institutions. Most of their customers were in the Southeast, but a small number were located throughout the United States. Only two of their customers were located in other countries, one in Canada and the other just across the border in Mexico. The customer awaiting delivery in Mexico was the reason the man was here.

He walked deeper into the warehouse, taking care to stay out of the wide corridor down the middle of the warehouse. This was the main driving area for the forklifts that hurried about moving pallets loaded with various chemical containers as the warehouse workers filled customers' orders and loaded them in tractor trailers backed up to the loading dock at the other end of the building. The man stuck to the aisles that ran between the rows of loaded pallets and racks of shelves as he headed for the loading dock area. As he walked he could hear other workers talking back and forth among the rows of shelves over the steady beep of the alarms on the forklifts that indicated they were moving.

He continued to walk toward the loading dock area. He wasn't worried about being seen. Like most of the workers in the warehouse, he wore jeans, boots, and a tee shirt. The only difference someone might notice was that his tee shirt was a different color from the ones the workers wore and it didn't have the Easton Chemicals logo on the back and over the left breast. He also wasn't wearing one of the reflectorized safety vests that the warehouse workers wore as a safety precaution in the dim interior to make sure the forklift operators saw them. If anyone stopped him, he would claim to be a new employee who was looking for the foreman so he could get the shirt and safety equipment he needed. He doubted anyone would stop him, though. He had learned a long time ago that, if you were somewhere you weren't supposed to be, it was better to act like you WERE supposed to be there. Confidence fooled a lot of people.

He made it to the loading dock area where five large roll-up doors opened to the loading dock where the tractor trailers backed up to be loaded or unloaded. All five doors were up and each had a tractor trailer backed up to it. Only three of the trailers actually had the rear door open so they could be loaded or unloaded. Lights on extendable arms that allowed them to be moved to illuminate the inside of the trailers were mounted by each door and the three open trailers had the lights on and extended, meaning that the workers were actually working inside the trailers. Just past the open roll-up doors was a small office with large glass windows that looked out at the loading area. Through the window he could see an older man with glasses looking at something on a computer screen at a desk covered with papers. A sign by the office's closed door identified it as the Shipping/Receiving Office. A normal metal door set into the wall just past the bay doors went out to a set of steps. The drivers of the trucks used that door to come in to the office when they needed to.

The man in the baseball cap stayed on one of the aisles between the rows of shelves as a beeping forklift emerged from one of the open trailers, turned down the center of the warehouse, and drove away. The driver of the forklift was busy looking at a clipboard mounted on a small stand near the forklift's steering wheel. The man figured it was the manifest listing what the driver was supposed to be loading on the truck he was working on. Once the forklift was past him, the man stepped out of the aisle and walked to the open bay doors. The two doors closest to him revealed trailers that were already shut and sealed with the metal load tags. The next three were where the lights were extended to illuminate the trailer interiors. He looked into the first one, but he didn't see what he was looking for. He continued on to the next open trailer.

He found what he was looking for in that open trailer. The interior of the trailer was about half full with plastic and metal drums in various colors sitting on wooden pallets and shrink-wrapped with plastic. The last two pallets the forklift operator had placed in the truck each bore four blue plastic drums wrapped tightly in clear plastic. Each of the drums on the pallets had two prominent stickers on the side. The smaller of the two stickers on each drum warned that the chemical supposedly contained inside the drum was corrosive. The larger sticker depicted a skull and crossbones, the international symbol for a substance that was deadly, in eye-catching colors with warnings in multiple languages that the drums' contents were deadly.

Moving quickly, the man moved the extendable light out of the way and closed the trailer's open doors. The two trailer doors opened to the side instead of the usual roll-up door. He was glad for that because closing a roll-up door made a very unique and identifiable sound that might draw attention. Once the two doors were closed and latched, the man dropped down off the loading dock to the concrete in front of it. He walked to the tractor, a newer model light blue Peterbilt with a sleeper cab and the Easton Chemicals logo on the door, and opened the driver's door. Just as he had expected, the cab was empty. He climbed into the driver's seat and closed the door. The keys were still in the ignition. He had expected that as well; no one expected their truck to be stolen in broad daylight in a secure facility with a guard at the gate while it was being loaded. He started the truck and the big diesel engine roared to life.

The man in the baseball cap drove slowly away from the loading dock and headed for the gate. A single, bored-looking Easton County sheriff's deputy in full uniform sat in the guard house. His marked police cruiser was parked on the wide median right in front of the guard house. The deputy looked up curiously as the truck drove up to the exit gate. The man in the baseball cap looked him right in the face through the window, smiled broadly at him, and waved. The deputy gave him a thumbs-up signal and raised the metal barrier arm that blocked the exit lane. The blue Peterbilt drove slowly past the guard house, turned left, and drove away down the street toward the main road that would take him through Easton.

Back inside the warehouse the truck had just left, a heavyset Hispanic man named Jorge walked into the shipping and receiving office at the loading dock. "Hey, Pete," Jorge said in his barely accented English as soon as he walked through the door, "where's my truck?"

Pete, the man sitting behind the desk, looked up at Jorge in confusion. "What do you mean?" he asked. "It's over there at door three being loaded for your trip."

Jorge, a native of Mexico, was the only Easton company driver allowed to make the delivery to the remote facility just over the border from Texas. Supposedly it was because Jorge knew the area and spoke Spanish. In reality, it was because Jorge worked with the Baja Cartel. The warehouse he was delivering the load of chemicals to was a legitimate business that made automotive paints and finishes. The cartel actually owned the company through several layers of intermediaries. Only Jorge and a few of the workers in the warehouse in Mexico knew that eight of the barrels being delivered there didn't contain what the label on the barrel claimed. Those workers were paid to separate those certain barrels and then make sure they were delivered to the right people. "Man, don't be screwing with me," Jorge warned, only half-jokingly. "I've got a long trip ahead of me."

Pete looked back at him from his seat behind the desk. "What do you mean?" he asked. "I'm not following you."

"My truck is not at door three," Jorge said impatiently. "There's nothing at door three."

Pete turned and looked through the window out at the inside of the warehouse and the loading dock area. Outside he could see one of the company forklifts sitting there at door three with a pallet on the skids. The driver, Franklin, had shut off the forklift and gotten off of the machine. He looked confused, alternately looking out through the roll-up door and then back at the shipping office. "It was just there. Franklin has been loading it for the last forty-five minutes."

"I know that," Jorge' said impatiently. "I'm the guy who backed the truck up to the door to be loaded. I came in to get some coffee and do my paperwork while it was being loaded for the usual trip. It's not there anymore. Did someone move it?"

"You know we don't move a driver's assigned truck," Pete said irritably. "Only the driver assigned to a truck can operate that truck. It is company policy and all of my guys know that. I barely trust some of these idiots to drive a forklift. Do you think I'd let them move your truck, Jorge'?"

"Well, somebody moved it," Jorge's said just as irritably. "My truck ain't there."

Pete jumped up from behind his desk and stormed past Jorge'. He walked out of the office to the open bay door and looked out. The space where the tractor trailer had been sitting a few minutes ago was empty. "Hey, boss," Franklin said from behind him. "Where's the truck? I still have over half a load to put on it."

Pete stormed over to a telephone mounted near the office door and punched in a number. There was a loud beep as the warehouse's intercom system activated. "All warehouse employees and all drivers come to the shipping office now!" Pete said. His voice echoed through the warehouse from speakers hooked to the beams that held up the roof.

It took about three minutes for all of the employees scattered through the warehouse to gather. While that was happening, Pete walked outside and looked around the concrete and gravel lot where the Easton Chemicals delivery trucks were normally parked. He fully expected to see Jorge's light-blue Peterbilt sitting somewhere off to the side where one of the other drivers had moved it as a practical joke. When he did find it, he planned to tear everyone in the warehouse a new one and threaten to fire them all if anything like that ever happened again. The planned butt-chewing session evaporated when he didn't see the truck anywhere outside. Pete felt the first faint strings of unease as he stormed back up the steps and into the warehouse.

Everyone was gathered near the shipping office. "Listen up, guys," Pete said firmly. "I love a good prank as well as anybody, but this one has gone too far. Who moved Jorge's rig and where in the hell is it?" All of the men assembled in front of him just looked confused. Several of them shrugged while a few others looked around at their coworkers. "This is the last chance, guys. If you moved it, speak up. I'll write you up, but that's as far as it goes. If I have to ask again, someone's losing their job. I ain't kidding either." No one spoke up. They all just looked back at him placidly.

Pete turned to Jorge', who was standing beside him looking as angry as Pete felt. "Jorge', did you leave the keys in your truck?' he asked.

"I did," Jorge' replied. "We all normally do that. The truck was sitting at the dock in broad daylight with men working on it, for God's sake. Who would take a chance on trying to steal it?"

Pete felt his stomach sink. He rushed over to the telephone on the wall and punched in the number for the guard house at the warehouse entrance. The deputy on duty there answered. "Did you just let a light-blue Peterbilt leave the property?" Pete asked.

The assembled workers could tell Pete didn't like the answer when he cursed and slammed the telephone back into its cradle. They slowly drifted away to get back to work as Pete ran into his office and slammed the door behind him.

Ronny Easton was in his office in the building next door when the telephone on his office desk rang. As the owner and chief executive of Easton Chemicals, Ronny occupied the biggest office on the top floor of the two-story office building that housed the company's offices. Despite the spacious office and grandiose title, Ronny really didn't do anything; he mainly used the office as a place to hang out and feel important. The general manager kept the company running and the money rolling in. Ronny usually came by the office for a few minutes each workday to put in an appearance before vanishing to play golf, hit the gym, or do anything other than work. Since Amanda had left him, he'd been spending more time there at the office than usual. He wasn't there to distract himself from his troubles with work, however. The office had a fully-stocked bar and was the only place where he didn't see something that reminded him of that bitch who'd left him and their bratty kid.

He'd spent the morning drinking bourbon and snorting crystal meth he'd gotten a couple of days ago from Stoner, so he was as high as a kite when the telephone rang. The ringing telephone surprised him because the receptionist knew he didn't take calls. He thought about ignoring it, but then realized that it must be important if the receptionist did let it get through. With that in mind, he grabbed the telephone. "Yeah?' he slurred.

It took a few moments for what he was hearing to slash its way through the drugs and alcohol, but when it did he was suddenly a lot more sober. "A truck?" he asked. "Stolen from the loading dock? Well, damn, call Sheriff Garrett. That's what the police do."

He was about to slam the phone back into its cradle, but then the man on the phone told him which truck was missing. The news that it was the truck going to Mexico caused his knees to buckle and he had to lean on the edge of the desk. Part of him wanted to burst out laughing hysterically, but he fought it back by clenching his teeth. "I'll call the sheriff personally," he mumbled. "Thanks for calling me."

He managed to hang the telephone up just in time to turn and vomit into the trash can beside his desk.

CHAPTER 28

Greenville County Sheriff's Deputy Ted Sarr spotted the truck as soon as he turned into the parking lot of the long-abandoned shopping center on Highway Twenty-five just a few miles from the Easton County/Greenville County line. The tractor-trailer, a light blue Peterbilt pulling a white trailer, was parked at the far edge of the empty parking lot, exactly where the anonymous caller to Greenville County's 911 Emergency Communications Center said it would be. The caller, an unidentified male calling from a cell phone, had told the dispatcher that he had discovered the truck while looking for his lost dog in the area around the vacant shopping center. The caller said it sounded like someone was being held captive in the back of the truck because he could hear banging and screams from the trailer. The 911 center had dispatched Deputy Sarr and another unit to investigate. Sarr was closer than the other unit so he'd arrived first.

Deputy Sarr, a slender, precise man with neatly-parted dark hair and military bearing, drove across cracked asphalt that was already sprouting weeds through the cracks toward the parked truck. He stopped several yards away from the truck and stepped out of the marked police car he drove. He stood there behind the open car door and carefully examined the scene. The truck and attached trailer were parked at the edge of the parking lot near an embankment that separated the shopping center from its next door neighbor which was, ironically enough, the newer, bigger shopping center that replaced it. The truck was at least a football field's length away from the vacant building that had once been a Wal-Mart and a row of smaller, attached stores. Sarr didn't see anything that raised any red flags. He figured that the driver had probably pulled over to get some rest or maybe for some sort of mechanical issue.

Sarr used his car's radio to let the dispatcher know that he was on scene and out with the vehicle. Once the dispatcher acknowledged him, he closed the car door and slowly approached the cab of the truck. His eyes moved constantly as he headed for the truck, looking for anything that might be a danger signal. Sarr, a fifteen-year law enforcement veteran, knew from hard experience how fast a seemingly benign situation could turn dangerous. There was no such thing as a routine call. Not anymore.

Sarr noticed the logo on the side of the cab as he approached the driver's side door. The truck apparently belonged to the Easton Chemicals of Easton County, the next county over. The truck's engine was shut off. The engine wasn't ticking as it cooled off and he didn't smell exhaust, so the engine had obviously been shut off for a while. Sarr stepped off to the side so he was out of the line of fire if someone in the cab of the truck started shooting through the door or window. He banged loudly on the side of the truck right at the sleeper. If the driver was inside sleeping, the noise would be sure to awaken him. Nothing happened. Sarr cocked his head and listened carefully, but he could hear nothing from inside the truck. He banged on the side one more time and waited for nearly a minute. Still nothing.

Deputy Sarr reached up and tried the driver's door handle. The door opened easily. "Police," he said loudly. "Is anyone inside the truck?" The inside of the cab was as quiet as a tomb. Sarr moved so he could see more of the cab's interior. The curtain that separated the seats from the sleeper was pulled back and secured, enabling him to see almost the entire interior of the cab. No one was in the cab. He noted that the truck's cab was very neat and organized and didn't appear to have been rifled through. He also didn't see any blood or other signs that might indicate something bad had happened. He stepped up on the steps like he was getting into the truck so he could see the center console. He noticed the keys in the ignition. The keychain was a metal charm featuring some kind of saint and some words that appeared to be Spanish.

Seeing the keys in the ignition but no driver immediately raised Sarr's suspicions. He had a big rig parked in a vacant parking lot nowhere near an area where such trucks would normally be with no driver around, the cab doors unlocked, and the keys in the ignition. The parking and unlocked cab doors might be explained if the driver was in the cab chilling out, but the lack of a driver and keys in the ignition definitely was unusual. He stepped back down and gently closed the cab door. He kept his hand near his holstered gun as he moved down the side of the cab and down the side of the trailer. He stopped about halfway down the length of the trailer and banged on the side of the trailer. He could hear the blows echoing inside the trailer. The anonymous caller had claimed that he heard screams from the back of the trailer and thought someone might be trapped inside. There was no response to the blows. Sarr listened carefully, but he didn't hear anything that might indicate someone was inside the trailer.

Now thoroughly puzzled, Sarr continued to the rear of the trailer. When he reached the rear of the trailer, he found one of the doors unlocked and standing open about three inches. It looked as if someone had unlatched the door and opened it to get into the trailer. "Hello? Police," Sarr called. "Anyone inside the trailer?" There was no answer. Sarr placed his hand on his gun, stepped to the unopened door side so he was out of any potential line of fire, and used his free hand to push the open door further open. The door swung wide and stayed open due to the slight incline the trailer was parked on. Sarr tensed as the door swung open, expecting everything from gunfire to smuggled humans jumping out to potential hijackers. Nothing came from inside the trailer but silence and the strong smell of chemicals.

Deputy Sarr took a quick peek through the open door into the interior of the trailer. The interior of the trailer was surprisingly well-lit, thanks to the translucent plastic that allowed daylight to enter but kept out the elements. He could see that the trailer was only about half full with drums and boxes on pallets. Some of the drums closest to the door where he was standing had fallen over and the tops of the drums had been knocked or pulled off. There was some type of liquid in the floor of the trailer. Sarr immediately leaped back when he saw the open drums in case the liquid that had spilled out was toxic. The trailer door remained open, giving him a clear view into the trailer as he backed away from the trailer.

Sarr had backed away almost twenty feet before he stopped. There was something spilling out of the fallen drums. It wasn't liquid, though; it appeared to be thick bundles of something wrapped in plastic. Curiosity made Deputy Sarr cautiously step back closer to the open door so he could get a better view and try to determine exactly what he was seeing. A few steps forward were good enough to verify his initial impression, the one he could barely believe. He was looking at thick bundles of what appeared to be United States currency that had been vacuum-packed in thick plastic. Each one of the visible bundles appeared to be a one-foot- square cube. He counted at least twenty bundles spilling from the tops of the fallen barrels.

Sarr gave a low whistle and hurried back to his cruiser. The situation had escalated from a possibly abandoned vehicle to something much more serious and much more puzzling. For some reason the driverless big rig parked in front of him appeared to have possibly millions of dollars packed into fifty-five- gallon drums in the trailer. It didn't take Sherlock Holmes to figure out that he was looking at attempted smuggling. The big question was why was the truck parked here and abandoned?

Sarr grabbed the radio microphone and notified the dispatcher. When she answered, Sarr requested the fire department hazardous materials team to handle the possible spilled chemicals inside the truck. He followed that up with a request for a supervisor and detectives. The detectives could figure out what was going on. That's what they got paid for.

CHAPTER 28

The arrival of Garcia, the Baja Cartel's feared enforcer and all-around troubleshooter, in Easton County went completely unnoticed, just like he'd planned it and just like he liked it. Carefully-crafted anonymity was the reason he was so successful at what he did. Upon hearing the words cartel enforcer, most people pictured the image Hollywood had taught them to expect: a young Hispanic man with numerous tattoos all over his face and body, a shaved head, shirt buttoned up to the throat, and using words like 'vato' and 'hombre' in every mumbled sentence. Garcia was a handsome, bi-racial man in his mid-thirties, the son of white man and Mexican mother, and a natural- born American citizen. He was clean-shaven and his jet-black hair and smooth, even features wouldn't have looked out of place in an ad for men's cologne. He had a college degree in economics, dressed tastefully in designer jeans and expensive shirts, and preferred cowboy boots. He lived in Phoenix, Arizona in an upper middle-class subdivision where his neighbors thought he was a successful real estate developer. The successful real estate developer cover story explained the nice house, designer clothes, and the expensive Porsche he drove around when he was at home. Even better, it explained his frequent travel and the weird hours he seemed to keep.

The expensive Porsche was sitting in his garage back home in Phoenix at the moment. He was currently driving a white Toyota Camry sedan with four doors and a South Carolina license plate. The car had been rented using a fake Georgia driver's license and credit card under the name Bradley Grant. Bradley Grant was real man who lived in Atlanta. At thirty-two years of age, Bradley Grant was the same general size and age as Garcia. The real Bradley had no idea that his identity had been stolen by hackers several months earlier and used to make a fake driver's license good enough to fool an expert, nor that his credit history and name had been used to get a credit card that never would be traced back to the man really using it. The real Bradley, a dentist, would have been truly horrified to know that the man currently using his identity was personally responsible for the deaths of thirty people and indirectly responsible for dozens more.

Garcia's real name was a surprisingly ordinary James Wilson Hartman. He's been born in San Diego, California and been raised in a middle- class household there until the age of ten. His parents divorced and his mother moved back to Mexico with her son in tow. His father, a career Navy man and borderline alcoholic, hadn't even tried for custody or visitation. His mother had moved into her uncle's palatial home outside of Tijuana. His mother's uncle's last name was Garcia and he was a widower with no children. He had taken an instant liking to James and quickly became the father James lacked. James had started calling him Papa Garcia. James had even stayed behind when his mother moved back to California.

James had been around the age of thirteen when he realized that his new father figure was involved in something sinister. It would take another few months before he realized that Papa Garcia was a founding member of the Baja Cartel, a dangerous criminal organization that he kept reading about in the newspapers and hearing about at school. At fifteen, James came right out and asked Papa Garcia if he was involved. Papa Garcia hadn't denied his involvement; instead, he'd seemed proud of it. From that moment, James Hartman had wanted in. Papa Garcia had recognized something in young James that could be used to benefit himself and the cartel as a whole, so he'd let the young man into the organization. At sixteen, James was delivering verbal messages to cartel associates for Papa Garcia because the old man refused to use cell phones or other traceable means of communication. James had displayed animal cunning, natural intelligence, and a vicious streak that quickly helped him rise through the organization.

From the age of eighteen into his early twenties, James had lived a bizarre double life. Most of the time he was a college student earning high grades at San Diego State University. However, when the cartel needed him, he served as a ruthless and highly-effective hitman. His normal appearance, a talent for weapons, and a tendency to plan that bordered on being obsessive, had made him very successful as a killer. Targets who were on the lookout for tattooed Mexican gangbangers never looked twice when the clean-cut, nicely-dressed young white man who looked like he wanted to sell them insurance approached them. He had racked up a number of high-profile hits and never even come close to getting caught.

As time went by, James Hartman had become known simply as Garcia, a homage to the great uncle who'd raised him. He was long past being a simple hitman; now he was the man the cartel called on when they had situations that needed to be handled with intelligence, discretion, and anonymity. Garcia was the man who bribed politicians and police officers, blackmailed judges, and kept the cartel under the radar and its bosses out of prison or the morgue. Garcia didn't show up and kill people, although he would if that's what the situation required. He played the long game, setting in place plans that might take a while to bear fruit, but when they did the harvest was spectacular. With a reputation for handling situations quickly, quietly, and effectively, he had earned the respect of the cartel's bosses. Rumor had it that when Papa Garcia died, he would take his place.

A sign up ahead on the right shoulder of the road welcomed him to Easton County. Garcia wasn't staying in Easton County; he had checked into a hotel just over the county line in Greenville County using the same fake driver's license and credit card. Once he figured out what exactly was going on in Easton County and handled the situation, he would return to Phoenix. There he would become James Hartman, real estate developer, again. His friends in the neighborhood he lived in thought he was in Florida looking at some property he was thinking of buying.

Garcia frowned as he passed the sign and entered Easton. He was not happy to be in Easton because having to come to Easton meant something was going wrong. Sheriff Garrett had called the number he'd been given if he needed help with a situation. He was only to call that number if the cartel's operation was in trouble and it was a situation he couldn't handle himself. The sheriff had called that number and now Garcia had to be in Easton. Garcia really didn't know what exactly was happening. The information Sheriff Garrett had relayed to the person who answered the call wasn't exactly clear. Supposedly someone was working against the cartel's smuggling operation and the sheriff needed it handled discreetly. Garcia would find out more as soon as he talked with the sheriff. He planned to do that as soon as it could be arranged. Garcia's reputation depended on it.

Garcia was the man who'd started everything in lowly Easton County. Originally the Baja Cartel was using Easton as just a smuggling route for the people they were smuggling to major cities up north. The major interstates were faster and easier routes, but they were also more heavily policed, not just by locals but also the federal agencies. The cartel had appointed him to find a better and safer way for them to smuggle their human and drug cargoes. Garcia had spent days driving back roads in places like Easton County and mapping routes with a GPS system. Staying off the interstates and using the routes Garcia had plotted had worked very well for the cartel. There was less of a police presence and even when there was, small-town cops were often too dumb to realize what they were dealing with. There were a few smarter local cops out there. Garcia dealt with them, either through bribery or a bullet. Cops who didn't take the bribes and kept interfering with the cartel's business often ended up getting killed on duty by suspects who were never apprehended.

That was how Garcia had made the acquaintance of Sheriff Lynn Garrett and Deputy Dwayne Cothran. They had been smart enough to take the money. The relationship had worked out exceedingly well. The sheriff and his men got paid and the cartel had a safe route to smuggle people, drugs, and weapons through the upstate of South Carolina. The Horde, the biker gang that worked with the Baja Cartel, were also allowed to set up shop and establish drop sites for the cartel's human cargo and illegal drugs and various legal businesses that could be used to launder the cartel's money.

Out of all the success he'd had in Easton County, Ronny Easton and the Easton Chemicals had been Garcia's greatest success. Smuggling cash back into Mexico had gotten harder and harder since September 11th, 2001. Following the terror attacks on that day, the federal government had stepped up border enforcement and also passed numerous laws regarding financial transactions with foreign entities. No longer were the cartels able to send hundreds of thousands of unexplained dollars back to Mexico with a few simple clicks on a computer keyboard, not unless they wanted that money tracked to places they didn't want it to be tracked. The cartels' only option then was to smuggle cold, hard cash into Mexico. The problem with that was that cash was surprisingly hard to smuggle, especially when there were literally tons of it,

Because of his success with the smuggling routes, Garcia was tasked with the job of finding a way to smuggle the Baja Cartel's cash back into Mexico. The answer had come to him by way of a news story about a tractor trailer crash that had resulted in dangerous chemicals being spilled and a number of people going to the hospital for chemical-related injuries. The news story included an interview with the fire chief whose department had responded. During the interview, the fire chief explained how trains and trucks carrying chemicals were always treated with great caution by police and fire personnel because of the potential danger from what they were carrying. Those comments and a little more research had helped him determine that a truck loaded with chemicals had a very low chance of being thoroughly searched by the border patrol or any other law enforcement agency. The chance of getting caught dropped even more if the truck was from a reputable company and all of the necessary paperwork for the delivery was legit. With that in mind, Garcia had started looking for a chemical company he could exploit.

Sheriff Garrett was the one who'd suggested Easton Chemicals. Due to his friendship with Ronny Easton, the sheriff knew that Ronny was in financial trouble and was in over his head following the death of his father. The old man who'd run the company for years wanted to buy it and Ronny was planning to sell. The sheriff had arranged a meeting between Ronny and Garcia. Garcia didn't want to buy the company. Instead, he wanted Ronny to run it and use its trucks to smuggle cash into Mexico. The cartel, through several intermediaries, owned a company in Mexico that had a legitimate need for chemicals. That legitimate company would start buying their chemicals from Easton Chemicals. Along with the legitimate load of chemicals shipped monthly would be a few other barrels that happened to contain cash. Those barrels would be labeled as some chemical that the cops checking trucks at the border wouldn't dare mess with. The barrels would be listed on the necessary paperwork, all nice and legal. Only a handful of warehouse workers at the company receiving the load in Mexico would know the truth. Ronny, eager to keep the family name on the company, had jumped at the chance. The company not only prospered from the new contract to supply the company in Mexico, Ronny was paid fifty thousand dollars a month in cash for his involvement.

It had worked like a charm. Once a month eight blue plastic fifty-five-gallon drums were delivered to the Easton Chemicals warehouse in a panel truck similar to the ones UPS used. The blue drums were labeled as an especially corrosive and deadly acid, but they actually contained sealed bundles of cash, the proceeds of the cartel's illegal activities in the United States. The shipment arrived at night, long after the warehouse had shut down for the night. Ronny Easton himself was there to open the loading bay doors. The two men in the panel truck would use a forklift to take the drums from the truck to a special storage area. Ronny would doctor the appropriate paperwork to make it look like a normal shipment of chemicals. The drums would then put on the truck heading to Mexico. The rest, as they say, was history.

Garcia had no idea exactly what was going on in Easton County, but he was there to handle it. He hoped handling it didn't involve having to shut down the operation he'd worked so hard to build. The cartel was smuggling over ten million dollars a month through Easton Chemicals. They would not be happy if that was compromised. If it was compromised however, then he was there to clean up the mess and make sure it didn't come back on the cartel. If it looked like it might, his back-up plan was basically scorched earth. Anyone who might be able to link the Baja Cartel to Easton Chemicals, The Horde, and the Easton County Sheriff's Office had to go. That included the sheriff and possibly some of his deputies.

Garcia's expression remained neutral as he continued driving toward the town of Easton, but his mind was buzzing. Killing police officers was always problematic because it usually brought a lot of heat. The cartel would have to abandon Easton County and possibly upstate South Carolina for a long time, meaning other routes and places would have to be found. However, if that's what it took to clean up the mess, so be it.

Garcia's mind continued sifting through different scenarios as he drove. When he reached the Easton town limits twenty minutes later, he pulled over into the parking lot of the first convenience store he came to and parked at the edge of the lot out of the way of the cameras that watched the parking lot and pumps. He opened the briefcase on the passenger's seat and removed a cell phone. He punched in Sheriff Garrett's personal cell phone number and then typed a simple text message. The message was *I am here*. He hit the send button. The phone's screen showed the message was sent successfully.

Now he would wait until he heard from Sheriff Garrett. It might be minutes or it might be hours, but when the call came he would be ready.

CHAPTER 29

Sheriff Lynn Garrett's hands shook slightly as he placed the telephone gently back in its cradle on his desk. He glanced over at Ronny Easton, who sat slumped in the chair in front of his desk, to see if Ronny noticed the shaking as he settled back into his chair behind the desk. Ronny hadn't noticed the sheriff's nervousness. That was a good thing because Ronny was drunk, strung out, and on the verge of a nervous breakdown already. Sheriff Garrett knew that if Ronny saw that he was also nervous, Ronny would probably shift into full-blown nervous breakdown mode. That was the absolute last thing Sheriff Garrett needed right now.

To say that it had been a horrible day for the sheriff was like saying the Grand Canyon was a hole in the ground somewhere in Arizona. The death of Stoner and the fire that destroyed The Boy's Club in the early morning hours of the day was just the start of a day that had turned into one disaster after another. Dwayne's interview had been the second disaster. They had carefully rehearsed Dwayne's version of events several times and Dwayne had sworn that any evidence that might reveal what had really transpired before he shot the girl had been destroyed. Despite that, BCI Agent Holliday had gone out to Dwayne's place and very easily found some very damning evidence that contradicted Dwayne's carefully rehearsed version of events. As if that wasn't quite enough, Dwayne had lost his temper during Agent Holliday's interview and probably said enough to warrant an indictment for murder. They would be lucky if the BCI's investigation stopped with something as simple as a murder indictment for Dwayne.

After sending Dwayne home, Sheriff Garrett had spent the few peaceful minutes he had before the frantic telephone call from Ronny Easton trying to figure out a way to salvage everything. If anything, the disaster of an interview with Agent Holliday had proven something the sheriff had feared: Dwayne couldn't be relied upon to keep his mouth shut. If Agent Holliday kept digging and found out the truth about Dwayne and the girl, Dwayne might try to save himself from life in prison or maybe even the death penalty. One way he might try to do that was to use information about the sheriff's illegal activities and those of his fellow deputies. He could even throw The Horde and the Baja Cartel in for good measure.

While Sheriff Garrett was pondering this doomsday scenario, his cell phone had rung. On the other end was Ronny Easton with the news that one of Easton Chemical's trucks had been stolen right from the warehouse loading dock. Ronny was practically babbling and the sheriff was about to hang up on him because he wasn't in the mood to listen to Ronny whine. However, just as he was about to hang up, Ronny managed to explain that it wasn't a truck missing, it was THE TRUCK, the one with THE SHIPMENT TO MEXICO. Sheriff Garrett had been standing by his desk as he was about to walk out of the office. That was a good thing, because when he heard that news his knees nearly buckled under him. He'd had to sit down on his desk to keep from falling in the floor. He'd managed to tell Ronny to head over to his office before ending the call and letting his cell phone slip from his suddenly-nerveless fingers and fall with a clatter to the desktop.

Sheriff Garrett had managed a quick sip of whiskey from the bottle he kept in his desk before Ronny arrived in his office just fifteen minutes later. Ronny was drunk and nearly hysterical. He'd managed to calm Ronny down long enough to get what little information he could. The truck's driver, a Mexican national who secretly worked for the cartel, had discovered his truck was no longer at the loading dock being loaded when he returned from the company break room. When the driver, Jorge', asked about his missing truck, no one at the warehouse knew what had happened to it. Deputy Henderson, one of his men who worked extra duty as one of the gate guards, had seen the truck leave and even waved at the driver. One the truck was through the gate, it had seemed to vanish. The sheriff immediately put every available deputy to work scouring the county looking for the truck, but the big rig seemed to have vanished completely.

His question about where a tractor trailer could vanish to and remain hidden had been answered just a few minutes ago. The telephone on his desk had rung and he'd almost ignored it until he saw on the caller identification screen that it was from the Greenville County Sheriff's Department. He'd answered it and found himself talking to a detective with the Greenville County

Sheriff's Office. The detective was calling regarding an Easton Chemicals tractor trailer found parked at a vacant shopping center just a few miles over the Greenville County/Easton County line with no driver around. The unspoken question the sheriff had about why they were calling him and not the company's office was answered when the detective on the phone told him that they believed the truck might be involved in some sort of illegal activity.

Luckily, Sheriff Garrett had been born with the ability to think on his feet. He had hastily explained that he'd just been notified of a truck reported stolen from Easton Chemicals. As a matter of fact, he was speaking with Ron Easton, the owner of Easton Chemicals, and working on the stolen vehicle report at that very moment. The Greenville County detective then told him to let Easton know that the truck had been located. Unfortunately, it was also being impounded by the Greenville County Sheriff's Office at the request of the FBI and Drug Enforcement Administration. The deputy who'd responded to an anonymous call about a suspicious vehicle and located the truck had opened the trailer to find what appeared to be a large sum of money stashed in such a way as to indicate a possible attempt to smuggle it out of the United States. The FBI and DEA already had agents on scene. Sheriff Garrett had thanked the detective for the information and assured him that he and his office would assist the agencies involved in every way possible.

Sheriff Garrett looked up from the telephone on his desk and glanced across the desk at Ronny. Ronny was staring back at him. Ronny's eyes were wide with fear and his face, previously flushed with alcohol, had grown deathly pale. He'd obviously overheard some of the conversation, but only one side of it. Still, he'd heard enough to get the gist of it. "What's happened?" Ronny asked in a quavering voice.

"The truck's been found parked in the parking lot of an empty shopping center in Greenville County just over the line," Sheriff Garrett said without preamble. "The money has been found. The FBI and DEA are involved now."

Ronny's mouth moved a few times, but no words came out for a few seconds. "How did they find the money?"

"Whoever took the truck must have driven it there, opened the trailer, and opened the drums with the money," Sheriff Garrett said numbly. "The same person then called in an anonymous call about the truck. The deputy who responded found the trailer door open and looked inside. He found the money."

"But...but they're not supposed to be able to find the money," Ronny stammered.

"Well, you're not supposed to let the truck get stolen from your warehouse, either, Ronny, but that happened, didn't it?" Sheriff Garrett replied bitterly.

Ronny looked back at the sheriff like the man had slapped him across the face. "Are you blaming me for this?" he asked incredulously. "Whoever took it drove by one of your men at the front gate!"

There was a faint tinge of something in Ronny's voice that could have been hysteria or rage. The sheriff couldn't tell which one it was and he didn't care. "Someone walked into your place of business and made off with one of your trucks in the middle of the workday in broad daylight," he spat at Ronny. "Whoever it was took about five million dollars of the cartel's money. They'll probably hold you responsible. Congratulations, Ronny, you now owe five million dollars to some people I would be terrified to owe 5 dollars to."

Ronny jumped up out of the chair. The pallor had vanished from his face and been replaced with red. "You think they'll just blame me, Lynn? You're the one who's been sitting on their ass while someone took out Judge Cooper, killed Stoner, and burned their bar. Now the same person has stolen their money. I promise you, brother, I'm not the only one who needs to be worried."

The sheriff started to bolt out of his chair and stomp Ronny through the floor, but he knew it was pointless. He also knew that Ronny was most probably right. They were all up the proverbial creek without a paddle. There was a very good chance that the cartel would indeed hold them responsible. The theft of the cartel's money had happened under their noses. The cartel paid him a lot of money to keep their precious shipments safe and Ronny a lot of money for enabling the shipments. The only thing that might save them was to find the person or persons responsible, turn them over to the cartel, and let the cartel exact their vengeance. That might satisfy them or it might not. Sheriff Garrett figured it was a fifty/fifty shot at best. If that didn't work, then Ronny and he would probably be on the hook to pay back the stolen money. Sheriff Garrett had a huge sum of money stashed in a secret place at his farm, but it was nowhere near five million dollars. Ronny might have it or might not.

No matter what happened, he and Ronny were now, unfortunately, on the same team. Once this was over, providing they all survived, he would have plenty of time to deal with Ronny. For now, it was better to mend fences. "Look, man, I'm sorry for that," he started to say, but before he could finish the sentence Ronny had turned and stormed out of the office. He slammed the door behind him.

The sheriff sat there and looked at the door in disgust. Ronny could run off and sulk for a while if that's what it took for him to pull himself together. Unfortunately, he didn't have the same luxury. Despite what he'd told Ronny, Sheriff Garrett knew that he was the one who would be the main target of the cartel's blame. He and his deputies were supposed to keep everything running smoothly and they had failed miserably. Since they couldn't prevent the events of the last twenty-four hours, the least he could do was determine who was responsible and deal with them. The problem with finding the person responsible was that he didn't have the slightest clue who was responsible for the series of unfortunate events that had befallen their operation in the last few days. The thing with Judge Cooper could have just been a fluke because it really didn't fit the narrative that someone was targeting their operation. The same thing applied to Sam Walker, the guy who'd thrashed the three bikers. Maybe the three bikers had just screwed with the wrong person. It happened sometimes. The attack at the bar, Stoner's death, and the theft of the truck, though, was definitely aimed at the bikers and the smuggling operation respectively. The big question was who was responsible. He would have bet his last dollar it was Sam Walker, the mysterious new arrival in town, but Agent Holliday had pretty much shot that down rather quickly.

The news about the truck and the load of money being found really had him confused. Whoever had taken the truck must have known about its secret cargo. That person had stolen the truck, driven it to a nearby county, made it so that the hidden money would be found, and then simply left it. The alleged anonymous caller who'd alerted the police in Greenville County was most likely the same person who'd taken the truck to begin with. That person had wanted the money to be discovered by the police, taking the money away from the cartel while simultaneously destroying the smuggling operation in one master stroke. If it was a rival criminal organization, they would have taken the money in the short term and made moves to take over the smuggling operation in the long term. The last thing they would have done is left the money and tipped off the police. With a rival cartel ruled out, who did that leave who might be trying to bring the whole thing down? How were they getting their information and staying hidden?

Sheriff Garrett felt his head start to pound as he tried to figure out who might be behind it all. It was a legitimate whodunit and he was baffled. Fortunately, he did have one ace in the hole. That ace in the hole was Deputy Chris Henderson and he was standing outside in the hallway waiting for his chance to talk to the sheriff. Henderson had been a deputy for five years and was one of deputies who was in on the operation. He was the deputy who was working the warehouse gate when the truck was taken. Deputy Henderson claimed that he had looked up through the window as the guy drove past him in the stolen truck. He swore that he'd looked the guy full in the face and would recognize him immediately again if he saw him.

Sheriff Garrett stood up from his chair and walked to his office door. He opened it and motioned for Deputy Chris Henderson to enter. Henderson was a tall, powerfully-built man in his early thirties with short blonde hair and blunt features. He looked subdued and nervous as he entered the office and came to stand directly in front of the sheriff's desk. The sheriff sank wearily down into his chair and looked up at Henderson. The deputy stared down at the surface of his desk. "Have a seat, Chris," the sheriff said. "We need to talk."

"Yes sir," Deputy Henderson said. He sat down in the chair Ronny had bene occupying just minutes earlier. He leaned forward. "Sheriff, just let me explain what happened from my end."

Sheriff Garrett held up one hand to stop him. "There's no need to explain, Chris," he said. "I'm not angry at you. You saw a truck leaving the warehouse, just like you see numerous times a day every day you work the gate there. No one in the warehouse raised an alarm or did anything that might have let you know something suspicious was happening. I don't think they even know where the guy came from or how he got the truck. We know he didn't come through the gate you were guarding, so it's not on you. It's on them."

Deputy Henderson looked relieved. "Thank you, Sheriff. To me, it was just a big rig leaving the loading dock area. It's not like the dock employees were chasing after it screaming. I didn't even know anything had happened until the guy had been gone for fifteen minutes or so."

"Now, Chris, this is important," Sheriff Garrett said gravely. "I know you told the guys at the warehouse that you got a good look at the guy as he drove by you."

"Hell, Sheriff, I looked him right in the face and he smiled and waved at me," Deputy Henderson said.

"Did you recognize him?" Sheriff Garrett asked. "Have you seen him anywhere else?"

Deputy Henderson looked at him, his face a mask of confusion. He was quiet for several seconds. In the silent interlude, Sheriff Garrett's personal cell phone buzzed in the case on his belt. The sheriff ignored it. "Is this a joke or something, sir?" Deputy Henderson finally asked.

Sheriff Garrett felt the anger start a slow burn in his chest. "What do you mean?" he asked. "What would I possibly be joking about?"

Deputy Henderson learned forward in his chair and pointed at the sheriff's desk. "That picture laying on your desk right there is the guy who was driving the truck," Henderson said. "I thought you had already found out who it was."

Sheriff Garrett looked down at the top of his desk where Deputy Henderson was pointing. The two photos they had taken of Sam Walker when he was brought in for questioning earlier that morning lay on top of a pile of other papers. Detective Roberts had brought him the photos earlier that morning when he came by to tell the sheriff he was releasing Sam after Agent Holliday gave the man an ironclad alibi. The sheriff had lain the single sheet of paper with the two printed photos, one full face and the other a side profile, off to the side and forgotten about it.

Sheriff Garrett snatched the paper up and shoved it across the desk at the deputy. "That's the guy who took the truck earlier? You're sure?"

Deputy Henderson took the picture and studied it carefully. "I'm sure," he said. "I saw him in profile and then he turned directly to me and waved through the window. It was weird, like the guy wanted me to get a good look at him. What kind of thief does that?"

Probably the same kind who would leave a truck loaded with money sitting there open and call the police, Sheriff Garrett thought to himself. "Are you absolutely sure it's him?" he asked Deputy Henderson. He didn't doubt the man; he just couldn't believe he'd gotten that lucky.

"That's why I thought you were messing with me, Sheriff," Deputy Henderson replied. "You're asking me about a guy whose picture is laying two feet away on your desk. He's our truck thief, that's for damned sure."

"That's great," Sheriff Garrett said enthusiastically. "I can't believe we identified him that easy. Good job, Henderson."

"Glad I could help, sir," Deputy Henderson said. "Sometimes you just get lucky. Anything else?"

"No, you can leave," Sheriff Garrett said. "Now that we know who's behind everything that's been going on, I've got some calls to make."

"I'll be glad to go with whoever you send to arrest him," Deputy Henderson said as he stood up and started for the office door. "I can still see that big smile he gave me as he drove by. He made me look like a fool and he was enjoying it. I wouldn't mind a chance to wipe that smile off his face."

"Don't worry, son," Sheriff Garrett said. "That's coming for sure."

Deputy Henderson left the office and closed the door behind him. The sheriff sat there behind his desk and studied Sam Walker's picture. He felt a small measure of relief now that he knew who had stolen the truck, but that knowledge brought with it more questions that swirled through his brain. He now knew who had taken the truck and left it to be found. The question of why remained. Also, was he the one who'd killed Stoner and burned the bar? Agent Holliday had sworn Walker was asleep in his hotel room at the time the incident at the bar was happening, so Walker must have an accomplice. Either that or Agent Holliday had lied about seeing him. Maybe he and Holliday were a team. They had shown up in town at practically the same time and in the same place. What were the odds?

The cell phone in the case on his belt vibrated again. Sheriff Garrett put the picture down and took out the phone. There were two text messages displayed on the phone's screen. The first message read simply *I am here*. The second read *we need to meet*. It was Garcia. The sheriff recognized the number as the one he'd dialed several hours ago from the burner cell he carried in his SUV. He now had that burner phone in his desk drawer close by because he'd expected Garcia to contact him on it. Somehow or another, the man had his personal cell phone number, even though the sheriff had gotten a new number just a couple of months ago.

The sheriff's mouth was suddenly so dry he couldn't swallow. It had been slightly more than fourteen hours since he'd made the call. "How in the hell did you get here so fast?" he muttered under his breath. He hadn't expected the man for a couple of days at least, but here he was, already in Easton. That could be either good or bad. It could be good because he could use Garcia's help and advice in dealing with the day's disastrous turn of events. It could be bad because Garcia would see just how bad the situation was now that the sheriff didn't have time to attempt some damage control on several different fronts. Considering that the theft and discovery of the truck had now effectively ended the cartel's smuggling operation, Garcia, the man who'd helped create it, was going to be understandably angry. Very dangerously angry.

Sheriff Garrett sat there for several moments as he fought to get his nerves under control and tried to figure out how to reply. Finally, he sent a text that read *major bad developments, will meet in person very soon.*

His phone buzzed with a reply almost immediately. It read simply *I'll be waiting.*

CHAPTER 30

The office at White's Hotel where guests checked in consisted of a small lobby with a couple of chairs, a waist-high counter the clerk stood behind, and then a small office through a doorway behind that counter. The door between the reception counter and the office was kept shut at all times and marked with a sign denoting Employees Only. Just through that door there was a second doorway inside the office that led to a small kitchen area complete with a table and chairs, refrigerator, and a microwave oven. A couch stood along the wall in the kitchen area as well. A small adjoining bathroom completed the area, which was reserved for employees of the hotel to take breaks when they needed to. Caleb sat on the couch at the moment playing with some of his dinosaur action figures. Amanda was over at the table, putting out dishes and cups for their pizza dinner with Mace Holliday.

Amanda hummed to herself as she set the table. She didn't even realize she was doing it until she saw her son looking at her quizzically. "You're making a happy noise, Mommy," he said as he looked up from the dinosaur battle he was enacting that had a stegosaurus busily stomping on a T-Rex.

It took a moment for her to realize that he meant she was humming, but when she realized she actually was, it surprised her. It had been a long time since she'd been in a good enough mood to feel like humming or singing or really even smiling, yet she was indeed humming away. "I am," she said softly. "I didn't even know I was doing it."

Caleb smiled at her. "I like it. It means you are happy. Are you happy, Mommy?"

Amanda thought about that for a moment. It was a question she really didn't know how to answer, perhaps because it had been so long since she'd felt truly happy. She was in a good mood, however, for the first time in way too long. She was also somewhat hopeful about the future as well. Logically, she had no reason to feel either emotion when she thought about it. She was in the middle of a nasty divorce from an abusive man who seemed to take special delight in trying to make her life as hard as possible, she had no job, and was back living in her grandparents' house. Also, given the way Ronny acted toward Caleb, she would probably end up being a single parent while her son's interaction with his father was nothing more than a monthly check for child support. Given those things lingering like storm clouds on the horizon, her pleasant mood surprised even her.

"I am, Caleb," Amanda said as she stopped putting out the dishes and walked over to plop down on the couch beside her son. "I'm happy because I'm your mommy and you are here with me right now."

Caleb cocked his head and looked at her. It was a little habit that he'd had since he was a toddler. It reminded her of the way a dog cocked its head when you spoke to it and it was adorable. "Are you happy because we're eating pizza with Officer Mace?"

Caleb sat there, surprised and unsure how to answer the question. Her five-year-old son had always been precocious and constantly surprised her with both his insight and some of the things that came out of his mouth. "Well, he's a nice man," she ventured. "He's fun to talk to."

"I like him," Caleb said. "He's not mean like Ronny is."

Amanda looked at her son. Refusing to call Ronny 'Dad' had been an issue with Caleb since the child was old enough to talk, despite both Ronny and herself trying everything to get him to call him that. He'd had no problem with calling her Mommy or any issue with any other labels like that, only with "Dad'. She wondered if it might be psychological because Ronny was so distant with Caleb on good days and outright mean to him on bad days. More than once she'd caught herself wondering if it was Caleb's intentional response to Ronny's tendency to refer to Caleb as 'it' or 'the kid', but that was hard to fathom given his age. Still, Caleb constantly surprised her so it was possible. Scary that he might be that smart, but possible.

"He is nice," Amanda conceded.

"Can Sam have pizza too?" Caleb asked innocently. "Is he coming to?"

Amanda really wished she knew the answer to that question. Sam had left the sheriff's office on foot following his interview. She knew that from talking to Mace. Sam had then walked to Smith's Garage and picked up his newly-repaired motorcycle. He'd told Jack Smith that he would take it for a test drive to see how it did before he continued his cross country trek. That had been hours ago and Sam hadn't returned. If Sam had a cell phone, he'd never given them the number and she'd forgotten to ask, so she had no way of checking on him. She'd even used her pass key to let herself into his room to see if his stuff was still there and make sure he hadn't slipped away. It was still there and the room was as neat as a pin. Given the length of time he'd been gone, she was starting to get really worried. She planned to ask Mace what he thought they should do if Sam didn't turn up soon.

"I don't think so," Amanda said. "After he got done talking to the nice police officers this morning, he went by and picked up his motorcycle from the garage. He planned to take it for a test drive, so he might not be back in time to eat pizza with us. But we will save him a few pieces. Okay?"

Caleb looked crestfallen. "I like Sam. He keeps us safe."

Caleb's choice of words was odd and Amanda was about to ask him what he meant, but before she could a buzzing noise filled the kitchen area. The buzzer was the door alarm for the office's front door. It buzzed every time someone opened the front door. "That must be the pizza," Amanda said. She had called in their pizza order to the local Domino's just before she'd started setting the table. "I'll be right back."

Amanda got up off the couch and walked through the doorway into the hotel office. She paused long enough to grab the money she'd laid on the desk for the pizza and then walked to the closed door that separated the office from the reception counter and lobby. She opened the door and stepped through it into the area behind the counter. As she did, she glanced down at the money in her hand to make sure she'd picked up all of the bills she had lain there. Because she was distracted, she didn't realize that the person waiting in the lobby wasn't the delivery person, but Ronny, her estranged husband.

Amanda had a split second to recognize that it was Ronny waiting there at the edge of the counter separating the lobby from the area where the clerk normally stood behind the counter and react before Ronny hit her. That split second gave her just enough time to partially bring her left hand up and jerk her head away from Ronny's incoming fist. That saved her from taking the blow squarely in the face where it most likely would have broken her jaw and knocked out several teeth given the strength and rage behind it. Instead his fist hit her on the side of the head just above her ear. Her world exploded into a hot flash of pain and she saw stars. She cried out and started to fall, but caught herself on the check-in counter. Ronny followed up with a punch to her ribs that drove the breath from her lungs and sent her to the floor.

"I told you I would get you," Ronny snarled as he towered over her. "You don't take what's mine and just walk away."

Amanda's first thought was of Caleb. He was just on the other side of the wall behind her. Once Ronny was done beating her, he would probably try to take Caleb. That was not going to happen, not while she was alive and conscious. As she landed on her back on the floor behind the counter, she kicked out with all of her strength. Her foot struck Ronny in the thigh and sent him stumbling back against the lobby wall. He laughed at her and started back toward her with his fist drawn back. "Bitch, you can't hurt me," he barked at her with savage glee.

Amanda scooted back on her butt and clambered to her feet. She stood up and faced Ronny. She glared at him with pure hatred. "Get out of here, Ronny!" she screamed. Ronny stood there just a few feet away breathing like an enraged bull. His eyes were wild and shot with red. He was obviously under the influence of something. She could smell alcohol, but this was something more. Ronny had always been abusive, but his appearance and behavior now had her wondering if he might actually kill her.

"Come back with me," Ronny said. "If you and Caleb come back now, I'll forgive you both. This is your last and only chance. You two belong to me."

"I'll never come back to you," Amanda replied. "And I'll die before I let you lay a hand on Caleb. Get out of here, Ronny, before you do something you'll live to regret."

Ronny took a menacing step toward her. "I'll drag you out of here," he said. "You and Caleb need to come home with me." His eyes suddenly teared up. "I'm going to die," he said out of the blue. "I've gotten involved with some people who are going to kill me and possibly you and Caleb too. You need to come home so I can keep you safe."

Ronny's moods were see-sawing wildly, going from rage one moment to what seemed to be fear the next. Normally Ronny was just mean and abusive, but now she wondered if he'd finally slipped over the edge to just flat-out crazy. She held up her hands in a calming gesture. Her head was pounding from where his fist had caught her. "Ronny, you're not making sense. Please, just go home. You can call tomorrow and we'll talk about this."

Ronny instantly flipped back to anger. "This is all your fault," he said bitterly. "Everything was going good until you left. Now everything's falling apart. You caused this!"

Amanda caught a flash of movement out of the corner of her eye. That flash of movement became the lobby entrance door opening and Mace Holliday stepping into the lobby. His attention was on Ronny. "Step away from the woman," Mace said instantly. "Do it now."

"You stay out of this!" Ronny yelled at him. "This is a husband and wife having a talk. It's none of your business!"

"You're under arrest," Mace said. "Turn around and put your hands behind your back."

Ronny took a menacing step toward Mace. "Fu..."

Ronny never got to complete the statement because Mace took two quick steps forward and drove his knee into Ronny's groin. It was one fluid motion, so fast and smooth that Ronny never knew what hit him. Ronny's face bore a comical look of utter surprise that morphed within moments into a look of pain as his mind processed the knee strike directly into his testicles. He gave a strangled groan and fell to his knees. Mace followed the knee strike by stepping around Ronny and forcing him down on his face into the lobby floor. Mace knelt on the small of Ronny's back, retrieved a pair of handcuffs from a case on his belt, and cuffed Ronny's hands behind him. The whole process took less than fifteen seconds.

"Ronny Easton, you are under arrest for criminal domestic violence," Mace said as he stood up from kneeling on Ronny's back.

"You can't arrest me!" Ronny said as he tried to roll over and sit up.

"Said the man lying in the floor wearing handcuffs," Mace retorted. He put one foot in the small of Ronny's back to hold him down. Ronny flailed and cursed loudly, but he couldn't budge. "Amanda, are you okay?" Mace asked over his shoulder to Amanda.

"I think so," Amanda said. She touched the side of her head with a trembling hand. There was already a lump there. "He hit me pretty hard."

"Mommy?" Caleb said as he peered around the doorjamb. His eyes were wide and he was shaking all over. "Are you okay?"

Amanda's pain was forgotten as she stepped forward and picked up her son. "Mommy's fine," she assured him. Caleb buried his face in her shoulder and began to cry. "It's okay, baby. Everything is okay."

Mace pulled his cell phone from the clip on his belt and dialed nine one one. When the Easton County 911 dispatcher answered, he identified himself and requested assistance. "I need a local police unit to transport a subject I have arrested for criminal domestic violence." He looked down at Ronny, who had stopped struggling and cursing and was now crying loudly, with disgust as he gave the hotel's address. Once the dispatcher had the information, Mace ended the call.

"Do you need medical assistance?" Mace asked Amanda with concern in his voice. "You still look a little dazed."

Amanda shook her head. "I'm good," she said. "Is he really going to jail?"

"Yes," Mace replied. "You're his wife and he hit you. By South Carolina law, that's domestic violence. I rounded the corner as he was preparing to strike you again. He's going."

"Amanda, tell him I didn't hit you!" Ronny insisted from his spot in the floor.

Amanda glared down at him. "He hit me," she said grimly. "I want to press charges. Enough is enough."

Mace nodded. "Take Caleb back into the kitchen there," he said. "He doesn't need to see or hear any more of this than he already has. A child shouldn't see their father dragged away in handcuffs."

"What happens now?" Amanda asked.

"Once the deputy gets here to transport him to jail for me, I'll have to follow him to the jail in my car to do the necessary paperwork and sign the warrant," Mace said. "That might take a while." He leaned close so Ronny couldn't hear. "I guess our pizza date will have to be postponed," he whispered.

Amanda nodded. She took Caleb and ducked back into the office and then to the kitchen area. She sat there, quietly consoling her son until she heard voices and movement in the lobby outside. She left Caleb on the couch and went back into the office. She opened the door just in time to see a uniformed Easton County Sheriff's deputy putting Ronny in the back seat of his car while Mace watched. She recognized the deputy as the one with the attitude who'd come by earlier that day to pick up Sam. Once Ronny was in the car, the deputy drove away.

Mace popped back into the lobby. "I'm leaving to go to the jail now," he said in a low voice.

To her own surprise, Amanda stepped forward and hugged Mace fiercely. "Thank you," she said. "I honestly think he would have killed me this time. He's completely out of his mind."

Mace hugged her back and then released her. He looked down directly into his face. "He's been taking something. His moods keep swinging from rage to paranoia to fear and back to rage. He swears someone is going to kill him."

"He'll be back," Amanda said. "Something has pushed him over the edge. I don't think it's just me and Caleb leaving either."

"If he comes back, he'll go back to jail," Mace said. "He's managed to get on my last nerve."

"Be careful at the jail, Mace," Amanda urged as she released her grip and stepped away from him. "The sheriff and many of the deputies are his buddies."

"I will be," Mace said. He turned and started toward the door, but then stopped. "By the way, you seen or heard from Sam?"

"No," Amanda replied. "I'm getting seriously worried."

"Me too," Mace said. "One problem at a time, though. Lock the door and I'll be back as soon as I can. If Sam isn't back by the time I return, we'll figure it out."

"Hurry, Mace," Amanda said as she followed him to the lobby door.

Mace nodded and walked out to his car. Amanda locked the door behind him.

Just a mile or so from White's Hotel, Deputy Cleveland pulled over onto the shoulder of the road and used his cell phone to make a call. The number he dialed belonged to Sheriff Lynn Garrett. The sheriff answered on the first ring. Cleveland quickly briefed the sheriff on what had happened at the hotel. "I've got Ronny in the back of my cruiser in handcuffs and I'm on the way to the jail,"

Cleveland said. "The BCI agent arrested him and is pressing charges. He's coming to the jail. He's supposed to be following me. Anyway, Ronny wants to speak with you right now."

The anger in Sheriff Garrett's voice was evident through the phone. "Let him. Put your phone on speaker and hold it up to the cage," the sheriff said. Deputy Cleveland put his phone on speaker and held it up to the wire mesh barrier that separated prisoners in the rear seat from the front seat. "What the hell, Ronny?" the sheriff demanded. "This is really the last thing we needed."

"I'm not sitting in jail, Lynn," Ronny said angrily.

"This ain't us making the charge, Ronny," Sheriff Garrett replied testily. "You messed up bad when you decided to punch your old lady in front of a South Carolina Bureau of Criminal Investigation agent, dumbass. I can't help you now, even if I wanted to."

"You either find a way to get me out of jail or I swear to God I'll be on the phone with the FBI," Ronny yelled into the speaker. "I'll start naming names. If I go down, we all go."

"Deputy Cleveland, this call is over," Sheriff Garrett said through the speaker. "Ronny is obviously suffering from some type of mental breakdown. When you get him to jail, book him in and have him placed in psychiatric lockdown in isolation. No visitors and no phone calls."

"Copy that, Sheriff," Deputy Cleveland answered. "It will be done."

Deputy Cleveland ended the call and tossed his cell phone into the passenger's seat. He turned up the radio so he didn't have to listen to Ronny rant, rave, and curse as he pulled away from the shoulder and continued on the way to jail.

CHAPTER 31

Sheriff Garrett tapped the screen, ending the telephone call with Deputy Cleveland and Ronny. He turned and tossed his cell phone onto the hood of his SUV with a disgusted sigh. "I assume you heard that," he said to the man standing beside him.

Garcia nodded. "Ronny is going to jail for attacking his estranged wife in front of a cop," he said somberly. "He wants you to save him. If you don't, he plans to roll over on you and, by default, us."

Sheriff Garrett and Garcia were meeting at the same place he'd met Stoner slightly over twenty-four hours earlier, the future site of his dream house. The site was secluded and the chance of them being seen together were practically nonexistent. Sheriff Garrett had gotten in contact with Garcia shortly after Ronny and Deputy Henderson had left his office. Any good feelings he'd had from identifying Sam Walker as the man who'd taken the truck and was probably behind everything else had vanished with the call he'd just gotten regarding Ronny. As evidenced by the call, any chance he had of keeping a lid on the situation and himself alive was vanishing quickly.

"He's a fool," Sheriff Garrett said hastily. "He's freaking out about the situation with the truck and money being found. Plus, he's been at it with his wife for almost a month. The man is wound way too tight."

Garcia turned and stared into the woods around them. Sheriff Garrett stood there and waited for him to say something. Garcia being quiet was a dangerous sign. The sheriff had already given him the details about the recent events in the county regarding the bikers, the truck theft, and the identification of Sam Walker as the truck thief. Garcia had looked troubled, but thus far he had just listened quietly. The sheriff was glad he was wearing his gun on his belt. There were no signs of a gun under the designer jeans and shirt Garcia was wearing, so Garcia didn't appear to be armed. That gave Sheriff Garrett a small measure of comfort, but not much. Being around Garcia was like being around a coiled-up and ready-to-strike rattlesnake; you couldn't relax for a moment.

"It appears to me, Sheriff, that the situation here is not something we can recover from," Garcia finally said as he turned back to face Garrett. "I have to say I am shocked by how thoroughly and quickly things here have fallen apart."

"It has hit the fan," Sheriff Garrett conceded. "What's Murphy's Law? Everything that can go wrong will. At least we know that this Sam Walker character- if that's even his real name- is the one who took the truck. I thought he might also be responsible for Stoner and the bar, but his alibi is a BCI agent here in town over Dwayne's shooting. So, either Walker has someone helping him or this Agent Holliday is in on it too."

"The odds of the BCI agent being involved are almost nonexistent," Garcia said. "He was sent here because Deputy Cothran killed that girl. Walker either has someone else helping him or the agent was mistaken. We need to get our hands on Walker and interrogate him. We need to know who's helping him, who he works for, and how he knew about the money shipment."

"I haven't met him face-to-face, but I understand he's pretty tough," Sheriff Garrett said. "He might not talk."

"I have some men I can bring in who will make him talk. There might not be much left when they are done, but they will get the answers we need out of him," Garcia said. "We'll need to know what he knows so we can clean up this mess." He walked over and leaned against the hood of his car. "I have to tell the boss about this," he added. "He's not going to be happy. He might order me to make a clean sweep of this whole mess. You know what that means."

Sheriff Garrett did indeed know what that meant. It meant that the cartel would kill anyone they had to kill to make sure nothing from the fiasco in Easton County would come back to haunt them. He figured he would be on the short list of victims. For a moment, he was tempted to just go ahead and kill Garcia, simply because he knew that Garcia would probably be the one who would kill him when the time came. However, he knew that doing that would just delay the inevitable. The cartel had an army of assassins they could send at their leisure. His best option, if he wanted to stay alive, was to keep Garcia on his side and use the man's evil brilliance to help fix the mess.

"You're talking about the nuclear option, Garcia," Sheriff Garrett said with forced calm. "The problem for you is that your bosses might not stop with us locals. Some of the blame might end up on you, no matter how unfair that is. But if we can somehow fix this, you will look good and I will look good. If we save this operation, it benefits everyone."

"And how do you propose we fix this?" Garcia asked. "I agree that I might also end up tainted by this catastrophe. I do not want that to happen. Our business, like any business, has its share of office politics, treachery, and egos. I have been told that I may one day be one of the big bosses. Because of that, I have people within our organization who would like to take me out because they want a chance for themselves. If I am responsible for redeeming this mess, my place will be assured."

"Then we are on the same page," Sheriff Garrett said quickly. "On the way over here, I was analyzing this situation and I don't think it's as bad as it seems. Take the situation with the truck being stolen and the money found in it. All Ronny would have to claim is that he knew absolutely nothing about the money on the truck. The money could have been put there by the person who took the truck from the warehouse. The guy who stole the truck might have been trying to put money in the drums where they found the truck. He got overcome by the chemicals and fled or something might have spooked him. I can cover Ronny's ass on our end with a stolen vehicle report. All Ronny has to do is keep his head together and we can pull it off. That gap between when the truck left the dock and when it was found in Greenville is a ton of reasonable doubt. We get Ronny a good lawyer and he'll be fine. Even better, we might can go back to using Easton Chemicals again in the future if he can convince the feds he and the company knew nothing about it. We will have to shut the operation down for a while, but maybe not forever."

"I would have thought that was a good idea until I heard your call with him," Garcia said. "He's unreliable. I don't think he's smart enough or tough enough to make it work."

Garcia had a valid point, but Sheriff Garrett wasn't going to give up that easily. His life literally might depend on it. "The other problem is Dwayne. The BCI is not buying his story on the girl. At the bare minimum, he might get charged with manslaughter for the shooting. If they really dig deep, they'll find out the truth. Dwayne will be looking at the death penalty, so I figure he'll do whatever to save himself. The big problem is I don't think we can wait and see how it goes. If they charge him and take him into custody, getting to him before he does some serious damage will be very hard, if not outright impossible."

"You're saying we need to deal with both Deputy Cothran and Ronny," Garcia said. "I don't want to, but I would be willing to write off our operation here in Easton. However, I will not take a chance on anything that might come back on the cartel."

"I think the only safe option is to take out Dwayne and Ronny," Sheriff Garrett said grimly. "However, if both of them are suddenly murdered, that's just going to prompt an even deeper investigation, the one thing we don't need to happen. Their deaths need to either look natural, like suicide, or be explainable under scrutiny. The good news is that if we can do that, it should put an end to everything."

"What about this Sam Walker fellow and the stolen truck?" Garcia said.

"The only people who know about Sam Walker taking the truck is the deputy who was manning the warehouse gate and me," Sheriff Garrett said. "We know he's staying at White's Hotel. We snatch him up, turn him over to your people, and you find out who he's working for. After they're done, bury what's left somewhere where it won't ever be found. I file the official stolen vehicle report on the truck without putting anything in it about a possible suspect. That's an easy fix on my end. That leaves Dwayne and Ronny. If Dwayne kills himself or something like that, the inquiry into the girl's death will end with him. Ronny's death could be a suicide because of his wife leaving him and taking the kid, plus the added stress of being investigated for smuggling."

Garcia thought about it for a few silent moments. The sheriff could almost see the man's brain working. "Two suicides would look too suspicious," Garcia finally said. "We need to find a better way to deal with both men that won't look so.....convenient. This Agent Holliday has already proven that he's pretty smart. He probably wouldn't stop digging until he found the truth."

"I'm brainstorming here," Sheriff Garrett said. "Thanks to Ronny getting arrested by Agent Holliday, I have him contained for now. He's on psychiatric lockdown at my jail, which means no phone calls and no bond hearing until we release him from that. I sent Dwayne home earlier today after he botched his interview with Agent Holliday. I assume he's still there, sweating bullets. I assured him I'm working on an idea that might save his ass."

"His size makes staging Deputy Cothran's death a problem," Garcia said. "Given advances in forensic science, staging a suicide is a lot more difficult than it used to be. Perhaps it would look better if we just made him vanish. We could make it look like he fled and is on the run from possible charges."

Sheriff Garrett thought about it. "That's possible, and easier than staging a suicide, but there's a good chance the BCI might not buy it. Plus, it means they would really dig deeply into Dwayne. That could still come back on us."

Silence lapsed between the two men as each of them tried to think of a possible solution to their mutual problems. The silence stretched for nearly ten minutes before an idea came to the sheriff. The out-of-the-blue idea quickly became a rough plan. The plan would require a number of things to fall into place, but if it went as well as he hoped it would fix all of their problems at once. With one fell swoop, they could deal with Ronny, Dwayne, Sam Walker, and even Agent Holliday.

Sheriff Garrett turned to Garcia. "I've got it," he said triumphantly. "I know a way we can fix this whole mess. The answer literally fell into our hands a little while ago."

Garcia cocked an eyebrow. "What answer would that be?"

"Ronny Easton," Sheriff Garrett replied. "He's the key to solving all of our problems at once. We'll just need some good luck and timing."

"And how is that?" Garcia asked.

Sheriff Garrett told him.

CHAPTER 32

Deputy Dwayne Cothran was sitting at his kitchen table using his laptop computer and the Internet to research state laws regarding obstruction of justice and manslaughter when his cell phone rang. He looked at the number displayed on the screen. It was Sheriff Garrett. He smiled for the first time that day. He'd been hoping to hear from the sheriff since Lynn had sent him home following the interview with Holliday. The sheriff had been furious at him because of how the interview went. Dwayne knew he'd screwed up bad, especially in hindsight, but he didn't think it was as bad as the sheriff acted like it was. He'd spent the hours at home researching state law on his computer and then on the phone with a friend who was a criminal lawyer. The lawyer didn't think they had enough to charge him with anything, but just in case the friend had suggested a criminal law firm in Spartanburg. Dwayne had an appointment for eleven tomorrow morning.

Dwayne answered immediately. "Yes?" he said. He was still kind of miffed about how the sheriff had treated him.

"It's me," Sheriff Garrett said without preamble. "I have a solution to our problems. Meet me in the rear parking lot at the office in one hour. Bring your tactical gear."

"What's going on?" Dwayne asked. "I heard about the truck today."

"It's related to that," Sheriff Lancaster said. "We've identified who took it. That's going to help us fix your situation and deal with Ronny at the same time. You in or not?"

"I've talked to a criminal lawyer about the shooting thing," Dwayne said. "He thinks I'll be fine. I have an appointment with a big law firm tomorrow."

"If this works out, you won't have to worry about it at all," Sheriff Garrett said. "You in or not?"

Dwayne didn't even have to think about it. "I'll be there," he replied.

"Don't say a word to anyone," Sheriff Garrett added. "Also make sure you bring a non-issue weapon with you in case this gets dirty. Understand?"

Dwayne knew exactly what Sheriff Garrett meant: He needed to bring a gun that couldn't be traced back to him or the department if he had to use it. That was not an issue; during his time on patrol Dwayne had collected a box full of weapons from people he'd arrested and never officially reported. The people being arrested didn't mind because it meant they avoided a firearms charge. Some of the guns were stolen, other were just in the possession of someone who shouldn't have had a gun. Regardless, they were untraceable. "Got it," Dwayne replied. "I'll be there."

With that, the call ended. Dwayne laid his cell phone down on the table. He had no idea what the sheriff had up his sleeve, but he trusted him. If the sheriff said he could help him with his current situation, he believed him. Lynn Garrett had been his best friend for many years for a reason. Dwayne glanced at his watch and saw that it was almost eight PM. He shut off the computer and hurried to the closet where he kept his department-issued tactical gear. As Chief Deputy, he was in charge of the special weapons and tactics team. If the sheriff wanted him in his gear, something big was going down.

The evening sky was just growing fully dark when Ronny Easton emerged from a side door of the Easton County Detention Facility. His anger at being arrested, along with most of the effects of the booze and drugs he'd ingested, had worn off while he sat in a padded cell reserved for psychiatric and suicidal inmates. He'd been booked into the jail, given an orange jumpsuit, and then put in that cell at the sheriff's orders where he was left alone and isolated. No one had checked on him, even though he'd cursed and screamed until he was hoarse and his throat was sore. Despite an epic tantrum that would have made a hyperactive three-year-old proud, no one had so much as walked by his cell. As the drugs, alcohol, and emotion started wearing off, Ronny had finally dropped off into an exhausted sleep about three hours into his stay in the padded cell.

The next thing he knew, he'd been awakened by his cell door opening. One of the detention officers had given him his clothes back and told him to get dressed for his bond hearing. Once he was dressed, he was taken to a small room set aside for bond hearings. The judge, one of the assistant county magistrates had released him on his own recognizance. He was taken back to the booking area and placed in a holding cell while his release paperwork was processed. He'd been given back his property, including his watch. To his great surprise, he'd only been locked up for about five hours. It had seemed much longer. The detention officer who unlocked his cell door told him that he had a ride waiting for him just outside the side entrance.

Now that he was outside, he stood there for a few seconds enjoying the fresh air and the breeze. It took a few seconds for his eyes to adjust to the dark parking lot following the bright fluorescent lights inside the jail. Once he could see, he saw that the small side parking lot was empty except for a few parked police vehicles and Sheriff Garrett's unmarked Chevy Tahoe SUV. Sheriff Garrett was leaning nonchalantly against the side of his unmarked Chevrolet Tahoe. "What's up, Ronny?" Sheriff Garrett said. "I'm your ride."

The moment he saw the sheriff, Ronny's temper flared back up. He stalked toward the sheriff, who continued to lean against his truck. "What the hell, Lynn?" Ronny demanded as he approached the sheriff. "Why did you have them put me in a padded cell?"

"Because you were acting crazy, Ronny," Sheriff Garrett said calmly. "Not only did you go and get yourself arrested at the worst possible time, you were talking out of your head, claiming you were going to roll over on us. What was I supposed to do? Let you call and spill your guts to the FBI simply because you were drunk and angry? What do you think would have happened to you in the long run if you had done that? I saved your life."

The sheriff's honest answer brought Ronny to a screeching halt. He stopped and stood there, his anger gone as suddenly as it had appeared. Now that he was little more sober and calmer, he could see the sheriff's point. He'd been so mad and scared over the events of the last few days that he was almost out of his mind. The drugs and alcohol he'd been using to help him handle the stress of his separation from Amanda, coupled with even more of both following the news about the truck, had pushed him to the edge. Even now, he still felt ragged and out of it, almost like part of his brain had burned out like a light bulb. "I was mad and panicking," he said. "I was just talking junk."

Sheriff Garrett smiled disarmingly. "We're friends, Ronny, and I know how you are," he said. "I figured the events of the day had you freaked out. I imagine the truck thing piled on top of your marriage issues had you on the edge. I'm sorry about the psychiatric cell, but I couldn't take a chance on it. I hope you understand."

"I have voice mails on my phone from the FBI and DEA," Ronny said. "They are going to come after me hard over the money in the truck, Lynn. I'm screwed." His voice had taken on a whining tone. "What am I supposed to tell them?"

"Well, now that you're sober and calm enough to comprehend what I'm about to tell you, I've got good news for you," Sheriff Garrett said. "I've had some time to think things over and I've come up with a plan that will keep you from having to worry about the feds or the cartel."

Ronny looked at him hopefully. "Really?" he asked. "What's the plan?"

"I'll tell you about it on the drive to your house," Sheriff Garrett said as he opened the driver's door. "Hop in."

"Thank God," Ronny said. "I could use a shower after that place."

Sheriff Garrett opened the driver's door and climbed into the vehicle. Ronny walked around to the passenger's side, opened the door, and got into the front passenger's seat. Due to the darkness and the truck's darkly-tinted windows, Ronny never noticed the man in the back seat right behind him. He never realized anyone was there until he felt the barrel of a pistol as it was pressed into the back of his skull. "Don't move a muscle," Garcia said as he pressed the gun firmly into the back of Ronny's head.

Ronny stiffened as if he'd touched an electrical wire. "What's going on?" he asked in a wavering voice.

Sheriff Garrett turned and looked across the seat as Ronny. As he did he clicked the button on his armrest that automatically locked the doors. "Ronny, this is Garcia. He represents our friends from south of the border. You need to sit very still and do exactly what I tell you to do. If you do, you'll be fine. If you don't, Garcia here will shoot you in the head. You understand?"

Ronny opened his mouth, but no words came out. He finally just nodded. Sheriff Garrett put the truck in gear and casually drove out of the parking lot. "Where are we going?" Ronny finally asked in a voice barely above a whisper.

"Your house," Sheriff Garrett said.

Forty minutes later, Dwayne and Sheriff Garrett stood in the rear parking lot of the sheriff's office building along with Deputy Cleveland and Deputy Henderson. All four men were heavily-armed and wearing black tactical gear complete with body armor, face masks, and helmets. The reflective panels with the words Sheriff and other identifying features had been removed, making all four men practically unidentifiable. The mood was quiet and somber, with none of the usual macho banter cops exhibited before a tactical operation. The sheriff had just gotten done detailing his plan and the men assembled around him were digesting it.

"I know what I'm asking of you three," Sheriff Garrett said quietly. "The reason I asked you three is because, like me, you all have a lot to lose. We've taken a lot of money from the cartel. Now we have to step up and earn it. I told you all from the beginning, when you wanted in, that this day might come, and it has. Due to circumstances beyond our control, this situation we're faced with can bring us all down. I'm not just talking going to jail, I'm talking death. Not just for us, but our families too. Either we handle this situation or the cartel handles it. I'm a single man with no kids, Dwayne is too, but Henderson, Cleveland, you two have wives and kids. Do you want to take a chance on something happening to them because we failed?"

"You know this is going to be investigated six ways from Sunday," Deputy Henderson said softly. "If it comes back on us, we'll be on Death Row."

Then we need to make sure it doesn't," Sheriff Garrett said gruffly. "I think we'll be fine as long as it goes the way I planned it. We have to make sure that it does. The margin for error is very slim." He looked at the three men. "If you want out, now is the time to speak up."

Deputies Cleveland and Henderson looked at each other, but then both nodded reluctantly to signal their agreement. "I'm in," Dwayne said while the two deputies were still nodding. Unlike the two deputies, Dwayne didn't seem to be reluctant in the slightest.

Sheriff Garrett breathed an internal sigh of relief. He'd never had any doubt about Dwayne, but Cleveland and Henderson were somewhat questionable. The two deputies had gladly jumped onto the cartel's gravy train shortly after beginning their careers with the sheriff's office. As a matter of fact, the sole reason the sheriff had hired them was because he had known both men since they were teenagers and knew that they would be willing to play the game. He knew Dewayne was a killer, but all the other two deputies had ever done was rough up some people. Tonight, they would be going way past simply roughing up someone.

"Let's go," Sheriff Garrett said. "Everybody ride with me. I have another vehicle for us to use waiting for us."

The four men got into the sheriff's SUV and drove away into the night.

CHAPTER 33

Amanda was sitting on a stool behind the counter in the hotel lobby when Mace's car pulled into the parking lot and parked. She watched as Mace got out and walked up to the door leading into the lobby. When he came in, she smiled wanly at him. "Hi," she said. Her head had finally stopped hurting, but she had a small knot where Ronny had struck her.

Mace walked up to the counter and stopped right in front of her. "Hi, yourself," he said. "I'm sorry it took so long for me to get back. Once I got to the jail, I had to write an incident report, then take it to the magistrate's office and sign a warrant. The magistrate was at dinner, so I had to wait. Once he finally signed the warrant, I had to take it back to the jail."

"How's my dear husband handling jail?" Amanda asked.

"Apparently not very well," Mace replied honestly. "They had him in a special cell on psychiatric hold. According to Deputy Cleveland, the deputy who transported him for me, Ronny started screaming and talking about killing himself on the way to jail, so they put him in a cell for inmates suffering from possible mental issues."

"He was probably just so mad that someone finally put a stop to his behavior that he threw a tantrum," Amanda said. "He's an overgrown five-year-old. Actually, I take that back. Caleb is almost five and he's more mature than Ronny."

"Speaking of Caleb, where is he?" Mace asked. "Is he okay with what happened earlier? It can be pretty traumatic for a little kid to see one of their parents hauled off in a cop car. I hate I had to do that in front of him."

The concern in Mace's voice was apparent and the fact that Mace was so concerned about Caleb touched her. "He's okay," Amanda said. "He's asleep on the couch back in the kitchen. He actually wasn't that upset, believe it or not, about his father going to jail. He was far more concerned about him hitting me." She shook her head. "Caleb has never really been close to his father. I suppose it's because Ronny was always so mean to him. Ronny has never called Caleb anything other than 'the kid' or 'the brat.' Caleb, in turn, only calls Ronny by his name or refers to him as 'him'. It drives Ronny crazy."

"Kids can be a lot more perceptive and smarter than people realize," Mace said. He looked directly into Amanda's eyes. "How do you feel about me arresting him? I probably should have asked you if you wanted to press charges, but I didn't want to put you on the spot. Since I actually saw him hitting you, your testimony is not required anyway."

"I'm very grateful," Amanda said. "I knew that eventually the day would come when he would snap and possibly hurt me bad or kill me. Thank God you came in when you did. Personally, I wish you would have beat on him a little while before handcuffing him. It would be refreshing to see him get a taste of what he loves so much to dish out."

Mace thought she was joking at first, but then he realized that she was dead serious. "I wanted to," he said. "I have no tolerance for a man who abuses anyone weaker than him, especially a woman or child. The fact that I know that woman and child and genuinely like them made it worse. It took every bit of my self- control not to give him a taste of his own medicine."

Amanda didn't miss the genuinely like them part of what Mace said. Hearing it made her heart leap a little, but good sense and reason brought her heart crashing back down. *He's just passing through and will be gone as soon as his investigation is complete,* her inner voice of reason said in her mind. *I'm a married woman with a child in the middle of what's going to be a very nasty divorce. What I'm feeling right now is just gratitude because a man is actually being nice to me. That and he just saved me from getting the crap beat out of me.* "That's so sweet," Amanda said. "You're a good man, Agent Mason Holliday."

"You're a good woman, Amanda Easton," Mace replied instantly as he looked across the counter into her eyes. "I know you're dealing with a lot of personal stuff right now. I just want to tell you to keep your head up. You're a beautiful woman, you're smart, tough, and obviously a great mom. Don't let one mistake, namely marrying someone like Ronny Easton, define who you are. Put him in the rearview mirror and find some happiness."

Deeply moved, Amanda spontaneously reached across the counter and placed her hand on the hand Mace had resting on the counter. Mace didn't pull his hand away. "Why couldn't I have met you about six years ago?" she said softly.

Mace was about to reply when the dark figures appeared from around the corner of the office and stormed through the door into the lobby.

Caleb was awakened from sleep by the voice in his head, the friendly male voice that he'd been hearing inside his mind for as long as he could remember. The voice didn't scare him because he knew who it was. The voice belonged to the man he'd learned about at church. The man was his friend and always took care of him and his mom. His calm voice had helped Caleb make it through all of the bad things Ronny had done to him and his mom. Caleb trusted the voice completely.

Instantly wide awake, he pushed off the blanket his mom had covered him with and sat up. He looked around and his eyes immediately settled on the back door. The back door opened to a sidewalk that led to his grandpa's workshop where he kept his tools and then to the dock and the boats there. The door was always locked because if it wasn't people could sneak in and steal stuff from the kitchen, the office, and the money drawer at the check-in counter where his grandpa checked people into the hotel. *Caleb, go to the door and unlock it,* the nice voice in his head said. *Hurry, little one.*

Caleb slipped off the couch and hurried over to the door. He had to reach up over his head to turn the little button that unlocked it, the one above the doorknob. Luckily, he was tall enough to be able to get to it and turn it. As soon as it clicked, Caleb reached up and turned the knob below it. The door opened with a slight creak. Caleb stepped back just as the man outside the door pushed it further open and stuck his head into the room. The man smiled at

Caleb and then held his finger to his lips in the gesture that Caleb knew meant that he needed to be quiet.

"Hey!" Caleb whispered excitedly as Sam slipped into the kitchen. "Mommy was worried about you. Where have you been?"

"I had something important I needed to do," Sam whispered. He looked over at the closed door between the office and the kitchen. "Caleb, I need for you to come with me. Some bad guys are coming to take your mom and Mace away. I'm going to stop them, but I need to make sure you are safe first."

Caleb's bottom lip started quivering. "Why are bad guys coming after my mommy and Mace?" he asked as his eyes teared up.

"Because they are bad," Sam explained simply. "Your mommy would want for me to make sure you are safe, and that's what I'm going to do. We are going to go and find you a secret place to hide where you will be safe. Once you're safe, I will rescue your mommy. Just like I did that day at the gas station. Okay?"

"Save my mommy and Mace first," Caleb insisted stubbornly.

On the other side of the wall behind the couch, they heard a brief cry and then the sounds of a struggle. "We need to go now, Caleb," Sam said urgently. Before Caleb could reply, Sam snatched him up, pulled him close to his body, and vanished out the open back door into the darkness.

Caleb struggled at first as Sam hurried through the darkness towards the marina and dock, but he quit as Sam pressed him into his body. It took barely thirty seconds for Sam to reach the marina office. Just past the marina office was a small storage building where Jacob kept tools and supplies for the marina. The door to the building was normally locked, but Sam still had the key in his pocket. He opened it and stepped inside into the dark interior. Once the door was closed behind him, he put Caleb down. Caleb whimpered in fear and confusion, but other than that he was silent in the darkness.

The storage building had a single small window that allowed light from a floodlight at the dock inside. It wasn't very much light, but it was enough for

Caleb and Sam to see each other's faces. "Caleb, do you trust me?" Sam asked softly. Caleb nodded. "Good. This is like a very important game of hide and seek," Sam said. "I want you to hide here until I come back for you. It will be just a few minutes, tops. I'm going to lock the door behind me just to make sure the bad guys can't come in, okay?"

"I want my mommy," Caleb said softly.

"Then I need to go help her and Mace," Sam replied. "It's what I do. I'll be back, little buddy. I promise." Caleb nodded reluctantly. Sam took his hand and guided him over to one of the corners where an old ice chest sat. He sat Caleb down on it and hugged him. "You're very brave, Caleb," he said.

Caleb nodded. The soft light filtering in through the single window made his eyes huge and luminous. "Go get my mommy, Sam," he said.

Sam nodded. He stood up and slipped out the door of the storage building. He closed the door behind him and Caleb heard the soft click of the lock. Left alone in the darkness, Caleb began to say the prayers Papa Jacob had taught him.

Mace saw the shock on Amanda's face as she reacted to something behind him. Mace reacted instantly, spinning around just as the lobby door flew open and four armed figures charged into the small lobby area. The first thing Mace noticed was their body armor, helmets, and masks. The second thing he noticed almost simultaneously was the absence of badges or anything else to indicate that the four figures might be law enforcement. Mace saw their guns and knew he needed to pull his own gun, but the first figure through the door was already too close to him for him to do that. That was still registering in his brain as Mace reflexively kicked out with a straight kick into the abdomen of the closest armored figure to him. The masked figure's body armor absorbed a lot of the blow, but the force rocked him back on his feet and sent him stumbling off to the side where he fell.

Taking out the first one through the door gave Mace a couple of seconds to try to draw his pistol. He had barely touched the grip of his holstered pistol when the second figure through the door fired the weapon he held in his gloved hand. The weapon was a Taser stun gun. The probe struck Mace in the chest and stayed there as the wire attached to it conducted a powerful electrical jolt through it and the probes and onto Mace's body. The effect was immediate. Mace's muscles instantly shut down as the electrical jolt short-circuited his muscles and nerve reactions. The pain was intense and Mace cried out as he crumpled to the floor. The jolt subsided momentarily and Mace tried to move. The figure holding the Taser pulled the trigger again following the first jolt with a second one. In severe pain, dazed, and unable to make his muscles obey his brain, Mace was helpless and another masked and armored figure stooped down over him and quickly handcuffed him. The gun in the holster on his hip was quickly removed. He heard Amanda scream and then she was thrown to the floor beside him and quickly handcuffed as well. She lay on her stomach in the floor beside him, her face turned to him, and her eyes wide and terrified.

A couple of minutes of confusion followed. Two of the figures stood over them and kept them at gunpoint while the other two hastily searched the lobby. "Where's the kid?" one of the figures asked in a male voice. The voice confirmed Mace's assumption that the four intruders were all men. "He's not here. The back door was open though," another male voice answered.

The voice was immediately familiar. Mace rolled on his side and looked up at the figures around him. The moment he saw the massive figure that had just walked from the office into the lobby, he knew who it was. Mace didn't say anything, however. He waited until he was pulled to his knees. The men did the same to Amanda. The two of them knelt in the lobby floor in front of the four intruders.

"Deputy Cothran," Mace said in a low deadly voice to the largest of the dark-clad figures, "I must say this visit is unexpected. I know that's you. The chances of there being someone else in Easton your size with access to what's obviously police-issued tactical gear are miniscule." He looked at the other masked figure that had just emerged from the office. "Sheriff Garrett, I know that's you as well."

Sheriff Garrett stepped in front of Mace and pulled down the mask that concealed everything but his eyes. He turned to the largest of the masked figures. "I told you he was good," he said to the figure. "I warned you, didn't I?" Deputy Cothran didn't reply as he removed his own mask. The other two figures kept their masks on.

"You two have just royally screwed up," Mace said as he glared dangerously at the two men. "You'd better have a damned good explanation as to why you burst in here and why I'm in handcuffs."

"Where's Sam Walker?" Sheriff Garrett asked bluntly. "We've already checked the room he claimed he was staying in when we interviewed him this morning. There's a back pack and some clothes in there, but that's all. Where is he?"

"We were wondering the same thing," Mace shot back. "The last time I saw him was at your office. I know he left on foot and that he went by Smith's garage and picked up his motorcycle. We haven't seen or heard from him since. We have no idea where he is or what he's been up to."

"I'll tell you what he's been up to," Sheriff Garrett said menacingly. "He went to Easton Chemicals around eleven this morning and stole one of their tractor trailers. We know it was him because the person at the gate positively identified him as the driver."

"This is news to us," Mace said. "That still doesn't even begin to explain why this woman and I are in handcuffs. We had nothing to do with that."

"Where's Caleb?" Amanda demanded. "He was asleep back on the couch in the kitchen. What have you done with my son?"

"I didn't see your brat," Sheriff Garrett replied. "All I found was a crumpled blanket in the floor and the back door of the kitchen open. I assume he heard us come in here and took off running."

"Why would a five- year-old take off running from a police officer?" Amanda asked in a wavering voice. "You better not have hurt him! He's a child."

"Amanda, we didn't find your kid," Sheriff Garrett answered. "Either you're lying about where he is or he's a lot more capable of some things than you think. It's a good thing for him that he's not here, though. Take it as a blessing."

"What do you mean?" Amanda demanded. "Why are we handcuffed? Neither of us has done anything wrong! He's a police officer just like you for heaven's sake! Somebody better tell me what's going on."

While Amanda was talking, Mace was observing the four intruders and putting it all together in his mind. A lot of the things he was seeing just weren't making sense. Two of the intruders were known lawmen, so he assumed the other two were as well, given their matching tactical gear and the way they had stormed the office and secured them. It was obvious to his trained eye that all identifying markings on the four men's outfits had been carefully removed so that they wouldn't be recognized as cops if someone saw them. He also noticed that each man carried a variety of guns ranging from holstered pistols on their belts to the assortment of assault rifles each man held. A legitimate police tactical team would all have the same issued weapons. The way the other two men kept their masks on and hung back told him that those two were having second thoughts about what they were doing. The intruders' stealthy approach and seeming nonchalance regarding a potential missing child further confirmed that these men were not on the level.

It only took seconds for him to put two and two together and what he came up with chilled him to the bone. "They won't tell us what's really going on, Amanda, because they aren't here for official reasons," Mace said. "This isn't really about Sam Walker or an alleged stolen truck. This is about me and my investigation of Deputy Cothran. They are here for me because I wasn't buying Cothran's story about the girl. They are afraid that I will keep digging. If I do, their whole operation might be found out."

Sheriff Garrett stepped back and applauded. "God Almighty, Agent Holliday, you're a regular Sherlock Holmes," he said sarcastically. "I guess it was just bad luck for everybody when Dwayne here had to cap that girl and they sent you. Why couldn't you be some old, burned-out agent close to retirement who would make a big show out of investigating, rule it justified, and head back to your office in Columbia? You didn't and now look where we are. In between you playing Super Detective and this Sam character showing up and messing with everything, drastic steps had to be taken. That's why we're here."

"I've got to know," Mace said as he looked up at Cothran. "What was the deal with the girl? It's obvious that your story about her just showing up randomly and stealing your truck is a bunch of bull. What was she to you? A girlfriend that you had a spat with and she took your truck? A local prostitute that ripped you off? My personal theory is that she is one of the illegals your biker buddies smuggle through your county. I think you were helping them smuggle her and she escaped, made it to your truck, and fled. Which one?"

"You're not as smart as you want to think you are," Deputy Cothran smirked.

Mace smirked back. "It's C, isn't it? That's the most logical explanation. Cothran, you, the sheriff, and these other two officers are getting paid off by the bikers to allow human trafficking through Easton. The girl you shot managed to escape and get your truck. You chased her down, but unfortunately there were two North Carolina Highway Patrol Officers right where she crashed your truck. You couldn't risk her telling her story. Luckily, she gave you a chance and you shot her, claiming you were protecting a fellow officer. It should have been a quick, easy investigation and then a ruling of justifiable homicide in the line of duty, but I showed up and messed it up."

Deputy Cothran stepped forward and stuck his pistol right between Mace's eyes. "I'll end you right now," he snarled. "Then, I'll take Mrs. High-And-Mighty Ronny Easton back to my place and make her wish I had killed her."

"Dwayne!" Sheriff Garrett said as his grip tightened on his own pistol. "We stick to the plan. We've already been here too long. Let's get them and go."

"Do you really think this will end here? By this time tomorrow the BCI will be so far down your throat, you'll be choking to death," Mace said as he calmly looked up at Dwayne past the pistol leveled between his eyes. "You other two guys better listen up. Sheriff Garrett and Dwayne here are going to get you both put on Death Row. Killing me is going to bring them all: BCI, FBI, and everyone else. Whatever plan the sheriff claims he has better be one thousand percent foolproof."

"It will be, Sheriff Garrett said firmly. "Get them both and let's get out of here."

Dwayne removed his pistol from between Mace's eyes, holstered it, and replaced his mask. Once his face was covered, he jerked Mace roughly to his feet. Sheriff Garrett replaced his own mask and grabbed Amanda. Dwayne wrenched Mace's arms behind him using the handcuffs as a grip. The sheriff wasn't quite as rough with Amanda, but he was exactly gentle either as he hustled her toward the lobby door. One of the other masked men walked out and held the door open. The second masked man led the way as Dwayne and the sheriff dragged their two prisoners out into the parking lot. A white Dodge van with Easton Chemicals painted on the side sat in the shadows just out of view of the lobby's plate glass windows. Amanda immediately recognized the van; it was a company van that Ronny usually kept at his office to pick up office supplies. Mace and Amanda were forcefully marched toward the van as the masked man in the lead hurried toward it to open the side door.

The group was just a few feet from the van when Sam Walker stepped from the shadows just beyond the van. "Looking for me, Sheriff Garrett?" Sam asked in a loud voice as he stopped several feet away.

Amanda felt the sheriff jump in shock at Sam's sudden appearance. The sheriff shoved her to the ground, clawed his gun from its holster, and aimed it at Sam. "Don't you move!" he barked at Sam as he stood over Amanda's sprawled form. 'You're under arrest!" The other two masked men drew their weapons and followed suit. Dwayne stopped as well, but he kept his firm grip on Mace.

"I'm being arrested? What a shock, Sheriff Garrett," Sam said casually. He grinned at the sheriff. "Are you arresting me because I stole the truck from Easton Chemicals? Or is it because of your business partner Stoner and the bar I burned down?" He rubbed his chin as if he was trying to think. "Maybe it was because I thrashed those three biker clowns the other day? Maybe it's because of Judge Cooper? After all, I'm the reason he wrecked. Which is it, Sheriff?"

"Don't you move!" Sheriff Garrett barked as he kept his gun trained on Sam. Sam's utter lack of fear at having a gun aimed at him from just feet away was making the sheriff very nervous. Most people would have been petrified and doing whatever they could to make sure they didn't get shot. "Get down on the ground right now spread-eagled!"

Sam looked at the sheriff and shook his head sadly. "Which is it, Sheriff, get down on the ground or don't move? I see now why you are a much better crook than you are a cop. Of course, you've never really been a good cop, have you, Lynn? You took the job because you were lazy and wanted to use the uniform to get women."

"Do what I tell you or get shot, man," Sheriff Garrett said with an edge to his voice. "I knew it! I knew you did the bar. That means Holliday here lied for you. You and him must be partners. That explains everything."

"We're not partners," Sam said as he took a menacing step toward the small group. He directed his attention to Mace who stood in front of Deputy Cothran. The deputy had a death grip on Mace's arm. "Just for the record, Mason, I didn't kill Stoner. He tried to pull a gun on me and we fought over it. In the process he accidentally shot himself in the femoral artery with his own gun. He bled out very quickly. There was nothing anyone could have done. I'm also sorry about tricking you into giving me an alibi. I made you see what I needed you to see."

Mace wanted to ask how Sam had managed to pull that one off, but now wasn't the time. Out of the corner of his eye he saw one of the masked men ease his Taser out of the holster on his belt. "Run, Sam!" he yelled.

"Pop him, Henderson," Sheriff Garrett yelled.

Sam didn't run. He just stood there and waited. A red dot appeared in the center of Sam's chest as Henderson, the masked man closest to the van, aimed his Taser stun gun and fired it. The red dot was a laser aiming device that showed the person firing the Taser where the probe would strike on the suspect. The probe and attached wire streaked toward Sam's chest. With amazing speed, Sam's hand shot up and caught the wire just a few inches behind the probe when it was just a foot or so from his chest. The probe dangled in the air and sparked uselessly as its energy charge discharged. Sam then jerked the wire and snatched the Taser unit completely out of the masked deputy's hands. The Taser clattered uselessly onto the pavement in front of the group. Sam dropped the wire and smiled. "If you boys are going to take me, you're going to do it the hard way." He looked at Dwayne. "You first, big boy," he said. "Or are you only tough when you've got some helpless girl chained up in that room in your basement?"

Mace felt Dwayne stiffen as if he'd just been suffered an electrical jolt. A low sound similar to a groan came out of the deputy's throat behind him. Sam noticed the deputy's discomfort and his mad smile widened. "Take notes on this, Mace. Deputy Cothran is a serial killer. That girl he shot had escaped from his homemade dungeon. She would have been his fifth victim. Her name was Lisita Gomez. She's from a small town just outside Matamoros in northern Mexico."

A stunned silence, made even more profound by the darkness and shadows around them, enveloped them all. "How do you know that?" Deputy Cothran asked in a shocked voice.

"That Easton Chemicals truck Sheriff Garrett is so mad about was loaded with cash going to the Baja Cartel," Sam continued. "They make a trip about every six weeks, carrying the money in drums marked as dangerous chemicals. The Greenville County Sheriff's Office has the truck right now."

Sam was about to say something else but Sheriff Garrett shot him twice in the chest with a Colt forty-five pistol he'd personally taken from Ronny Easton's gun cabinet earlier. The powerful rounds struck Sam squarely and sent him pitching backwards to the asphalt behind him. Sam landed on his back and lay crumpled there like a lifeless rag doll some angry kid had thrown. Blood immediately soaked the front of his shirt and began to pool around his body. He twitched a couple of times and then lay still.

The entire thing had taken only a couple of seconds, but to Mace it seemed to happen in slow motion. He heard the two loud booms as the sheriff fired the pistol in his hand. The noise momentarily deafened him. By the time his hearing returned, he could hear Amanda screaming and crying. She tried to get away from the sheriff but he slapped her back down to the pavement. One of the ejected shell casings rolled and landed beside Mace's foot.

"Check him," Sheriff Garrett ordered one of the masked men with him.

The masked man rushed forward and squatted down beside Sam's body. He reached over and checked Sam's throat for his carotid pulse. "He's dead," the man said. He stood up and retrieved the Taser from where it had landed nearby.

"So much for finding out who he's really working for," Sheriff Garrett said. "Garcia is going to be pissed, but it was unavoidable. The shots are going to draw attention, so let's get out of here now."

Amanda was dragged to her feet and hustled toward the van along with Mace. One of their captors opened the side door and the two of them were shoved into the back of the van on their stomachs. Sheriff Garrett jumped behind the steering wheel and Cothran rode up front with him. The other two men jumped in the back with Mace and Amanda. One of them slammed the side door. The moment the door was closed, Sheriff Garrett started the van and sped away from the hotel parking lot.

"Where are you taking us?" Amanda asked the man closest to her.

"Shut up," the man replied roughly. "You'll know when you get there."

Amanda looked at Mace. "They are going to kill us, aren't they?" she asked. Her voice shook and her face was deathly pale. She looked like she might faint at any moment.

Mace wanted to lie to her so her last few minutes on earth wouldn't be filled with terror, but he couldn't make himself do it. Amanda wasn't a fool and she would figure out what was going to happen. "I'm sorry about this," he said softly. "At least they didn't get Caleb." He turned his head so he was looking directly at the masked man closest to him. The two men in the back with them had taken seats with their backs against the van walls. They were just a few feet away from Mace and Amanda. "Rest easy knowing that the people responsible for this will never know a minute's peace for the rest of their lives. They are crooked cops. Even if all that happens to them is a prison sentence, it's still the death penalty. Instead of a nice quick needle in the death chamber, it will come to them in a prison shower room or in a cell."

The man Mace was making eye contact with turned his head to the side as if he couldn't bear to look Mace in the eye. "Shut up," he said. There was a faint tremor in the man's voice.

"I don't want to die," Amanda whispered softly. "I want to see my son grow up." Tears steaked down her face.

Mace slid over so that his body was right next to Amanda. In the dark interior of the van his face was just inches from hers. "This night's not over yet," he whispered softly. "I'm not going without a fight. Be ready when it breaks out."

"I'm with you," Amanda whimpered.

"If we survive this, I want that dinner date," Mace whispered.

"If you get us out of this, I'll marry you one day," Amanda whispered so softly that Mace barely heard it even though he was just a couple of inches away.

Mace nodded. He looked down his body toward the front of the van. He could see the faint outlines of Sheriff Garrett, Deputy Cothran, and the other two in the darkness. Lying there in the darkness with his hands cuffed behind his back and outnumbered four to one by armed men, he made a silent vow. No matter what, Amanda Easton was going to survive this night and go home to her son. He didn't care who he had to kill to make that happen or if he died in the process.

While Mace weighed the odds and tried to formulate some semblance of a plan that might work, Amanda fought back her terror and began to pray quietly for her missing child, herself, and Mace.

CHAPTER 34

Sam listened to the squeal of tires as the Easton Chemicals van containing Mace, Amanda, and the others sped away into the night. Once it was out of sight, Sam slowly sat up and took a deep breath. He sat there for a moment as the two entrance wounds in the center of his chest closed up, followed by the single exit wound on the left side of his spine. One of the bullets had passed cleanly through his body and exited through that hole. The second slug remained inside his right lung. Sam got to his feet, sucked in a deep breath, and gave a single violent cough. The dented and bent slug flew from his mouth and he caught it in his hand. He held it up and studied it carefully. It amazed him how much damage to a human body the little bits of metal could do. If he was actually human and capable of being killed, he knew he would be dead right now.

He tossed the deformed bullet into a nearby flowerbed. He looked down at the front of his blood-soaked shirt. He didn't really bleed; the blood on his shirt was nothing more than an illusion to fool anyone who saw him get hit by the bullets. With a simple thought, his bloody shirt disappeared and was replaced with another spotless tee shirt that looked exactly like its predecessor. He couldn't go and get Caleb with blood all over him. The poor child was already scared enough. With that done, he raced back around the building toward the marina and the storage building where he'd left Caleb.

Sam made it to the storage building and opened the door. Caleb was still sitting on the ice chest where he'd left him. "You okay, Caleb?" Sam asked.

Caleb nodded. "I heard shooting," he said softly. "Where's my mommy?"

"I'm going to get her," Sam promised, "but first I have to make sure you are safe. I'm going to take you to a place where I know you'll be safe while I'm gone."

"Papa Jacob's not home," Caleb said. "Where can I go?"

"I know a place I can take you," Sam said. "How would you like to ride on my motorcycle?"

Caleb's eyes widened. "That would be cool," he said enthusiastically, but then his face fell. "Mommy says they're not safe and I should stay away from them."

"Caleb, I promise you that I will keep you safe. You can even wear the helmet," Sam replied.

"Will you have a helmet too?" Caleb asked. Sam shook his head. "How will you be safe then?" Caleb asked.

Sam smiled and winked. "I'm hard to kill," he said as he scooped up Caleb and headed for the door.

CHAPTER 35

Jeff Bradley sat at his daughter's bedside and held her hand. His daughter, Lizzie, was in a coma. The child had gone to sleep about four hours earlier after a sizable dose of the medication they gave her for pain. Normally, Lizzie slept for a couple of hours and then awakened, whimpering from the pain in her head and unable to see because she'd lost her sight the day before, thanks to the tumor pressing on her brain stem and optic nerve. When she awakened, Jeff or Melanie would give her some more of the medication, then one of them would hold her hand and sing or talk to her until she lapsed back into sleep. Lizzie had not awakened for her last dose. They had called Mary, the hospice nurse, and she'd come to the house. After checking Lizzie's vitals, Mary had confirmed what both Jeff and Melanie already feared: Lizzie was dying. Their daughter was now in a coma and her breathing and heart rate were starting to slow. It was now just a question of how long.

Mary, the hospice nurse, was staying with them for the end. Mary was a petite woman in her late thirties with blonde hair cut short and pretty features. She had been a godsend since being assigned to Lizzie a couple of weeks earlier, becoming almost a member of the family over the last few days with her frequent trips out to check on Lizzie. Mary was now in the kitchen with Melanie, his wife. The two of them were drinking coffee and Mary was making Melanie eat something. Melanie had been at Lizzie's bedside for hours without eating or resting. Jeff was now alone with his daughter. The only light came from a small lamp on the bedside table. That table, the chair Jeff sat in, and the hospital bed where Lizzie lay were the only things that could fit in the small room given the size of the bed and the other medical equipment. Jeff was also tired, but he was afraid to go to sleep in case his daughter happened to wake up and need something. According to Mary, that wasn't going to happen, but he was unwilling to take the chance.

Jeff was staring at Lizzie's face when he heard the sound of a motorcycle pulling up in front of his house. He glanced at his watch and saw that it was nearly eleven PM. He had no idea who would be coming to his house at this time of night, especially on a motorcycle. The only people he knew in Easton who rode motorcycles were members of The Horde. Jeff felt his face flush and his heart quicken at the thought of one of the bikers coming to his house. He'd had a few run-ins with them in town, but it was just a part of his job as a law enforcement officer. It was nothing personal. However, if it was a member of the biker gang who'd dared come to his home, it was going to get personal really quickly. In a way Jeff hoped it was one of them because he wouldn't mind a good fight at the moment given the anger and grief inside him.

Jeff stood up, leaned down to kiss Lizzie's forehead, and walked out into the hall. He was walking down the hall toward the living room and the front door when he heard heavy steps on the front porch and then someone rang the doorbell. Melanie and Mary both walked out of the kitchen with looks of confusion on their features. "Who in the world….," Melanie said as she emerged from the kitchen with Mary behind her. Jeff held his finger to his lips, silencing her, and waved her back into the kitchen. He stopped at the coat closet in the hallway, opened the door, and reached up to the top shelf. He kept an extra pistol there in the event that he might need it one day. He took the pistol, checked the chamber, and went to the front door. He held the gun down by his side while he switched on the front porch light. He looked out the window beside the front door. Mary and Melanie watched nervously from the kitchen doorway.

There were two people standing on his front porch blinking from the sudden brightness of the porch light he'd just switched on. Sam Walker stood at the front door with Caleb Easton by his side. Sam was holding Caleb's hand. Thoroughly puzzled, Jeff unlocked his front door and opened it. He kept the gun down by his side and out of view. "Chief Bradley," Sam said as soon as Jeff opened the door. "Hey, Mr. Bradley," Caleb added as he looked up at Jeff.

"Walker," Jeff said casually, "what in the world are you doing here?" He looked Sam over from his head to his feet. He didn't see any weapons. "Caleb, it's good to see you. Where's your mom?"

"Amanda and Agent Holliday have been kidnapped by Sheriff Garrett, Deputy Cothran, and two other crooked cops," Sam answered immediately. "They came to the hotel and kidnapped them both. I was able to get Caleb out of there and run for it. They intended to take all four of us. I brought him here because this is the only safe place I could think of."

Jeff stood there, disbelief and confusion evident on his face. "Do what?" he asked. "What in the world are you talking about?"

"Chief, can we please come in?" Sam asked. "I know this is weird, and an incredible intrusion given your circumstances right now, but you are literally the only other person in Easton County I know and trust with Caleb's life. You can keep the gun you have in your right hand concealed behind this door trained on me the whole time if you want, but please let me come in and explain."

"How did you know I have a gun?" Jeff asked incredulously.

Before Sam could answer, Melanie appeared in the hallway behind him and peered over his shoulder at Sam and Caleb. "Hello, Mrs. Bradley," Caleb said cheerfully when he saw her face over her husband's shoulder.

"Hello, Caleb," Melanie said softly. She nudged her husband in the back. "Jeff, let them in," she added firmly. "They need our help."

Jeff wanted to say no, to tell her that now was the absolute worst time he could possibly imagine to have someone else in their house, but something inside him wouldn't let him. He tucked the gun into the waistband of his jeans at the small of his back. "Come in," he said reluctantly. "Mr. Walker, you've got two minutes to explain all of this to me. It had better be good." He opened the door and waved Sam and Caleb inside to the living room.

"Mrs. Bradley, could you take Caleb into the kitchen and get him something to eat?" Sam asked as he cut his eyes toward the kitchen. "I imagine he wouldn't mind a cookie or something."

Melanie took the hint. "I bet you're right," she said softly. She reached down and took Caleb's hand from Sam's grasp. "What do you think, Caleb? Chocolate chip cookie?" Caleb nodded enthusiastically. Melanie led him away into the kitchen.

"Talk," Jeff said flatly once Caleb was out of earshot. "My daughter is lying in a hospital bed right down the hall in a coma, so I don't have the time or patience for too much right now. Give me the short version of that story you told me at the door, especially the part as to why you, a complete stranger, have Caleb with you without Amanda."

"We need to sit down for a few minutes while I explain it all," Sam said.

"Not happening," Jeff said brusquely. "Like I said, short version."

"Okay then," Sam said. He took a deep breath. "Sheriff Garrett and a sizable number of his employees at the sheriff's office are part of a criminal conspiracy that also involves an extremely dangerous criminal cartel in Mexico and The Horde, the biker gang we're both so fond of. The sheriff and his men have been getting paid off to facilitate human and drug trafficking through Easton County, just like you and pretty much everyone else in this county always suspected. Ronny Easton is also involved. He's been using Easton Chemicals to smuggle the cartel's money back into Mexico. They hide the cash in drums marked as chemicals and the drums are shipped to a cartel-owned business in Mexico. For his help, Ronny also gets paid an obscene amount of money. Now, it's all crashing down around them and the sheriff has to clean up the mess to save his own skin. The sheriff's way of doing that involves killing several people, including Agent Holliday, Amanda, Deputy Cothran, and Ronny Easton in an effort to cover his tracks. Sheriff Garrett also would have killed Caleb if I hadn't intervened."

Sam paused for breath. Jeff blinked a couple of times. "Uh, we need to sit down for a minute," he said. "My head is spinning." He sat down in the closest chair, a rocking chair where he'd spent many hours rocking his infant daughter and reading her stories. Sam took a seat on the edge of the couch beside the rocking chair. "How has it come crashing down around them?"

"Because of me," Sam said simply. "I was sent here to kick-start a process that would have a specific result. Everything is in play now. Now I just need to wrap it all up nicely."

"Who are you?" Jeff demanded numbly. "I know your real name isn't Sam Walker. Who are you and who are you working for? What process are you talking about?"

"There are some things going on that would be difficult for you to wrap your mind around," Sam continued calmly. "Some evil people need to be dealt with and some people and events need to be nudged along in the right direction. I'm talking real big-picture stuff, Jeff. By tomorrow morning, people will be dead and others will be picking up the pieces. You're the last honest lawman in this county. All I need from you is for you and Melanie to watch over Caleb until someone comes for him. That's all."

"You said Sheriff Garrett and his men have taken Amanda and Agent Holliday," Jeff stammered. "Why would they do that?"

"Deputy Cothran is a serial killer who's killed six people," Sam replied. "Cothran shooting that girl a few days ago was the final piece of the puzzle and it kicked everything else into high gear. That girl was an illegal immigrant smuggled into this country and given to him as part of his payment for his involvement. He holds them captive in the basement of his house, rapes and tortures them until he's tired of them, and then kills them."

"How do you know this?" Jeff asked incredulously.

"I'm the one who unlocked the girl's shackle so she could get free and make a run for it," Sam answered. "I was watching her and waiting for the right time. I hate she had to die, but her death- like all deaths- served a purpose. Her death brought Mason to Easton. He saw through Cothran's lies. Because of that and other events I set into motion, the sheriff fears a major investigation that would uncover his corruption. The sheriff plans to kill Mace and Amanda. Mace because he was getting close to the truth. Amanda is collateral damage. The sheriff plans to make it look like Ronny Easton killed them."

Jeff's head was spinning. "What do you plan to do?"

"I know where the sheriff is headed," Sam said. "I'm going there to put an end to this. I just need for Caleb to be in good hands while I do it. I also need for you to give me about ten minutes head start and then call the South Carolina

Bureau of Criminal Investigations headquarters in Columbia. Identify yourself and tell them that one of their agents has been kidnapped by corrupt cops and his life is in grave danger. Send them to Ronny Easton's house."

"They will think I've lost my mind," Jeff said. "How do I know this isn't some made-up story? You could be crazy. You could have kidnapped Caleb for all I know. Besides, why did you bring this nightmare to my house with my daughter at death's door? Damn you!"

Jeff's raised voice brought Melanie into the living room from the kitchen. "I'm sorry, but I was eavesdropping," she said forthrightly to both men before she directed her attention to her husband. "Jeff, I think you should trust him," she said. "I just tried Amanda's cell phone and it went straight to voice mail. You know she wouldn't let Caleb out of her sight unless something bad has happened. Just now, in the kitchen, Caleb said he heard loud noises in the hotel lobby right before Sam came and got him. Do you think he would bring Caleb to another police officer's house if he'd kidnapped him from his mother? Something weird is going on!"

"Thank you, Melanie," Sam said as he stood up. "I've got to go. Take care of Caleb. Give me ten minutes and then call the cavalry, please."

Jeff sighed wearily. He looked pale and exhausted, but also determined. "You've put me in a bad spot. I need to go with you," he said. "I can't sit here idly while Amanda and a fellow officer get killed. However, I don't want to leave Lizzie." He looked at his wife in anguish. "Baby, I can't leave you here to face this alone and I can't sit by and let someone be murdered. What am I supposed to do?"

Melanie stepped forward and gently took her husband's face in her hands. "You heard what Mary told us earlier," she said softly. "It could be hours or days before Lizzie passes." Tears began to fall from her eyes. "And nothing either of us do here will make a difference. You can make a difference for Amanda and Agent Holliday, however. Go do what you swore an oath to do: Uphold the law and help others."

Jeff's own tears began to flow. "I don't want my baby girl to die without her daddy being there for her."

"You're always with her," Melanie said softly. "Not even cancer and death can take you out of her heart and mind. You know that deep in your heart."

"I should be here for you," Jeff protested.

"You have been and you will be," Melanie answered. "We both know that. If you can make something good out of this terrible night, go do it."

Jeff nodded, then leaned down and kissed his wife fiercely. "I love you," he said as he broke the kiss. Melanie nodded and stepped away. "Give me five minutes," Jeff said to Sam.

"I'm taking my bike," Sam said. "They are at Ronny's house on Canaan Road where he and Amanda lived. You need to wear body armor and bring some serious firepower. Get that stuff, call the BCI, and head that way. I'm going now."

"You're going alone?" Jeff asked.

"Amanda and Mace are running out of time," Sam said. "I can't wait."

"You're either going to get them or yourself killed," Jeff said. "Wait for me. If we were both smart, we'd wait for the BCI."

Sam simply shook his head and started for the front door. He had almost reached the door when Caleb bolted out of the kitchen and ran to him. Caleb grabbed Sam's leg and held on fiercely. "Don't leave, Sam!" Caleb cried. "Please!"

Sam squatted down so that he was face to face with Caleb. "I'm going to get your mom, little buddy," he said gently. "Jeff is going to help me so he can arrest the bad guys. You stay here with Melanie and the other nice lady and keep an eye on things, okay?" Caleb looked as if he was about to start crying, but he fought it back. "There is one more thing I would like for you to do, Caleb," Sam added.

"What?" Caleb asked.

Jeff and Melanie watched as Sam leaned in and whispered something into Caleb's ear. Caleb's eyes grew wide as Sam whispered to him. Once Sam was done, Caleb nodded vigorously. Sam hugged the child and stood up. He nodded to Jeff and Melanie once before turning and walking out the front door. A few moments later they heard a motorcycle start. Jeff went to the door and watched as Sam rode off into the night.

Following Sam's departure, the next several minutes flew by in a burst of frantic activity. Jeff vanished into his bedroom and emerged wearing the bulletproof vest and gun belt he wore on duty, jeans, boots, and a tee shirt with Police on the back. He stopped in Lizzie's room, whispered softly into her ear, and gave her a long kiss on the forehead. His daughter's breathing was still steady and strong, almost as if she was just in a deep sleep. "Just hang on until I get back, Lizzie," he said softly to her.

Melanie was waiting for him with his cell phone in hand and a number written on a scrap of paper. "That's the BCI's emergency number," she said as she pressed the paper into his hand. "I looked it up for you."

"I'll call them on the way there," Jeff replied. He stopped and hugged and kissed his wife. "I guess you should find Caleb a place to sleep. I don't know what's going to happen or how long I'll be," he said as he looked down into her eyes.

"I'll handle everything here," Melanie promised. "I've got Mary here to help me. All of us, including Lizzie, will be okay. Just make sure you come home to me, Jeff."

Jeff nodded, grabbed the keys to his police cruiser, and headed for the door.

Jeff had been gone for barely five minutes when Melanie realized that she had lost track of Caleb. She had put the exhausted child in the master bedroom on their bed in hopes that he would get some sleep. Once he was dozing off, she'd stepped into the bathroom that adjoined the bedroom to use it. When she emerged a few moments later, the bed was empty. Puzzled, Melanie hurried out of the bedroom and down the hallway to the living room. Mary, the hospice nurse, was sitting on the living room couch working on her laptop. "Mary, have you seen Caleb?" Melanie asked as she hurried down the hall into the living room.

"No," Mary said. "I'm sorry. I was on my laptop updating some files and I wasn't paying attention."

Melanie continued down hallway into Lizzie's room. Caleb was in there. He had pulled up a chair beside Lizzie's hospital bed and was sitting in it. He was holding Lizzie's hand and studying her face intently in the dim light of the small lamp by her bed. "I thought you were asleep, Caleb," Melanie said as she stepped in to Lizzie's room.

Caleb looked at her. "Is Lizzie still sick?" he asked. Melanie nodded quietly. "Will she feel better?"

Melanie stood there, too drained by her own emotions and the events of the night to think of anything else to say but the truth. "She's going to die," Caleb," she finally answered. "She's going to Heaven soon. There's nothing the doctors can do to make her better."

Almost as soon as she said the words, Melanie regretted them. The poor child was already dealing with his mother being abducted, not to mention the previous events with his father. The last thing he needed was to know that Lizzie, his favorite playmate on Sundays in the youth program at church, was dying. Remarkably, Caleb seemed to take the news with surprising calm. "Can I stay here and pray for her?" he asked simply.

Caleb's request moved her beyond words. "For a few minutes," Melanie answered, "but then you need some sleep, Mister."

Caleb simply nodded. Melanie took a seat in the recliner Jeff had moved into the room. She settled back into the chair's cushions as Caleb bowed his head. She'd planned to give Caleb a few minutes before she carried him off to bed. However, she was the one who dozed off almost instantly as the exhaustion, stress, and grief of the last few weeks hit her like a ton of bricks.

CHAPTER 35

Mace and Amanda felt the van slow and then make a right turn. A couple of minutes later the van stopped and the engine was shut off. Sheriff Garrett and Deputy Cothran got out of the van first. Once those two were out, the two men in the back with them opened the side doors and got out. "Both of you get out now," one of the masked men ordered Mace and Amanda.

"How are we supposed to do that with our hands cuffed behind us?" Mace asked from his position in the floor of the van. Amanda lay right beside in the van's floor as well.

One of the masked men swore angrily. He gave his partner his rifle, reached into the van, and dragged Mace roughly over to the side door of van. "Put your feet on the ground and stand up," he said. Mace complied and was able to stagger to his feet. The masked man did the same with Amanda. The second masked man kept his rifle trained on Mace as Amanda struggled to stand up straight.

Mace took the opportunity to check out where he was. Even though it was dark, lights from the inside shining through the windows and exterior floodlights enabled Mace to clearly see his surroundings. He was at a large house that appeared to be sitting on top of a small hill somewhere out in the country. The house was only one story and built to resemble an Italian villa. The exterior was pale brick and stucco, the windows were large and numerous, and the door and window frames were arched. A paved driveway ended at front courtyard and entrance paved with brick. A lion stature flanked each side of the steps leading from the courtyard to the home's massive wooden front door. The grounds he could see were carefully landscaped and well-maintained. Ronny's Range Rover was parked in the front courtyard. Beside it were an inconspicuous Toyota Camry and a dark-colored Chevrolet Tahoe that Mace recognized as belonging to Sheriff Garrett.

"Why are we here?" Amanda asked Sheriff Garrett when he came around the front of the van to the side door. "Why did you bring us to my house?"

"You'll see soon enough," Sheriff Garrett said as he took Amanda by the arm and led her toward the front door. "Dwayne, get Agent Holliday and bring him. You two guys stay out here and keep an eye out until we're done," he added as he pointed to the other two men. "This won't take long."

Mace and Amanda were marched up to the front door. When they reached it, the door was opened by a handsome young man with a tan complexion wearing designer clothes. He wore latex gloves. He stepped back out of the way as Mace and Amanda were forced into the house by the sheriff and Deputy Cothran. "Where is he?" Sheriff Garrett asked the man at the door as Mace walked by into the house.

"Living room," Garcia said. "I'm glad you're back. He was really getting on my nerves."

"That's Ronny for you," Sheriff Garrett said.

Cothran forced Mace into the house through the foyer and into a large, open area that was the house's living room. The room was beautifully furnished and the artwork on the walls was tasteful and looked valuable. A couple of lamps illuminated the room. A family picture of a younger Amanda posed beside Ronny Easton hung on one wall. The glass in the picture frame was broken as if someone had punched the picture in a fit of rage. Despite the abundance of chairs and sofas in the room, Ronny Easton sat on the floor in the living room with his back against the wall just a few feet from a massive fireplace. His hands were secured behind him with a pair of handcuffs. He looked up when the others came in. "Amanda!" he cried. He glared at Sheriff Garrett. "Why is she here?"

Sheriff Garrett ignored Ronny's question as Mace and Amanda were marched over to one of the couches. "Sit down," Sheriff Garrett ordered. Mace sat down on the edge of the sofa. Amanda took a seat beside him. Once the two of them were seated, Cothran, the sheriff, and Garcia stepped back. They huddled together and seemed to be conferring.

Amanda leaned over to whisper to Mace. "What's going on? Why are we here?"

Mace had an idea what was going to happen, but he did not want to tell Amanda. The fear etched on her face was enough to break his heart and he did not want to add to it. Still, he felt like he owed her the truth. "I suspect this is where they're going to kill us. If we're going to make a move, it's going to have to be in the next few moments."

Amanda nodded grimly. "Ronny always kept a gun in the top drawer of that set of drawers over there by the archway that leads into the foyer," she whispered. "It's a revolver. He claimed it was for home protection. It used to worry me one Caleb started toddling around. He refused to move it. I'll bet it's still there."

Mace looked over and saw the square chest with several drawers on the front Amanda was referring to. It was only about fifteen feet away, but with his hands cuffed and their three captors between him and it, it might as well have been on Mars.

Mace was weighing his other options when the sheriff turned to Mace and Amanda. "I bet you're wondering why you're here."

"You intend to kill us," Mace answered. "I had an idea of what you had planned when I saw Easton Chemicals on the van. As soon as I saw Ronny sitting over there handcuffed, I put the rest of the pieces together. If I wasn't in the position I'm in, I'd almost be impressed with your creativity, Sheriff."

Sheriff Garrett smiled. "Would you care to enlighten the others?" he asked.

"You're going to shoot Amanda and me with guns you've taken from Ronny," Mace surmised. "Then you're going to shoot Ronny with your duty weapon. Your story will be that Ronny abducted Amanda and me from the hotel, brought us here, and killed us. The whole jealous-estranged- husband- kills- wife scenario. I assume I'm collateral damage? Wrong place, wrong time?"

"Ronny getting himself arrested by you today was a godsend," Sheriff Garrett answered. "You went from simple wrong place wrong time collateral damage to the victim of a revenge killing."

"Somehow or another, you found out we had been abducted," Mace continued. "What's the story going to be? That Ronny called you admitting what he'd done? That's the easiest way."

"On the way here, I received a call on my cell phone from Ronny's home telephone," Sheriff Garrett said proudly. "It had to be something verifiable."

"Ronny calls and confesses what he's done to you, his good friend," Mace said. "You came here with Deputy Cothran and the other two guys who I assume are your deputies as well. Upon arriving here, you were confronted by Ronny and you were forced to shoot him. Tragically, you were too late and we had already been killed."

The sheriff applauded. "God damn you're good!" he said to Mace. "I hate this. I really do. Why couldn't you just come in, do some paperwork, and then leave, Agent Holliday? If you had, we wouldn't be here. I've got to know, are you in cahoots with your dead friend, Sam, or is it all bad timing?"

"Never seen the man before in my life until I arrived in your county," Mace said calmly. "If what Sam said back at the hotel before you killed him true?"

"Every bit of it," Sheriff Garrett said gleefully. "I would love to have known how he knew so much about everything and I wish like hell we could have turned him over to our Mexican friends so they could find out who he worked for, but it didn't go that way. Regardless, he's not a problem anymore."

"I guess that worked out for you then," Mace said. "Just like me arresting Ronny earlier today. I guess you were worried about him ratting you all out once the whole smuggling thing was discovered today. I figure you're killing me because if I kept digging on your deputy there, the truth would come out. Amanda here is the real collateral damage."

"Afraid so," Sheriff Garrett said. "Waste of a good woman, but some things can't be helped."

"So, who is your Hispanic friend there?" Mace asked as he looked at Garcia. "I assume you're from the cartel? What are you, a hitman?" Garcia didn't answer. "One last question," Mace added. "Which of you plans to shoot Deputy Cothran?"

Deputy Cothran was standing just a few feet away. "Huh?" he asked when he heard Mace's question.

"I'll bet there's another part of the plan you don't know about," Mace said. "You're going to die tonight too, Cothran. You shooting the girl caused all of this. The only surefire way they can be sure you won't roll over on them if you're charged in the girl's death is to kill you too." He looked back at the sheriff. "What was it going to be, Sheriff? Cothran gets hit by a lucky shot from Ronny as he breached the door?"

Sheriff Garrett drew the pistol he'd used to shoot Sam earlier at the hotel. He aimed it squarely at Mace. "Ignore him, Dwayne. He's trying to save his own skin."

"Think about it, Dwayne," Mace said. "Even if I'm dead, supposedly by Ronny's hand, do you think that ends the investigation into the girl? There will just be another BCI agent to take my place. I've got another news flash for you: We're all pretty smart. Chances are the next agent will spot the same inconsistencies in your story I did. But if you die tonight in a shootout with poor, old, deranged Ronny Easton, the case is over. The BCI will stop investigating because you are dead."

"You're full of ...," Dwayne started to say.

"I've already emailed my updated reports about what I found today to the chief of the BCI," Mace shot back. "Think about it, Dwayne. This morning he was furious at you and ordered you out of the sheriff's office building. All of a sudden, he calls you and gets you to take part in this. I'll bet he told you that killing me would end it. That's a lie because I told him I would be sending my findings to my boss at the BCI today. Also, the most damning evidence I have on you is the bottle of nail polish. It's locked in the trunk of my car at the hotel. I noticed no one even tried to get that and destroy it."

Dwayne stood there for a couple of seconds as if he were thinking about what Mace was saying. "You're a lying son of a bitch," he said as he raised the M-14 assault rifle he held in his hands and took aim.

Deputy Chris Henderson stood in the front courtyard where the vehicles were parked with his back to the house. He was glad that he wasn't inside and taking part of what the sheriff had planned for the captives inside. Henderson was already seriously regretting being involved in what had already transpired, and he definitely wanted no part in shooting a BCI agent and an innocent woman. Even more sickening to him was the realization that Sheriff Garrett had also planned to kill the kid if he'd been there. Thankfully the child wasn't there, but the sheriff's willingness to kill him if he was had really opened Henderson's eyes to just how dangerous the man was. A man willing to kill a child would do anything. Not for the first time, Deputy Henderson wondered just how far he'd fallen down the hole of being a bad cop. Taking bribes to ignore a crime was one thing. Killing other cops, women, and children was another. He wondered where it would stop.

Deputy Henderson already knew he was in too deep. What had begun as simply accepting a few extra hundred dollars a month to make sure no one bothered the vehicles transporting illegal immigrants, the money truck, and the bikers had now become taking an active part in murder. The sheriff's plan seemed pretty smart and like it would work, but if it didn't and the truth came out, they all would be lucky to get life in prison with no parole. Of course, life in prison for a cop would, in reality, be a death sentence anyway. The thought of getting raped to death in a prison shower room didn't appeal to Henderson in the least.

Henderson looked over to where Deputy Jimmy Cleveland stood several yards away near the steps that led from the courtyard to the front door. Henderson knew from talking to him earlier that Cleveland was in the same boat as him: drafted into doing something he wanted no part of but unable to find any way out of it. Henderson knew that it was really bothering Jimmy too because the man hadn't said much since the hotel. Cleveland was one of those guys who wouldn't shut up, always bragging about something they had done or planned to do. Another sign that Cleveland was terrified was the fact that the man had already vomited twice into the grass. He claimed that he'd eaten some bad food earlier in the day, but the fear on his face told the real story. Cleveland, like him, knew he was now in over his head and he was terrified.

Henderson's attention was focused on Cleveland, so he didn't see the figure appear out of the darkness until the man actually touched his shoulder from behind. "Hello, Deputy Henderson," a sinister male voice hissed into his ear. "You ever heard the phrase 'there will be hell to pay'? Guess who's here to collect."

The sudden presence behind him and the voice so close to his ear caused Henderson to react with pure, reflexive terror. Henderson gave a loud scream and tried to spin around to bring the rifle he held to bear. However, a forearm shot around his throat and pulled him back as if the man behind him planned to use him as a human shield. The man's other arm reached around Henderson's body and caught the rifle as Henderson tried to bring it up. With no discernible effort at all, the man holding him pivoted both of them so that Henderson was facing Deputy Cleveland. Henderson's finger reflexively tightened on the trigger. Henderson's rifle wasn't on safety. He fired a wild three-round burst before he even realized his finger was on the trigger.

The last spent shell casing was still falling to the grass when whoever had a hold on him released him with a little shove that sent Henderson sprawling to the grass. Henderson fell to the ground, rolled over, and came up firing wildly into the darkness behind him. He emptied the fifteen-round clip in the rifle. When he ran out of bullets, he tossed the rifle down and drew his sidearm. With his other hand he removed the flashlight he carried in a case on his belt and switched it on. The super-bright LED beam revealed nothing around him but grass and flowers. Whoever had grabbed him had completely vanished into the darkness. He stopped and listened for the sounds of movement. He didn't hear movement, but he did hear a horrible gasping sound behind him.

Henderson spun around and shined his light toward the sound. Deputy Cleveland lay at the foot of the steps. "Oh shit," Henderson said when he saw that Cleveland was down. That first three-round burst he'd fired out of sheer instinct when he was grabbed from behind had been in the general direction of where Cleveland was standing. "No, no, no," Henderson muttered desperately as he ran to where Cleveland lay and shined his light on him. The bright beam of light revealed a scene that would be etched in Henderson's mind for the rest of his life. One of his stray bullets had hit Cleveland in the face right under his left eye, leaving a small, neat hole about the size of a dime. The bullet had then exited out the back of Cleveland's skull, spraying blood, skull fragments, and brain tissue all over the neat brick steps behind his head. The gasping sound was Deputy Jimmy Cleveland breathing his last. That gasping stopped as he died.

Deputy Henderson stood there and watched Cleveland die in the crisp white light from his flashlight. He stood there for a few quiet moments as his brain processed what he was seeing and its implications. Someone had grabbed him from behind. Someone was here. That meant it was all over. There would be no explaining this, and by this he meant his part in the kidnapping and murder of a fellow cop and two other people and the accidental shooting of Deputy Cleveland. No lawyer in the world could keep him out of prison. It was over.

Deputy Chris Henderson turned off his flashlight and slipped it back into the case on his belt. He took a deep breath, jammed the barrel of the pistol he held into the soft flesh under his chin, and pulled the trigger. The forty-caliber jacketed hollow-point bullet tore through his brain, killing him instantly. His last conscious thought was that at least he wouldn't be going to prison.

Sam stood in the darkness several feet away and watched as Deputy Henderson killed himself. He'd known that Henderson was the weakest mentally and emotionally, thus making him more prone to make a mistake, so Henderson was the one he'd snuck up behind and grabbed. The rest was just pure panic on the man's part. It had worked out just as he planned. *Two down, the rest to go,* he thought as he started toward the house.

CHAPTER 37

Deputy Cothran aimed his rifle at Sheriff Garrett's chest. "Is what he's saying the truth?" he snarled. His eyes had taken on a wild, animalistic look.

"Dwayne, we've been friends since grade school," Sheriff Garrett replied nervously. "He's just trying to save himself. The reason we didn't take that evidence from his car is because it's not important enough to worry about. That's all. Now, don't point that thing at me."

Dwayne didn't lower the rifle. He started to say something else but a sudden burst of gunfire from outside interrupted him. Garcia, who was standing closest to the front door, gave a startled yell at the sudden explosion of sound. Dwayne spun around toward the front foyer and front door. At that moment Ronny Easton, who was handcuffed and sitting in the floor, struggled to his feet using the wall behind him as leverage and made a run for the front door. Sheriff Garrett saw Ronny running for the door and opened fire at him with the pistol in his hand. The sheriff's first shot missed, striking the wall behind Ronny. The second shot hit Ronny and he fell to the floor with a scream. All of this happened behind Dwayne, whose attention was on the foyer. When the sheriff opened fire, Dwayne instantly assumed the sheriff was firing at him. He spun and opened fire with the assault rifle at the sheriff.

Mace and Amanda were sitting on the edge of the couch about seven feet from the sheriff. As soon as the shooting started, Mace dove to the side and used his shoulder to push Amanda to the floor. He landed on top of her. "Stay down," he yelled at her and he tried to shield her with his body.

A couple of Dwayne's shots hit the sheriff in his armored vest. The heavy tactical vest stopped the rounds, but the force of the bullets was enough to knock the sheriff backwards. The sheriff stumbled sideways and fell over a chair near his legs. The sheriff landed on his side. He tried to bring the pistol he held up to shoot at Dwayne, but before he could Dwayne stepped forward and kicked the pistol out of his hand. Dwayne aimed his rifle at the sheriff's face. "Don't do this, Dwayne," Sheriff Garrett begged. Dwayne's answer was to fire a single round directly into the sheriff's face at nearly point-blank range. Most of the sheriff's head vanished in an explosion of blood and gore.

While this was happening, Mace was moving. He rolled off of Amanda onto his side in the floor. Once he was on his side, he brought his handcuffed wrists down and pulled his legs up, enabling him to slip his chained wrists under his butt and then down his legs. Once he pulled his feet through, his wrists were in front of his body. He was still handcuffed, but at least now his hands were in front of him so he wasn't totally helpless. While Dwayne was distracted by the sheriff, Mace scrabbled to his feet and lunged.

Garcia watched the end of the shootout between Sheriff Garrett and Deputy Cothran from his position in the foyer. Following the burst of gunfire outside, Garcia had run to the front door and peeked out the window beside it. He could see two bodies sprawled at the end of the walkway where the steps led to where their vehicles were parked. Judging from the blood and gore visible on the steps, he could tell that the two officers who were outside were most likely dead. He couldn't see who had killed them, but the area beyond the range of the outside lights was pitch black. It could have been an attacker on foot or a sniper who'd killed the two men. There was no way to tell.

He was still trying to decide what to do when the shooting started in the living room around the corner. The successive cracks of gunfire were so fast and close together that he couldn't tell how many shots were fired, only that there were many. He jerked away from the window, drew the pistol he'd been carrying in the waistband of his designer jeans, and quick-peeked around the corner into the living room just in time to see Deputy Cothran shoot the sheriff in the head with his rifle. He could also see Ronny Easton lying in the floor near where he'd been sitting in the floor earlier.

Garcia had no idea what had happened both inside and outside, but common sense and survival instinct told him that he needed to get out of there. Sheriff Garrett's plan had obviously fallen apart. Now, not only was there someone outside killing the sheriff's men, the men inside were killing each other. Garcia was smart enough to realize that, if he stayed, he would most likely be killed. Sheriff Garrett had already told him that the man called Sam Walker was dead. Obviously, the man must have had accomplices. That had to be who was attacking them outside.

Garcia turned and ran down the hallway that led the opposite way from the foyer. The hallway brought him into a dark kitchen. The kitchen had a back door that led out to a large cement patio area and an in-ground swimming pool. Garcia didn't turn on the light as he ran to the back door. With his gun in hand, he peered through the blinds over the window in the back door. He saw nothing but the glimmer of moonlight on the water in the pool. As quietly as possible, he opened the door and slipped out onto the dark patio. He took a few seconds for his eyes to adjust to the night. Once he could see, he slipped across the patio and hurried across the grassy back yard towards the line of trees several yards away.

Garcia was almost to the tree line when a blinding beam of light came from nowhere, blinding him instantly. "Police! Put the gun down and get on the ground now!" a voice screamed at him from just beyond the light. Garcia stopped immediately. He realized that he still had the gun in his hand. For a moment he thought about opening fire in the direction of the light source and the voice yelling commands at him, but he knew that ultimately he would just be committing suicide.

Garcia gently dropped the gun onto the grass, took a couple of steps away from the gun, and dropped down on his face in the grass. He remained there as a man with a rifle approached him and handcuffed him quickly and efficiently.

Once the man on the ground was handcuffed, Jeff Bradley switched off his light and pulled the handcuffed man up onto his knees. Jeff had made the call to the BCI's Emergency Communications Center just like Sam had asked him to and relayed what Sam had told him. It had taken a couple of minutes to convince the dispatcher that he was who he claimed and it wasn't a prank call, but once he convinced her he was sincere the reaction was swift. Multiple BCI agents were on the way from nearby counties and a hostage rescue team was inbound by helicopter from BCI Headquarters in Columbia. With help on the way, Jeff had driven to Ronny's address. As luck would have it, Jeff was familiar with the forests around the Easton family home because as a teenager he and his friends had hunted there. He'd parked his car several hundred yards away and hiked through the woods toward Ronny's house. The plan was to simply reconnoiter the situation and relay information to the BCI via his cell phone, just as the dispatcher at the BCI Emergency Communications Center requested. Unfortunately, the sounds of gunfire had blown that plan away.

Jeff had reported the gunfire to the BCI dispatcher and was making a plan to move on the house when the man he now had in custody ran from the back of the house. "Who are you?" Jeff asked as he leaned close to the handcuffed man.

The man looked up at him from his position on his knees. "I want a lawyer," he said.

Another faint gunshot from inside the house caused Jeff to nearly jump out of his skin. Whatever was happening in the house was happening now and he didn't have time to play games with his captive. He jerked the man roughly to his feet and marched him to the closest tree, a small pine tree with a trunk about a foot in diameter. He shoved him face first into the tree trunk. "If you try anything stupid, I'll shoot you," he said fiercely. He took the handcuff off the man's left wrist and used the handcuffs to drag the man's right arm around the tree trunk. "Give me your other wrist," he ordered. The man complied and Jeff re-cuffed him with his arms around the tree. The man was now effectively trapped. "I'll be back," he said.

With his rifle in his hands, Jeff hurried toward the house.

Mace's hands were still restrained, but he wasn't helpless and he wasn't going down without a fight. He plowed into Dwayne with all of his power, knocking the big man off balance. Dwayne was so big and powerful that he didn't fall, but as he stumbled back and tried to regain his footing, it gave Mace a chance to grab the barrel of the rifle Dwayne held. The handcuffs on his wrists meant that Mace was forced to use both hands on the rifle, so he was forced to use his legs. He kicked out with his left leg, trying for a straight kick to Dwayne's groin, but the deputy turned to the side and blocked it with his thigh. To Mace, it felt like he'd kicked a brick wall. Dwayne barely grunted. Mace followed that up with a head butt aimed at Dwayne's face. Given the height difference all he managed was a glancing blow to Dwayne's chin. That stunned him enough for Mace to rip the rifle from Dwayne's grip. Any feeling of triumph was short-lived, however. Any thought Mace had of using the rifle was foiled by his own restrained hands and Dwayne's speed and power. He had barely torn the rifle away from Dwayne when the huge deputy swatted the rifle from Mace's hands. The rifle flew across the room and landed somewhere near Ronny Easton's prostrate form.

Before Mace could react, Dwayne went for the pistol he had holstered at his hip. Dwayne drew the gun and was bringing it to bear on Mace. Before Dwayne could aim and fire, a fierce kick struck his hand and sent the pistol flying from his grip. The kick came from Amanda. She had rolled onto her back as she lay on the floor and kicked with all of her might. The kick had connected with Dwayne's gun and sent him flying. "Bitch!" Dwayne screamed in rage as his gun went flying. He lunged over and punched Amanda in the side of the head. The blow connected solidly and she went limp. "When I'm done with him, you're going to wish you were dead."

While Dwayne was distracted, Mace used that chance to attack. He stepped toward Dwayne and tried to strike him in the face with his cuffed hands. Unfortunately, Dwayne was ready. Dwayne caught his wrists with one hand, grabbed Mace's throat with the other, and then swept his legs out from under him with his leg. Mace slammed down onto the floor. Luckily for him, he took most of the force from the impact on his upper back and shoulders; if his head had struck the marble floor his skull would have split open. The impact drove the air from is lungs and dazed him, however, and that was enough for Dwayne to get the upper hand.

Dwayne stepped over Mace and then dropped down so that he was straddling Mace's chest. He grabbed Mace's throat with both hands and clamped down. "You should be ashamed," Dwayne said as he squeezed down on Mace's throat, shutting off his air. "You're supposed to be some badass super cop, but those girls I killed fought harder than you did." Mace tried to buck Dwayne off of his chest and to fight back, but his restrained hands and Dwayne's weight and power made doing that nearly impossible. Mace already had the wind knocked out of him by the impact to the floor and with Dwayne's grip on his throat shutting off his windpipe, there was no way to get any air into his lungs. Blackness hovered at the edge of his vision and he could feel his body shutting down.

Dwayne could tell that Agent Holliday was losing consciousness. Just a few more seconds and the man would be dead. Once he was dead, Dwayne would kill the woman. Once she was dead, he would get out of here and head back to his house. He had always assumed that one day he might have to disappear, so he'd planned accordingly. He had almost a hundred thousand dollars and several sets of fake identification, including passports, stashed in a hidden cache on his property. Given his size, it would be hard to vanish, but it wasn't impossible. There were things he could do to downplay his size and disguise his appearance.

Agent Holliday had almost quit moving entirely when a set of hands seized Dwayne by the back of his tactical vest. He felt the hands grab him and sensed a presence behind him. To his immense shock, he was lifted off of Agent Holliday and thrown bodily. He flew across the room and struck the wall on the far side of the room about twenty feet away from where he was moments ago. His back hit the wall, leaving a huge hole in the plaster, and he toppled onto his face in the floor. He landed there, stunned and gasping for breath. He had never been manhandled like that before in his life. Ever. He felt the first faint stirring of fear in the back of his mind. The fear turned to full-blown panic as soon as he saw the person responsible for pulling him off of Agent Holliday.

"You're supposed to dead," Dwayne said as he struggled to his feet.

"Surprise," Sam Walker said sarcastically.

"How?" Dwayne stammered as he faced Sam.

"No human being can kill me," Sam replied casually. "I am an angel of God, sent forth to enact God's will in the world of men. I have walked the earth since God created mankind, doing whatever is necessary to ensure that what He wills happens. His will has brought me here, just like it has brought you and all of the others here."

"You're crazy," Dwayne said.

"And you're finished," Sam said as he took a step forward toward Dwayne. "Your reign of murder, torture, and mayhem is at an end. Ask God for mercy and you may yet save your soul. You will, however, face punishment for the things you've done."

Dwayne's reply was to charge toward Sam with his fist raised and a cry of rage. Sam stood his ground and never flinched. When Dwayne was within arm's reach, Sam threw a straight punch squarely into the center of Dwayne's massive chest and the tactical vest covering it. There was a loud crack similar to wood splintering as the force of Sam's punch shattered Dwayne's sternum and ribs. Dwayne stopped as if he'd run into a brick wall. He staggered backwards with a strangled scream and hit the wall in almost the exact spot he'd already left an impression in the plaster. He came to rest sitting on his butt in the floor. His face wore an expression of stunned surprise. He tried to get back up, but couldn't. He tried to take a deep breath, but it wouldn't come. When he tried to breath, it felt like his lungs were full of glass. He coughed up a mouthful of blood.

Sam walked over and squatted down beside Dwayne. His face was expressionless. "Normally, I can't kill people. Only certain ones of us can do that. However, I got special permission for you."

"Who?" Dwayne gasped. His mouth kept filling with blood and the pain in his chest was incredible.

Sam's answer was to point upward. "You're dying, Dwayne," he said. "I know what awaits you on the other side. I would suggest you ask Him for the mercy He is willing to give all through his son, Jesus, the Christ." Dwayne's reply was to raise his fist and extend his middle finger up into the air. He held it for just a few seconds before his hand fell down into his lap. He took one more ragged breath and then his head lolled to the side as he died. "So be it," Sam said softly.

Sam stood up just as Mace managed to stagger to his feet.

CHAPTER 38

"Sam?" Mace asked hoarsely.

Sam reached down and removed a set of keys from Dwayne's belt. He stood up and turned to go to Mace. "Mace," he said as he took Mace's wrist and used the deputy's handcuff key to unlock the handcuffs.

"I saw them shoot you," Mace said, "but here you are. I know I also saw you in your motel room, but you said you were at the bar. How?" The last part was more of a plea than a question.

"I can make you see what I want you to see," Sam answered. "Trust me when I tell you that I don't really look like this."

Mace's eyes widened. "I saw and heard everything that went down with him." He pointed toward Dwayne's body with a shaking finger. "Please, tell me what's happening so I know I'm not crazy."

"Let's get Amanda first," Sam said gently. "I don't want to explain this twice. Are you okay?"

"I feel like I just lost a fight with a bulldozer," Mace said weakly," but I think I'll be okay." He hurried over to Amanda. She woke up with a little cry when he touched her. He used the key to quickly remove her handcuffs. She still seemed dazed, so he helped her to the couch. She sat down. Her eyes grew huge when she saw Sam. "It's Sam," Mace said to her unspoken question. "He's about to explain all of this."

"Sit down, Mason," Sam said. Mace sat down beside Amanda. Almost unconsciously, she reached over and took his hand. Sam remained standing. "First of all, Caleb is fine. He's at Chief Bradley's house right now. I'm the one who took him from the office and to Chief Bradley's house where he would be safe."

"Oh thank God," Amanda sobbed. "I saw you get killed. How are you alive?"

"I'm alive because I'm not really human. Sam Walker is not my name," Sam said gently. "It's just the name I used here. I am angel sent by God Almighty. I was sent here to put an end to the horrible things Sheriff Garrett, Deputy Cothran, and the others were doing. They preyed upon the innocent and powerless. It had to end. "

"That happens everywhere every day," Mace said. "What's so special about here?"

"Stopping them was the secondary part of my mission," Sam explained patiently. "The main reason I was sent here was to protect you and Caleb, Amanda. All people are special to God, but some are meant for marvelous things in His service. God has a special plan for Caleb. Everything I have done here was to make sure Caleb was raised in the right environment by the right people, people who would make sure he was equipped to do what God wants him to do."

"And what is that?" Amanda asked shakily.

"The clue is in what you named your son," Sam added with a slight smile. "What's Caleb's middle name?"

"Elijah," Amanda answered. "His full name is Caleb Elijah Easton."

"Did you ever wonder why you gave him that middle name?" Sam asked.

Amanda thought for a moment. "I just liked it," Amanda said. "I guess because my grandfather is a preacher. I heard it in a sermon when I was younger and liked it."

"And what was Elijah in the Bible?" Sam asked softly.

"Elijah was a great prophet in the Old Testament who performed many miracles and turned many toward God," Amanda answered. "He's the one who foretells the return of Jesus Christ"

"Exactly," Sam said.

It took a few seconds for Sam's words to sink in. "But Caleb's just a normal little boy," Amanda said.

"And Peter, James, and John were normal fishermen, Moses and David were normal shepherds, and Mary was a normal girl," Sam retorted cheerfully. "The Living God can do whatever He wants, including putting people exactly where they are supposed to be at the right time," he added with a pointed look at Mace. "Everything that has happened in both of your lives has brought you to this place at this time. Mace, that's why you survived what happened in Laurens. That's why Director Keller sent you here. "

Mace digested this silently. His mind was reeling. He had so many questions, but he couldn't find the words to ask them.

"Amanda, one of Sheriff Garrett's shots killed Ronny. It was his time, just as it was for the others who died tonight," Sam said matter-of-factly as he directed his attention to Amanda. "Mourn him if you wish, but that part of your and your son's lives is over."

Amanda looked over at Ronny. Her husband lay face down in the floor, unmoving. "How do you know he's dead? You haven't checked him," she said.

Sam looked at her. "I know. Trust me," he said.

"Now what?" Mace asked.

"All of the bad guys are either in custody or dead. Their criminal organization and everyone involved in it will face justice," Sam said. "In just a few seconds, Chief Bradley will come through the back door, followed very shortly by a bunch of your fellow officers, Mace. Tell Jeff to check his phone. It's about his daughter."

With that, Sam Walker vanished from right before their eyes. One moment he was there, the next he was gone. Mace and Amanda both gasped loudly at the suddenness of his complete disappearance. They were still sitting there in disbelief when Jeff Bradley slipped from the kitchen into the living room area with his rifle at the ready.

When Jeff Bradley made it into the living room area after sneaking in through the back door, he found a slaughterhouse. Blood, spent bullet casings, and bodies were everywhere. A quick visual check confirmed that Sheriff Garrett and Deputy Cothran were already dead. Ronny Easton lay face down and unmoving in a pool of blood close by. Judging from the blood on the floor around him, he also appeared to be dead. Jeff feared that he would find both Amanda and Holliday lying somewhere in the floor dead as well. He about wet himself when he found them both sitting beside each other on the couch. They both looked like they'd been roughed up, but he didn't see any blood or bullet wounds. Both of them looked as if they were in shock.

"You guys okay?" he asked as his eyes swept the room. He didn't see any other obvious threats so he lowered his rifle.

"We're okay," Mace replied. He seemed dazed. "All of the bad guys are down."

Jeff looked at the broken furniture and carnage. "What happened? How are you two not hurt?"

"Jeff, check your cell phone," Amanda said numbly. "There's something there about Lizzie."

Jeff had about a million questions, but he took his smart phone from his pocket and looked at it. He had two missed calls from home and then a text message that read *Going to emergency room. Meet us there ASAP.* The calls and messages were from Melanie. He looked up from the phone. "How did you know that?" he asked Amanda.

"Brother, that ain't even in the top five for the weirdest things that have happened to us in the last few hours," Mace said numbly as he stood up. "Give me that rifle and get to the hospital."

"The BCI is on the way," Jeff said desperately. "I'm supposed to be here."

"Jeff, go!" Amanda said. "It's okay."

Jeff nodded. "There's a guy handcuffed to a tree in the back yard at the woods," he said.

"I'll tell them," Mace said. "Run back to wherever your car is and get to the hospital."

Jeff nodded silently and rushed back through the house. As he ran he prayed silently. *Please, God, don't let her be dead. I should have been there.*

Left alone in the bloody living room, Mace went over and checked on Ronny Easton. The man was dead. One of Sheriff Garrett's wild shots had apparently found its mark. Mace went back over to the couch where Amanda still sat. "He's dead, just like Sam told us," he said. "I'm sorry."

Amanda nodded. "I don't know how to feel about it," she said honestly. "He was so mean to me and Caleb. Part of me is glad he's gone because of that, but the rest of me doesn't know how to feel."

Mace looked around. "You have the right to feel that way," he said. "Let's get out of here. We can wait for the cavalry outside." He reached down, took Amanda by the hand, and pulled her to her feet.

The two of them stumbled outside. Off in the distance they could helicopters approaching and down the hill where the road was they could see a stream of headlights rushing their way. "I can't believe we're not dead," Amanda said hollowly. "I guess I owe you a date."

"I don't know," Mace said. "We went out together tonight and it sucked."

Amanda turned and looked up at Mace's face. She saw that he was grinning. "Look who's being funny," she said as she reached and hugged him fiercely. "Thank you for saving us," she said.

Mace hugged her back just as fiercely. "I think I had very little to do with it. It was all Sam."

The helicopters were getting closer. They could hear the screech of tires and motors accelerating as cars turned off the highway into the driveway leading up to the house. In just a few moments they would be swarmed with BCI agents. "What are you going to tell them about all of this? About Sam?"

"If I tell them that an angel saved us, they'll lock me in a mental institution," Mace said. "I'm going with we were kidnapped and brought here by the sheriff and his men. They had a falling out and a big gunfight and brawl ensued. They all killed each other."

"Works for me," Amanda said.

"I do plan to ask for that date, though, after a respectable mourning period," Mace added.

"I plan to say yes," Amanda said, "after a respectable mourning period."

CHAPTER 38

Four Hours Later

Jeff Bradley sat in the second pew in the small chapel on the second floor of the Easton Regional Medical Center. The chapel was really just a large room that the hospital had decorated with a small altar bearing a crucifix and some wooden pews. A large painting of Jesus Christ standing on a hill holding a shepherd's crook and carrying a single lamb hung on the wall behind the altar. A spotlight on the ceiling illuminated the picture. A small brass plaque identifying the painting's title as The Good Shepherd and giving the artist's name was mounted below the painting. At three in the morning, the chapel was completely empty, except for Jeff. He didn't mind the silence and solitude. He would have been embarrassed if someone else had been there to see and hear him as he sobbed.

Jeff had slipped into the chapel just a few minutes ago in an effort to find some peace and quiet to gather his thoughts and pull himself together. Almost as soon as he walked in, however, he'd broken down and started crying like a baby. At first, he'd tried to stop the tears, but it was futile, so he'd just surrendered and let them flow. He'd quickly soaked through the tissues he'd brought with him and then his shirt sleeve. He'd finally just buried his face in his folded arms on the back of the pew in front of him and let it go.

"Jeff," a voice said from somewhere behind him.

Jeff raised his head and spun around. Sam stood in the middle of the aisle between the rows of pews just a few feet away from Jeff. Jeff hadn't heard him come into the chapel. Of course, the way he was blubbering, he wouldn't have heard a group of tap dancers. He jumped up and ran his hand down his face to wipe away the tears. "Amanda called me and told me what happened," he said.

"Yes," Sam said.

Jeff stumbled out of the pew into the aisle. He fell to his knees. "Thank you so much," he sobbed as his voice broke.

Sam immediately pulled him to his feet. "Don't bow to or worship me, Jeff," he said. "Worship God for giving the power to heal. He performs miracles, not me." He smiled. "I just work for Him."

"My daughter is fine," Jeff choked. "She woke up and told my wife that her head had stopped hurting and she felt good. It threw Melanie and the hospice nurse for a loop and they rushed her here. They've run CT scans, x-rays, and everything else. The tumor is gone. Every bit of it. The ER doctors even called her oncologist in because they couldn't believe it. It's all gone!" He choked back a sob. "She's sitting in a room in the emergency room eating a bowl of ice cream and laughing with her mother. Five hours ago, she was in a coma and about to die."

"Then why are you crying, Jeff?" Sam chided.

"Happiness, relief, fear? I don't know!" Jeff said. He fought to bring his emotions under control. "Amanda claimed you're some kind of angel. That sounds nuts, but you have to be! My daughter is alive. Not only that, but she's perfectly healthy. The doctors are all looking at each other and scratching their heads." He reached out and touched Sam's arm with one trembling finger. "Are you really an angel?"

"Yes," Sam said, "but I had nothing to do with healing Lizzie. That's not my cup of tea, I'm afraid."

"Then how? Who?" Jeff stammered.

"Caleb," Sam replied. "It was Caleb. Now you know why I came here and why protecting him and putting him on the right path was so important."

"Caleb healed my daughter?" Jeff choked.

"God did it through Caleb," Sam said. "Caleb is special beyond words. Trust me."

"Wow," Jeff said. "I feel like I need to sit down."

"You've had a big night," Sam said with a smile as he guided Jeff over to the closest pew and motioned for him to sit. Jeff sank down into the pew. "I have to go, but I just wanted to come say goodbye to you personally and thank you for your bravery and sacrifice." He extended his hand.

Jeff took it and shook it weakly. "I'm touching you, so this must be real," he said shakily. "If you're leaving, how do I explain all of this when the BCI questions me about you?"

"Even if you tell the truth, no one would believe you anyway," Sam said. "But don't worry. It all works out in the end. There is one thing I must ask of you."

"Anything, sir," Jeff stammered. "Do I call you sir?"

"Don't tell anyone that Caleb healed Lizzie," Sam said. "His time will come, but until then just let him be a normal kid."

"Absolutely," Jeff said. "What about Melanie and Mary, the nurse? They were there."

"They had both dozed off and were sound asleep," Sam said. "They have no idea how it happened. They just know it happened. Now, go back to Melanie and Lizzie and enjoy this wonderful gift God has given you."

With that, Sam was gone. The only person in the chapel was Jeff. He looked around for a few seconds as if Sam might have somehow ducked down and tried to hide, but he was gone. Completely disappeared. "Wow," Jeff said in genuine awe. He turned slowly and looked at the painting on the wall behind the altar. Jesus Christ gazed back serenely at him, His face the picture of peace.

Jeff stood there, studying the picture. He felt like he should say something. "Your ways certainly are mysterious," he finally said, "but I just wanted to say thank you with all of my heart. I'll never forget this, Lord. I promise that. Thank you. Thank you. Thank you."

The picture didn't answer back, but if it had Jeff wouldn't have been shocked, given some of the things that had already happened tonight. In the silence, Jeff wiped the tears of joy from his face with his sleeve and hurried out of the chapel.

His wife and daughter were waiting for him.

CHAPTER 39

ONE YEAR LATER

The angel who called himself Sam Walker sat in a booth at The Diner in the town of Easton, sipping coffee and reading the local newspaper. The headline on the front page read NEW SHERIFF CLEANS HOUSE. According to the story, Easton County's newly-elected sheriff, Jeff Bradley, had fired a substantial number of sheriff's office employees on his first day on the job in an effort to be rid of the last vestiges of corruption and restore the agency's reputation. The article followed that by noting that most of the people who had taken bribes or worse during Sheriff Garrett's tenure had already been fired from their jobs and were serving time in prison, thanks to former sheriff's detective Roberts turning informant on his fellow crooked cops and spilling his guts to the BCI. A related article on the same page from the Associated Press wire service detailed how The Horde, the biker gang that had once occupied the county, had been decimated by arrests following an extensive investigation by multiple federal and local law enforcement agencies. The remaining members of the gang who weren't in prison were either on the run or dead as a result of shoot-outs with the police or other criminal gangs.

Near the end of the article about Sheriff Bradley's first day, one small paragraph also mentioned that Mason Holliday, the heroic former BCI agent and Bradley's new chief deputy, would be starting his new job following his return from his honeymoon after marrying Amanda Easton, the widow of Ronny Easton. Sam smiled as he read that last part. It had worked out just like it was supposed to. Mace Holliday was a good man and he would be a good husband to Amanda and father to Caleb. He was the right man to make sure Caleb grew up to be the man he was supposed to be.

"More coffee, honey?" the waitress asked as she walked by his booth with a fresh pot of coffee in one hand. According to the nametag on her shirt, her name was Amy.

"No thanks," Sam said as he smiled up at her from his seat. "I'm just passing through and thought I would check out the local news."

"There's a lot of news to be had around these parts lately," Amy said pleasantly. "Things went crazy around her for a time about a year or so ago. There were crooked police officers, bikers, smuggling, and all kinds of other crazy stuff. A bunch of people got killed, including the old sheriff and some of his men. They all turned out to be crooks, though, so I guess they got what they deserved. One of them even turned out to be a serial killer! He was getting girls from these folks who were sneaking them into the country and killing them. They found their bodies on his farm. Crazy stuff," she added with a shake of her head. "It put Easton all over the national news."

"Wasn't there a guy that got arrested that was supposed to be some kind of hitman for the cartel or something? Sam asked. "I remember that from the news, I think. He had some kind of Mexican name."

"The FBI linked him to a bunch of other crimes all across the country," Amy said. "He went by Garcia, but he was an American. He's locked up somewhere awaiting trial."

"Crazy," Sam said. "That's not the kind of thing you normally find in places like this."

"It all passed," Amy said. "Thank God. Things look like they're getting back to normal, sleepy little Easton."

"That's good to hear," Sam said as he put a five- dollar bill down on the table to pay for his coffee and stood up. "You have a good day, Amy. Keep the change."

Sam walked past Amy toward the restaurant's main entrance. "Mister, you look familiar," Amy called to him as he headed for the door. "You ever been to Easton before?"

Sam smiled as he reached the door. "I get that a lot," he said politely. "I just have one of those faces, I guess. Have a nice day."

With that, Sam stepped out into the morning sunshine and walked away.